J. L. Fraser grew up in Saskatchewan, Canada. Reading almost to a fault, her books portray adventure and are full of love, lust and wild imagination. Through her own writing, she has been able to bring those wild adventures to life.

Living in rural Alberta with her husband and four book-obsessed children, she spends her days training and playing with her dogs and running a dog hotel, called Paradise Kennels. To relax at the end of the day, Jennifer dives into writing, reading and seeking the next great challenge that life may present to her.

To my husband, Les, who as crazy as he knows I am, still helps my insane dreams come true.

My rock, my man, my love.

J. L. Fraser

EXIMIUS

I hope my book keeps you ~~warm~~ HOT at night Emma! ♡

AUSTIN MACAULEY PUBLISHERS™

LONDON • CAMBRIDGE • NEW YORK • SHARJAH

Ordering Information
Quantity sales: Special discounts are available on quantity purchases by corporations, associations, and others. For details, contact the publisher at the address below.

Publisher's Cataloging-in-Publication data
Fraser, J. L.
Eximius

ISBN 9781647503529 (Paperback)
ISBN 9781647503512 (Hardback)
ISBN 9781647503536 (ePub e-book)

Library of Congress Control Number: 2022915080

www.austinmacauley.com/us

First Published 2023
Austin Macauley Publishers LLC
40 Wall Street,33rd Floor, Suite 3302
New York, NY 10005
USA

mail-usa@austinmacauley.com
+1 (646) 5125767

Chapter 1

Sabastian was not the best multitasker, yet he was doing an outstanding job while he propelled the black sedan down the highway. For the last several hours, he had been able to keep the car on the road while trying to plan his next step without punching his loquacious passenger in the face. Sabastian had been trying to go over the scenario in his head, however, he could not figure out the last bit of instructions or lack thereof and needed silence to think clearly.

The partly cloudy night sky sped past them as the car smoothly took the two men to their destination. Running out of patience, Sabastian tightened his grip on the wheel, twisting his palms around the slick black leather trying to control himself. Even though Sabastian hadn't responded to him in the past hour, Edward hadn't stopped talking since they got into the lush sedan. He was past being polite and finally turned to his passenger.

"For Christ's sake, Edward, would you shut up for five minutes?" Sabastian asked smoothly, in control of his temper as always.

Sabastian did not yell. He rarely raised his voice, but no matter how soft spoken he was, he usually made his point. Edward, however, was not that observant tonight.

One of the meatier men that worked with Sabastian, the torn jean jacket stretched across Edward's broad chest and his arms looked like they would tear through the thin worn material. Both men had donned clothes designed to make them look shabby and the attire was not something the men would normally wear. The clothing had been chosen with care, especially for this assignment before they had left the manor.

Edward's face, obscured by a thick black mat of facial hair, looked very different than normal. The facial hair made his car mate look even more intimidating than usual, which was the point and why both men had given up shaving for the last few weeks. Sabastian was sure he looked just as gruff but only used mirrors to shave and since he had not picked up his razor in weeks, he had no idea of what the mat of extra light brown hair did to his facial features. He only knew he could not wait to get this over with if only to get the scratchy coarse hair removed from his face.

Edward bounced back from the rebuff and continued, "What? Don't tell me you think that the Yankees will take it this year? Come on, they need to lose one of these days, they always win, it drives me nuts. You know who I think will…"

Sabastian mustered his will power and restrained himself from doing bodily harm to Edward. He liked Edward; however, being in a vehicle for this long with him was quickly changing his opinion of the man.

Truth be told, he was anxious. Sabastian knew what was required to get ahead in this business but that didn't mean he had to like it. He just didn't like the assignment he'd been given after all these years. He would never dispute the system or his boss and truthfully, he was thrilled the time had finally come for him to advance with his given task. However, that did not change his feelings about the test that very few men had been given to move ahead in this game. The task was routine, but that still did not make it right. A collection like this was immoral, it had been done before and had usually worked out, but it still felt wrong. Morality had never been a strong personality trait of Sabastian's, but he felt this was coming dangerously close to crossing the line. Edward had helped collect before and did not seem stressed about the task at hand, but seeing how this would be Sabastian's first chance at this kind of opportunity; he needed it to go well.

Another quiet warning was all Edward needed.

"I need to think, stop talking!" Sabastian whispered gruffly.

Pronouncing the last two words slowly got the point across and Edward wisely ceased his incessant chatter about the Yankees.

"Christ, man, how hard can this be, we collect and go home. I just don't get why the hell we had to go so far for this one."

"You know we have to keep a low profile closer to home. They had the list and this one just happened to workout with the timing and was the one that was viable enough to work for what we need. Besides, Mr. D insisted on this one for some reason. Now, shut up, I need to think."

Edward rolled his eyes and looked out the tinted window.

Sabastian sat in the driver's seat uncomfortable in the worn denim jeans and flannel shirt covered with a cheap leather vest. He tried to think clearly but felt almost claustrophobic in the layers of torn mismatched attire. Perhaps it was not the clothing, but the mission he had almost unwilling accepted that made his feel edgy. He was thrilled, of course, this is what all the men at the manor hoped for. A promotion to get them more integrated and obtain more power and control within the company and of course money, an obscene amount of money. He felt like a wannabe gang member who had to kill someone in order to be welcomed to the gang. A feeling he was far too familiar with and it twisted his gut. It was thrilling yes, but wrong!

Sabastian's broad sculpted face held a slight crease in his forehead while his dark green eyes narrowed at the road ahead of him. Even working in a business full of gorgeous guys by anyone's standards, he stood out. He was not the biggest man when it came to muscles but compared to any other man, his mass was substantial. Sabastian shoulders, legs, and arms were cut like Michelangelo's David if you broaden the chest, doubled most of the limbs and intensified the face. His normally wavy light brown hair was slicked back with too much heavy gel to make it look greasy and unwashed for this task. Sabastian also could not wait for a shower to get the unwashed look from his head as well as his face. He was not vain in the least and was never one to preen in front of a mirror like several of the men he worked with. However, wearing heavy tattered clothes, being unshaved with thick heavy hair only made him feel that much more uncomfortable.

Sabastian reassessed the situation, there were too many variables. The snitch that had disappeared with his payment was not entirely reliable. He was the only one who could confirm the details, which were shady and full of holes. Sabastian went over and over the last part of the assignment and he could not figure out a way to make it work for both parties involved. One thing was certain, not completing the task wasn't an option.

"Okay, now what?" Edward asked as the car slowed.

Edward had stayed quiet long enough that Sabastian had had time to organized his thoughts, but he was still overly impatient with his passenger. How could Edward not know the next step in the plan? Was he not mentally at the meeting when Mr. D called them in? Or was he going through baseball stats in his head while the information had been relayed? Sabastian didn't blame him, Edward was a simple guy and did his job well, but the man could rarely think past his perks at the manor.

"We have to meet Frank first and change cars," Sabastian replied coolly.

Sabastian pulled the car off the highway and headed to Leader, a small town off the highway several miles from Denver. It was still dark outside, with large rolling clouds obscuring the bright shine of the full moon. Sabastian turned off the cars head lights and turned into the far end of an old parking lot. He quickly glanced around and confirmed the area was not being monitored by security or surveillance cameras so at least that information was correct. He hoped all further information about this undertaking would prove as reliable.

Edward glanced around the abandoned parking lot.

"I thought you said we were switching cars?"

"Christ Eddie, we are, come on," Sabastian answered annoyed.

Sabastian locked the doors of the Sedan and together, the men started east. They used the sporadic light of the moon and were able to jog to the auto wreckers within ten minutes with ease.

The men squeezed through the partially closed, dilapidated chain link gate and noticed a tiny worn out shed, lit with a soft yellow light to the right of the entrance. Sabastian approached the shed and tapped lightly on a small sliding window. Before they saw a face, they heard a voice.

"You're early," a gruff voice wheezed from behind the yellowed cracked glass.

"You got what we need?" Sabastian asked, cutting though the niceties.

"Ya, give me a sec."

The two men heard a sharp scraping sound of metal against metal which resonated sharply in the quiet junkyard as a side door of the shed opened to their left. A thin, ragged man stepped out of his booth in what used to be blue overalls, now black with oil and dirt. His skin appeared darker next to the white hair that topped his head and white unshaven beard betraying his age. The wrinkled man craned his neck to look up at the pair of men standing before him, both of who were at least a foot taller than him.

"Here you go, plates are good, registered, and not stolen."

He offered no introduction, nor asked for one, but tossed the keys to Sabastian and pointed to a beat-up beige Grand Am to his right.

Sabastian glanced at the pathetic rusted out car the old man referred to and gave him an unsure look.

"It'll drive fine, being wrecked cause a guy died in it. Ain't nothing wrong with it, but can't be resold. Worth more dead than alive," he said without humor. "You got five hours. I wanna go home, so I ain't waiting longer than that to crush her," the old man coughed as he turned back into his shack.

Sabastian looked at his companion with raised eyebrows. Edward looked bored, so Sabastian just shrugged and tossed him the keys.

"Okay, let's roll," Sabastian said, his feeling of unease deepening.

Over an hour and a half drive later, the men parked the car in an abandoned part of Denver, known for its unsavory environment. There were a few scattered street lights around, most were broken or burnt out. The city, probably hoping to forget this neighborhood, had not bothered replacing the bulbs.

Donning baseball caps low over their faces, Sabastian and Edward knew they would go unnoticed in their street clothes, blending in easily with the locals. It was a cold tonight and Sabastian quickened his pace to keep his blood up, Edward easily matching his stride. They walked another mile in silence, hyper aware of their surroundings. Sabastian glanced around subtlety reading what numbers he could find on the buildings. This was not easy, seeing most buildings weren't numbered and Sabastian guessed that they were mostly abandoned.

Rounding another corner Sabastian slowed in front of an abandoned apartment building and said low, "Here."

"Okay, where do we go?" Edward asked, glancing around for a sign of where the collection should take place.

"Well, the problem is it's a surprise collection. This will be the first time anyone has gotten close so we're just going to collect," Sabastian said with a worried shrug.

Edward frowned, "So what, it's a grab and go situation?"

"Ya, I guess," Sabastian looked up the building.

This was the part he didn't like. It was wrong and someone could get hurt and that would mean "mission-failed" according to Mr. D. Even if the collection was successful, anyone getting hurt was unacceptable and an injury could risk his test and promotion. Nothing but perfection was good enough for Mr. D. His boss was very proud of the high standards he offered his clients and he demanded excellence from everyone who worked for him. However, Sabastian and Edward were walking into this job blind and that kept the high standard difficult to live up to. Sabastian did not like it. But really, how hard could it be, there were two of them and they had the element of surprise.

Chapter 2

Shit, shit, shit, it's not supposed to be this damn cold, Victoria thought to herself.

The small figure curled up tighter in a ball, wrapping her blanket around her neck and cursing silently to herself, again. It was nights like this when she looked back on the choices she'd made that brought her here. Even freezing outside, behind the building in the alley that was now one of her many sanctuaries, she didn't regret the decisions she'd made. Victoria looked around, it was late and dark, except when the thick clouds let the full moon shine through. She shivered again and considered her options for getting warm.

She couldn't risk a trip down to the shelter, she'd already used it once this week and didn't want to be a regular there with a routine. A routine would get her noticed by others that frequented the streets. She could get up and walk to the nearest fire pit, however, the last time she tried that, she was almost beaten and robbed. Thankfully, sharp words and another altercation close by had given her the opportunity to slip away.

It's all about keeping a low profile, flying below the radar and never going to the same place predictably. Stay safe and don't make the same foolish mistakes.

The first time Victoria had been dragged back, she had been young and stupid. She'd gone to the same shelter every night and he had quickly tracked her down. He couldn't watch her every second, so she slipped away a month later. However, he had found her again and she'd been hauled back. Being taken back both times was disastrous and she knew she had to be smarter. So far, she had been lucky in this new city and it gave her a shred of hope that she was finally safe from him.

This new life was unbearably difficult and, in turn, it made the once sweet and gentle girl, hard on the inside. Things that used to make her cry and feel helpless, made her strong, tough, and indifferent. Cruel situations on the street where she used to help others had either gotten her beaten, stabbed, robbed, or she had simply made the situation worse. Victoria had stopped long ago trying to help others, it made her feel sick when she had to pass someone who needed help. It went against everything she was thought was right.

In the beginning when she was young and she first broke free, she swore to herself that if anyone needed help, she would try her best to assist. But after a few years, she was no longer the person she used to be when she first started this lifestyle and time had educated her on what life was really like on the streets. Survival was her only goal, stay safe and move around as much as possible. That's why she lived in several different places and never went to a shelter more than once a week. She only went to soup kitchens when absolutely necessary and scavenged when she wouldn't be seen. She couldn't be caught again because she knew next time he would kill her.

Victoria was smart and learned fast. What she researched when she first considered leaving had foolishly made her feel prepared. Mistakes had almost cost her life, but being physically capable had saved her many times. She was small, but very strong, agile, and athletic. Almost this alone had rescued her, as the men and women who tried to assault her had underestimated her abilities and she was able to get away. Being more than proficient in self-defense had made her body taut and flexible. However, years on the street had robbed her of most of her muscle mass and had left a thin, fragile shadow of her former self.

That was why keeping a low profile was so important. She no longer had her old strength as backup when she got into trouble. Also, using the trench, as she called it, was so valuable to her safe keeping. It lay on her now and was her best defense when someone got too close. Right now it was keeping her from freezing, though it filled the space with a stench that would turn away even the rats that frequented the alley. She was used to the smell that permeated around her, a combination of feces, dead rodents, and garbage, which was stuffed into the folds of the two old trench coats.

She had spent hours sewing them together and making pockets for which she would hide revolting treasures that gave off the strongest smells. It was like being a skunk, once someone got a whiff, they would always move away and give her space. The trench was her security blanket in more ways than one and it made her feel safe.

Mildred was also an effective safeguard that had not failed her yet, so she felt secure. Freezing, but safe.

Pulling the trench closer, breathing in the scent, goose bumps ran up and down her skin from the chill that would not cease. She was exhausted from shaking, but didn't have the energy to get up and find warmth. When she heard voices nearby, she curled herself even tighter and quietly stayed where she was and hoped the shaking and rustling of the garbage bags that made up her bed would not draw attention.

Chapter 3

She heard them before they got close to her sanctuary, although she couldn't make out their shadows until well after she first heard them speaking. She knew there were two men, but could not hear what they were saying, only a faint mumbling drifting to her from around the corner. Victoria did what she always did. She tensed and with freezing shaking fingers she grabbed a knife in her right hand and twisted a rope around her left wrist. She had done this so many times that she was on autopilot.

Her eyes, barely visible under her trench, were glued on the two tall shadows standing at the end of the alley. They were sixty feet away, but even that was too close for comfort. This had happened several times before, others trying to claim her spot, but her trench always worked so she was not overly concerned. They started moving toward her and her chills were suddenly gone, replaced by adrenaline warming her blood. Her eyes narrowed, assessing the situation. Should she play up her act or bolt? She stiffened and waited, willing the energy that she did not feel into her body.

"This isn't right," Edward murmured squinting into the darkness. "There can't be anyone here."

Sabastian looked past the piles of garbage bags to the back of the alley, somehow among the bags, boxes, and bins, it looks organized. He could just make out something deep in the alcove, surrounded by a wall of bags and boxes that looked like an arranged space.

Sabastian looked closer. "We might as well try," he said in a low monotone.

"Hello, is anyone there? May we speak to you for a moment please?" Sabastian called out softly.

Wound so tight, listening to their words, Victoria nearly yelped when they addressed her. Knowing it would be a mistake to let them know exactly where she was, she bit her tongue and stayed silent. She was perplexed by the man's soft deep voice and his manners, either they were not homeless or they were trying to fool her into exposing herself.

Well, she thought, *let's see whose act is better. I'll bring Mildred out and see if she can talk my way out of this one.*

Victoria had done this countless time and it had worked before and she had no doubt Mildred would work again. But, first, she wanted to see if she could convince them no one was here.

Sabastian tried again, his patience wearing thin, "Please, we know you're there and just want to talk to you."

Keeping his tone in check as always.

Sabastian took a couple of steps toward her, but took a step back when he caught a whiff of a disturbing smell. Edward caught it too and coughed, gagging.

"Christ, what is that?" Edward mumbled under his gloved hand. The men covered their noses and started walking forward determined.

His tender deep voice and politeness still threw Victoria off, but she did what had worked every other time there was a potential for a conflict, she brought Mildred out to play. She had to act fast, she could not allow them to get too close or she wouldn't have enough time.

"Go away!" came the hoarse voice from her throat. This was the voice she used anytime she felt threatened. It was the voice of an ailing old woman. It was the only voice she'd used in the past two years, once she figured out the best way to stay safe on these harsh streets. Be someone you would want to avoid, like the drunk you see puking on the street or the battered smelly old woman who talks to herself.

"Come on, let's just go. The info's wrong or we're in the wrong place," Edward mumbled under his breath. "Besides, I'm freezing and it fucking stinks here!" he said, rubbing his arm and covering his nose at the same time.

"There's no harm in at least checking and maybe she'll know where the girl went. If not, we can at least give her some money and find her a place to get warm," Sabastian said, reaching into his pocket.

"Excuse me, ma'am, we just want to help."

Sabastian took another step closer when the old woman's voice shouted out.

"Go away. I don't want you here. I don't need your help. Piss off!" Victoria had mustered all the vehemence she could summon, but it was hard to keep her voice from shaking and not from the cold. These men were no good Samaritans, they were looking for a girl. He must have sent them and it sent terrifying chills running down her spine.

Sabastian sensed something wasn't right, the voice was that of an old woman, shaky, and raspy, yes, but there was strength that could not be hidden. If it truly was an old woman, she would be bored with them and not care. This voice had too much passion and panic, someone who cared about her life, not an old veteran of the street who just wanted to sleep.

He stepped closer carefully navigating through the narrow passage, "Okay, I know who you are and you're not kidding anyone. Please, just come out so I can talk to you."

Victoria was stunned and a new wave of adrenaline rippled through her body.

Shit, she thought. He found her again, this time she wouldn't survive and she concentrated on controlling her emotions to focus on what needed to happen next.

Victoria tighten the grip on her knife, prayed the device would work as tested and hoped she still had the element of surprise on her side. With one swift movement, she cut three thin cords in front of her and turned to slice through another thicker one and was quickly propelled skyward.

Chapter 4

"Hey!" Sabastian yelled as he saw the swift movement before him. He was ten feet away, too close to react quick enough, as three heavy garbage bags were hurtled toward them. He was able to slap the first one away, but the other two slammed into his chest and legs. Completely thrown off balance, Sabastian stumbled backward into Edward who couldn't see anything but Sabastian's back hurtling toward him. Edward was able to catch him before being knocked over as well.

"What the hell, Sabastian," he exclaimed, hoisting Sabastian to his feet.

"What happened?" Edward asked, looking around Sabastian to where the bags came from.

Sabastian was not looking down; he was looking up. The clouds had parted for a split second and he had seen a flicker of movement above him. His eyes caught a dark figure disappear over the wall of the alley and onto the roof.

"She's on the roof," he said pointing up.

"What? How?" Edward asked, looking up, and seeing nothing.

"Quick, you watch the front of the building, I'm going up."

Sabastian grabbed the swinging rope and hand over hand, feet on the brick wall, he started to climb up, strong and fast.

How did she do that? He thought. *No way could she climb that fast, she was up the building in mere seconds.*

It took Sabastian less than a minute to reach the top of the six-story building and was barely winded when his feet hit the roof. The building was an old brick apartment and the roof was worn with holes dropping to the floors below. He listened quietly and heard only a squeaking door to his right. He bolted toward it, knowing he would lose her in the darkness if he didn't reach her fast.

The girl was quick, he would give her that, but no way was some girl going to get away from him. The chase had become a challenge, a game. One he was hell-bent on winning.

Sabastian could hear the occasional scrape and rustle below him and took the stairs down fast. It was pitch black in the stair well, as most of the windows were covered. He decided that if she could run blind, he would simply follow the noise she made and catch up. She was right in front of him, he would reach her in seconds. He sped up perplexed when he heard a heavy grinding noise. He turned the corner and ran face first into a wall in the middle of the stairs, bouncing off it severely and falling hard on his left shoulder.

Oh come on, he thought, getting up and slamming his right shoulder into the makeshift wall, feeling it budge. Sabastian hit it three more times finally breaking through. Stepping over the debris of wood and metal racks he took the steps more carefully now. The next time the stairs turned, he slowed slightly, looking up making sure there was nothing to block him. Suddenly, he was sent flying down the stairs in a heap, something wrapped around his ankles. He reached down and felt a thin rope twisted around his boots, he yanked it off and got up. After only a few steps he fell again, another rope tangled on his feet. He couldn't see the rope on the stairs, it was too dark, but he could hear the girl moving effortlessly in front of him. She must have set up tripwires all along the stairs. Knowing where the ropes were, she increased the distance between them. Sabastian was blind in the darkness and his frustration grew.

"Move faster," he told himself. His feet became tangled again but this time he managed to stay upright. He was starting to gain again when he heard a door close. She had fled the stairwell and he was glad to get away from the web of ropes that were still loosely wrapped around his ankles.

Going through the door, Sabastian silently cursed again, he was standing at the end of a long hallway with no sight or sound of the girl. He took a deep breath, kicking the rest of the ropes off his boots. Moonlight shone through the dank quiet space, let in by loose boards, which had come free from the broken windows at the far end of the hallway. Sabastian didn't move, but grabbed his phone and shot a text to Edward "3 floor *now*."

He started forward, looking down the hall for any sign of where she might be. He knew she would be hiding as he could no longer hear her. Worried she might have set more traps; Sabastian was cautious as he moved forward as

19

clouds had covered the only source of light. Heading down the musty hall that smelled of rats, his shoes kept crunching beneath him effectively giving away his position. He stopped, closed his eyes and listened. The only sound he heard was Edward noisily making his way up the stairs behind him, ensuring the girl would not be able to double back. Two things alerted him to her presence, one was a distinct smell, the odor he had recoiled from in the alley. And two, when the clouds shifted the moon shone through the window again and onto the wooden floor and he could see fresh scuff marks in the dust. She may as well have drawn a map and handed it to him. He motioned to Edward to follow him and they moved toward the third door on the right.

Chapter 5

Victoria was outright pissed; how could this be happening? He must have sent professionals after her. She might feel flattered if the thought of being tracked by head hunters didn't nauseate her.

Her escape plan had worked so far, the spring-loaded bags and pulley system that hauled her up the side of the apartment worked like a charm. She had distracted them with the thrown bags long enough for her to cut the rope, which held the counter-weight to lift her to the top of the building. She spent over a month preparing and it was worth every second. However, she didn't think that Spiderman would be after her. How did he get to the top of the building so fast?

She was now improvising. She knew the make-shift wall she created in the stairwell, would work, giving her a little more time. Even knowing where the ropes she placed every third or fourth step in the stairwell, helped her get down the stairs fast. But she had not planned to go down into the building and through her own traps. She never thought that someone would be able to climb up the building after her. She couldn't stay on the roof and hop to the next building as planned. Her panic had blinded her and she had not been able to think quickly enough to cut the rope that had propelled her up and had run when she saw the man climbing fast up the building behind her. Now she was on an unknown floor and trapped, her final escape route was blocked.

If her assailants had not seen her go up the building, she would have been safe. If they did happen to see her, they were supposed to think that she was trapped in the apartment and come up the stairs. Then she would simply stay on the roof and jump from building to building getting away while they struggled through her maze of traps on the staircase. But no, they had followed her up the wall and now she was trapped from above and below.

She huddled in the back corner of a small dark cluttered apartment. The only light came through a window to her right. With adrenaline still coursing through her veins, she sat thinking and clutching her knives. She could get out the window to the fire escape, but that would be too risky. There was no guarantee the rusted-out stairs would release down to the ground and they would be too loud if they did. She could take a chance, climb halfway down the un-extended stairs and jump, hoping she didn't break her leg. Victoria stopped thinking, she was out of time, the door to the small apartment was opening and she bolted.

No longer worried about making noise, she reached the window and was more than half way out when a pair of strong arms wrapped around her waist. With her knife held in her hand to strengthen her blow, she twisted and her fist connected with something hard. Shooting her leg out, she connected again and heard a low groan. One of her knives was suddenly ripped out of her hand. She couldn't see anything with the low light and Mildred blocking her view, so she fought on both training and instinct and hoped it would be enough.

While the men struggled to get a good grip on her. Her right knife hand swung back and felt resistance as it ripped through clothes and flesh. She heard a male voice curse in her ear and the arms momentarily loosened around her. She swung her knife again at the man in front of her in a downward stroke and saw him disappear to the left, away from her slicing motion. She felt strong arms release her waist and clamp down over her arms above the elbows so fast she didn't have a chance to slip away. She twisted her knife in her hand and drew it down, sinking it to the hilt in the man's thigh. She heard a scream and was thrown to the ground leaving the knife behind in the man's leg. She quickly reached down and grabbed her ankle knife, and jumped to her feet, but another set of hands reached out to her, knocking the small knife to the floor.

She was grabbed again around the waist, but her arms were free this time. She swung her empty fist forward at a figure in front of her, this time seeing his face. She slammed her fist into his face at the same time she brought up her knee hard. She was a mess of leveled punches and thrusting knees and elbows barely missing their target. But she was held in a vice grip that would not loosen, no matter how hard she hit and struggled. She knew she was making good connections, but it felt as though her strikes were completely ineffective, like she was attacking a brick wall. She was weak and these men were no light weights, but still she fought hard letting adrenaline rule her. Victoria pushed off her feet and threw her head back missing connecting with the man holding her. She was suddenly lifted off the ground and lost all the momentum for most of her defensive moves.

What confused Victoria the most was that the men were not fighting back, only trying to hold her or defend themselves! She couldn't fight them if they didn't fight back. Most of her defenses were for a fight, using momentum against her attackers and they hadn't even tried to hit her once.

She glimpsed movement in front of her and threw her forehead toward an oncoming face and connected, her head throbbed painfully and started to spin. She knew either of the men could win easily against her, but still they did not fight back. They only restrained her and tried to keep her still. Suddenly there was a bright white light in the room, and she saw the face of a man who was beyond pissed, someone who, if you met him in a dark alley, you would run for your life, which ironically, she was attempting to do. She only saw him for a spilt second and then there was a cloth over her face and she couldn't breathe. She let out a grunt as she kicked again and connected hard. The last thing she remembered was the smell of a sweet, pungent aroma pressed into her mouth and nose, then blackness stole over her, and she knew nothing more.

Chapter 6

"Holy hell, what the fuck was that!" Edward exclaimed, dropping the dead weight of the girl to the floor heavily.

"Nice," Sabastian said, motioning to the helpless heap on the floor. He grabbed a cloth from his pocket to stop the blood that flowed from his nose.

"You didn't need to drop her like that," he said, bending over the small figure who had given them so much trouble.

"Are you kidding me?" Edward exclaimed. "She stabbed me; the pint size bitch stabbed me!"

Edward grabbed the knife handle still imbedded in his thigh and yanked it out, biting his lip.

"Damn it!" he said, looking at the knife.

"Well, at least, it was a small blade," Sabastian chuckled.

"It doesn't feel small," Edward mumbled, holding his blood-stained hand over the wound.

"I think she broke my nose."

"Please, she couldn't kill a cockroach, let alone break anything on you butch boy," Sabastian said.

"Well, my fucking balls are throbbing."

"Suck it up, princess, so are mine," Sabastian retorted.

It had not been Sabastian's best night either. He knew this was going to be a shit-show, right from the beginning. He held the cloth over his bleeding nose while mentally checking his body. His shins were bruised, as well as his face when she had connected a solid punch to his cheek. However, it was the cheap head-butt to his nose that almost made him lose it. His groin was throbbing and he felt sick. He looked down at the unconscious heap in the stinking pile of clothing and considered what to do next.

Sabastian, hearing Edward's groan realized Edward was worse off than himself. He tore off a piece of his shirt and tied it tight around Edward's leg.

"Shit," Edward said, grimacing. "How the hell did she do all that?" He asked, looking at the pile on the floor.

"She's on something, either speed or cocaine or maybe both, she didn't feel a thing…" Sabastian was an expert on narcotics. But he knew it was more than that, she had fighting skills, he had seen it before and a lot of her moves were calculated and well trained, as weak as they were.

"How's the leg?" Sabastian asked.

"I'll live, but it's going to be a pain in the ass getting her to the car."

"I can handle her on my own, as long as you can walk there?"

"I should be able to handle that," Edward said, putting weight on his leg. "I'm glad I don't have to carry her, she stinks and I don't want to ride with that smell in the car," he complained.

"Okay, get my flashlight and shine it over here."

Sabastian bent over her trying to get a better look. Edward picked up the small flashlight that he had lost during the struggle and shone it on the heap on the floor. Sabastian turned the pile of clothes over and gasped at the old woman that looked up at him.

"What the hell!" he cried, peering closer.

He was looking into the distorted face of an old woman, but something didn't seem right. Looking closer, he realized it was a very convincing mask. The disguise was hiding the girl's face well and he tore it off and a small gaunt face appeared beneath. He moved on, not interested in this female who had caused him so much hassle. His hands moved across her body quickly. Sabastian found clasps, running from chin to knees and started undoing them roughly, yanking the stinking overcoat from her body. He was shocked to see how much bulk the over-coat took away from her small frame. He could tell by her face that she was thin, and she still wore several layers of clothing. He could see her hands, neck, and face and how meager they looked. He took off the coat and handed it to Edward, who was still holding the flashlight over the girl.

"I don't want it," Edward said, holding the garment away from his body.

"Relax, we just need to get rid of it."

Sabastian reached down and scooped up the limp girl, he was surprised how heavy she was, it didn't make sense.

Sabastian felt around her back and found the reason. He gestured to Edward as he slung her onto his shoulder.

"Take her bag off."

Edward struggled with balance on his injured leg as he slipped the bag off the girl's shoulders.

"Man, what does she have in here?" Edward asked, weighing the bag in his arms.

Sabastian's burden lighted considerably. He guessed she carried around thirty pounds in the pack and was even more impressed she was able to fight with that amount of weight on her.

"Okay, Edward, your turn."

Edward reached into his pocket and took out a syringe.

"How much do you think she weighs?"

"Ninety pounds at most," said Sabastian, adjusting his load.

Edward squirted clear liquid out of the needle on to the floor and injected the helpless female in the neck.

"Okay, we are good to go," Edward said. "I'll try to clear the way. There's a bunch of shit you didn't see in the stairwell."

"It couldn't have been any worse than what I went through," Sabastian said.

Sabastian could not have been more wrong. There were fridges, washers, dryers, and oil spilled all down the staircase. He had to concentrate and watch his step so as not to slip and drop his burden. There were ropes at different heights, ball bearings, and debris everywhere. The little hellion must have spent weeks creating this little playground.

Sabastian had to set her down several times to help Edward cut ropes, move furniture, and balance him when the terrain was too difficult for his injured leg.

Out on the street, Sabastian said, "The bottles."

Edward took out two small whiskey bottles from his jacket, handed one to Sabastian, and held the other in his hand. Both men began to sway back and forth down the street. Edward limping considerably added to the drunk act. They had to look intoxicated, hoping that anyone watching, would only see a couple of drunks hauling another drunk home. With empty whiskey bottles in their hands, the stink of the overcoat Edward carried and the occasional slurred word, no one looked twice.

Once the men reached the car, Edward put the overcoat in the trunk as Sabastian stashed the still unconscious girl in the back seat along with her backpack. All that was left was to transfer her to their original car, return the

26

borrowed car, and leave the unpleasant coat and the Grand Am for Frank to dispose of, then head back to the airport. All Sabastian could think about was, she had better be worthwhile. He could very easily dump her in a ditch on the way back, promotion be dammed, and not think twice about it. She was already way more trouble than she was worth!

Chapter 7

"Well, Roman, how does it look?" Sabastian asked, grabbing a rolling chair and sliding in beside the broad man who was watching several colored monitors.

"Nothing so far. She's still passed out," Roman answered, looking bored.

Roman was a fine example of the type of man that worked at the company, well-built, strong, and sculptured. He was the typical tall, dark, and handsome male employed by Mr. D. Handpicked and trained to do an expert job according to his skill set. It was not one sided, the women also had to be utterly beautiful and very intelligent just like the men so at least the company wasn't biased.

"I'll let you know if anything changes," Roman continued.

Sabastian frowned. "Michael checked her vitals…" he said, flipping open the report in the file folder he held.

"She's fine, just really small, so the drugs will take a while to wear off, plus, whatever's in her system will affect when she'll wake up. Hey, is it true?"

"What?" Sabastian asked.

"That she has purple eyes?"

"That's what Mike wrote down but I don't believe it, I'll have to see for myself," replied Sabastian.

"I thought only cats had purple eyes?" Romans asked.

"Well, that's what she is, a wild cat for sure," Sabastian said yawning.

"Go get some sleep. I'll give you a call if she wakes up?"

"Fine, she's a pain in the ass anyway," Sabastian tried to turn away from the monitors but the small figure in the huge bed completely intrigued him. As much as he would have loved to send the girl packing, he admired her tenacity. He had to remember it must have been the narcotics fueling her. What kind of a female takes on two full grown men and almost gets the better of them? Miss Cherry was going to have fun explaining the situation to her. Sabastian smiled.

"What are you smiling at?" Roman asked.

"Oh, just thinking that Miss Cherry is going to need bloody body guards when she goes in to talk to her."

"Was she really that much trouble? Come on, she must weigh less than a hundred pounds," Roman scoffed.

"Ya, well, you weren't there, that chick is crazy. I've never seen someone be so savage. I think Miss Cherry will have her hands full with her."

"Do you think she'll work for you?"

"I don't know, but one thing is for certain, I am staying the hell away from her until she's fully educated because if I go anywhere near her, I will be paying her back for my balls," Sabastian winced, rubbing his crotch.

"Well, you don't have to concern yourself about that. Only Miss Cherry talks to the test girls, so you don't have anything to worry about her for at least a few months. Go get some ice for your balls," Roman said smirking. "I've got this."

"Okay, let me know, I need to wrap up my report," Sabastian said, waving the folder in his hands, turning to leave when Roman asked.

"Hey, how's Eddie doing?"

"He'll be fine, just a knife wound, he's with Michael now getting stitched up."

"Man, she really laid into you guys."

"You weren't there, the girl is wild."

"Well, I'll keep a close eye on her then," Roman said turning back to the screen.

Sabastian pulled his eyes away from the monitor, scowled, and hoped the vagrant female would never wake up so he wouldn't have to deal with her any time soon. Secretly, he was excited of the challenge of becoming her trainer to see if she would be the one that would give him the promotion he desperately wanted. Walking out of the monitor room, he turned to the stairs to try to get a few hours of sleep before having to report to Miss Cherry on their so-called routine collection he and Edward had just finished.

Chapter 8

This was different, something was wrong. This was not like the last time, this was so much worse. He had never used thugs or drugs before and she was in an unfamiliar place even though she couldn't open her eyes, at least not yet.

She was lying on a soft surface but her eyes wouldn't operate, even though she was conscious. She concentrated on her other senses. Touch, sound and smell were slowly kicking in and the one thing that started to worry her was that her security blanket was gone. The putrid trench coat that had kept her safe for so long was nowhere near her. The scent that had kept her protected for so long was replaced with the soft smell of lavender and roses. She couldn't see, but it was the lack of garbage, feces, and rotting flesh that made her panic.

Victoria was lying flat on her back and that also meant the bastards had stolen her backpack. All the possessions she owned were in that pack and they were gone and it pissed her off. Breathing hard, her emotions at the injustice finally getting to her, she realized she was also breathing fresh air, not the stuffy air that she was used to from Mildred. Her old woman mask was also gone, she was completely exposed and felt naked!

The adrenaline was kicking in now and Victoria's eyes finally flew open but were instantly blinded by a harsh light and her eyes shut reflexively. She tried opening her eyes again, this time slowly. The lights were so bright at first it took several seconds for her pupils to adjust and to start to see shapes come into focus. The bright light was actually a soft yellow glow that was hidden in the corners of the room and reflected off the ceiling. She could see that she was lying on a large four poster bed with sheer material laced throughout the canopy which confused her even more. She controlled her panic and concentrated on breathing deeply in and out and closed her eyes again.

Not hearing anything but her deep breaths, she kept willing herself out of this paralysis. She assumed she must be tied up, but couldn't feel her body or any restraints on her wrists or legs.

She lay there for what could have been minutes or hours trying to wiggle her fingers when something finally changed.

She felt her fingers twitch. *Yes,* she thought.

Victoria was careful, she didn't want someone to discover she was awake and kept her eyes closed. She had a feeling she was being surveyed. That someone was hovering close by, watching and waiting for her to wake up. She was scared. What would happen to her once they, whoever they were, found her awake? She needed to figure out how tightly she was bound, but didn't dare move her arms or legs to find out. She decided not to move at all until she was sure that she had mastered her body again.

Slowly and with as little movement as possible she tested every part of herself. Being careful not to move the only parts of her body that were visible outside her layers of clothes. She needed to be subtle. She could not show them she was awake as she was hoping to regain the element of surprise. She flexed every muscle feeling major tenderness and pain in her legs, arms, and back after the fight she had put up. After moving her shoulders, back and thighs at the same time, she came to the conclusion that she was ready to get up or at least test the strength of any ropes holding her down. She cracked her eyes slightly so the soft ceiling light didn't make her shut her eyes automatically again. She then moved her hands slowly and the horror of what she felt shocked her into a state of pure panic.

Her hands had come into contact with thick plastic and she verified what sent a cold chill through her by reaching out again slowly with her fingers. She had been put onto a plastic tarp. Whoever had taken her was going to make a mess with her and wanting to keep his bed and house clean after he had done chopping her into little pieces or raping her so much she bled out or…

Her mind went in to overdrive and she knew she needed to move fast. She had to fight and escape while she still had the upper hand of them thinking she was still passed out.

In one swift unsteady movement, she grabbed the only thing she could use as a weapon and yanked hard at bonds that were not there! Momentary flustered, she flung herself clumsily off the bed, and stumbled to a door in the far corner of the huge room with the plastic tarp tightly in her hand.

Shock was replaced by amazement that she had not been tied down on the plastic covered bed. Victoria swayed heavily but maintained her balance, her back slamming into the wall behind the door. She assumed whoever was in the room would pounce, but she was taken aback that she was alone.

There was a large bathroom to the right of her position, door open, she could see it was empty. Being alone in the room meant they didn't think she would wake up so quickly. She was now in the perfect position to hide behind the only door when it opened. She reached down her leg instinctively for her knife but grasped nothing. She looked down at her ankle, the knife strap was in place but the knife was gone, looking at her other ankle she realized both knives were missing.

Of course, she thought.

Quickly and as quietly as she could Victoria wrapped both ends of the plastic tarp tightly around her hands and wrists. Intending to use the tarp around the neck and face of whoever came through that door first, praying that only one person would enter. Watching the door, ready to jump at any noise or movement of the doorknob made her unsteady. Victoria's eyes were going in and out of focus, she had moved too fast and her body was not as in control as she had hoped. Her hands started to shake first and her legs followed after only a few minutes.

How long could she maintain this position ready to defend herself? She was staring unseeing at the door knob, waiting for it to move and listening hard. She couldn't hear anything and her shaking hands were starting to noisily shake the plastic she held. She couldn't let the noise alert them she was waiting for them right behind the door. Her eyes started to water, her legs in pain, her arms hurt from holding them at the ready. She was too weak and she would be completely useless if they came in now. Her arms fell first and the tears that she had been holding back followed. She couldn't take this; it was too much. She let her knees give out and she let herself sink to the ground. Better to be on the floor resting, then fainted, unconscious again. She tried to regain some control of the situation and placed her ear tight to the door and listened. She swiped at the tears, frustrated with herself. She was stronger than this.

Blinking the tears away, she took her eyes from the door to focus on the room looking to see if there were any other weapons she could use to her advantage. She looked where she had come from. The bed was rumpled from her leaping from it but the room itself was stunning. A gold and cream shrine of a bed, decorated in an old Victorian motif.

At least she was not in some wooden shack and she was certainly not back at home with him. The windowless room reminded her of the basement she used to be kept in, but the lack of windows was where the resemblance ended. The room was huge and very tastefully decorated. The furniture was artfully carved in a dark mahogany and layers of sheer cream draperies enveloped the beautifully carved bed. Just the headboard alone looked like it took hundreds of hours to carve. Detailed swirls and loops and a large cream padded backboard stood out below the decorative carvings of the bed. On either side of the bed, there were matching wooden nightstands with cream marble tops with dozens of white roses in gold-colored vases. There was a sitting area on the other side of the open concept room with a large mahogany couch, loveseat, and carved chair, embellished with gold accents and cream pillows. A huge, floor to ceiling mirror was hung across from an ornate wardrobe, also carved from dark wood with gold accents. There was a large dresser with a second mirror perched on top. The walls boasted a cream chair level wainscoting with gold trim and it matched both the crown molding and the baseboards.

Taking in the room allowed Victoria to calm down slightly and she ran her hands through the soft, plush cream carpet beside her hips. She knew this kind of luxury existed but had always been prevented from experiencing it for herself. Even the door she was leaning up against was thick and ornately carved mahogany. Looking around the room and admiring the many fine things had cleared her head and she was able to think and see clearly, the adrenaline driven panic finally subsiding. Her adrenaline slowed with every second and she was now noticing it was too warm in the room, which was did not help considering the layers of clothing she still wore. The heat started to make her sweat and a fresh wave of dizziness swept over her. She was too hot, sweating, and starting to shake harder still.

Gazing around the room her eyes fell once again on the door, she was puzzled to see a bright orange note just to the right of it, several inches above her head. She had been too panicked to notice it before, even though it stood out so sharply in this lush setting. She got up slowly and moved closer to the sign still in tune with the outside noises she still couldn't hear and read "You are safe, no one will harm you. No one will come through this door without your permission. Please stay calm."

She blinked and was taken aback, she looked up at the door again and saw there was a lock on her side of the door. It was a deadbolt and under that a slide chain. She unwound the plastic tarp from her wrist and reached tentatively toward the door and with shaking fingers slid the slide bolt into place to the right, then latched the chain to its place on the wall. Trying to understand and still untrusting, she knew that a key from the other side and a swift kick could dislodge the chain, but that did not explain the floor bolt she saw. Staring at it she reached down and pushed the thick metal bolt into the floor, securing the door tightly. She was completely baffled.

Even though the door was clearly impregnable, she did not trust the situation. Why would anyone grab her and stick her in a room that only she could control? This was too weird and thinking hard it took her a long time to finally relax her muscles again, but not her mind.

Would no one be able to get in?

She considered the door again before deciding to see if there were other ways to enter the room.

She didn't want to venture from the door so Victoria scanned the room looking for any seams along the walls, thinking there might be a hidden entrance. Seeing nothing, she got up slowly and began to walk toward the bathroom. A crunching sound made her freeze in the quiet room and she saw that the plastic tarp was still wrapped tightly around her wrist. This reminded her, why would someone cover the bed in plastic?

She ambled toward the bed, dropping the plastic behind her. She reached out and placed a hand on the bed and saw the answer immediately. Right where she had rubbed the luxurious light-colored duvet was a dirty smear from her fingers. She looked and saw another stain of dirt where she had rolled off the bed. She glanced behind her and saw filth from her boots staining the cream carpet behind the door and on a path from the bed and back again. The plastic was protection from her!

Here she was in the most beautiful room she had ever seen and she was polluting it by bringing her grime from the streets with her and whoever had brought her here wanted the room to stay tidy. This completely threw her off balance, she wished she was drugged again, as that unbalancing made more sense. She could not register this, she looked at her hands and then at her feet and self-consciously she reached down to undo the laces on her oversized army boots. She reached over to pick up the plastic and placed it back on the bed before sitting down to remove her boots.

Victoria was still too hot and sweating, making her feel even filthier. Glancing at the door, she proceeded to take off her outer layers of clothes. Taking off her large winter jacket, then a thinner jacket, there were two sweat shirts under that. With each layer taken off, she felt lighter and could finally feel cool air touch her moist skin for the first time in a very long time. She walked over to the door to check the locks and look around again for another entrance before removing the hooded sweat shirt over her head. She now wore a pair of leggings and grey sweat pants, a sports bra with a tank top, and a blue t-shirt over top.

Apprehension made her hesitate to take off the one thing that was still keeping her much too warm. A tight black winter cap with a large bulge at the back of it wrapping her neck. The room looked secure and Victoria knew that if these people wanted to hurt her, they could. Still worried, she slowly lifted the woolen cap from her head and for the first time in months, a cool breeze hit the back of her neck and she was able to let her hair down. Her tightly braided hair fell heavily around her, falling past her knees before stopping.

Her hair was one of the things she desperately tried to keep hidden on the streets. Not only was it a telltale sign of her youth, but it could be grabbed, and she could be trapped by whomever held it. She had learned that the hard way, however, she had refused to cut it. She found that the security she felt of it wrapped around her and the warmth it provided was worth keeping the long mane intact.

Victoria still had a few layers of clothes on but she was now in clean clothes, at least on the outside. She hadn't done laundry in over four months and she knew she stank but the smell was only that, a smell and the clothes themselves had very little street grime on them. She gingerly piled her other clothes beside her boots on the floor, wincing at the smug of dirt they left on the carpet.

She had never been more ashamed of her appearance and general lack of personal hygiene, but, of course, living on the streets, who had cared? She had made herself repulsive on purpose, it was a survival method that worked well. But being in a room that was so clean, fresh, and well cared for, the last thing she wanted was to contaminate it. She felt humiliated and ashamed and it brought back terrible memories of being back home. Victoria desperately longed to feel clean again.

Her gazed traveled to the bathroom and she took a tentative step toward it, she could at least wash her hands. Watching the bedroom door nervously as she passed, her feet led her to a bathroom that was unbelievably more stunning than the bedroom.

The floors were covered in a rich cream marble that swirled in patterns which was warm on her feet. A huge vanity had a new packaged toothbrush and toothpaste beside a deep marble sink. Next to the sink was an elaborate make-up desk with a Victorian chair, both had their own mirror that was wrapped in carved mahogany like the bedroom decor. Straight across the room from the door was a monstrous jetted tub with a frosted glass steam shower to the right. In the middle of the room, directly in front of her, stood a large pedestal table with an oversized woven basket containing all sorts of creams, soaps, scrubs, cloths, oils, exfoliators, and more.

It is like the bathroom you would see in a rich and famous magazine, she thought.

She looked down into the basket hoping to find normal soap for her hands and reached in and grabbed a small pink bar of soap in the shape of a swan. She carried it over to the sink and unwrapping the little soap treasure, she turned on the hot water. She looked up from the sink and stopped. Staring back at her was a haggard, skinny girl, she looked into the mirror at her reflection and saw only despair and hopelessness.

Her hair which used to be a lovely shade of dark blonde was heavy with grease and limp. Her face was dirty and unrecognizable. She could see lines where the sweat had rubbed the grit off on her neck and tear lines down her cheeks and her unusually colored eyes were lifeless. Looking away repulsed, she glanced down at her hands. The swan which was so pretty before was now caked in dirt. Everything she touched, she ruined, her face contorted, and she started rubbing her hands furiously, trying desperately to get at least one small part of her body clean. Tears streaming down her face, she scrubbed until her hands were sore and raw. Thoroughly frustrated she threw the soap across the room and tossed the pedestal table with the basket in a rage, collapsing onto the floor sobbing uncontrollably.

What happened to me? I'm ruined, disgusting and now I'm trapped in this heaven of a place that just reminds me of the hell I've come from. I don't belong here; I have to get out. I need control. I can't be here and don't deserve to be here.

She felt gross, and unclean and being in a place like this reminded her how no good, white trash she was. She couldn't cope and curled into a ball on the bathroom floor defeated and cried.

Chapter 9

"What the hell happened?" Sabastian glared at the monitors grabbing Roman hard on the shoulder. "I told you to call me when she woke up."

Roman and Sabastian were watching the small girl on the bathroom floor through the screens in the monitor room. A room filled with TV's monitoring almost every area of both the manors.

"I thought you said you wanted nothing to do with her, beside Miss Cherry should be on her way down, I just texted her," Roman replied, shrugging his shoulder out of Sabastian's tight grip.

"What's wrong with her? And what is that?" Sabastian asked staring at the curled-up figure on the floor and pointing to something beside her.

Sabastian had been heading to see Richard after his nap when curiosity had gotten the better of him and he decided to check on the little wild cat.

"You are going to love this. And I thought the eyes were an anomaly," Roman said, working with the controls and another monitor popped up.

Sabastian looked up while the monitor rolled back and watched her from the time she gained awareness on the bed, to the table throwing episode. He was impressed she was ready to take on any attackers that came through the door with only a plastic tarp as a weapon. Then he watched as she finally focused and locked the door. He was startled on how many layers of clothes she had on when she started to undress, she kept getting thinner and thinner with each layer she took off and it worried him.

"Jesus," Sabastian was amazed as he watched her pull off her cap and her hair fell heavily.

"Ya, that's what's wrapped around her on the floor," Roman said pointing to the monitor that Sabastian was referring to, answering his earlier question.

Watching her in real time now, Sabastian asked, "All that is hair?"

"Yup, not only does she have freaky eyes, but she has longer hair than Rapunzel."

"She must be crashing," Sabastian noted.

Watching her on the many expertly hidden cameras in the room, Sabastian squinted at the monitors. Not one of the women who had been in the room over the years had ever noticed the cameras. He was sure almost all the girls had suspected and even looked for them but they were undetectable even to him. Hidden in the wood work, the walls and the furniture. Timothy, their local tech expert, had been a genius when he designed and installed them.

"Have you got the results back?" Roman asked still fiddling with his instruments.

"No, not yet. I won't have to deal with her for a few months, so what drugs she's on doesn't matter. I just need the tox report before I can submit my paperwork and finish up with her until the real testing begins. I could care less what she's on, that's Michael and Miss Cherry's job. They are the ones that get to clean her up. I'm going to recommend we dump her anyway, I don't think she's worthwhile."

"You're going to throw your test away and start over?" asked Roman looking at Sabastian with raised eyebrows. "That could take months!"

"Ya, it's not worth it. It'll be faster if I find another girl," Sabastian shrugged. "Okay, send Miss Cherry to me once she's seen the footage. I can give her my report and my recommendation and hope she listens and also hope that Mr. D lets me try again. Have fun watching the psycho chick."

"Okay, see you around."

Roman turned back to his monitors and checked his phone waiting for a response from Miss Cherry that should have been sent almost immediately after he had texted her. *'She must be with Mr. D,'* he thought, and settled into his book with his feet up on the desk waiting for the small figure in the golden bathroom to finish her breakdown.

Chapter 10

Miss Cherry, like all the other women that worked at her company, was the type of woman people would stop on the streets to stare at. This was a feat considering she was over fifty. However, her company and Mr. D had taken very good care of her all these years and she did not look a day over thirty-five.

Her shoulder length copper hair fell in waves around her face. Her golden eyes were kind and had an exotic slant to them. Standing at five foot nine inches, naked before the mirror, she contemplated what to wear.

When discussing the situation with her Mr. D, she would need every bit of confidence she could muster. She also knew that he wouldn't be as hard on her if she came before him stunning and beautiful. It would show him respect and in turn, he would show at least a little restraint if and when he started to browbeat her.

She had sent the long correspondence of e-mails she had been working on for the last few hours trying desperately to back-track where things had gone wrong and knew it would not take Mr. D long to finish reading through it. She reached into her closet and unhooked a light emerald short sweater dress with a plunging neck line. She also put on her pearls and a touch of light make up while brushing her hair out. She wanted to time her entry into his apartment perfectly because if she kept him waiting it would only fuel his temper.

Ten minutes later, she was riding up the silver elevator with her cell phone and notes in hand. The doors to the artfully decorated elevator slid open with a soft ring to alert Mr. D of her arrival. A grim-faced man was facing her a few feet to the right of the elevator. He nodded to her and led her toward the office.

Jeremy Wright was in his forties and was Mr. D's right-hand man and had served him for over twenty years. Jeremy was slender and tall but not without muscle, his face was cleanly shaven topped with short salt and pepper hair and his clothes were always immaculate. He was almost constantly stoned faced and took everything in stride without any emotion. It was rare to ever see the man smile or show any kind of passion at all. He was impeccable at his job and it had always been that way and everyone respected the man greatly.

They walked through the top floor of the largest apartment in the men's manor. Everything was steel or glass, white or black, the ultimate bachelor pad. The decorating was tastefully done, without going over board and she loved this most manly of spaces. Hardly anyone got to see it and she thought that was a shame since she had put so much work into decorating it for her beloved boss.

Mr. D liked his privacy and rarely left the manor, except to ensure the other chapters of his business were being run to his level of excellence. He enjoyed the life and business he had built here and since everything ran smoothly, until today, there was no reason for him to leave his sanctuary unless absolutely necessary.

Mr. D was hunched over his computer, he was a heavy-set man. His six pack long forgotten he boasted a slight belly that didn't hang over his belt. His shoulders were wide and he had a good collection of hard muscles under a layer of padding. Being six foot three and two hundred fifty pounds, he was still a healthy man who got plenty of exercise. Cherry saw to it that he followed a diet of good food because quite frankly without Mr. D this thriving business would fall apart.

So many people relied on this passionate man with a temper and it was her job to see that the business he had struggled to build ran flawlessly and there had rarely been any major problems.

Cherry could not see his face behind the monitor but his oversized hand was clutching the computer mouse so tight she was afraid that one more ounce of pressure would lead to the small electronic device collapsing in his hand.

She had only seen Mr. D really mad one other time, yes, he had raised his voice, mostly to the men that worked for him and the occasional client, but not to her or any of the women. She knew that he had the potential to make tough, hard men quiver with his short temper and his rules of perfection, but only when the situation called for it and she knew that this particular complication more than called for it.

She stood before him on the other side of the desk, trying to read his expression around the computer screen waiting for him to address her. Jeremy had faded into the corner of the room so she knew he would be of no help. Mr.

D slowly raised his head and looked at her concerned face and she saw his rage softened slightly.

His face was handsome and was only lined around his eyes and mouth, impressive since he was in his early sixties. Short black hair was thick and frazzled on his head from resting his head in his hands while he read her e-mail. He was unshaven with at least three days of growth and she could see mostly grey in his whiskers. His eyes, normally a soft brown looked almost as dark as his hair, were narrowed as he spoke.

"Is this all of it?" He demanded harshly.

"Yes, that's all the information I have," Cherry squeaked, clearing her throat.

"You could not find anything else?" his voice getting louder, incredulous.

"I wanted to bring Timothy in on it, but I thought I should wait to see who you would want to know about the situation."

"Yes, I want him in on it, Cher, fuck, I'll do whatever it takes to get this fixed. And if a few more guys know what's going on, then maybe it will be the God damn wakeup call they need to remind them we are not fucking selling flowers here. This is a dangerous business and this is what happens when you forget that."

Cherry saw his face was red now and that he was clearly losing it. The scope of the situation did not take long to hit him.

Mr. D took a breath and Cherry held hers. Regaining control, his face started to return to a normal color.

"What's the next step?" he asked, leaning back in his chair, exasperated.

"I have three first class seats on the next plane out there," she replied.

"Who?" he snapped.

"I was thinking Sabastian, Timothy and I," she waited for the rebuke.

It took Mr. D a second to respond, then the explosion erupted.

"No way, are you going, are you insane?" Mr. D scowled at her, his face turning pink again.

"We're going to need a woman over there and I know you wouldn't risk any of the other girls and I certainly wouldn't risk it either. I am the only viable option."

"How about no women and we send just the guys?" Mr. D said this slowly, trying to calm down and think out the situation, but knowing she was right as he spoke the words. He lowered his head into his hands and tried to see a way out where his Cherry would not be put into jeopardy.

Cherry waited, letting him process the scenarios in his head, knowing he would come to the same conclusion she did hours ago. After a few silent minutes, he looked at her again with worry in his eyes.

"Okay, you have to go. Shit, you're right, but I am not letting you out of my sight. Those baboons have already screwed this up. I will not risk it. I'm coming with you and we'll take Tim as he has the skills we need to dig up what the hell happened."

Mr. D watched her and waited, he knew this news would not go over well but, of course, her opinion in this case did not matter.

"What? No, you have to stay here," Cherry almost choked on her words.

Mr. Do softened, "Look if you're going, so am I. Besides, this needs to be unfucked and taken care of properly. I will not sit on the sidelines while they are missing. What would happen if word got out that I stayed here while they were gone? Left the dirty work to others."

Mr. D looked kindly at Cherry, their relationship had always been so close and they were both worried about each other. Together, they were unstoppable and they needed the best team possible to fix this.

Cherry was speechless and looked at Mr. D wide-eyed.

Not looking away from Cherry's face he spoke to his assistant.

"Jerry, get Sabastian," he ordered.

Jeremy, who had been unseen or heard during this conversation, faded from the shadows on his new assignment.

Cherry watched him go, then went to Mr. D who held out his hand to her. She slipped her hand in his and sat on his knee, leaning her back into his chest.

"How are we going to fix this? Even if we find them, the word will get out and we'll be ruined," Cherry whimpered, tears rimming her eyes.

Mr. D held her close and felt the warmth of her body seep comfortingly into him as he wrapped both his arms around her slight frame.

"First things first, we have to get them back, that is the only thing that matters right now."

Chapter 11

He had gotten her successfully and now he was filled with the thrill of anticipation of what would be his. Every time someone new came he had to keep himself in check until she was ready. He knew once collected; it would be months before he could introduce the new girl to his specialty. The anticipation as well as working though the scenarios in his head was one of the best parts.

As much as he would love to perform his unique skill over and over again, it could only happen once. The first and only time is what built him to a frenzy of expectation.

He would need to visit the other manor several times over the next few months to gain some measure of control until he could unleash himself and be fully free. He took a deep breath and tried to calm himself, but he was sick of controlling himself. The constant control with this job was maddening.

He loved his job and it wasn't only for the opportunity to vent, but also to enjoy a part of life that so many people never fully discovered.

Breathing hard, he decide to see if he could take over Roman's job for a few hours to enrich his imagination and begin his pursuit.

Chapter 12

Victoria didn't know how long she had laid on the floor. There was no way to even tell if it was day or night without windows. She only knew that her side was throbbing and her tears had run dry.

This is ridiculous, I need to figure what I'm going to do, she thought as she slowly got into a sitting position. She rubbed her cheek and almost choked when she saw the smear of dirt that had rubbed off from her face to her once clean hand.

She sighed.

Getting up, Victoria found the soap she had thrown and headed to the sink to wash once more. Slowly scrubbing her hands under the warm water, she glanced again at the door, still no noise or movement coming from her room or beyond.

She looked up at the mirror and saw one clean spot under her eye where she had rubbed her face. Looking at the mess on the floor from the basket she had thrown, she saw a face cloth and picked it up. Moving to the elaborate marble sink, she proceeded to wash her face but water soaked into her greasy hair, which caused dirty droplets to run down her face again. She slowly put the cloth down and stared at her reflection, defeated. She was so uncomfortable and out of her element, it unnerved her.

She turned her gaze through the bathroom to the bedroom door again and walked over to it. She checked the locks to see that nothing had been disturbed from when she had locked it.

Hoping no one answered, as she felt too drained for a confrontation, Victoria knocked tentatively on the door. After hearing nothing, she banged on it and yelled.

"Hey!"

Nothing.

No one wanted in or was trying to get in. The only way anyone was getting in here is if there was another entrance which she still couldn't find. She looked once more around the walls for any seams and since there were no windows, the only door in or out was the secure one she had locked tight. Walking along the wall, she noticed a long horizontal box seam that looked out of place beside the large mirrored night dresser. It was about two feet long and one foot high at chest level. The area was too small for anyone to get through, so she dismissed it.

"Screw it," she said. Glancing at the door once more, she started to undress. If she was going to get cleaned up, she was going to do it right. Striping off everything she was wearing; she placed the clothing in a pile beside her boots and walked quietly over to the sitting area on the other side of the bed. There stood the huge full-length mirror, she walked in front of it almost scared of what she would see.

Her eyes are what she focused on first, they were her very best feature and she didn't want to look at the rest of her body. Staring into her own eyes, she saw they had lost their luster and looked dull and sad. The color was there, but not as bright. Her eyes were ringed in a usually rich dark blue but that is where the normality of them ended, around the pupil was a thick ring of a striking purple color that took up more than half the color of her iris.

Even when she was being teased for being white trash in grade school, all the other girls still admired her. They had asked why such worthless trailer trash had been lucky enough to get that color of eyes. Her eyes were the only thing about her that made her truly proud of herself. They were her mother's eyes.

Glancing down reluctantly, she was right to be alarmed as her eyes pooled with fresh tears looking at her emaciated body. Her tiny frame of only five foot four had been robbed of her proud muscles, her arms and legs were thin with bones sticking out all over. Her body was bruised almost everywhere from the fight in the apartment and she was horrified at the patchy dark colors on her otherwise pale skin. Her ribs, elbows, knees, and hips protruded and her spine was sticking out of her back when she turned. Her once large and full breasts were reduced down to nothing and looked weepy and her butt was non-existent.

She had no idea she was so far gone, she looked retched, sick, and pale. She must be well under a hundred pounds and it shocked her to the core. She could see her war wounds from past street fights where she had been assaulted protruding pink on her pale skin. Her lank hair was greasy, hanging down past her knees and dirty droplets of water from her recent face washing streamed from her hair alongside her now falling tears. She had to look away. Still looking through the mirror she stared at her dirty feet, which were also boney. Eyes teary and unfocused on the floor she saw something in the background that made her heart leap.

She spun and dove for the dark green bag that she thought had been taken from her. She couldn't believe it, her back pack with all of her possessions had been in the room the whole time.

She frantically grabbed at the bag and opened it, rummaging through it make sure everything was indeed in her precious sack. She reached through the bag and saw that it had been almost untouched. Her water bottles and beloved books were still there. The rest of her clothes, her treasure box full of her mother's memorabilia's and several photos were intact and what little money she had was all there. Even her realistic old lady Mildred mask was there.

She opened the outer pocket of the pack and wrapped her hands around a rolled leather case and knew before opening it that it was empty. She untied the string and unrolled the case, the four pockets were empty, except for one. Curious, she tugged at the folded piece of paper within one of the pockets and opened it.

"We apologize, but these needed to be removed, they will be returned to you at a later date."

Well, of course, they wouldn't leave these knives behind, just like they wouldn't let her keep her ankle knives. They must have known if anyone would have tried to enter the room she would have stabbed them in the face and made a run for it. She sighed, stood up, avoiding glancing toward the mirror, and placed her bag down carefully beside her pile of clothes.

She looked at the pile of meager possessions. Dirty, smelly, and completely distasteful in this setting; she glanced around the room for somewhere to put the mound where it would not make her wretch. Everything in this room screamed that she was tainted, it was so spotless, so clean and she was so foul that she wanted to scream. She saw a large woven laundry basket with a clear plastic garbage bag in it and practically tackled the dirty pile of clothes and tossed them in with her boots tightly shutting the lid.

Satisfied, Victoria headed to the bathroom to get the grime of the street off her skin and hair, hoping that would also make her feel better.

She checked the bedroom door once again, still paranoid someone would find a way in now that she was completely naked and defenseless. But at this point, she did not care. She closed the bathroom door behind her and was thrilled to see two locks on the door and quickly locked them, doubling her sense of security, relaxing a bit more.

Walking onto the warm bathroom floor, she slowly started to pick up the mess she had made. Carrying the oversized basket in both her arms she carefully laid everything that was strewn on the floor back in, except for the things she would use for her shower. Most of the items she had no clue what they were used for, even when it had a tag on it telling her what it was. Items like bath bombs, skin conditioner, and oiled hair treatment, she had no idea how to use. So she stuck with grabbing what she knew was shampoo and soap.

Undoing her long tightly braided hair, it fell in waves another foot to her ankles. She glanced at the door once again before turning tentatively to the shower. The marbled, glassed shrine had more dials than the average airplane and she had to experiment for several minutes before being able to step into the hot water. Still not sure if she would be able to stay long without someone disturbing her, she quickly washed her hair and rubbed her body down with the bar of soft soap.

She wanted desperately to stay, but seeing how she hadn't had a shower that had lasted longer than two minutes in years, she figured she was clean enough and reached for the knob to turn off the water. She was surprised when she was sprayed with cool then hot water from a different side of the shower, now there was a shower head and four jets spraying her body. She smiled and reached for another knob and another till she was being sprayed by two shower heads eight body jets and a large square overhead shower, dousing her in water. The feel of the jets and the hot soft water was so heavenly, Victoria gave into temptation and stood for a long time soaking up the luxury of the shower. Her body had not been properly cleaned in months and she decided that she needed this.

Making up her mind to treat herself, Victoria stepped out of the shower, looking toward the door, and listening once again for any sound in the room beyond the bathroom. Hearing nothing, she walked over to the basket of bath goodies and did her best at guessing what she could use to scrub her skin clean with the products offered. She found three different types of body cleanser, two different shampoos, and a rich apricot conditioner. She also hit the jackpot when she found a pair of abrasive gloves that she could lather and scrub her skin to her hearts content.

Stepping into the steaming shower with her treasures, she decided to think of nothing else but the water and soap and the feel of a private shower all to herself for the first time in years. More confident on how to work the shower, she worked on getting the water as hot as she could stand and proceeded to scrub every square inch of her body with the sweet-smelling soft soaps until her skin glowed pink and burned as hot as the water steaming around her. Shampooing her hair three times and leaving the hair conditioner on for ten minutes felt heavenly.

She was contemplating experimenting with the steam aspect of the shower but she had started to feel light headed from sweating in the hot water. She turned all the dials off but one, turned down the hot spray to cool, and she soaped the sweat from her skin one last time before turning off the flow and stepping out.

With conviction, she grabbed a light-colored cream towel and scrubbed the water off her body, happy to see the towel came away as clean and as fresh as she felt. She then wrapped an oversized towel around her head. Grabbing another soft thick towel, she wrapped it around her chest and tried tucking it between her breasts like she had seen in a magazine. Apparently, wrapping a towel to hang by itself around your body required both finesse and boobs, both of which she lacking at the moment so she ended up holding the towel until she saw a thick cream-colored robe hanging beside the bathroom door. She threw the large towel in the general direction of a laundry basket in the corner and sighed heavily as she enveloped her body tightly in the silk lined heavy cotton robe, not letting it bother her that the robe could have easily wrapped around her twice. Still feeling light headed, she felt completely drained so she filled a glass beside the sink with cool water to replenish her fluids.

Jesus even the water was perfect, she thought, drinking three glasses thirstily.

Victoria saw the packaged toothbrush and toothpaste beside the sink and preceded to scrub her teeth and the inside of her mouth for a full five minutes, making sure every single inch of her mouth was as clean as the rest of her. Loving the sharp taste of the toothpaste and mouth wash, she even flossed a bit, not wanting to miss a single spot of her entire body, determined to wash every inch of the streets from her.

She sat down at the elaborate Victorian style make-up desk and picked up a hair brush which was laid out along with combs, creams, hair ties, and all sorts of jars and spray bottles. Enjoying her time alone she knew this was something she would probably never experience again and she focused on brushing out her long, wet hair that had not been properly cleaned in years. Not wanting to think about the unknown and dreading what was to come, she forced her mind into fantasy and happy times with her mother and drifted in her own world while she brushed her long mane of hair dry.

Chapter 13

At the insistent knock on the door, Sabastian rolled over in bed.

These cat naps are going to kill me, he thought.

"Ya, come in," he yawned, still half asleep, eyes closed.

Jeremy walked in and turned on the lights.

"Mr. D requires your presence immediately."

Sabastian eyes popped open as those words jolted him awake. Getting out of bed, he looked at Jeremy alarmed.

"Um. Okay. Can a have a minute?"

"No," Jeremy answered sharply, "follow me."

Sabastian was stunned.

Why would Mr. D want him? Was there something wrong with the girl? Was he about to get busted for the way the collection went down?

Question after question bounced around his head, trying to figure out how he was going to talk his way out of this one. He threw on a shirt and jeans and followed Jeremy into the private elevator in a daze.

Sabastian knew Jeremy wouldn't give him any additional information if he asked so they rode the elevator up in silence.

The doors opened and Sabastian followed Jeremy into the office. He saw Miss Cherry standing to the left of the desk.

Shit, this is bad, he thought dismally, trying to compose himself.

"Yes, sir," Sabastian said smartly, trying to hide his wariness, fisting his sweating hands behind his back.

"I hear you have your test subject downstairs waiting to be introduced to Miss Cherry, is that correct?" Mr. D asked.

"Yes, sir, I have yet to complete the report, as I am waiting on the toxin analysis," Sabastian answered professionally.

"It did not go well," Mr. D stated.

"No, sir."

"How badly is Edward hurt?"

"Five stitches to his leg, a cut to his arm and minor bruising. He has already been treated by Michael."

"And you? You don't look so good yourself." Mr. D said, referring to his red swollen nose.

"No, sir. I'm fine. Just a lucky shot," Sabastian said, trying not to go red from embarrassment.

"She had training, sir, martial arts or something, plus the drugs she's on fueled her."

"Was she hurt at all?" Mr. D asked sternly.

"No, sir, we restrained her only and kept her from hurting herself and took most of the assault until we could sedate her."

"Normally, there would be an investigation in this complete failure to attain a collection safely, however, there is more pressing business that I have to get to."

Sabastian was on the defensive, the only reason Edward and him got the better of the attack was because they couldn't hurt the girl. He wanted to say that they didn't even get the chance to talk, as she had run, then attacked them with no warning. Yes, they did not expect it and had underestimated her, but it was not like they could fight back. They could only try to get a hold of the infuriating female.

He resented the small woman more than ever. She was not worth it and he wanted to pass working with her, so he wouldn't have to deal with her again. It would mean months of waiting for another opportunity to attempt his test again on a different girl. Perhaps never if his boss deemed this a failure and he would be stuck in the same job again, all because of that train wreck of a woman.

"Sir, allow me to explain, we did not get the chance to even talk to…"

"That's fine, Sabastian, it doesn't matter now," Mr. D said cutting him off. "I wanted to inform you that Miss Cherry will not be available to explain the situation to the girl, so you will be the one handling her introduction."

Still frustrated at not being able to defend himself, Sabastian was flustered.

"I am not sure I understand, sir."

"Instead of just training her to work at the manor, you will also be pitching to her once she's clean."

Mr. D said this like it was an everyday occurrence, but he couldn't ignore both Miss Cherry's and Sabastian's reactions. Cherry, knowing better than to argue, kept her silence, but Sabastian was quick to respond.

"Men never talk to any of the newly collected, ever! How can I? I've never even witnessed the initial talk with a test girl. I can't do it…"

Mr. D cut him off again, "Miss Cherry and I will be leaving within the hour for an undisclosed amount of time, you will be in charge of the new girl and Jeremy will be taking over my job."

In a rare show of emotion, Jeremy raised both his eyebrows, turned his head, and looked stunned at his boss. It took him only a second to regain his composure and continued to stare straight ahead like he had not been listening.

"Sir, my recommendation is that we let her go."

Trying to get a hold of himself, he swallowed and took a breath.

"Sir, it will take months to clean her up to even start to think about pitching to her," Sabastian finished.

"Well, consider that a great opportunity to prove that you are ready for this challenge. If she is suited to the work and you can get her to take the job, your test will be passed and you will have your pick of which city you want to branch our company out in. I will not tolerate anything less than her cleaned up."

Mr. D smiled knowingly. He knew with a new girl to care for, Sabastian would not have the time to worry about why he and Cherry had to suddenly take off. He needed to know the girl was here, cleaned up and taken care at the very least as he had special plans for her. It would also be a great way to see how his favorite employee, Sabastian would handle a situation like this when he was in control of his own chapter, a good test all on its own.

Sabastian looked at Miss Cherry, who shrugged and smiled encouragingly.

Thinking hard, Sabastian said, "Mr. D, can I at least have one of the other girls with me to help…"

Mr. D cut him off again. "Not their job," he stated flatly.

Sabastian tried again, "Sir, she's crazy, she went into a complete frenzy when we came only to talk to her. She acted as if the devil himself was after her. If I were to approach her, I would get nothing but a fight on my hands, I wouldn't even be able to get close to her, let alone talk to her."

"Did she see your face when you grabbed her?" Mr. D asked.

Sabastian had to think, there was a moment when their eyes met but it had been dark and she had only seen him through her mask.

"I don't know how good of a look she got," Sabastian started.

"Well, you better hope she has a bad memory after detox. They hardly remember anything, especially if she was high when you got her. I'm sure you'll be fine."

"Sir, I will not be able to work with her. I want another girl to work with. If I waste all my time with this one, it will take over a year to get another shot at the test."

"Part of the test is working with who you have collected. It may be harder to work with her without Miss Cherry pitching, but I want you to try to see what you can do. When I return, I may reassess the situation."

"Now I need you to get Timothy in my office in three minutes. You're dismissed," Mr. D brushed him off before turning to Miss Cherry.

Sabastian spun and headed to the elevator in a daze following Jeremy, still trying to process what had happened. Something was wrong as Mr. D was not usually that abrupt, he was generally a good man and easy to talk to if you did your job well. He felt a little better when he saw his own puzzlement reflected on Jeremy face.

"Have you ever been left in charge?" Sabastian asked Jeremy.

"Not in twenty-two years," he stated.

"Have you ever seen anyone talk to a new girl who was not Miss Cherry?"

"Only Miss Cherry," Jeremy replied.

"Okay, Jeremy, spill it, what the hell is going on here?"

"I do not know, but I suggest you focus on the task at hand," Jeremy answered unhelpfully.

"Shit, I don't even know where to start," Sabastian stressed. "Any suggestions?" he asked. Doubting that even Jeremy would have a clue where to start.

"First thing you should do is read the pitch until you have it memorized, then I suggest you talk to Roman and watch the tapes of all the previous pitches, just to watch reactions. Then read the conversations that have been documented on hard copies. After that is done, watch her and try to get to know her before barreling in there like you always do."

"Shit that doesn't sound like much," Sabastian said sarcastically.

Putting a hand on his shoulder, Jeremy looked him in the eye and said, "You have two minutes, don't make him wait."

It took Sabastian a second to realize what Jeremy was talking about, but then the doors of the elevator opened and he sprinted down the hall toward Timothy's apartment.

Not bothering to knock, Sabastian barged into Timothy's room and went straight to his office. Timothy lived on his computer and had to continually be dragged away to go to the gym or go jogging to keep himself in shape for his job. Timothy looked up from his laptop at Sabastian.

"Nice," Timothy said sarcastically, gesturing to his open front door. "Come on in."

Sabastian grabbed his arm and yanked him up out of his desk chair. "Let's go, brainiac, Mr. D wants you and I mean now!"

Timothy was one of the bigger men next to Mr. D at the manor but he was still heavily muscled, he had freckles which the girls loved and light red hair, he was also the shortest of the men at five foot eight. On average, if you were to compare Timothy to the average man he would win every time. But in a household of sculptured, muscled, and model looking men, he was at the bottom scale, however, that never stopped the girls from fawning over his freckles, red hair and sweet demeanor.

As soon as Timothy heard Mr. D's name, his face paled, yet that didn't slow him down from grabbing his dark blue laptop.

"What? Why?"

"Don't know, buddy, but I think you are going on a little trip," Sabastian answered.

Sabastian also grabbed Timothy's red laptop with the skull on it, knowing that it was his serious laptop and they both jogged out the door toward the elevator.

Jeremy was waiting with the elevator doors open, Timothy went inside and Sabastian handed him his laptop. Holding both computers, he gave Sabastian a worried look as the doors slid closed.

Well, could be worse, thought Sabastian, *I could be Tim.*

Chapter 14

Sabastian needed to get to work but he also needed to focus and be alone. He turned down the hall and headed to Richard's lab.

Knowing he was probably too early to get any results, he stuck his head through the door and said, "The tox report on the new girl, come to me as soon as you have it, Okay, Richard?"

Richard stayed concentrating on his vials, not bothering to look up, "It's going to take at least four more hours, I'm backed up with clients right now," Richard replied in his overly deep baritone voice.

"No, Richard, she gets moved to the top of the list, this girl needs food in her system and I won't know what drugs to give her for the detox program without a report, Got it."

"Okay, you got it, but don't come crying to me when we have clients who have to wait and start belly aching to Mr. D."

"Since Mr. D will be gone for an undisclosed amount of time," Sabastian said, quoting his boss. "I don't care what they bitch about. Get them to stall until you can send them their results. New girl first!"

Richard finally lifted his head, "Mr. D is taking off?"

"That's what I was just told and with Miss Cherry, don't ask me why. All I know is that they'll be gone, Jeremy's in charge and I get to pitch to the new girl."

"You...a guy? The same guy that had to hog tie her to get her here? Damn, man," Richard said, laughing, "Well, this will be entertaining at the very least."

"Ya, that's what I thought. I'll send someone in to help with the clients results so you can focus on my girl. I'll be in bed, wake me up with her results, ASAP."

"Okay, what's her name, so I can label the samples Michael got from her?"

"Hell if I know," Sabastian replied turning to leave, he turned back again and said, "On second thought, name her wild cat."

56

"I heard she was a handful," Richard smirked. "I thought you were a tough guy."

"You want me to prove I still got it," Sabastian said sarcastically, threatening the big man.

"Get out, I'm working," Richard said, turning back to his vials.

"Ya, that's what I thought, later," Sabastian said with a smirk.

"Later," Richard mumbled already moving to the fridge to dig out her samples.

Sabastian knew if put to a fight between him and Richard it would be pretty even. Richard was built like a brick house, overly wide in the shoulders and chest with thick legs and biceps that stretched out most of his shirts. Sabastian would have to use his speed and skill to beat a man as large as Richard. However, Richard was a pussy cat and loved his work too much to risk losing it by fighting. That was why Richard was so great in the lab, doing what he loved along with the rest of the perks that came with working here. Sabastian was itching for a fight as he knew it would blow off the tension he had at the moment.

Sabastian walked down the hallway and upstairs toward his apartment. Opening his door, he kicked off his shoes and slumped on the bed.

He had personally designed and decorated his apartment and it suited him well. His dark, navy-blue king-sized bed in the middle of the room faced a wall of windows showing off the massive acreage with a glorious city skyline in the distance. Black slate covered the floor, which was heated on his feet and a gas fireplace stood beside his bed. There was a sitting room large enough for six people with a large flat screen and an office to the left of his bed. Curled up on his bed was a small soft black shape that he walked over to. Sabastian was one of the rare people in the manor that had pets and one was currently stretched out on his bed. A pure black female cat with green eyes peered at him lazily.

"Hey, Sketch," he said, rubbing the cats head affectionately. The cat had been aptly named because it had been very sketchy how he had rescued the four-week-old kitten from a garbage container late one night.

Of course the name really came to him when he was sketching out an outline of the skyline and the kitten had knocked his tin of charcoals all over the floor. Instead of the small black feline being scared of the noise she had created, the cat had jumped down and proceeded to knock the charcoal all across the floor. Sabastian was laughing so hard as he tried to race the tiny black kitten to pick them up before she rolled them under the bed. Finally, he had to pick up the kitten to collect all the sketching implements as she was clearly faster and more agile than he was.

Sabastian also had salt water fish, mainly bought for Sketch when he was working, but he found the lazy swimming of the fish soothing and learning how to run a salt water tank was a very rewarding hobby. So much so that his twenty-gallon starter tank had turned into a two-hundred-and-fifty-gallon feature wall in his room that many others enjoyed when invited, which was not often.

It was one thing that he and Mr. D had in common, they both liked their privacy. Sabastian rarely did anything with the guys and didn't mingle with the women or the other staff. He focused on his job and did it to perfection as required. He spent the rest of his time in his room, reading and working out or at his easel.

Sabastian received more respect from the other men as he was often in charge of the men's behavior and assigned jobs to the guys. However, all the men knew how to do their jobs and what was required on a daily basis, so Sabastian rarely had to push his weight around. He was personally trained by Mr. D and many considered him third in line after Miss Cherry and Jeremy. It was rumored that Sabastian had not been given a chance for a promotion because Mr. D wanted him to stay at the manor. But this test opportunity had finally come and Sabastian was more than happy to have a chance to get out on his own.

Keeping the guys in line was only his second job, his first job was much more important to the company and more fun, but after so many years it was starting to wear on him. He knew he was longing for more and a VP position was an excellent solution to the melancholy feeling he got when training new recruits to the business.

It was his job to not only train, but assess to see what a particular girl could bring to the manifesto of skills currently in the company's portfolio. However, he had never pitched to a girl before. He was only introduced to them once they had accepted the internship and had begun training, then he would see if they fit in and find them a position with the company. He was not the only trainer on site, there were other men that also specialized in his field, but Sabastian was the first the ladies had to go through before being handed over for further lessons.

Sabastian looked down across the massive lawn at the busy city. He started stripping his clothes off and readying himself for a long hot shower. Walking over to the mirror first as he still had not assessed the damage that had been done to him by the small female. Her punches had the will of a power fighter behind them but even when she caught him square in the face, he had barely felt its blow. He still could not get over the ferocity in which she went after them. He looked at himself in the mirror assessing; both his figure and any flaws the wild cat may have inflicted on him.

Sabastian was one of the finest members of the team, hard and wide in the shoulders, lightly tanned with a sprinkle of light hair on his chest. His eight pack beneath his broad chest was as impressive as his arms and legs, which were also heavily muscled and defined. He had the growth on his face to play out the role of a bum and the thick hair made him look even more forbidding. His hair was a light brown that fell in soft, layered waves to his ears and always sat perfectly no matter what he did to it, which was good, because he was never one to fuss with his hair.

Sabastian was not vain. Treated like dirt early in life, being taught he was worthless, had erased any vanity that would come with a face and body like his. Standing at six foot four, he was an impressive male. He enjoyed working out because it let off steam and it was a job requirement. He did not exercise to get good looking muscles like most the other guys he worked with. His face was strong with a slight cleaved chin, bright white teeth and a slightly larger than average nose that match his facial features nicely. His eyes sparkled a brilliant light shade of green that would turn to emerald when passion over took him and it was the sweet soft eyes that usually won over any of the women he had to work with.

The one thing he hated on his face were his dimples that would stand out even when talking, he didn't even have to smile to bring them out and it drove him mad. The girls said it made him look cute but that was not the image he was supposed to project so he avoided mirrors most the time. That small flaw, that women loved, he could not stand and he had even tried to take a knife to his face while completely intoxicated one night. The guys had saved him from himself and after that episode they had stopped harassing him about his "cute" dimples.

Looking closer at his face, he saw he still had dried blood in his nose from the wild cat's cheap head butt. A long scratch on his neck and a slightly swollen cheek from a side swing she had handed him.

Knowing he had hours, he decided to finally shave the scratchy beard off his face, take a shower and get some real sleep. He tossed Sketch a half a dozen treats on the bed before heading to the bathroom.

Sketch lazily watched the stunning naked man cross the room with interest before delicately nibbling her goodies.

Chapter 15

Sabastian woke with a weight on his chest and a pair of green eyes two inches from his face. He smiled and rubbed Sketch who was perched on his chest and looked at the clock on the wall. He rolled his eyes and swore to himself.

"What the hell was going on around here? Where is Richard's wakeup call?" he asked Sketch.

Reading his mood correctly, Sketch gently leaped off her master's chest and curled up on the edge of the bed. Sabastian was pissed. Judging by his clock, his new charge had been without food for at least eight hours and God knows how much longer it had been since she had a decent meal before he had collected her. He grabbed a pair of jeans and a white T-shirt from his closet and had just reached the doorknob when he heard a knock. Swinging the door wide, a surprised Richard stood there with papers in his hand.

Scowling at him, Sabastian snatched the papers from his hand and asked, "What the hell took so long?"

"I checked twice, then once more, just to be sure," Richard said.

"That bad, huh?" Sabastian asked, scanning the pages.

Sabastian's scowl deepened with every page he flipped through, checking twice he looked at Richard who had both an amused and worried look on his dark face.

"Are you sure about this?" Sabastian demanded.

"I checked three times because I knew you wouldn't believe the results the first time, so unless Michael gave me someone else's samples, that's one hundred percent correct."

"But how?" Sabastian was astonished. He was silent, thinking what this meant. They had never had a test girl with these results before. It was unheard of, especially seeing her behavior upon collection.

"Completely clean? Nothing in her system at all? Not even pot?"

He couldn't believe it.

"You got it, Sabastian, she is clean as a whistle. A new born wouldn't have as good of results."

Richard was boasting for the girl like he was proud of her.

"Well, shit, there goes protocol. How am I supposed to go through the process of cleaning her up if there is nothing to clean?"

Richard shrugged, "Well, I would tell you to talk to Mr. D but since that option has flown the coop, you are on you own."

Richard gave a hoot backing up, "You have fun with that." And with that, he turned to get back to work.

Sabastian called after him. "Don't you want these?" he said, waving the papers at him.

"No, I made copies so you can have that same look on your face that you have on now every time you look at them."

Laughing down the hall as he went, the very large man gave a little skip as he disappeared around the corner and Sabastian glowered after him.

"Ass," he muttered to himself, flipping through the stack of papers again.

Clean, he thought. *Completely clean.*

Of course all of their staff were always drug free as it was one of the bare minimum requirements to work with the company. But that was completely different from a test girl from the street.

Well there is no use waiting with my thumb up my ass, Sabastian thought as he made a bee line to the kitchen. He knew he was skipping about a hundred steps and didn't know what would happen, but he was on his own and no one would know what to do with a crazy, wild cat of a girl whose system was completely clean of any toxins in her body.

Chapter 16

Suddenly awakened from an accidental nap, Victoria's eyes flew open and she stiffened. She had heard something! She bolted out of bed; her body wound tight ready for an assault. Scanning the room, it took her a second to see she was still alone and a second more to notice a change in the room. Beside the marble top mirrored dresser, across from the bed was a large tray with a round silver lid that had not been there before she had laid down.

She looked to the left and right of the table tray, then tightened the silk robe rope around her as she slowly approached. She saw that the tray was resting on a small table that had popped out of the wall where she had noticed the long two-foot, thin box seam before.

She ran her hands along the seams and tried to dig her fingernails into crease unsuccessfully. She dug and scratched at the wall and pushed as hard as she could but it wouldn't budge. Someone must have opened a hatch and put a hotel like serving tray in her room. She banged on the wall.

"Hello, anyone there?" She asked, her voice raised apprehensively.

With no response, she took the silver tray away from the wall and brought it to the bed.

The smell coming from it was mouthwatering, so she slowly lifted the lid. The strong scent of food wafted up into her face and she closed her eyes inhaling deeply. She was wary of eating food, but she was too hungry to turn it down. On the tray was a chicken breast, brown rice, spinach salad, and green beans all in miniscule servings. There was also small cup of yogurt with granola, whole grain bun, still warm and a little bite size chunk of dark chocolate. For drinks, there was what looked like a small energy drink, milk, and a large bottle of sparkling water.

She didn't know where to start. Beside the plate were two packages, one contained aspirin and another chewable digestive tablets, two tablets in each package. At the head of the plate was a tent style note, she picked it up completely intrigued. What was with the notes? How come they didn't just come and talk to her?

Small portions so you do not get sick. Please eat slowly and know that the food is safe to eat and there will be more, enjoy.

Well, she figured that the food would be safe, unless they wanted to drug her again. But why would they drug her when they could not enter her room and would have no problem over powering her if they did get in. She hesitated, froze, and a thought entered her head that gave her chills, worse than anything in the freezing alley.

What if they needed her healthy for a reason? What if they were going to do something awful to her once she had regained some strength? She had heard of underground companies that harvested healthy human organs for huge amounts of money or even horrible experiments done but only if the person was healthy. She even heard one story about women who were kidnapped and impregnated so they could sell babies to rich people. She trembled at the thought. That couldn't be real, could it? She pushed the food away and looked around at the plush furnishings. Were they were trying to lull her into a false sense of security? Was that why they were trying to feed her and get her healthy. Of course, it all made sense now. She shuttered and slowly put the lid back on the tray, almost in tears that the food could not be trusted. That is why they did not attack and hurt her in the alley. That is why the drugs had been temporary and that is why they were trying to get her comfortable and stress free. They were going to cut her up and take parts out of her or use her like a bitch in a puppy mill to pop out babies! She could not eat, she would not. That would only speed up the process. Victoria started to panic again, not thinking clearly. Her only thought was that she had to get out of here.

Chapter 17

"What the hell is she doing?" Sabastian cried out in frustration. "Why isn't she eating?"

"Hell, if I know, you said it yourself, she's psycho," Roman replied.

"Well, what the fuck am I going to do now?" Sabastian exclaimed; this wild cat was driving him crazy. "It's not like I can go and talk to her."

Both men watched the girl back in the monitor room frustrated and confused. She was on the bed just staring at the tray of food that had been prepared for her. Sabastian put his head in his hands and tried to come up with a viable solution.

"Look," Roman said, pointing at the screen they had been watching.

The girl had gone over to her bag by the bed and pulled out a small object. They watched her as she lifted the note from under the meal lid. After writing something down, she walked over to the wall and worked the object into the seam in the wall, where the tray had come through until she had jammed it far enough to fall.

Almost not daring to say, because clearly Sabastian was not in the mood, Roman still couldn't help it.

"Looks like you have a love note," Roman said, laughing.

Sabastian raced out of the room, cuffing Roman on the back of the head as he ran out.

He reached the kitchen and the chef Nickolas, looked up from the counter in surprise.

"Is she done already? I wrote to eat slowly," the chef said to himself, continuing to chop up the veggies he was currently working on.

"Not really," Sabastian muttered distractedly, as he went over to the corner of the kitchen, where the serving tray slot was.

"Don't tell me we have another food fight in there? I perfected that meal for her, the least she could do is eat it, not use it to paint the room, like the last girl," Nickolas was frowning, shaking his head.

Looking where Sabastian had gone, Nickolas followed him over to the corner of the kitchen, still holding his knife. Nickolas was another tall fine man with short jet-black hair, hazel eyes, and one of the few men in the whole complex that got away with not shaving for the ladies.

Walking over to where Sabastian was, pausing to watch him on the floor, he asked, "What are you looking for?"

"Got it," Sabastian cried and lifted the note in his hand.

"What? She sent you note, why?" Nickolas asked.

Sabastian ignored him and opened the folded note.

No way are you going to gut me like a pig once you have fattened me up! Fuck you!

Wow she had a potty mouth, he would give her that or she was covering up the fact that she was really scared.

"Shit," Sabastian said.

"What is it?" Nickolas asked.

Sabastian handed him the note and got up off the floor.

Reading the note, Nickolas said, "Another one, hey?"

"Another one what?" Sabastian asked, looking for any shred of hope what this insane girl was thinking.

"Well, a few years back, we had this girl. Rita was her name and she was a test girl for a guy named Josh from Russia. She didn't make it to the next step of the program, too paranoid, but she was completely convinced we were going to either eat her, or harvest her organs. It took a lot of work to talk her down off that ledge, but in the end, she was convinced enough that we were trying to help and not chop her up."

Nickolas's brows came together at the memory.

Sabastian looked at Nickolas wide eyes, completely offended. He would have never met Rita if she didn't make it through the first part of the program. He had never worked with her; however, he did remember hearing the name.

Slowly, Sabastian asked, "Well, how did they do it? How did they convince her that we were not going to kill her?"

"It was Miss Cherry mainly, she spent hours talking to her and walking her around to show her what we were all about here, it took a few days but, in the end, she started eating," Nickolas replied. "Although I don't think, you have that kind of time judging but the weight you gave me earlier, what is she, eighty-four pounds?"

"Yah, that was our guess once we estimated how heavy her clothes were on her."

Sabastian looked hopelessly at the thoughtful chef, dumbfounded on what to do next. He had to get her to eat no matter what it took.

"Okay thanks, Nick," Sabastian turned and ran back to the monitor room, Roman spun around.

"So?" Roman asked.

"She thinks we are going to harvest her organs," Sabastian said tossing the note to Roman.

"What? That's insane," Roman said, disbelieving as he grabbed the note.

"Ya, that's what I thought, but apparently, it's not the first time."

Roman was silent for a minute as he read, then said, "Rita, ya I remember her, she was put on twenty-four seven watch to make sure she didn't kill herself, which she tried three times."

Sabastian was shocked, if this girl killed herself not only would he not get promoted, he could be out right fired.

"God, damn it," he swore, slamming his hand on the counter.

This girl should have been dumped from the beginning, but now it was for totally different reasons. Running both his hands through his hair, he knew he couldn't talk to her and he also couldn't get anybody else to talk to her. How in the world would he be able to convince this crazy wild cat to eat? Then it hit him.

Running out of the room again, Sabastian said, "Watch her close and wait for my text."

Sabastian bolted out of the monitor room and was back from his room and in the kitchen within minutes.

Holding a pen and sketch pad in his hand, he hesitated. What would he write to her that would calm her and set her mind at ease? He slid a chair over to the slot in the wall and sat down with Nickolas watching him curiously. Sabastian looked worriedly at the chef, frowned, cursed, and started to write.

He tossed out the first draft after signing his name.

Christ, he thought, *I can't even use my first name.*

He was sure Edward had said his name in the alley when they were grabbing her and of course now he could not rely on the drugs to affect her memory.

Knowing she was clean, he knew that if the girl had even glanced his face, that would have been the last thing she saw and that it would be burned into her memory. He was screwed and he knew it, but he had to try, if the little bitch died, there would be hell to pay. This piece of work would be his undoing and when he did meet her, it would take all his restraint not to toss her off the roof of the manor.

Chapter 18

Victoria couldn't help it, her eyes kept drifting to the plate of food on the bed as she frantically scanned the room looking for escape. She had tried the door after unlocking it, but of course, if no one could use the door to get in, she couldn't use the door to get out. She had been through her bag twice, but a collection of trinkets, treasured books, and pictures of her mother was no help to her and neither was a pile of dirty clothes.

She sat on the floor gazing around the room. She could use the vases by her bed for a weapon, but that would only work if there was one person coming after her and if she was a good shot. She was drained and couldn't think. Her adrenalin was going down after it spiked again and it left her even shakier than before. The fact that there was a tray of food tempting her didn't help.

After only ten minutes, she was too tired and unsteady that she was ready to sleep again, until she heard a noise behind her. There, on the table tray where the food had been, was a grey spiral notebook. She walked over and picked up the book before running her hand along the crease in the wall that was sealed tight again. Confusion written on her face, she walked with the book over to the bed.

She sat on the bed facing the wall to keep the secret slot in her sightline, hoping to see how it worked the next time it opened.

The book was a small professional looking sketch book. Opening it, she saw the paper was thick and there were several tattered edges from pages that had been ripped out.

She flipped the first page to find a cursive hand-written note.

'I know you are scared and you don't know why you are here, but I assure you we will not harm you in any way. We are here to help and want you to get better and be healthy, only for you and not for any other reason. When you have your strength up you, will be given a choice of being able to walk out of

here free and healthy or possibly work with us if you would like a job with our
company.

    Sincerely,

    Mr. Greene.

    P.S. Please eat for no one but yourself.'

The hand writing was beautiful and it flowed like water over the page, but she was baffled. A job? That made zero sense. How could she be sure? These were only words on a page and if she didn't eat then what? If she refused, would they bust in here, tie her down and hook her to machines forcing her to eat? They could, she knew that, she had no control of this situation. She felt helpless once again and it made her face hot and her rage flared. She threw the book across the room and swore to herself.

"Shit, now what?" she asked herself.

She curled her legs up and put her face down on her knees wrapping her arms around her head, trying to clear the rage and think of how to get back in control. She always had such good control of herself in almost any situation these last years. Control of herself was usually the only control she had, but this was so bizarre of a scenario that she was at a complete loss.

Sabastian looked down at his phone waiting for a reply from Roman who was texting him from the monitor room, he was waiting for a response to his note. He needed to know if she would write back or if she would do something drastic to the point of him having to get in there. Finally, his phone pinged.

"She tossed the notebook." Roman's text read.

Tilting his head up to look toward the heavens, "Oh come on," he begged.

Thinking hard, he decided it was better to keep her thinking about him, the notes and food than anything else and tried something different.

Sitting on the bed frustrated, she heard a soft sliding noise and a click and looked up. The slot with the crease had slid back into the wall and had rolled to the side and the tray now had a black pen sitting on it. She couldn't see past the hole in the wall as it blocked. Sliding off the bed, she tried to look closer but only saw a flat black steel backing attached to a mechanism.

"Whose there?" she demanded, she waited.

"For Christ's sake, answer me!" she yelled directly into the slot.

Silence.

She was talking to a wall, if someone was there and could hear her, they were choosing to keep silent.

She sighed with resignation, grabbed the pen, and picked up the book.

Fine, she thought, *I guess we are going to have to do this old school.*

Picking up the book, she flipped the page and wrote sloppily.

"Why won't you speak to me, can you not hear me? Come and talk to me, coward! This is bullshit, if you are going to let me go why not do it now? What do you want from me? Let me get the hell out of here, I do not care what you want with me. I do not want or need a job; I need to be gone. Let me go!"

She placed the book on the table tray and stood back waiting, in seconds, the table disappeared and the wall slid back into place.

She felt like she was in school again, passing notes in class.

This was dumb, how big of a wuss were these people that they could not send someone to talk to her, what were they hiding? She fumed frustrated.

Backing up toward the edge of the bed, watching the slot, she sat down and waited. She didn't have to wait long for the wall to move and the table to slide back into her room.

She grabbed the grey notebook that was placed there and read the perfect smooth handwriting.

"I wish I could come in and talk to you, I want to, but we have to wait for that. All I need you to do is eat so I know you will not pass out, we can't enter without your permission and if you are sick or unconscious on the floor, we will not be able to help you. Please help us, help you and eat, nothing bad will happen to you I promise.

Mr. Greene."

Picking up her pen, she responded.

"These are just words, prove it. For all I know, you will be hacking me up once I'm healthy. I heard about places like this, organs for huge money; well, you will not be making money off of me. Go to hell!"

Taking her note back from the kitchen slot, Sabastian read and it took a lot for him to hold onto his temper, this girl was infuriating. He had to control himself and not go busting in her room to force feed her. He wanted to threaten

71

that very thing but thought better of it and went with an educated, soft touch, which was the last thing he felt like at the moment.

"We are not going to harvest your organs, that is a horrible thought, please take it from your mind. If we were going to do that, you would be tied down and knocked out. Not free in a beautiful room, with one of the greatest chefs working hard to cook you a meal that will give you back your strength. We will do whatever it takes to make sure you are safe and healthy. What will it take for you to trust that eating will only benefit you and it is not some underhanded trick on our part?"

Passing the notebook back, he waited with bated breath. It only took seconds to get the text from Roman that she had put the book down on the table and he pressed the button to return the table back to him.

"Prove it!"

She wanted proof that they were not harvesting organs!

Come on, this is crazy, just eat the food, you crazy chick, he thought.

How the hell was he supposed to prove that? He had to think, perhaps talk to Jeremy and follow his advice about reading the pitch and going through the recent reports.

He blinked. *Of course,* he thought, scribbling something in the book and sending it back, he raced out of the kitchen, Nickolas watching him go with raised eyebrows grinning.

Texting Roman as he ran, he hoped his last note would do the trick, but needing Roman to see if the girl would respond. He ran down the hall, thinking what he would need from Gregory and hoped that he had what it took to convince this girl without giving her too much information.

Chapter 19

Gregory was quickly pulling all the files that he thought would help after Sabastian's text. Trying to narrow down the ones that he knew would give the most information without letting the new girl know what the company actually did.

"Here take these," he said handing a stack of papers to Sabastian, who was rifling through files picking out the ones that would work the best.

"Try to find ones of mostly test subjects. You know, the ones the guys pulled off the streets for their promotions and none from the professional pool."

Sabastian didn't know if this would work as some of the files spoke in code, but it was the only thing he could think of to give her. He needed to somehow verify that they were not going to hurt the stupid female.

Once he thought Gregory had given him all the files that might work, he sat down and started to eliminate the ones that had failed the program, except for a few. Hoping to show her that many girls took the job opportunity presented to them. He still needed her to not only finish the cleaning process, which was the first steps to getting detoxed and healthy, but in her case, only healthy was needed. He also needed her to enter into the internship program and hopefully be successful in it, to prove to Mr. D he had what it took to be a VP. Several minutes later, Sabastian received a text from Roman.

"Finally," he sighed with relief.

"What?" Gregory asked.

"She's eating," Sabastian declared, one battle won.

Sabastian collected the stack of files they had compiled and asked Gregory to send him the pitch and proposal documents, so he could study the conversations given to new recruits. He was hoping to get a chance to study at the same time she was reading the files. He had thought he would have nothing but time to review and prepare himself to pitch to her but skipping the detox program had drastically shortened his prep time by several months.

Sabastian grabbed his laptop from his apartment, fed Sketch, and jogged lightly to where he would be staying in the kitchen for god knows how long, to babysit the brat he had been saddled with.

He was thrilled to see when he pushed the button to the pass through to bring back the hidden table in the wall that the notebook was on top of a completely empty food platter.

He scanned the last two things written. The first was his note.

"I will prove it and will have the proof to you as soon as your meal is done, one meal will not fatten you up enough anyway, eat, and you will have your proof.
Mr. Greene."

Under his message was:

"I'm waiting."

Jotting under her message, he wrote:

"Here is the proof you asked for, please forgive the time it took me to get it. Some are old and some are recent. As you read, you will see almost every person we have brought here has either received our help and moved on or have taken a position with us, enjoy and I hope it will help you pass the time while you get better.
Mr. Greene."

He wanted to ask her name but he felt it would be too intrusive, she was just starting to trust and if he asked, she may become even more guarded then she already was. Anyway, to him, she had been aptly named wild cat until he found out her real name.

Chapter 20

Victoria was startled from a light nap when she heard the sound of the table move back into the wall. She had been hoping she had not been tricked into eating the most delicious food she had ever had. Eating heavy fatty food would make her sick and apparently, the chef knew that as well, but even so, the food had been delicious. She had to force herself to finish it because even though the amount would have fed the average six-year-old it was too overwhelming for her shriveled-up stomach.

She practically launched herself at the table when it came back through. There was a bowl of fresh strawberries sitting on top of a large pile of files, beside the gray notebook. The berries looked so good, but it was the files that fascinated her, she took both the papers and the berries and placed them on the bedside table and went back for the notebook. She read the note, then snuggled into bed, and started to read, trying to figure out what this Mr. Greene had gotten her into.

Flipping through the files, she learned that they were all young, eighteen to twenty-five and they were mostly woman who came from the streets, women shelters, or from half way houses. It was clear that every person were in need of help. She read their profiles, their back ground, and their skills, still trying to piece together what job they would be needed for at this company and why this company would employ them.

There were several files with codes beside their names that she didn't understand which must be some sort of position in the company. There were two codes beside every girl who had taken a job, one in the skills column, DM, SB, SM, and the other in the education column, ST, DS, SS, and so on. Unable to figure out the codes, she read on.

There were several pages of medical reports and the detoxifying program they had gone through to get them clean enough to work. Some girls did not have a work history in their file and under their medical records was the explanation. One girl Becky "had been too traumatized by an unfortunate episode in her past and opted not to pursue a career with the company."

Another girl was Stephanie who choose to return to her family, that one worried her. The other girl, Alison, had been pregnant and was being supported by the company. That one puzzled her, too. Apparently, they took this Alison girl off the streets, detoxed her, and have been supporting her and her baby for the last three years without her ever having worked for them? The other two girls had gone through the internship program and "were deemed not suited to the work." They were let go with a payout. That was another question, why, after putting so much work into a prospective employee, did they not only let them go, but paid them when they left?

It looked like this place helped others for good will or to perhaps advertise, but she had never heard of a company that did that. Something like that would be in the newspapers, which she read a lot on the streets. Although she didn't know the company's name, so maybe that's why she had not heard of the charity work they did. The files did set her mind at ease a bit, but it brought up more questions than answers. The only answer she got was that they were not in the business of chopping people up, which did make her stress level lower slightly, replaced by curiosity. What did they do and what did they want her for?

She read through the men's profile as well, there were only two and there was no detox report on them, only history, skills, and position in the company. This time there were real titles to their position and these guys were both Watchers.

She slowly read through every file again, taking her time while gingerly nibbling on strawberries, trying to figure out the scam. However, she was coming to the realization that the way the paper looked and felt that these files were not just whipped up to prove a point, they were genuine, some old, some newer. Wondering why they didn't use computers, because clearly this company was high tech, the hard copies also threw her off.

She reached over, took the notebook hoping to get some questions answered and wrote:

"Why are there so many more women, than men?

What is the company name?

What do the codes mean?

Why are all the girls "rescued"?

Why does everyone need to be detoxed?

Why did the one girl decide to go home?

Why are you supporting someone who never worked for you?

Why did you pay out the failed internship women?

Why hard copies of files? You seem high tech."

She got her answers back, with a few questions of his own after what seemed like forever.

"Dear miss???

We rely on strong women to make this company successful; the men are mostly here to serve the women and make them safe and comfortable. That is why there are more women than men. The company name is Eximius. The codes are used when a woman picks her specialty, which I will teach to you at a later date. I am already skipping so many steps with you that this is one step you will need to wait for, sorry.

Most of the women in this company who come from broken pasts do not have family or friends to fall back on and that is why we help them into our family. They have no ties, so starting fresh and leaving everything behind is a positive thing. It is beneficial for them to drop everything and come to work for us and to get the help they need and we are able to get staff that are completely dedicated to us. Detoxing is one of the things that our boss, Mr. D, is adamant about. Everyone here must be clean, no drugs, no alcohol, no smoking, no exceptions, and getting girls off those disabilities gets them to truly appreciate all we have done for them and gives them a dedication to the company that has helped them in so many ways.

Stephanie was scared to go home because she was on drugs; we solved that problem and she went home happily and is now in her fifth year of medical school, paid by Eximius. Even though Alison never worked for us, we felt she needed our help and since we have the means to support her, we are doing so, she is not the first person we have helped who has not joined us and she will not be the last. We are proud of the fact that she got clean and is staying clean even after our help and as long as she stays clean for herself and her baby girl, we will continue to support her.

The interns still worked hard for us but we felt they did not have what it took to continue working here, so after signing a non-discloser contract, we paid them for their silence and to give them a new start.

We cannot be hacked into with hard copies, it keeps our staff and company safe and anonymous, no matter what happens, if someone were to steal our computers or hack into our system, all our staff and especially our women would still be safe from any past that may be problematic for them.

I hope I have alleviated any worries you may have had and it would mean a lot if you would be so kind as to answer a few of my questions if you feel comfortable enough to do so?

Please tell me your name?

How old are you?

How long have you been living on the streets?

How did you get there?

Do you have family looking for you?

When was your last meal before this one?

Do you have any allergies?

Do you prefer any type of food?

Are you comfortable?

Do you need anything?

Thank you,

Mr. Greene."

Standing beside the wall, on edge, with her hair twisted in her hands, she snatched the notebook off the table when it came through and read quickly.

Wow, what a load of information. This Greene guy does not mess around, she thought as she read still standing beside the slot.

She loved the last part about keeping the girls safe, no matter who may get into their computer system. The girl who went home by her choice made her feel better, too.

She liked this Mr. D guy as she felt the same way about drugs and alcohol, they were the things in this society that made everything worse and she hated them to the core especially being surrounded by them for so long. The fact that she was not on any drugs had kept her alive and out of trouble for much longer than most other young people on the streets.

Greene also talked about steps, was she on some sort of program? The fact that this company had so much money that they could support a single mother just because she stayed clean and send someone through medical school floored her. Who does that? This was the one part she had doubts about. She had been surrounded by so many selfish people in her life that someone who would do something without asking anything in return did not exist in this world any more.

She had never heard of Eximius and did not even know what it meant. Well, Greene had taken the time to write this to her the least she could do is write back.

"Thank you for what I hope is your honesty. I will only tell you my first name which is Victoria and I am twenty-two. I have been on and off the streets for five years now, but only in Denver for two. I have no family. I ate on Monday and have no allergies. I don't care what kind of food I get but I am not used to fancy meals so simple is fine. There is no way anyone could be uncomfortable in this room but I would like my clothes cleaned if possible?

Thanks Greene, at least I will be able to sleep soundly tonight know you are not going chop me up.

P.S. is it true you cannot enter my room?

Victoria."

Taking the notebook back, Sabastian thought, *Yes, a name, some progress at last.*

He wrote an e-mail to update his report to Jeremy, her name, what little history he got from her, age, tox report, and her progress and asked him to forward it to Miss Cherry. He hoped she was able to read it and pass it along to Mr. D, even with both of them gone to show them he was making progress with his impossible assignment. He wrote a quick note back to her hoping he would be able to crash after this, he was wiped out and having cat naps that had been disturbed so many times today was getting to him.

"Dear Miss Victoria,

There are dozens of outfits, dresses, and night wear in the drawers in your room, enjoy picking one out tonight, they are as close as we could find to your size and will be yours to keep if you like them. Please enjoy a good night's rest knowing we will not hurt you. If there is anything you need, this pass-through will be left open and I will be alerted if you send any messages, for now I suggest you sleep and I will have our chef prepare something for you in the morning.

Take care,

Mr. Greene."

He waited and when nothing came, he shot a quick text to Roman who informed him she had gotten dressed and was turning off lights.

Good, he thought, stifling the feeling of guilt of the white lies and fuzzy answers he had given her. *I can't tell her everything,* he thought.

Sabastian got up and stretched, groaning. The chair he had been sitting in by the pass-through was killing his back and he as looking forward to a full nights rest.

Chapter 21

The next morning, Sabastian woke up early. He had gone to bed shortly after a superb meal from Nickolas, who had felt sorry for him and his aching back.

He checked the monitor room and said hi to Matthew who had taken over for Roman late last night. Asking him, if Roman had filled him in and to text the second Victoria started to wake up. Matthew gave him the thumbs-up sign and over exaggerated looking at the screen as Sabastian headed to the gym.

Sabastian decided to only do free weights as he didn't want to be pulled out of a running program to go to his female burden when she woke up. He always did his best thinking when in the gym and came up with a plan to continue to get his wild cat to eat and to also wiggle his way around giving the girl too much information, too soon.

Over an hour into his workout, he sent a quick text to Matthew asking if there was any change and got the replied that she was still completely out. So he showered and grabbed his computer, thinking that he really should crack down on all the reports and pitch research to make sure he was fully prepared for Victoria this morning.

He removed Sketch from his laptop on the desk and opened his computer with the documents.

He started with the pitch and was not happy to see the dozen or so rules he had already broken. Not to mention the information he had given her which was strictly prohibited. Also giving her the files with the personal information on several of their employees and failed interns was paramount to treason.

This was not an ordinary situation however and he hoped it would excuse his ignorance. Reading, he was reminded of the many rules he had been taught and followed every day since he had first come to Eximius.

Respect was always number one and there was a zero tolerance policy with this number one rule, especially toward the women who worked for Eximius. One slip in that department could get your ass put in the streets with several parts of you broken. He decided to copy and paste some respect rules to print to his charge so she would be able to see the dedication the company had toward treating all women right.

"Rules pertaining to the respect of Woman employed by Eximius:

Respect from men toward women at all times.

Complete and total respect must be shown toward all women at all times, unless otherwise requested of the woman.

Addressing each other formally with respect for both sexes:

All women must be addressed as such: Miss Joan, Miss Sara, Miss Jennifer, and so on.

There will be no shortening of any names within the women's manor by the men. Jennifer must not be shorted to Jen or Jenny. Men's names have the same rule within the women's manor, no shortening of names or nicknames are allowed. Nickolas cannot be shortened to Nick. This rule pertains when the sexes are intermingling and when together working at all times.

There will be no profanity at all within the woman's manor or in a woman presence.

It is recommended that men refrain from cursing in their own manor to ensure a slip is not made within the presence of the women.

Men are only allowed to address the women while on a job only if they need to relay vital information when working together.

Men are not allowed to touch or make any gestures toward the women that they deem inappropriate. This included rude body language, hand gestures, rude noises etc.

It is the men's responsibility to ensure that all the women in the manor and when out on a job have everything they need to be comfortable, safe, and to do their job to the best of their ability.

It is the job of the men whether they are Watchers or not to make sure that the women's safety is the top priority at all times.

Men must respond to any request by a woman immediately. This includes, but is not limited to, food orders, outing requests, item retrieval, information retrieval, change of assignment, personal care, or other services etc....

Any complaints of any women toward men will be dealt with openly and harshly. Men can lose up to a full year of pay or more if a breach of the respect contract is broken.

Men will be released from the company permanently with half their savings taken if there is an extreme violation of the follow rules:

Physical threat of any kind; no man will touch, hit, or grab any women in a violent or threating manor.

Mental threat; no man will verbally threaten or otherwise cause stress to a woman of any kind."

Sabastian stopped there as the document started to go over very detailed rules in the company that gave away too much. He added a note on the end of the document.

"Miss Victoria, please note that although these rules are only for the employees who currently work with Eximius, I want to assure you that you will be safe from harm while you are recovering."

He went over to his desk and took the piece of paper with the respect rules from his printer, when his phone pinged.

"Awake."

He texted back *"Tell Nickolas."*

"Done."

Sabastian grabbed the paper, his laptop, and his bathroom scale and headed down to the monitor room.

Poking his head in the door, he said, "Matthew, I need you to text me what she is doing in the room when I am down in the kitchen talking to her, Okay?"

"Ya, Roman told me, I have his notes and looked over the footage of the other night so I'm good to go."

"Thanks."

The great thing about Mr. D's excellent expectations in this company is no one slacked off or did things half assed around here. He could always count on his fellow team mates to do an exceptional job.

Reaching the kitchen, he asked what was for breakfast.

"Spinach and light Bree cheese omelet, whole grain toast with light peanut butter, blue, black and strawberry medley with kiwi, milk, water, and orange juice," Nickolas replied, bored.

"Not really a challenge, huh?" Sabastian asked.

"Not really but the presentation is always fun," he said gesturing to the plate which was artfully arranged in a lovely solar system pattern on the plate.

The omelet was the sun with the berries representing planets, and the toast had been cut into little stars round the plate.

"Cute," Sabastian said, grinning.

"Well, I needed something to do," Nickolas said, rolling his eyes.

"Well, how about making me something fancy. I missed breakfast with the rest of the guys today and I just worked out so I'm starving, do your worst," Sabastian said to the grinning chef.

Sabastian headed to his corner of the kitchen and pressed the button to get the notebook back.

When the sliding table moved back into the kitchen, Nickolas came in behind Sabastian and placed the breakfast tray on the table and then went to his kitchen studio to get to work on Sabastian's morning meal.

Sabastian took the notebook and scanned the conversation they had last night and went over all the information that he was not supposed to give her, and shrugged, it couldn't be undone.

Reading the notebook, he read:

"Thanks for the clothes, Greene, but I noticed you didn't answer if you can come into my room or not? I have thought of so many more questions for you but I would like to talk to a person and not a notebook, it's very frustrating."

He sent the food, the scale, and his notes, hoping the plan that he had come up while working out would buy some time with her. She wanted to get out and talk to him and was asking too many questions already, he knew her curiosity would not be sated for long at this pace. He had to slow her down and gain her trust.

Chapter 22

"What is this?" she asked herself as the table slid into her room. A tray of food was sitting on top of a scale with the notebook on top of it. She took the notebook first and read.

"Dear Miss Victoria,

I have the answers to all of your inquires but we need to slow down. The first thing we need to do is get you better, you are too weak and need to rest and get healthy again. If you are not one hundred percent, it is my fault and I need you to be strong enough to handle what this company will be offering you at a later date. That is, if you choose to accept an internship with us. This is my proposal, for every meal you eat and every pound you put, on I will answer one question. I realize it is a slow process but that is what I am asking. I also need your trust, as that is my job with this company, making sure the women trust me when entering the program and I hope you will be able to give me that.

This is your first meal today, you will be served a meal by our wonderful chef, Nickolas, every two hours so eight times a day and you will also be served drinks in between the meals. So with every meal, you may ask one question and with every pound you put on, another question. The scale will send your weight to my phone every time you step onto it, please weigh yourself three times a day, morning, noon, and before you go to sleep.

Since you are giving me your wellbeing as a payment for answers, I will not ask you anything until we are able to speak face to face. I will try to answer all your questions; however, some questions I cannot answer and I will apologize in advance. Anything you wish to have in your room to pass the time I will obtain for you. Please do not think that a request is too big as I'm here to make sure you are at ease while you get better.

Please have patience with me while we go through the steps to ensure you are on the mend. I have also included the respect rules that women receive once employed with Eximius, so I hope you will see that we are an honorable company with only the women's best interests at heart.

Have a pleasant day.

Mr. Greene."

Victoria stared at the note.

He has got to be kidding me. I have to weigh myself to get answers and he will not talk to me face to face, that's bullshit, she thought.

She picked up, that if she didn't get better, it was his fault. It looked like he was put in charge of her and if she didn't put on some weight he would be in trouble and looking at the respect agreement, they took the care of women very seriously.

It was all so foreign to her, the amount of respect they showed to the women baffled her, what kind of company had rules like that? Taking the tray and the notebook over to the bed, she opened the round silver cover and smiled at the colorful solar system on her tray. Not wanting to wreak what someone obviously took a lot of time and care to prepare she started to only nibble at the outside of the arrangement and reread the rules and the notes Greene had written.

Eight meals a day, she hoped she would be able to eat all that food. She usually averaged five meals a week and now she had to try to eat eight a day, it was crazy.

She also didn't think one question was enough, maybe she should try to get the number up to five questions per meal and per pound. She could think of over twenty questions already and more kept popping up after reading the respect rules.

She scanned the questions in her head trying to think of the best question to ask seeing how she only got one. She felt like Aladdin wishing to a genie and wondering if she could wish for more wishes.

Eating slowing, she took the book and wrote.

"Okay, Greene, one question, come on? I would like at least three answers per meal and per weigh in and if I gain weight or not, I want to be able to ask

a question as I cannot control my weight, even if I eat everything. I have too many questions and it will drive me insane without the answers I need. According to you, it's your ass if I get better or not so I want more questions. So three for a meal and three for a weigh in this morning.

1. *What is your first name? Because this Mr. Greene is bullshit?*
2. *Where am I?*
3. *What does the company do?*
4. *What is your position in the company?*
5. *What kind of internship will I be going into?*
6. *Why does the company stress so much about respecting women and the men are treated like servants?"*

She put the notebook on the table, turned on the scale and stepped on, eighty-five pounds, "Well, I better start eating," she said and turned to her meal.

A few minutes later, the book came back.

"I am sorry, Miss Victoria, but one question is all I am permitted to give at this time, all your questions will be answered in due time. I will however grant your questions no matter what the scale says, but only if you are able to eat all of your meals.

I am sorry to say that the only questions I can answer are 4 and 6: that my job title is 'Trainer,' I train women in the skills they need to do their job in this company. I cannot tell you what skills I train so don't ask. The men are not treated like servants, all the men working here absolutely love their job and are paid very well to do it. Some men working here would do his job for free as they relish the tasks they perform here.

Respect toward women is the base of what this company is all about. Without respect, we would not be successful and our ladies who work for us would not be happy and therefore would not do a good job. Respect is what they require to feel needed and valued. Their dignity is very important to all of us as well as appreciation for the hard jobs they do with the company. I know this will not satisfy you but that is all I can give at this time.

I will return in two hours to see if you need anything and to answer your next question after your meal is served. Have a good day.

Mr. Greene."

Well, she thought closing up the notebook, *it was worth a try.*

At least she would get scale questions answered no matter what. She sat in bed and read their conversation hoping the next hours didn't drag for her.

True to his word, an hour later the table reappeared with a small fruit smoothie and a large sparkling water. Another hour after that a plate of fancy crackers and cheese, pineapple, and sweet peas popped out of the wall. Once again artfully arranged with the food cut to display a colorful water lily on the plate.

Taking the tray to her bed, she was able to ask the only question she could ask.

"Why won't you tell me your real name? I like to read; can I get some books?"

Sabastian was baffled on the other side of the wall, why would she be focused on him? She must have dozens of other questions, why ask his name?

"I will bring you some reading material.
Greene."

Frustrated, she took the notebook and wrote.

"Okay, fine, 'Greene.' When can I get out of here and what job do the women do here?"

Having to wait over fifteen minutes drove her mad, however when the note came back with several books, she understood why.

"When you are healthy and strong, you will be let out and shown the job we do here, eat up.
Greene."

Annoyed, Victoria flipped through the books she'd been given. She was so pleasantly surprised to see several classics that she had read years ago but was unfortunate not to have them in her personal collection. Flipping through the

88

titles, she knew that whoever had picked out the books – she assumed Mr. Greene – had gone through her bag and saw what she liked to read. Pride and Prejudice, A Tale of Two Cites were both there which she had read and loved so long ago. Then there was The Secret Garden, Crime and Punishment and Moby Dick three books among several others she had been desperately trying to afford while on the streets.

She didn't know whether to feel violated that he had rifled through her belongings or pleased that this Greene person had taken the time to see what books she liked and ensured she received what she would enjoy.

Feeling defeated over her lack of answers and still feeling trapped, she took her meal to the bed. Confused and a little unnerved with this whole new situation she found herself in, she reasoned she had little to complain about as she was warm, clean, and well fed for the first time in a long time.

Chapter 23

He lay on his back in his large navy bed looking up at her as her soft hair covered his naked body. Long dark blonde wisps of it trialing from his feet all the way up to his neck. The hair was cool on his hot skin and was a welcome contrast to the heat running through his veins. He reached for her and wrapped large hands around her feather light frame as she lay with her hair between them. Stroking her creamy back up and down lightly, he could feel her sweet breath in his ear as her breasts pushed into his chest.

Running his hands through her mane, he cupped her cheek and kissed her, intent on owning her outright. His needy erection pulsed into her soft thighs and he could feel her heat penetrate him. He moved his body so that the head of his shaft rested in the welcoming wet warmth of her mound and rotated his hips until she was moaning with need. Kissing her again, he flipped her over to hold the dominate position as her hips reached for his. With deliberate slowness, teasing her, he framed her body in the silk like covering making her a shrine in the middle of her hair and lay slowly down on top of her. Feeling her body welcome him as he put gentle weight on the small demanding woman underneath him.

He could feel his sex reaching for her and throbbing as she ran her cool hands over his straining muscles. He bent down to claim her mouth and she opened both sets of lips as he plunged into her dripping sheath groaning with her. He entered her hard with a thrust that sent her light body across the bed so he held her down as he drove into her. He saw her eyes closed in ecstasy meeting him halfway. Grabbing her nipple between his teeth, he pumped into her soft flesh increasing the rhythm, amazed at the girl under him.

He felt her move in sync with him getting louder and louder as he increased his movements, feeling her strain with her own need as she cried out her longing. He gazed down at her trying to see her better, but she was suddenly fussy underneath him. He could still feel her wrapped around him and he felt his aroused flesh buck inside of the warm tight girl.

He began his climb to a glorious orgasm when he saw the pleasure he gave her turn quickly to pain in her eyes. She suddenly started to thin under him and become smaller and smaller. Horrified, he stopped moving to watch her slowly fade, her frame too small to take him as she disappeared altogether, still holding the pained look on her face as her body wasted away to nothing.

Sabastian jolted out of bed with a start.

"What the hell was that?" he asked himself, throwing the covers off his sweating body.

Sabastian knew exactly what that was. He had been watching the wild cat too much and had started to become consumed by her. His only thoughts were making sure she was happy, eating and well cared for. The monitors, though grainy could not hide the fact that Victoria was a beautiful woman, graceful in her movements and the feline quality in the way she did everything.

The last time Sabastian had seen her face to face had been when he had deposited her into Michael's care and since then had only seen her through the TV's in the monitor room with Roman. She had been weak, unconscious, and disheveled and she had given him such a hard time in the alley that he had not been at all interested in the small female and he had not looked twice at her. But now that she was under his care, he was in awe and admired her so much that he found himself dreaming about her. The fact she was clean of any drugs, brave, and strong is what held him and the fact that he had dreamt about her could not come as a complete surprise.

He couldn't wait to see her again, even though it had only been a few days he was sorely tempted to break her out if that room only to see her in the flesh and watch her walk and move in front of him. Everyone in the manor knew her story and had picked up the name wild cat for her. The men referred to her as such and it pissed him off to the point of wanting to hit someone. Being jealous was not only ridiculous, but it was against the rules. There was no excuse for him to be upset at his fellow employees because they used the same nick name he did.

Sabastian's thoughts revolved around Victoria and he hoped she would continue to get healthy and to gain enough weight for what lay ahead of her. Sabastian was only doing his job and had to keep a clear head. He needed to be professional and treat her like all the other women he had worked with, but it was so very, very hard.

Without even really meeting her and only talking to her on paper he had grown protective of her and as much as he knew he needed to handle this woman with distance, he realized now he might lose that battle.

Sabastian thought about his dream. Victoria under him, with eyes he had never seen, but was dying to see in person. Her soft skin, her long hair and her lips as he entered her both from above and below. She had been so willing, so passionate in his fantasy. She had welcomed him and he had taken her firmly with uninhibited passion. He could feel his shaft pulse again, filling with blood at the thought of her and he fought his thirst for her body. She could not be his and he could not grow attached to a job. He needed her to be healthy so he could talk her into taking a position with the company. He only needed to use her to get his VP promotion and open his own branch in whatever city he wanted and get out of here.

Repeating to himself that she was only a job, he knew that she had a long way to go and it was his responsibility to ensure she was safe, healthy and growing strong. His dream told him clearly what he was thinking, she was too weak for him to even consider her at this point. As much as he would like to have her, she was not his to have and needed to focus on his main priority.

They would be spending a lot of time apart and he should be able to keep himself at least physically distant from her. Fighting the need that had racked his groin, he rolled over in bed and tried to think of something else, anything else. But his mind always came back to Victoria and wished he could see her in person, only to put some detail into his elicit thoughts.

Chapter 24

Over the next week, Victoria mostly slept. She had not been able to fully sleep for years. Always afraid of being jumped or beaten, she had never had a full night's sleep and catching up on it now felt so good. When she was not sleeping, she ate and enjoyed the shower and the jetted tub. Snooping around her room, she found it filled with beautiful new clothes, everything from thick comfortable sweats to silky night gowns, beautiful evening gowns, jeans, and comfy t-shirts.

Being clean and warm and having the feel of new clothes on her body for the first time in her life that she could remember and her stomach full, she should have been content. But Victoria was uneasy and nervous. She knew this couldn't last forever and the premonition that something big was about to happen that would change her forever would not fade from her mind. She pushed those feelings back and focused on the now, which was something she was very good at doing.

Over the first week, she could feel her energy slowing coming back and was starting to crave more. Living the life of luxury with everything, she needed Victoria quickly got bored and she was starting to lose her patience with the whole situation. She had been given almost everything she has asked for, except answers. She had reading material, mostly classic books as well as the newspaper, which she had hoped would tell her where she was. The Denver paper was given to her daily but she didn't believe she was still in the city.

After a week of reading, she asked for a needlepoint kit and was working on stitching a field of flowers with a country home on it. Into the second week, she had asked for a TV and a computer, but had only asked trying to get them to open the door to bring those large items to her. She received a large screen laptop that she could watch movies and play games that fit through the food slot, unfortunately keeping her bedroom door firmly closed. Of course she was hoping for internet access but was not at all surprised when the computer could not pick up any signals or Wi-Fi at all.

Half way through the second week, she received a routine of a dozen floor exercises and a thick yoga mat as well as instructions to work out three times a day. She added her remembered self-defense exercises to the routine and loved the challenge and the freedom to be able to practice her old skills. That same week she noticed that her meals were bigger and started to get more flavorful and heavier.

She ate almost constantly and drank protein shakes in between meals. She was always full but needed the calories now that she was active again. Her portions were always well thought out, just enough to fill her up but not so much to make her ill. She was fed the very best food and many of her first tastes had been in the last week. Things like lobster, shrimp, and all manners of shell fish were something she had heard of but never tasted. Also prime rib, salmon, pasta in every variation as well as asparagus, lamb, and escargot were among her favorites. Every dish was always beautifully arranged, like a piece of art that she almost hated to ruin by eating them.

Every day, she was given new movies and enjoyed watching them while throwing herself into her workout routine. She was thrilled she had goals to work toward, even though she was very sore after pushing herself so hard, too fast. She also enjoyed the bathroom immensely, loving the feel of the water on her skin and soaking in the tub for as long as it took her fingers to wrinkle. She loved exploring the bath products and was thrilled when Mr. Greene replenished the products she had used up.

The beginning of the third week she was given a pair of light dumbbells along with a new exercise program of weight training written in the back of her notebook. She loved the feel of weights in her hands again as she relished the feeling of power when she worked out and loved the challenge. However, she never appreciated the jetted tub more, as her muscles screamed every time she moved after the first day of working out with the weights and she was stiff and sore all over again. On the third week, her muscles may have throbbed every time she moved but her meals were so much better and larger and she really started to notice that the scale was showing more pounds added.

She would have thought that with the amount of meals she was eating and weight she was putting on, that a lot of her questions would have been answered. However, she only knew a bit more about the place in which she was being held.

The company's name was Eximius which meant nothing to her as she had never heard of it. She learned there were forty-one women working in what she now knew was named "The Manor." There were twenty-five men working for the women and a small staff of serving women that helped the men. The men and women lived in different manors and the men were only in the women's manor when invited.

She was currently in the men's manor as it was the men who were taking care of her and they needed to be close by to ensure she got everything she needed. There was also a full-service spa and kitchen on sight that the men worked at. Most of the men did multiple jobs cooking, cleaning, serving the women, and working at the spa, along with other jobs that were their main priority. There was a doctor on site available twenty-four seven. She also learned the Watchers protected the women, but she didn't know from what. She was worried. How dangerous was the work the women did if they required protection?

Other jobs, Greene would not answer, he would simply write beside the question TMI, too much information. So she would move on to other less intrusive questions about the company. She found out that after only two years working at Eximius, you would be better off even if you had worked another job for thirty years which meant the pay was more than substantial. The women all earned the same amount of money and had the same living quarters. The men earned the same wage but Greene would not tell her the amounts.

She learned about the main people in charge as well. Jeremy, a right-hand man to Mr. D who shared the largest living quarters with Mr. D, and a woman named Miss Cherry, who was somewhat of a co-owner of Eximius. She learned they were on the outskirts of a major city in a very well-respected area that had other large manors but that were far away from their location leaving them isolated. But that information in no way narrowed down even which side of the country she was in or if she was still in the United States.

Every week, she received fresh flowers for her vases and every few days, something new to do like a puzzle, heavier weights, or a new game for her computer. After the fourth week, she was happy to see that the scale pronounced her weight at ninety-seven pounds. She had been working out every day for the last three weeks and getting larger more satisfying meals. Her muscles were starting to come back and her skin and hair had regained their luster. She felt strong and energetic and ready to take on any challenge.

She was a more than a little worried when she received a note that said. "Another five pounds and we will open the door and be able to meet, then all your questions will be answered."

She had felt safer here than she had her entire life and as much as she wanted to get out of this room, she was scared of what lay on the other side of the door. Greene and his team of merry men were taking very good care of her but she still worried what would be required of her to stay here. What if she did not pass into the internship? Would she be back on the street? Or would she be supported by someone who had deemed her inadequate for their company? She was still craving information and her curiosity drove her mad every time she received TMI for an answer. But still she was safe, happy, and healthy and after so many years on the street she appreciated the last four weeks more than anyone could know.

She could understand the loyalty an employee would have toward this company and its founder. She did not need help overcoming an addiction; however, just feeling safe and full for once in her life she was more than extremely grateful. She knew, once presented with the challenge that they would give her to work here, she would try damn hard to stay and pay back what they had given her. She still had a trickle of doubt in the back of her mind but pushed it away forcing herself to be optimistic for the first time in her life and hoping it would not bite her in the ass when all was reviled.

Finishing another meal she settled into a movie then began the weight training that had gotten more intense the last week, a sign that she needed to push herself some more. After her weights, she would get into the bath and then work on her stitching or play a video game. This routine was starting to get tedious, but there was consistency and harmony that gave her a feeling of security that she was not sure she would be willing to give up after five more pounds.

She had a feeling that this was all building to some huge climax and that over whelmed her, but the patience on the other side of the notebook was comforting. However, all the information she had received about the company was not quite enough to quench her thirst for what lay beyond those doors.

It was the man who had been caring for her the last month that she really wanted to know about. Who was he? Why did he care so much about how well she was and that she was happy and had all the luxuries she needed to stay that way? Was it really only his job to care? It was driving her crazy and as much as she hated to leave the sweet sanctuary, she was dying to find out who Greene was and what he and his company really wanted with her. Was it all just a made-up story to keep her relaxed or would it be true that a dream job and life waited on the other side? She was at a loss and only time would tell if she would be introduced to a fairy tale or a nightmare when her bedroom door was finally opened.

Chapter 25

Sabastian was surprised he had been able to keep his wild cat in the room as long as he had. It was several months less than every other girl who had stayed there but she didn't have to go through detox. She had stayed in her room content as long as she was getting some answers from him and as much as he could see her frustration, she was gaining weight and working out religiously.

He was taken aback when she had started self-defense moves when he first gave her the exercise program and had to bring in Maximus to ask what form of martial arts she was practicing.

Watching her on the screen, Maximus had to study her for over ten minutes before he told Sabastian that her form was three different types of self-defenses.

"Karate, kickboxing, and jujitsu," Maximus said surprised. "It's a combination of all three and look at her style, Sabastian, she's no beginner. She has great form; it looks like she had been studying the art for years. She might have as much skill as me."

"Shit, no way," Sabastian said, watching the small girl in the monitor go through a flawless routine.

"Ya, look at her," Maximus said pointing to the screen. "You can tell she has not practiced in a while but she still flows from one style to the next beautifully or she has combined moves with each other to allow for more damage. No wonder you had a hard time bringing her in."

Slapping Sabastian on the back, "I'll stop giving you a hard time, if she did any of that with knives in her hands when you collected her you are lucky you got away."

"I wonder where she learned it," Sabastian asked, fascinated.

"You should ask her, I want to know, too," Maximus said, still studying the moving figure on the screen.

"Ya, I will," Sabastian said slowly, trying to figure out how to ask where she learned the complex moves without letting her know that she was being monitored.

"Well, have fun with her, and if I were you, I wouldn't piss her off," Maximus said smiling, shaking his head as he left the monitor room.

Sabastian was shocked that Victoria had impressed Maximus, as that was not easily done. Maximus was not the only one in awe of this small girl.

He watched her each day on the screens when he was not corresponding with her through the notebook. He watched the dedicated routine she had set for herself and saw her strength return to her slowly. The monitors were not the best and he cursed that Mr. D had not gone high definition as Timothy had suggested. He was unable to really see her, the screen always fuzzy or obscured, but he could see how she moved and with each day, her confidence built, even the way she walked had changed and he couldn't wait to see her in the flesh.

Sabastian hadn't really had a good look at the girl after he had deposited her in Michael's office. He had stayed just long enough to ensure she wouldn't wake up during the examination and had gone to check on the injured Edward in the other room. After he had returned, he was informed she had been moved to the bedroom. So the only real look he had was at her peaceful dirty face passed out on the doctor's table.

Sabastian had other things on his mind and Victoria was distracting him, however, it was a pleasant distraction. He wondered when Mr. D and Miss Cherry would be back. He was so surprised that they had not returned weeks ago and only updates from Jeremy told him that they were fine and still focused on getting something important done.

Sabastian had been able to keep up with most of his duties at the manor as his wild cat was the least demanding person he had ever worked with. He wondered if that would change once he got her out. Usually when any new girl was recruited and was told anything they wanted was theirs, the girls turned into spoiled children asking for anything they could think of, but not her. Victoria was content with books, a few movies and as much information as she could get out of him.

Having someone to update him in the monitor room and Nickolas who was working hard to restore her with his outstanding cooking Sabastian was let off the hook for many hours of the day. His feeling of frustration and lack of patience with the small female had evaporated seeing how sweet she really was, at least on paper. She was grateful, understanding and after a few notes were passed, she had stopped complaining when she didn't receive the answers she craved. He no longer thought the best option was to dismiss her to start over with someone different, but to use her for his promotion and to possibly give her a chance at a better life with Eximius.

Sabastian knew the real work would begin soon and the first thing he needed to do before the door was opened was to give her a bit more information. He needed to see her reaction before he hit her hard with the internship that he would pitch, as well as the contract she would be forced to sign or leave.

Chapter 26

Victoria awoke early, invigorated like last few mornings and looked to see her breakfast sitting in its usual spot. She stretched and got up, loving the feel of the silk night gown as it brushed her ankles. She stepped on the scale before grabbing her tray and noticed two things different. First, there was a single red rose on top of the tray and second, there was a file folder under the tray with the grey notebook. She frowned, the consistency that had kept her in a state of serenity shifted and she worried that this was the first step to a change.

She smiled at the color the flower brought to the bedroom that was only shades of cream, gold, and mahogany. Placing the flower with the rest of the white roses on her bedside table enchanted on how lovely the deep red color contrasted among the white roses. She took out the file and stared at it. Glancing to see what Greene had to say about this new development she was stressed at the first few words.

"We need you to sign this before we can let you out in one week, there is no longer a limit on your questions, although I still cannot answer some, please question me freely as I hope to introduce you to the program soon.
Sabastian."

Vitoria stared at the signature for a long time. It was the same person she had been corresponding with as the penmanship was identical to the past pages. Although that name triggered something in the back of her mind and it took her several minutes to place it.

It was him, the man who had hunted her down like a fox. It was one of the only things she heard that night and she had memorized that name hoping to confront the bastard that had scared her senseless. She didn't know which man it was, as there had been two men in the alley. She had glanced one dangerous, violent face, the one that had drugged her and the other man, the one she didn't see, she had stabbed. Not knowing if she would prefer the dangerous man or the man she had stabbed, her agitation peaked drastically.

She had never thought she would be cared for so thoughtfully by the same men she had fought and that had man-handled her that horrifying night. Sabastian had brought her here and he was the very man she had been conversing with this last month.

She wasn't sure if she was outraged or scared or not. She had been enjoying herself here, even though her freedom had been taken away from her. The night she had been taken still gave her the chills, being hunted and attacked like that. Thinking that she was being dragged back to him again, knowing she would not survive had torn at her and made her feel utterly conquered to the point of giving up.

She focused on the memory of the man's face which she had seen only briefly. It had been so large and overwhelming as he had been so close to her. Seeing the formidable face had given her the instinct to head butt him and she could still remember her head ringing from the impact. The shear rage in his features had frightened her almost to the point of stopping her attack, afraid what he would do to her if she fought him, but unusual panic had taken over. She never really saw him, only a shadow of his face but his dark rage filled eyes had haunted her for the first few weeks until she had learned to calm down and try to trust the situation she was in.

She forced herself to relax and lifted the lid of her meal, settling down to read what looked like a contract. It was a non-discloser agreement, a lot of legal stuff she didn't understand. Basically it said if she spoke out about her experiences at Eximius, the manor, and the internship program she would be sued and jailed. The one thing that it said was after she was released from jail, she would be returned to her family and that was enough to get the pen out and fill in every single space that required her initials and her signature. She wrote her whole name several times as well as her birthday and her place of birth and her mother's maiden name.

She knew by reading this, that not only was this company doing something illegal or at least highly secretive, but that she would be destroyed if she spoke out about it and was unsure how she felt about that. She only hoped that they were not selling children or torturing baby animals for coats. She looked around her beautiful room and smiled. No way was this company evil as she signed her name on the last page with a flourish. She placed the file back on the table and got out the notebook scanning over all the questions she had asked the last month and wondered where to start.

"Is Sabastian the same person who had taken her?
Did I stab you?
Is the company hurting or killing anyone, selling drugs, guns, anything to do with children, or anything that would cause a war or to do with politics?
How illegal were the activities that the company was involved in?"

She thought if she didn't have to kill anyone or steal babies or something truly evil like that she could consider the job.

She was at least a little relieved to get back her answers.

"Yes, what the company did was illegal, but not everywhere.
We do not hurt anyone, physically or otherwise. No drugs or guns, nothing to do with children or murder. Yes, I was the one who took you. No, you did not stab me. I am sorry how it all happened that night, it wasn't my choice and hope you are okay both physically and mentally as we will be working together once you get out.
Sabastian."

Victoria took back the notebook. It was him, the terrifying one! That was unnerving. How would she be able to meet the man who had taken her? The rage in his eyes still scared her when she thought of it and she would have to not only meet him, but work with him. He had been in charge of her this whole time and had been nothing but helpful, patient, and understanding, she wondered just how closely they would be working together?

She wrote a quick note back.

"I'm ready when you are."

Passing the notebook back, hoping she sounded, at least on paper, brave enough to face him and whatever program he wanted to put her through. She had a week to think about her situation and devise some sort of a game plan. She knew when they came face to face, it would be another story and she began to twist her long hair in worry. The stress turned her off her half-eaten meal so she turned to her bed to think about the fact that she may have just signed her life away.

Chapter 27

Sabastian noticed right away in the monitor room that after reading his responses she had broken her routine and went back to bed with a half-eaten breakfast and worried what had gotten her so upset? Was it because she found out he had taken her? Was it the fact that the company was illegal? Or because of the contract she had signed?

"That must have put her on edge," he hoped.

Looking at the text he had received from Nickolas, who texted him what her last note said, he didn't believe it for a second. She was rattled and if she was reacting this badly to the fact that she was sworn to secrecy and that what she would be doing would not be totally legal, then she was a lost cause. He silently cursed and looked toward the ceiling running his hands though is hair and wondered if he should bring in Douglas, the company shrink, but thinking it was premature. He decided to play this out and see where she would be in a couple of days.

Later, Sabastian decided that after the fourth meal was sent back that day barely touched, that he had enough and would speed up the process. He had asked her with each meal if anything was wrong but of course she wrote back with the infuriating woman's reply of *"I'm fine."*

She had also stopped asking questions which was so unlike her curious nature. He said to Roman after the last meal was sent back with no response to his note.

"Today," Sabastian stated flatly.

Roman gaped at him, "What, you are going to pitch to her today? You have no idea what she's thinking or what she's planning. The behavior she's displaying is classic bolting behavior, she's going to take off on you."

"No, I don't think so," Sabastian replied thoughtfully. "But I do need to talk to her face to face and let her know everything, because not eating is not an option. At this pace, she might start to lose weight and I can't let her to do that. She still has another ten pounds to go, to satisfy me. Maybe after I see her face to face, I'll be able to read her better when I talk to her."

He was trying to figure out some way to regain the trust of the small female he was in charge of and needed to at least get her to settle down.

"Well, you better keep her under lock and key and not out of your sight," warned Roman.

"Get the word out, I want all security measures in place, protocol. Locked down within the hour," Sabastian said.

Chapter 28

Minutes later, Victoria held the notebook in her hand that simply said.
"I will come for you in an hour. Sabastian."

Victoria stared at the note and panicked, she thought she had a week not one hour. She scanned the room.

Now what, she thought.

Placing the book back on the table without an answer, Victoria started shaking. She still didn't know if she wanted to run away or stay in her room forever. She was still a prisoner but she was intrigued of what this place was all about. Her thoughts contradicted and ran into each other and she couldn't think clearly.

Wondering if she would be able to come back to her room, she jumped in the shower and enjoyed every minute of the soft soaking water. Feeling rushed, she got out, dried off, threw on her robe and started to pack, thinking that this may be the last day in this lovely room. She packed her clothes which had been washed and folded for her and placed them in her bag. The only thing she packed that had been given to her was the cross stitching she had been working on. She placed the books beside the movies and laptop in a neat pile on her mirrored dresser.

It didn't take long to organize, as she had kept everything in its place and orderly, seeing she had plenty of time to do so.

She jumped and gave a shriek when a low knock sounded on her door. She walked over to it and hesitated.

"I'm not ready," she managed to squeak to the back of the door.

She was still in her robe as she was debating if she should wear her clothes or theirs.

There was no reply and she wondered if the person had heard her or not. She decided to wear their clothes because even though her clothes were clean, they still didn't feel good enough. She quickly went over to the dresser and picked out a pair of black jeans, a light blue T-shirt, and an oversized lavender sweater. She also put on a pair of white sneakers and put her wet hair into a long loose braid over her right shoulder. The outfit was warm for her room but she was in the habit of always over dressing. She walked over to her bag, still wishing she had some sort of protection on her, and slung it onto her back.

It had been at least ten minutes since the first knock and she was surprised that the person had not knocked again or tried the door to get in. Her hands were shaking as she slowly undid the floor bolt and flipped the other lock. Trying not to be a complete coward, she undid the chain and opened the door wide and stepped back.

There was no one there. She was standing at the end of a twenty-foot, windowless hallway that was encased by dark wood on the ceiling and floor. The walls were large slabs of black marble with natural thin white lines of marble streaks running through them. She knew right away that this was indeed the men's manor, even the hallway was masculine. She saw her bedroom was the only room in the long hallway. The empty hallway opened into a large space at the end. She was tempted to turn back into her room when a voice alarmed her from around the corner.

"Miss Victoria, you will not need your bag, I am just around the corner. Come to me when you are ready."

The slightly familiar voice was so soft and deep she wondered if someone was faking the whispered huskiness to sound like some radio personality. The voice sounded both polite and commanding, like someone who was used to being obeyed and her mind flashed to the man who had called out to her in the alley what seemed like years ago.

She shuttered as she turned to put her bag down on the inside of the door. Taking a deep breath, she twisted her hair in her hands as she straightened her back and walked toward the end of the hallway. She pushed away the feeling she was being herded toward something that she could not escape.

The hallway opened into a huge perfectly round library filled with tons of books. The cavernous living space had an enormous glass blue skylight overhead and the late afternoon sun shone down into the room of black leather furniture placed in different sitting areas in the circler room. There were several hallways and stairs cases both up and down, leading out of the large room in the same black marble that had the layout of a 3D spider and she shivered. The walls were layered in dark wood to match the ceiling that boasted the high skylight. There were three levels of balconies completely surrounding the room, with a matching black metal and dark wood railing going all the way up to the skylight above. She had never seen anything so fine in her life. The space screamed masculinity and she felt like she had step out of a completely different world then from her soft cream-colored sanctuary.

She didn't immediately see the figure standing beside a couch across the room to the right of her, as his back was toward her, but once her eyes fell upon his frame, she couldn't tear her eyes away.

He was broad and tall with wavy light brown hair that stopped short of his ears, she could see muscles straining his long-sleeved tight navy-blue shirt and his tight dark jeans left little to the imagination. He blended into the surroundings like he was part of the room, dressed so darkly. He didn't turn around to face her, so she tentatively stepped further into the room bringing her slightly closer to the large man, but that still left over thirty feet between them in the huge space.

She thought she should say something to him but her mouth was suddenly dry and she couldn't speak. Victoria decided not to move toward him but to circle the room to her left and look around. Apparently, he was in no rush and she wanted to take advantage of checking out the room, plus she was too nervous to speak anyway. This room was obviously a common area for the men to share but the only people here were herself and the tall man seemingly ignoring her.

There were hundreds if not thousands of books, rows and rows of books covering every inch of the wall. One large section of a book case wall across from her had a long black sheet covering what was behind it and her curiosity peaked. She ran her fingers over the some of the books scanning the titles. She realized most were text books, English, physiology, sociology, psychology, math, science, law, and medical books all neatly arranged according to genre. There was also ethics and etiquette books and she wondered why a group of men would read such things. There was an entire wall just for games and movies with several missing spots where they must be being used elsewhere.

She had just crossed the half way mark of the room when her deep concentration of the books turned back to the man who had silently turned to watch her. She stared at him completely at a loss of words, his posture, and his size told her he was dangerous and threatening, he looked hardened past his age, thinking his life had been even more difficult than hers. His arms were crossed in front of his chest and his feet planted, looking like he was ready to leap at her if she moved too fast. She remembered those arms and that face from the day she was taken and shuddered.

The only thing that kept her from bolting back to her room was the look on his face and his soft, bright green eyes watching her intently. He looked so worried for her, like he was scared she was about to collapse or faint. His eyes, as intense as they were, held nothing but concern for her. He appeared to be at least thirty, but thinking his size and hardened features aged him. One thing she knew for certain this man was unbelievably gorgeous, stunning even. Even with her mind telling her to bolt for her life, her heart rate had increased dramatically and she was hungry for a closer look at him.

Victoria detached her eyes away from him. She had been staring and was embarrassed for her rudeness and choked, "I'm sorry," looking at her shoes.

She had not spoken with her real voice to someone in years as she had always pretended to be an elderly woman on the streets. She cleared her throat and coughed, trying to get her voice to work properly again.

Sabastian had barley heard her and uncrossed his arms taking a step toward the small girl across the room from him and asked, "Miss Victoria, are you okay?" in his rich monotone voice.

"Yes, I'm fine, thank you," she replied in her soft sweet tone, still looking at her feet. Happy that her voice box was operating at least a little better. She was distracted and surprised how much she enjoyed the sound of her name coming from his mouth, even though the Miss part was a bit much.

Christ, Sabastian thought, *this is going to be impossible, she's a frightened rabbit. Where did the wild cat go that almost stabbed me in the alley?*

He was watching her so closely, trying to figure out what she was thinking and saw her shudder and her eyes tear up. Her voice was so surprisingly sweet like something out of a cartoon but husky at the same time. He was used to training girls with zero manners, rude, selfish, vane, and uncaring of others. The other girls that came for the promotion test had been hardened and had lost themselves to drugs and the streets, but this woman had held herself intact through her experiences and his awe of her increased.

He had watched this girl for so long in the monitors and had witnessed her transformation, seeing her fill out and gain weight and start to be human again. However, seeing her in the flesh made his body warm at the sight of her. She was much shorter than him and so tiny. What skin he could see was so pale, almost translucent, and he vowed to get her outside as soon as possible only to see her skin glow and warm under the sun's rays. Her body had started to get back a few of its curves, but she was still too skinny for his liking.

She wore a baggy sweater that emphasized her small frame and he didn't like it, she looked like she was drowning in the material. Her sweet heart shaped face and her eyes were what held him entranced, he had never seen such angelic eyes in his life. They were large and wide and had an exotic shape that said this girl was something out of a fantasy, like a fairy or a wood sprite. The color of her eyes now seeing it in the flesh is what fascinated him the most. He desperately wanted to get closer to her to verify the fact that she really did have dark blue and purple irises, but didn't dare approach her.

She was too soft; Sabastian could not believe she had survived so many years in the streets. He had to remember there was another side of her, the wild cat that he had fought, but she looked too young, too sweet for what he had in store for her. What was he supposed to do with her, he was completely out of his element and she wouldn't even look at him now. He hoped his plan to give her back some control and confidence would work. Keeping his eyes intensely locked onto her face as he moved, he grabbed something on a shelf and then walked toward the table in the sitting area between them. There, he placed all six of her knifes neatly in a row on the table and stepped back.

He gave her a slight smile as he turned his back and asked, "Would you like to go for a tour Miss?"

Moving away from her toward a hallway.

Victoria stared at her newly polished knives, bewildered, *why would he give those back to me?*

She walked to the table and reached for one, hesitated, then quietly walked after him leaving the weapons behind. She knew even with six knives she would be no match for him. She would be able to do some damage, yes, but she had been told she was in a house full of men and to try and fight would be stupid. The fact that he had given them back, probably when he was not supposed to, gave her a least a little hope and her trust went up a notch.

Victoria would have liked nothing more than to go back to her room and lock the door, not ready for this. The man walked away from her leaving the decision completely to her, she could follow him or take her knives and run back to her room. She needed to follow him as her curiosity of the manor and this man intrigued her. She was drawn by some invisible force and walked behind him as he talked, gesturing where the kitchen was, the games room, the entertainment room, and the men's apartments.

There was no one in sight. Only the sound of male voices coming from the entertainment room let her know they were not alone. She followed him, looking around and taking in his low tenor, not really listening to the words but just enjoying the tone of his voice when an overwhelming feeling of frustration over took her. She needed answers, not a tour of this beautiful building, even though her surroundings, as masculine as they were, soothed her.

He had just started down a hallway and said that if she wanted to use any of the rooms, to let him know and he would have them cleared, when she said.

"You're the man who took me," she didn't ask, it was a whispered statement.

Sabastian turned to face her, not realizing she was so close behind him, and froze making eye contact so close to her he got the full effect of her incredible eyes and was lost for a moment in time. He blinked, then took a step back to give her space. She was looking up at him, apprehension on her face.

"Yes, I'm sorry, miss," he replied, having the decency to flush a little.

"Why?" She asked her violet eyes burning into his.

"Please," he said as he motioned behind them to head to the round room.

Turning to go back, she wished she had taken a knife. With him walking so close behind her, it made her feel as if she was being stalked and her nervousness increased tenfold.

He walked over to the couch and motioned for her to sit across from him in front of her knives. He was able to see her better and could not tear his eyes from her face. He watched her sink into the soft leather and saw her hands immediately take her braided hair and start to twist it in her lap.

Gesturing to the weapons, "You are welcome to take them back if you wish. If it will make you feel more comfortable," Sabastian said, sitting down.

"There's really no point, is there? If you need to force me to do something, there is nothing I could do to stop you."

She was soft with her words but the feeling of being under threat was clear. She didn't feel safe yet and that was something Sabastian was determined to fix.

"What are you afraid of?"

You, she wanted to scream, but she knew she didn't have a good reason. He was the one that had taken such good care of her and she was being irrational. It didn't change the fact that he was too dominating, too large, and in command that scared her to the point of chills running up her spine.

She was able to really see him now, his masculine face, his chin, and his tanned skin added to his threating features. His eyes were what held her, they were a brilliant shade of green and they sparkled and bore into her own eyes. He looked genuinely concerned for her and if she only looked into his eyes, she could not feel threatened. His body was taut, hard, and broad; she could see the definition of large muscles under his dark shirt and she shuddered at the memory of him grabbing her and restraining her in the darkness of the apartment. He was gorgeous but too masculine and he had hunted her. She shivered again.

She didn't answer his question but repeated her last one.

"Why?"

She had a sad scared look in her eyes and it made Sabastian's heart break, hoping that information is what she needed to come out of her shell. He had thought long and hard of what to tell her and started with a shadow of the truth as he dove into a rendition of what she needed to know, hoping not to scare her more.

"My boss is a very wealthy man because of this business and when he started expanding, it was hard to find the right employees. He needed young women, with no family ties, no close friends, and they all had to be unmarried, without children. That left a small pool of people, so he turned to recruiting off the streets as most people from that back ground fit the requirements he needed. He found that in helping people who joined the company they appreciated the life he offered them so much more and with that came a loyalty that he could never buy. When we recruit people from the streets, we clean them up and give them a new start at life either with us or on their own. The people he saved, work extremely hard for him, living up to his high standards and making his business thrive. Of course only a small percent makes it into the program as it is very hard to find young people on the streets who were not so heavily damaged that they wouldn't be able to make a life for themselves here. There are other ways to bring people into this business but Mr. D both needs the loyalty and gratitude he receives from rescuing his employees."

Sabastian paused to watch her reaction, so far, she was simply taking it all in, in silence, which he appreciated. The story he told was twisted, leaving out several important things but she was on a need-to-know basis. Until he had gotten his promotion, she would need to be kept in the dark about where the real women who worked for Eximius came from and what she was really here for.

Victoria raised her eyebrows, clearly trying to be patient for him to answer her original question.

He continued, "We have several snitches on the ground who are outsourced to find young women that fit our needs and that need help. The snitches have no idea why we want the girls but are paid for the information and that is how you were found. I think a local found you at a YMCA and followed you to your alley. He followed you for a few days and when he saw you were settled in a certain location, he called us and gave us the go ahead that you were there."

Puzzled, she asked, "So some street rat tracked me down, called you, and you came and kidnapped me?"

"Well, we do not like to use that word. We collected you," he said apologetically.

"Call it what you will, but how come you didn't let me go when you saw I clearly didn't need help?"

Shooting a confused look back at her, he asked, "You didn't need help?"

"Well, I'm not on drugs or anything, which I am sure you have figured out, so why would I need saving?"

Bemused, Sabastian repeated, "You didn't need help? You were freezing, starving, it wasn't even that cold the night we came. You would have been dead within a few weeks at the rate you were shriveling up. You didn't need to be on drugs to get yourself dead as your own stupidity would have done that," he was upset with her and tried to keep his voice level.

Anger flared in her eyes, "I would have been just fine. I've survived much worse than some cold weather and I know where I could get a good meal."

He liked this aspect of her, he wanted to see her angry and passionate and pushed her some more. Without raising his voice, he continued, "That's bull, how long would it have taken you to be raped, or killed, or just to waste away in that alley? How long would the old lady act last you? You knew you were in trouble, what was your plan anyway? To live out your life eating garbage, hoping no one would notice you existed? What were you hiding from? How did you even get there? Five years on the streets, why would you leave so young? What happened to make you leave?"

Tears sprang in her eyes and the fight left her suddenly, she turned her head away from him embarrassed.

Shit, he thought, he had pushed too far. The overprotectiveness he felt for her was so surprising and unexpected that he was confused and he frowned.

Victoria wiped at her tears, frustrated with herself and spoke low in a husky voice that was choked with emotion, without thinking the words flowed from her.

"Mom died when I was fourteen, then Gary, my good for nothing stepfather, turned to me for his sick pleasures."

Fuck, she was out of the program, no one can come back from that kind of abuse and work here, Sabastian thought. *There goes my VP position.*

Victoria continued, "He hunted me down just like you did, to drag me back home and continue to use me like a punching bag. After he finally killed my mom with one punch too many, she was no longer there to protect me."

Closing her eyes, she tried to shut down the pain of the hard subject she had never spoken about to anyone before. Talking about this subject to someone was disarming but she felt a weight lift off of her almost physically and she took in a deep breath.

Sabastian was confused and almost jumped at her with his next question.

"So he was not molesting you, only slapping you around?"

She looked at him shocked and he realized how that must have sounded.

"Oh, Miss Victoria, I'm so sorry, I didn't mean to lessen what he did, but I need to be clear that it was only physical abuse?"

"Ya, he only slapped me around a bit."

She sounded empty and sarcastic at the same time and Sabastian wanted to kick himself for being so obtuse.

"I'm sorry, Miss Victoria, I didn't mean to sound insensitive, but with this job, you can come back from getting the crap kicked out of you daily. Trust me, I know, but it is almost impossible to come back mentally healthy from being raped at a young age."

Victoria frowned, why did the kind of abuse matter? She was slightly distracted by the formal use of her name as it was really starting to annoy her.

"So if Gary killed your mother, why is he not in jail, did you not tell anyone?"

"No, I couldn't," she said ashamed, eyes brimming with tears.

"I was only fourteen when it happened and he had already laid into me a few times, besides no one would listen to trailer trash like me and my mom. Gary married my mom when I was six and we were in all accounts trailer trash. She was too kind, too soft and sweet and I think that is why Gary picked her. He didn't pick a wife; he picked an easy victim. Gary is a sick man. We lived in an incredible snobby area and Gary was very well respected, well connected, and very rich, but it's not like my mom or I ever saw that money. Within a year of their marriage, my mother was his nightly punching bag and I lived in the basement. My mom had tried to report him once when I was ten. He almost killed her for it, then proceeded to beat me bloody in front of her to prove a point. We both learned to keep quiet the hard way. He liked to drink and I was too scared of him to talk to anyone. After she died, it took me almost three years before I got the nerve to run away and escape him only to be dragged back two weeks later."

Victoria couldn't believe she was telling him all this, she didn't even know this man. It felt good to let someone, anyone know what had happened that would not treat her like worthless trailer trash and who would actually listen. She looked up at him, tears making her long lashes sparkle and only shrugged lightly.

"So that's why you fought so hard when we came to get you?" he asked, finally comprehending her reaction to that night when he grabbed her.

"He had caught me twice before. Once after only a couple of weeks and then it took three months to escape from the prison cell he had installed in the basement. I was kept in the same basement; however, everything that my mother had ensured I had when I was forced to live down there was gone. My bed, my clothes, dresser, any possessions had been thrown out. I only had an old mattress, a sink, and toilet and bars were installed on all the windows. He found me again a year later after I escaped that dungeon and it took another four months to heal from the beating he dished out and for me to figure out how to get away and stay away and now I have been gone for over three years."

Sabastian was outraged at the so-called father who had beat his wife to death and then started beating on a little girl just for fun, like a hobby.

"You must have gone to school," he asked.

"Yah, I did. A fancy prep school actually, but I kept my head down and missed a lot of classes when I was marked up from the visits Gary would give me in the basement every other week when my mother displeased him or when he felt like it. My mom had to hide whatever money she could to buy me anything as I was given only what would make me presentable when out in public. I was to be not seen or heard when he was home and was never allowed in the main house and he made sure of that by keeping the basement door locked at all times, but I did have the use of a separate outside entrance to come and go and avoid being seen. According to Gary, I did not exist unless my mom had displeased him and then he would use me to put on a show for her."

Victoria sighed, staring off into the distance almost talking to herself and forgetting there was anyone in the room. She felt like she was suddenly unburdened telling her story, even though her throat hurt from talking so much, she quietly continued.

"I was basically a prisoner locked up and ignored by Gary but loved by my mother who tried to protect as much as she could. My mom would bring me food only when Gary had gone to work and after they had eaten dinner and she would cash in bottles for money as Gary made sure he was in complete control of every aspect of her life. She had no car, no money, no freedom or friends. She was a slave and she could not break free. I also had no friends and no one ever came over to our house. I spent as much time away as possible I would take the bus to the city to walk the streets outside alone. I felt free walking the streets. Yes, there were bad things happening out there as well but at least the people were free. After my mom died, I stayed out after school as long as I dared as he would check to see if I was downstairs every night. He would stand over me and remind me of the trailer trash both my mom and I were. When he would get a rise out of me, he would use me like he used my mom and I would feel the abuse physically instead of mentally. I almost preferred the beatings as I could not stand to have that man talk about my mother that way and I felt like I could handle it, but it got worse and worse and when he started saying that I should move upstairs so that I could replace my mother fully, I started planning my get away."

She trailed off thinking about the life she had lived in the streets, free from the fear of the nightly beatings from her stepfather. She smiled internally at the thought of him still looking for her. She had beaten him and would never see that bastard again.

The silence was broken by Sabastian's next question spoken softly.

"You said you have been on the streets for five years."

She blinked and remembered she was still in a conversation with a strange, beautiful man and refocused straightening up.

"About that, on and off."

"Where is Gary now?"

"Still looking for me, living in Texas."

"How do you know he is still looking for you?"

"Because he is. He'll never give up, he told me he would kill me if I tried to run away again. I have him beat, but I know he is still out there hunting me. I got away and that will drive him mad, thinking that a little girl had beaten him for once," she finished with a slight smirk on her face.

"Male ego," she shrugged.

"Well, I am glad you are safe here with me," he said kindly.

She stiffened slightly, reminded she was in a strange house with a strange man in a house full of other strange men. She looked at him, glanced around, and looked back, trying to read him and wondering if she truly was safe here. She tensed when he got up and moved toward her. Victoria looked at the knives that were within grabbing distance and her fingers twitched toward them.

Sabastian approached slowly, got down on his knee before her and very slowly reached for her hand. He had to win some trust with her or they would be at a standstill, never moving forward.

Victoria's body jerked at his movement toward her, she had not been touched in years and she was instinctually mistrusting. She pulled her hand back out of his reach and froze. He was so close and the sweet strong aroma of him filled her senses and made her want to breathe deep, but she held her breath, waiting for his next move and thinking of a physical defense against this devastatingly handsome man.

Sabastian saw her reaction to him; trying to touch her and he was so pained for her. So he pulled his hand back, ran it through his hair and looked up at her. He said with as much sincerity as he could muster.

"Miss Victoria, I promise I will never hurt you. You will always be safe with me and you will be safe forever if you want to stay after I have told you everything."

He reached over very slowly letting her watch his every move. He took a knife slowly by the blade, offering it to her handle first, looking up at her.

"Please, if this will make you feel better hold it, I will do whatever it takes to make you feel like you can trust me. I am so sorry you felt like you were being hunted and I will never allow you to be hunted down again. I give you my word and beg your forgiveness, sweet Miss Victoria," he said this slowly, softly, and with honest sincerity.

Victoria slowly took the blade from his hand grazing his palm with her fingers tips and shivered at the first human contact she had had in years. Sabastian gave her a slight smile, stood up, and walked across the room to where she had first found him.

Victoria was completely taken aback; she was not expecting a forthright speech from this huge dominating man. No man had ever begged for anything from her, the only man that she had known had simply taken what he wanted and she assumed that was true of all men. Every man she had ever met had meant her harm, she had escaped being raped so many times, she had been stabbed three times, and robbed more times than she could count, mostly by men. They were brutal, selfish, violent brutes that she never wanted anything to do with. But this man had gone on his knees and begged for her to both trust and forgive him. She blinked, yes, he had hunted her but he had also rescued her from herself and she needed to try, at the very least to start to trust someone, she had to try to let go and start over.

Victoria felt the smooth metal blade in her hand, and slowly rolled it in her palm.

Sabastian stood with a file folder in his hands and watched her.

"Yes," she whispered, almost so softly that he did not hear.

Sabastian did not expect a response from her at all, watching intently, he gave a little smile.

"Yes," she said more clearly. "I can forgive you. You didn't know what I'd been through. It wasn't your fault I thought you were him." Referring to Gary. She closed her eyes.

"You are not him," she said to herself.

"No, I'm not and quite frankly, I'm insulted you would even think that," he said disgruntled.

She looked up at him alarmed; she had upset him but saw a smile lifting his lips and dimples deepen making him look instantly youthful.

"I've got to look way younger than that, and look at me," he said his smile broadening. "I am super-hot looking. No way is he as cute as me."

He had his arms spread wide and he gave her a dazzling smile with his dimples showing up impressively.

Victoria laughed, which made the room light up around Sabastian. She smiled at him, put the knife back on the table, crossed her legs, and visibly relaxed.

"Ya, I guess you are not bad looking," she said smiling shyly at him.

"Damn straight, I'm not bad looking," he said mockingly arrogant, a personality trait foreign to him.

Victoria liked this side of him, teasing and playful. His smile was infectious and made all his intimidating features disappear. The smile made him unbelievably more handsome, if even possible, and much younger looking and she knew she could start to try to trust him.

Sabastian walked back over to her and offered her his hand.

"Miss Victoria, will you please come with me? I want you to meet someone."

She looked at his large hand and hesitated. It was too big and she felt herself tense again.

"It's okay, miss, if you are not ready, we can wait another day. As long as you promise to continue to eat," he said patiently still holding his proffered hand out to her.

"Tell you what," she said. "I will come with you, but only if you stop calling me 'Miss Victoria.' It is really irritating and makes me feel like I am back in the 18th century."

Sabastian smiled at her in response still holding out his hand.

Taking another deep breath, she placed her small hand in his and let him lift her up gently. His hand was big, but it was also warm and incredibly comforting. She had not touched anyone in years and it felt strangely good to have contact with someone.

She remembered what he had said, and asked worried, "Who am I going to meet?"

"You are going to meet my very best girl. She's even cuter and more charming than me."

119

Chapter 29

Frowning, Victoria followed him up the stairs, her hand still wrapped warmly in his. She had heard the teasing tone in his voice but was still confused. She thought that the people working here had to be single. Why would he introduce her to a girlfriend? Wasn't this also supposed to be the men's manor? She realized she was slightly jealous that he belonged to someone else.

They walked upstairs, down the hallway, along the balcony, above the round room, and right into a huge bedroom. The room was the same size as her own room but with large covered windows along the far wall. The room smelled heavenly, and she recognized the scent of him, the soft smell of citrus soap, leather, and musk.

She lightly resisted his grip in the doorway, not wanting to go into his bedroom.

He let her hand go and walked straight to the bed.

What was he thinking? That I'm going to sleep with him because he helped me?

She panicked under the door frame.

"Come in and please shut the door," he said, his back turned to her.

She stood frozen thinking she should bolt again, but where, back to her room where she would have to start this process all over again.

"Close the door or my best girl will take off on me and I'll have to chase her around the kitchen again."

She was completely bewildered until he turned around with a small black cat in his arms.

Victoria smiled and turned to close the door and moved forward to pet the sweet animal who had already started purring.

"Here is my very best girl. Her name is Sketch and I rescued her, just like you," he said smiling.

"And like you," he continued, "you are both wild cats."

"She has your eyes," Victoria exclaimed, looking closely in the cat's face.

He shrugged. "It runs in the family," he said smiling down at the green-eyed feline.

He placed the cat gently in her arms and moved to the sitting room several feet from the bed, sitting on the far end of one of the couches.

The cat immediately put both its paws on Victoria's shoulders and started to rub its soft forehead on her cheek.

"She doesn't look like a wild cat," Victoria said, nuzzling the cat with her nose.

"Well, I had to tame her," Sabastian replied, lounging, and relaxed in the soft sofa. "I think taming her will be easier than you," he said laughing.

"Ya, good luck with that," Victoria answered walking over to the sitting area. She sat down lightly on the other end of the couch while Sketch proceeded to lie stretched out on her lap, feet in the air.

"Do you charm all your girls with Sketch?"

Sabastian was silent for a moment.

"Actually I haven't brought any women in here before," he said almost puzzled. "I did it without thinking, I just thought you would like to meet the first person I ever trusted before I was settled here. Of course, she's not a person, but don't let her know that," he said smiling at his cat.

"I wanted to show you that it took me a long time to trust as well and I know it's not easy. I started with Sketch and finally expanded to the other members of the team here."

Sabastian paused, "If you're not comfortable here, miss, we can go back down stairs."

"No, I'm fine, and stop it with the, 'Miss' stuff," Victoria said, stretching like the feline in her lap.

"Sorry force of habit when in the presence of a lady," Sabastian said, doing an over exaggerated bow to her.

"Yah, I read the respect rules," Victoria said rolling her eyes at him just as dramatically, causing him to laugh and for her to relax that much more.

Petting the cat, she glanced to the right to enjoy the gliding fish in their tank as well as taking in the sights of his room. The windows were covered from between the panes of glass, which was a shame because it might have given her an idea of where she was if she was able to look out.

The room was immaculately clean, except in front of the window where an art station was set up. There was an easel facing the window with several scattered drawings of cities and buildings around it on the floor. Looking closer, she could see most were of interesting structural and architectural designs. The only drawing that was not of buildings; however, was the outline of a female on the easel itself, in the beginning fazes of a portrait. She could see the curve of the women's body, faceless, but still sensual.

She tore her eyes away from the easel to gaze around the rest of the room. The massive dark bed dominated the room, but the space itself felt warm and soft. With pale ceiling lights and the glow of the fish tank, it was a very relaxing space, but it was clearly a man's space.

"Okay," he said, tapping the folder he had brought up with them, "I am going to try not to mess this up. I have never pitched before so please bear with me."

"You've never what?" Victoria asked amused, her eyes brows raised.

"Pitched, uh, is when we pitch the company's internship to a new recruit or a new collection after they have been detoxed, but in your case, healthy and fat."

She gave him an exasperated look, "Fat?"

"Oh, please, you have at least another ten or fifteen pounds to go before I'm satisfied," he said seriously.

"You've never done this before?" She asked.

"No man has ever done this. It is too hard for women to trust a man, no matter her history. Miss Cherry always pitches to the girls but she's gone and I was saddled with you."

He said this with a smile so she knew he was kidding.

"Okay, well, it'll be a first for both of us. I have never been pitched to before, let's hear it," she said, hoping to finally solve the mystery of this place.

Sabastian looked down at the file, he was fully prepared just to read it to her, but it was written to be read by a woman to a woman and it felt wrong. He knew most of it by heart and decided to put forth his version and hope he would not come off as too crude. He watched her with Sketch still in her arms and saw her curiosity over run any feelings of being uncomfortable. He opened the file so he would at least hit all the important points once he started.

"The first thing you have to promise is not to interrupt me. You need to hear all the rules and how this place is run before you make judgments, can you do that?"

"Umm, I can try," she said, thinking this is going to be bad and tried to prepare herself.

Sabastian cleared his throat, "Most of the people work for only out of necessity and for the money. They hate their job and would do anything to be able to afford not to have to work. Most people are forced to work because of bills, debt, and to be able to afford the things they think they need to be happy. When working makes them miserable, the possessions they buy with their money takes away some of that misery and distracts them long enough to not think about their hated jobs and lives."

"However, there is a percentage of very lucky people who absolutely love their job and would forsake everything else so they can continue doing what they love to do for a living. Money doesn't matter, they could be paid pennies as they are already doing what they love to do and do not need money to fulfill a happiness gap that is not there," Sabastian took a breath, watching her closely and started again.

"That is the main requirement of this job. You must love what you are doing and want to do it. No one here is forced to work. Everybody is free to leave at any time with or without a reason and they would be able to leave with quite a bit of money in their pockets. If a woman is given a certain job within the company, she has every right to refuse it, without having to give a reason, she can simply say no, without question or reprimand. And some women do pick and choose which jobs they want to take. Although most love the work so much that refusing is something they rarely do. But let's say a woman is not feeling well, is tired, or simply doesn't like the job assignment given, she says no, and that is the end of the conversation."

Sabastian paused, hoping he had made his point.

"Okay, so people like working here and have the freedom to work or not. I got it," Victoria said, understanding what he was getting at.

He continued; glad she was engaged and getting the important points he was making.

"However, not everyone would love working here. Most do not understand the passion it takes to work here; it is very subjective. Someone may say they absolutely love being a teacher and you may think, that's stupid, because you

123

don't like kids. Or same goes for a doctor, but you can't stand the sight of blood. So it all comes down to your life experiences and if you like the work we are doing here. But I wanted to stress that everyone here, is here because they love it and for no other reason. Most would work for free and the fact they are paid very well has no reflection on the work they do. The women work when they want to and make money at their own pace. Not one member of the team is more important than that rest. With maybe Miss Cherry being the exception and perhaps Jeremy, but they do not work with the team they work with the boss."

Victoria had put her feet up on the couch carefully adjusting Sketch with her. She was absorbing everything Sabastian was saying. She was trying to wait for him to get to the point remembering that this was his first time and didn't want to interrupt his flow. With Sketch on her legs and her feet inches from Sabastian, she was surprisingly very comfortable listening to his soft deep voice.

"Eximius is Latin for extraordinary, exquisite, rare, and superb," he continued. "We are the best at what we do. We run this company to perfection in both our services and the way we treat our women. Would you like me to go over the respect rules again?" he asked her.

"I have them memorized," she said simply. "I know how well all the girls are treated but I don't understand why? Why are the women more important than the men?"

"It's because they are the ones that make the money and the men are here to keep them happy. Think of it like a bee hive, the queen does all the work to keep the hive alive but she needs workers to make sure she gets everything she needs to provide for the rest of the hive."

Sabastian made sure not to mention that men also do the same jobs as the women as he did not want to confuse things just yet or give her unnecessary information.

Victoria looked at him expectantly.

Sabastian could not help it and trying to get the point across, he spit out.

"Our Eximius women are responsible for fulfilling the emotional, social, intellectual, and physical needs of our clients," he said slowly, trying to tip toe around the explanation hoping she would catch on.

Victoria stared at him, dumbfounded.

124

He watched her face, seeing she was still completely confused. Not getting it he blurted out.

"Physical Victoria. Including sexual needs," he said clearly.

Her face went from being confused to her eyes widening and her face paled slightly.

Bingo, he thought and waited for the explosion that must usually followed. This was the moment of truth and the next few minutes would determine everything about her and what she thought of him and the company.

"You mean this nothing but a whore house?" she spluttered.

Sabastian was clearly upset and put his head in his hands and wished he had done this better.

"I'm sorry, I didn't mean to insult you," Victoria was horrified at her bluntness. This business meant everything to these people and they clearly loved their work. But she couldn't get past the fact that this beautiful place was where men came to satisfy themselves physically. It both intrigued her and horrified her.

Sabastian raised his head. "No," he said, "clients never come here, this is our sanctuary, our home, our women do their business off site. That is only a small part of what they do as well, they are hired as intelligent, bright young women who can hold their own in a crowd of professionals. They are paid actresses who can play any role. They can participate in political debates, be experts in their field, and be a speaker at any event from crime to world peace. One of our women is on the Woman's World Union, they speak for women's rights and fight on anti-rape committees. You think it ironic, but what is right for women and our employees loving what they do for a living are completely different things. Some people think that only men truly enjoy sex, but it's simply not true and our company thrives on women who love sex and do it better than anyone. But like I said, that part of it can be a very small part of their job. There are times where they are hired, but do not end up in bed with the client, much to our women's disappointment."

Sabastian looked up at her, hoping not to see horror in her eyes. He was surprised to see her deep in thought, gazing at his aquarium.

"Ummm. Okay, so…it's like an escort service," she started slowly.

"Well, yes and no. We are so much more than an escort service, there is no one in the world that can provide the services we do in the grand scale that is required of our clients."

He was so glad she was not yelling at him or had run screaming from his room, both good signs.

"But it is against the law, right? I mean buying and selling sex is totally illegal," she stated.

Sabastian refrained from rolling his eyes since she was speaking so calmly about the work they did here. He knew some education was in order.

"Yes, in many parts of the world, prostitution is illegal. But, Victoria, there are so many countries where our kind of work is legal, regulated, and safe for everyone."

Victoria frowned at him skeptically.

"When governments have a legalized and regulated sex workers, it has shown to have so many benefits. It has been proven there are less violence crimes overall and much less sex crimes committed against woman and children in these legal countries. The woman themselves are much healthier and safer when taken care of like normal industry with rights and rules. There are less human trafficking violations and countries save millions of dollars in the court system and make millions with taxing the industry. A woman has a right to do with her body as she wishes and it is a victimless crime. It is really surprising that more countries do not regulate sex workers. But, of course, we are not in one of those countries, so we have to fly below the radar to supply the same services, but at a much higher value than all others."

Victoria mentally went through the list of benefits and it did make some sense, but it was something she had never thought of. Yes, her mind had strayed to the profession when she saw the girls making money on the streets. But seeing those same girls beaten by their buyers or pimps and being treated like they were trash had always steered her away from even getting close to the seemly dirty woman selling themselves on the garbage infested sidewalks. It always looked so unclean to her but she had never really thought of it as a business, just a way to survive on the streets. Victoria sat in silence and absorbed this information in a new light. Did women actually do the prostitution thing, right? Would it be possible to be safe and enjoy the work and do it, not to survive, but for something more gratifying? She had always thought of those women as being forced, threatened, and made to be a sex object for the pimps that ruled them and she had to admit this new take on the profession left her curious.

"The girls don't have to take a job if they don't want to?" she asked slowly.

"Nope."

"They really like, umm, sex and want to be with their clients?"

"Yes."

"What is their percentage?" she asked, knowing from experience on the street that most street walkers made less than ten percent or were just glad they were not beaten by their pimps if they had made enough money that night.

"Seventy-five percent."

She turned to look at him, "Seventy-five percent!" she was floored, "Really?"

"Yes, of course, they work very hard, they have to study almost constantly for several of their clients, they exercise all the time and are always working on perfecting their art."

"Wow," she said, "you guys don't mess around with your respect thing, hey?"

"The last thing we ever want our women to feel, is taken advantage of, you can imagine why," he said cracking a tiny smile, his dimples surfacing.

"I guess the respect rules make a lot more sense now. How do you know if someone is suitable for the work here?" she asked hesitating.

She had not really meant to imply how to find out if she would be suitable to work here. But knew that is what it sounded like when the question left her lips and she turned red from embarrassment immediately. But secretly, she was intrigued what kind of women it took to work in this kind of profession.

"Well…" Sabastian hesitated. How could he tell her that she needed to have sex to begin?

"Umm, the first part is to introduce a new intern to one of our trainers and talk about her likes and dislikes openly to see where she stands when having intercourse. She is supposed to ask as many questions about sex, so that everything is clear without any reservations or shyness. There is no room for modesty in this business, everything must be laid out in the open to ensure that a woman is not faking it and is truly enjoying the job. They also have a ton of studying to do, to hold their own when out with these much-respected men and be highly educated in several fields."

Sabastian had to be careful answering her questions now. Women that were collected for the men's promotions test, like Victoria, were a far cry from the actual professional girls. The professionals were mostly smart, young models and actresses or university students and they were the only ones actually hired to service their wealthy clients once trained. Eximius was the very best and their clients expected professional women who were beautiful, smart, and sexy and could do the job naturally. Hiring drug addicts, homeless women, and former street walkers would never be accepted.

The professionals at Eximius were the women who were put into the real training program that he was now practicing with Victoria, someone deemed unworthy by Eximius standards. It was the ultimate test. If a prospective VP like Sabastian could teach a drug addict, homeless woman then he was capable of hiring respectable women and training them to fill a new chapter.

Victoria was going to be trained for a position that she would never be offered, but she could not know that until he was finished with her. He needed to make sure that Victoria only thought she would be considered for a high paying career to get her through the program; just long enough for him to get his promotion. He could not let her know the truth till his new job had been secured. No test girl had ever been hired for their clients; Mr. D would not allow it. Sabastian could not let Victoria find out what would happen to her once she had completed the program. She could never know she would only be used as a pleasure girl for the men and a general worker for the Eximius girls at the end of the program with no option to do better.

Sabastian had to get his mind wrapped around this concept when he had been studying the pitch. Yes, he was a good liar and could fool almost anyone but deceiving Victoria now that she was in his room petting his cat, felt so wrong. He had to stifle that feeling to concentrate on her questions that were coming in quickly.

"So the girls who do not make it are the ones who had bad experiences with sex, like being raped? That is why you were making sure I was only beaten," she asked him matter of fact, snapping him out of his thoughts.

Sabastian had to concentrate to answer her.

"Yes and no, some women never learn to like sex or their bodies never learn to fully enjoy everything sex had to offer. A lot of the time their early experience was soured and that completely wreck how they looked at sex for the rest of their lives."

"So how does a woman learn to enjoy it?" she blushed, not wanting to say the word sex again.

"Most women have the potential to enjoy it, but it is like doing anything new, you have to be taught well so you are not turned off during the learning process. You can very easily be put off of driving or learning the piano if your instructor is an uncaring jerk. It could take a really long time to trust and to try to learn again with someone new. Some girls who have sex for the first time are with selfish guys who could care less about the girl and just satisfy themselves leaving the girl in need or worse, shock. It can take years for that girl to get over it. Some girls are lucky enough to have a partner that loves them and they learn together over a long period of time. Even better when that partner is experienced and caring and he puts both love and effort into the love making."

Wow it was like a sex-ed course in here, she thought and she was starting to feel her face warm up again with embarrassment.

Trying to get off topic she said, "But I'm not smart, I only finished grade nine and barely. I also was held back because I hardly went to school. I don't know about being intelligent enough to talk to these business men."

"That's bull," he said, sounding a little annoyed at her. "I doubt you got someone else to rig that catapult and pulley system that whipped you up that building like a shot. You also figured out how to stay hidden in plain sight in the streets with the old women act and that horrible coat you wore, which I thought was a nice touch. Don't tell me you are not smart, because you were an extremely hard collection and you almost got away. And your defensive moves, wow, where did you learn all that? It was very well executed. You, my dear, are brilliant. So reading up on a few books to learn some facts will be child's play compared to your little street drama you had me going through to get you," he finished smiling at her.

She smiled back, it had taken awhile to rig the system and it had worked so nicely. Only Sabastian was stronger and faster than her and his sheer strength and agility was what beat her, plus there had been two of them.

"Thank you," she said. "But that was done to survive, I would have been dead if I hadn't used the old women to save me, aka Mildred," she said seriously. "Being able to rig up a pulley system and play out an old lady act hardly makes me brilliant."

"But you're wrong, the fact that you thought of it and were able to play an old lady convincingly, for what, two, three years? Is exactly the type of intelligence you need to be here. You are smart, you are creative, and you can act! That sounds to me like a really good base to be very successful here," Sabastian said confidently.

"But I didn't walk away untouched I made tons of mistakes and…"

He cut her off, "Get over it, I'm sticking with my argument, you're brilliant, admit it."

"I was…"

"Admit it, no excuses, unless someone either taught you or showed you to do any of the things you did to stay alive these last years, it is all you."

She blushed and smiled at Sketch, "Okay, but…"

"That's good enough for me," he said, interrupting anymore argument.

Victoria was embarrassed thinking of her behavior that night, when something dawned on her.

"Oh my god," she said covering her mouth.

"What?" Sabastian asked alarmed, sitting up. "What is it?"

"How badly did I hurt the other guy?" she asked horrified. "Is he okay? I'm so stupid I completely forgot I…."

"Oh, he's fine, please don't worry," Sabastian said relieved, relaxing back into the couch.

"Edward is just fine; he was stitched up by our doctor and was up and walking around the same day."

"Are you sure?" she asked, she was so ashamed.

"Yes, and that leads me a very important question, how does a tiny eighty-pound girl almost get the better of two strong trained men?"

"Oh, um, another long story."

"I have time," Sabastian encouraged her.

Victoria remembered back and thought there was no harm in letting Sabastian know how she had acquired her fighting skills.

"Okay, well, my mom tried to keep me out of the house as much as she could. Keeping me away from Gary until it was time to go to bed or he passed out from drinking. She wanted me to be strong so I never had to go through what she was going through. She got me to volunteer at a karate school after I was finished my regular school day. I cleaned, helped the little kids get ready, and did laundry, things like that. After volunteering, I was able to get free classes. I went three times a week but it was not enough so I also started kick boxing the other days of the week. Same thing, volunteer, get free classes. I was there for about four to five hours every day during the week; either practicing, watching the advanced classes, or helping out. I also did specialty mixed martial arts classes on the weekend after collecting enough bottles for the lessons. I have been doing all of it the since I was eight. It made my mom so proud and I loved it. It was the only time I had any control or power in my life. I felt strong and I felt I could protect myself."

Victoria finished, leaving out the part where no matter how strong or skilled she was, her fear kept her from defending her mom from her stepfather. It was not her skill set that kept her from responding any time her mom had needed help, it was the uncontrollable fear that Gary had engrained into her for so many years that always kept her cowering the corner. No amount of training or self-defense she had could give her the mental strength she needed to stand up to him, even for a mother whom she had loved so much. It killed her to know that she could have helped even though she wasn't there when her mother was killed. That's why she threw herself so passionately into the exercises and the practice, she never wanted to feel weak again.

"Shit," Sabastian said reacting to her story, then after pausing. "Sorry."

"Sorry for what, swearing?" she asked, remembering the respect rules and smiling.

"Ya," he said. "So you're a lethal weapon."

Blushing, Victoria replied, "Maybe a few years ago, but I haven't trained properly in years."

"Don't be so modest, what level are you?"

"I don't know," she shrugged.

"That's bull, anyone who has studied for years knows the levels, tell me."

"Does it matter?"

Sabastian lowered his eye brows and gave her a stern look, however with his dimples showing, she smiled at him and replied.

"Okay, I used to be a second-degree black belt, in kickboxing and jujitsu and a third degree in karate," she said, her eyes lowered and pet Sketch again, not looking up.

"Nice," Sabastian said, looking at this small girl in a new light.

"Used to be," she repeated. "Like I said, I haven't trained in years, when you gave me the exercise routine, it was so boring so I started to practice like I used to at the clubs. I enjoyed it and it doesn't feel like I am working out, only having fun." She fibbed, knowing the real reason so pushed herself so hard.

"Would you be interested in working with our trainer?"

Victoria gapped at him, *what was he asking?*

"Oh sorry, I don't mean that kind of trainer. Maximus teaches all us guys how to handle ourselves and protect the girls when needed, we also train with him to stay fit. Anyway, I'm sure he would love to meet you and maybe you might want to practice your skills with him. You might even teach him a thing or two."

"Really? I would love to, I always loved training and it's been so many years," Victoria said passionately.

"Well, I'm glad you were rusty and I guess I should say thank you for not killing us that night," Sabastian said joking.

Victoria twisted her hair again, looking ashamed.

"I'm sorry if I hurt you guys, but it's not like you were fighting back. You were only trying to restrain me. If you had laid into me, I would have been toast."

"Well, we couldn't hurt you, even though I would have liked to flatten you, especially after the head butt you handed me," Sabastian said rubbing his nose.

"Oh God, I forgot about that," Victoria put her hand over her eyes covering her hot face.

"Trust me, it wasn't that bad. I've had much worse," Sabastian said, his eyes going unfocused at the awful past memories.

Shaking himself from his dark thought, he asked, "Okay, do you have any more questions about Eximius?"

Trying to ease her embarrassment.

"Oh right, so now what, do I have to sign something else? Do I go to a class? Do I watch porn and have someone commentate throughout?" she said joking, but worried. "I guess I would have to learn how to pleasure a man, that would be the first step," she said this with a hard blush in her cheeks not looking at Sabastian, now completely mortified she had said that.

"No, that would be the very last step," he said. "We need to make sure you are in tune with your body's sexuality and that your past experiences have not wrecked your openness to try new things. You have to learn to fully love being with a man and to give yourself completely to your trainer. Once you start to crave the feel of a man and want nothing else, then you can expand on your experiences and learn what kind of sex you prefer."

She didn't know if her cheeks could get any redder but she had to ask.

"There are different kinds of sex?" she asked swallowing.

"There are many variations of sex, yes, but you will learn them later in the program."

Something dawned on Victoria, Sabastian's title was a trainer. She looked at him and looked where she was and was suddenly unsettled.

"You are my trainer," she said; the statement she knew was true. She was so apprehensive that Sketch jumped from her lap and Victoria sat up curling her hands in her lap and started to twist and tug on her hair.

"Please, Victoria, I am not about to jump you," he said kindly. "Have you not heard what I have said, this takes time and I need to know so much more about you before we can even begin and that is, of course, if you would like to? The choice is one hundred percent yours; you are free to walk out of here. We will give you a few thousand dollars and fly you anywhere you want to go and even find a job for you if you don't want to do this. I sincerely hope you will consider the offer, as you don't have anything to lose by trying,"

"You would give me money and find me a job after putting so much work into me?" she was surprised.

"Yes, of course, no one is ever forced to enter into the program," Sabastian got up and offered his hand, which she took without hesitation, glad for its warmth.

Sabastian pulled her up and led her out into the hall heading back to her room.

"Take all the time you need to think this through. You are welcome to come and go as you please, however all the exterior doors are locked so you can't slip away. We still cannot let you know where you are and rat us out," he said with a smirk.

He opened the door to her room.

"This side of the door will not be locked, but the rule still stands that no one will enter your room without permission. Please think about it, Victoria, you have nothing to lose and everything to gain from staying here and at least trying."

Sabastian bent, kissing her lightly on the hand, and with his other warm hand on the small of her back, he guided her back into her room before closing the door behind her.

Victoria stared at her hand that he had put his mouth on and shivered warmly. *He's wrong,* she thought. *I have something to lose,* and she was not sure how he would take it.

Chapter 30

He paced his room, beyond frustrated. He had to have her and would be able to get away with it. With Mr. D and Cherry both gone, he should be able to go to the wild cat and fuck her senseless. His cock throbbed painfully and he cursed again. Just the thought of her hair wrapped around his arm or better yet, his cock made his head spin. He wanted to yank her head back with that hair and jerk himself off, until he covered her hair in his cum.

Fuck, I should have better control, he thought to himself.

It had been weeks of the girl taking her sweet time getting better and he was just waiting for the time to perform *his* test on her. The only time he could ever really let himself loose was when fresh meat was delivered. He had thought about all the things he would do to her with the limited time he would have. Hopefully, he would have hours to have her and thought about how he would take the intensity too far.

This was a delicacy, given to him so rarely. He was lucky to have this job as Mr. D knew what drove him, but he had been careful to always keep it in check and he was the best at what he did after all. When he found out Victoria was drug free, he knew it would be only a matter of time and he wouldn't have to wait until she was cleaned up to take her ruthlessly. However, the time was dragging on endlessly.

He could have his skill set requested and have other girls trembling under his touch but it wasn't the same. They were still willing and it only kept his real tendencies at bay and it was not enough for him.

"Fuck!" he yelled into the empty room.

He slammed out the door and strode downstairs and hoped that whatever woman would take him tonight would be able to handle him.

Chapter 31

Victoria sat in her room for hours after their conversation, just staring at the wall. Could she do this? Would she? Would she be any good at it? How could she sleep with just anyone? She sighed when her meal popped up, and walked over to retrieve it, still dazed. Finding that the conversation had drained her. For the first time Victoria did not notice the artful arrangement that was her meal. She ate and went straight to bed, needing the dark and quiet to think.

Sabastian watched her intently on the monitor.

Well, at least, she's not packing and heading for the hills, he thought.

"What do you think?" Roman asked.

"I've no idea. She handled it well considering, and she was smart about her questions, too. But she doesn't have much experience as she was blushing and wouldn't look at me almost the whole time."

"So now what? You're winging it and have thrown the program out the window? So what's the next step for her?" Roman asked.

"No idea, but maybe I'll wait and see if she'll come to me."

"Ya, good luck with that," Roman said grinning.

"Shove it," Sabastian said on his way out the door, heading down to the kitchen.

Nickolas was cleaning her tray when he entered.

"She ate everything tonight, so that's a good sign, means she is not panicking or stressing."

"You're not Douglas," Sabastian said, referring to the psychologist on staff. He walked passed Nickolas and toward the slot with the notebook on it.

"But I pick up on things over time. Food tells all," Nickolas said mystically with a wink.

"Ya, okay, Nick," Sabastian said writing in the book. "Give this to her after she is finished with her meal in the morning, please," handing Nickolas the gray notebook.

"You got it."

The next morning was like any other, the food tray with its delicious smells wafting around her, like the conversation yesterday didn't happen. Victoria was still in her room; she was still safe and it looked like her routine was the same. When she finished her meal, the table popped out again with the grey notebook.

Until she read the note she thought she could stay in here forever, ignoring the reason she was here.

"Good morning, Victoria, please meet me in the round room when you are ready for the day. Please only wear your robe and slippers if you are comfortable with that.
Sabastian."

"What the hell?" she yelled at the notebook.

Only wear her robe, was he insane? I thought he was giving her all the time she needed and that there was no rush. This was the opposite of taking it slow. She was suddenly nerve rackingly nervous. What did he have in store for her? Would she have to start today? She still didn't know if she could go through with it, her mind was not wrapped completely around it yet. Could she have sex with a man she only just met face to face yesterday? He was attractive, yes, breathtakingly so. She focused on him and him only, to try to imagine herself on the bed with him. His strong square muscles, his large arms holding her against his broad chest. Listening to his low deep voice as he talked her through the process. His dimples as he smiled down at her, he was so gorgeous and masculine, holding him in her imagination gave her the chills, but in a pleasant way.

It was too much though, as now he was telling her to come to him basically naked and start the program with Eximius. Did she want to stay or go, that was what he was asking her at this moment and she knew the answer to that question.

She washed her face and hands and debated getting dressed but thought that this was the only way to start trusting. If he wanted to, he could have grabbed her at any point during their conversation yesterday or for that matter any time during her stay here.

Looking into the full-length ornate mirror, she said, "Okay, I can do this and if I am going to do this I might as well go all the way," she was talking to herself in a mirror and took three long breaths, then stripped completely naked, pulled on the robe, and slipped on soft white moccasins.

Moving fast, so she didn't lose her nerve, which were on edge, she was in the round room in seconds.

Sabastian was waiting and was shocked it had taken her so little time, he thought for sure he would have to wait for her to decide to come, if at all.

"Good morning," he said with a smile that showed off his sweet dimples.

She could tell he was pleased to see she had listened and gave a shy smile back.

"Morning," she whispered all blushes and eyes submissively lowered.

"I bet you are a little worried," he said with a grin.

Victoria nodded her head still looking down at her slippers, her eyes starting to water with apprehension.

"Come on, sweet Miss Victoria," he said moving closer to her. "This will be fun."

Ya, for you, she thought. "Stop the 'Miss' crap, it drives me nuts."

"Sorry," he apologized grinning.

"I'm trying to trust you but, you are not making it easy," she whispered up at him, looking at his bright green eyes.

"You are in good hands," he grinned again down at her.

Victoria looked up into his mocking face and was suddenly annoyed, anger coming to her defense.

"Wipe that grin off your face, you know everything about this and I know nothing and that's starting to get old," she said boldly.

Sabastian was more than amused, her true self was coming out and that's what he needed today. Still he gazed into her stunning purple eyes that sparkled with salty tears and felt that he was teasing her too much, but he could not help playing with her.

"Please follow me," he commanded gently turning away from her.

Sighing heavily, she followed him down a flight of stairs and along a long hallway that was slightly chilly.

"We're underground now, this tunnel connects to the spa and I would like to give you a full-service spa treatment today if that is okay?" Sabastian said, breaking the growing tension that had built as they walked.

"The spa?" she asked raising her eyebrows.

"Yes, what did you think we were going to do?" he asked turning to face her in the narrow space.

"Umm, well I thought we were going to, ummm."

Sabastian reached out for her hand and held it warmly.

"I said I would give you all the time you needed to get comfortable with this idea if you wanted to stay."

"Oh," she replied, her nervousness being replaced with disappointment much to her surprise. "That sounds interesting but I've never been to a spa. I did not really have a sparkling social life if you remember. You can get things like nails painted and neck massages there, right?"

Sabastian, still holding her hand, led her further down the hall.

"Well, yes, and a very big no. A spa is where most women love to spend all of their time and money being pampered. Our girls can use it any time, night and day and get any service they want. It's a huge perk if you work here and I didn't want you to miss out if you decided to leave today. If you don't want to try, I'll understand but at least check it out. I'll give you a list of what you can get done and I'll let you pick one thing or everything, the day is yours. I have booked the entire place off so you can enjoy it without anybody else around. I will admit though, I am not good with nails, that's Blake's specialty."

They came to a large door with a key pad on it, Sabastian punched in the code and opened the door for her to enter. Victoria gapped at the tropical like room. There was a large ten-foot fountain with water fall in the middle of the marble room. There were large lounge chairs with tubs beside them, little tables and chairs with lights and nail polish on them, and what looked like a hair salon in one corner. Every few feet, there was a large dark mahogany door with engraved pictures around the outside of the room.

"So that's where you can get a pedicure," Sabastian said, moving into the room and pointing to the tub chairs.

She looked at him with an expression of total confusion, but did remember blurbs of conversation at her prep school and recognized the word.

"Sorry, um, a pedicure or pedi is when you get your feet rubbed and your toenails shaped and painted. Same goes for your hands, that's called a manicure."

"A mani?" she said smiling remembering her school mates comparing finger nails after a trip to the spa.

"Yup, the doors lead to where you can get a body scrub, we basically give you a scrub down with minerals to cleanse the skin and make your body silky soft and to get rid of any dead skin, then rub you down with oils and body butter."

"Body butter?"

"It's like lotion on steroids," he said.

"You also can get body wraps, where we wrap you in things like seaweed to pull out any toxins in your skin and mud baths. Facials are where we scrub the face and get rid of imperfections in the skin, all the women swear by them. We also do full body waxing as well, but I don't recommend that if you are here to enjoy and relax, as that can be painful. There are variations of each service but those are the basics. For each service, there are several different products to choose from so you could be here a thousand times and never get the same thing twice. Of course there is also the massages, full body, just legs, back, or neck and you can get Swedish, hot stones, therapeutic, aromatherapy, reflexology, deep tissue etc. Basically, we do every massage out there."

Sabastian smiled down at her. Being at the spa for women was like a kid in a candy store with unlimited money. It was where you entered a woman and left feeling like a goddess and he was looking forward to Victoria experiencing it for the first time.

"What would you like to try first?" he asked.

She was so overwhelmed and decided to at least eliminate the treatments where she would have to take off her clothes.

"How about a facial?"

Sabastian made a face.

"What?"

"Well, a facial tends to be painful, it's not an enjoyable treatment. It just makes your face glow and look younger, something you don't need," he said with a wink.

"Okay, um, can I get a pedicure?"

"Yes, but do not judge the pedi on me. I'm the worst at it, when Blake does it, you will know true art, however, I can try."

"I think any experience with you will be enjoyable," she said teasingly, lowering her lashes. She was shocked she was flirting. The more time she spent with this man, the more her tension faded and more strongly she felt herself growing more attracted to him. He was so strong, which, at first, had scared her, but his strength and good humor and the attention he showed her was starting to build her trust in him. She imagined kissing him softly on the lips and him holding her tenderly in his arms when he answered her flirting with some of his own.

"I hope so," he said looking at her intensely. He had to blink to break eye contact with her as he motioned which chair to sit in.

"This also gives us a chance to talk about yesterday, if you like?" he asked, filling the little foot tub with warm water as she sat down placing her feet in the tub.

"Any questions?"

"Well, I would like to try the program and see what I think, can I do that or do I have to commit fully."

"Of course, you are allowed to go as far as you want and can quit any time. You can opt to discontinue the program and even drop out after being hired."

"I guess that makes it an easy choice," she said slowly.

Victoria laid back and closed her eyes, absorbing this new information. Sabastian pressed a few buttons and her chair started to warm up and move under her. She opened her eyes and looked at him hilariously squatting on a very short stool in front of her.

"Massage chair," he said, handing her the remote and showing her how it worked.

"Can you pull your robe up please?"

She looked at him wide eyed, if she pulled up her robe, he was in the ideal position to see right up her legs.

"Umm," she muttered hesitating.

"Just to your knees, then tuck it under your legs from the inside," he said, enjoying her modestly. It was not something that he saw much in here as most women walked around naked in the spa. He busied himself looking away as she tucked her robe in and got to work on her feet and legs. She was tense at first but then relaxed as he gently rolled her small strong calves in his large hands. He worked on her toes and feet but kept running his hands along her legs. She was loving the feel of her slippery legs and feet in his warm palms.

Sabastian, wrapped up in the feel of her soft skin in his hands, cleared his throat, trying to focus, he asked. "What color?"

She opened her eyes and picked a soft pink polish from the color swatch he handed her and laid back to enjoy once more. Over an hour later, he was done, she looked down impressed.

"You said someone else does that better?"

"Much better, I had to clean up my sloppy polish work three times."

"Well, they look great, can I get nails to match?"

"Yes, but like I said Blake's better."

"Well, I think I'll be sticking around so I can find out later and compare the both of you," she said smiling.

She realized she was flirting with him again and blushed. She had to remind herself that this was not a guy that would become her boyfriend and fall in love with her. He was here to train her to enjoy sex and nothing more, however that idea made her fidget and she let her imagination take ahold of her again to fairytale soft kisses and sweet embraces. Holding her hand, he led her to the small table with the light on it. He motioned for her to sit down and sitting across from her, he started rubbing her hands in oil.

He was looking at her hands but they were sitting so close that it was even more intimate, then when he was down between her legs. She blushed at the thought. She was able to watch him closely here, his green eyes were darker than before and his wavy brown hair had light strands of bronze in it. He kept looking up at her, catching her looking at him and she blushed and looked away every time.

Sabastian couldn't believe this girl, the fact that she had trusted him so far, knowing her history and her bias against men really impressed him. Also the first test he had given her, she had passed with flying colors. The fact she had come to him in nothing but a robe had amazed him. He had only asked her to do that to see how much of a fight he would be dealing with. Just to give him an idea on what she was thinking and how long it would take to get to this point. She had not even complained but dove into his challenge. Whatever her history, she was stronger because of it and he was looking forward to seeing just how far she would go and how fast.

"So any thoughts on how you would like to start the program?" she asked him, trying to sound casual.

Glad to talk about work, Sabastian answered.

"Yes, I have books for you to read first, then we can move onto a few films and then a more direct approach."

She thought he was kidding, she thought she would just get into bed and let the learning begin.

"I have to study?"

"Yup."

"And where are these books, I didn't see them in the book case in the round room?"

"They were covered for you; we didn't want to scare you away without first talking to you. They are being placed in your room now."

"Oh," she said, thinking of the black sheet that had covered up a large portion of the large round library.

After several moments of silence with him concentrating on her nails, he said, "So I talked with Maximus and he said he would be more than willing to practice with you. He would clear the room so it would be just the two of you and you can train whatever skills you want. We have a complete gym as well as a training room for classes."

"Really? That's great, when can I start?" Victoria was thrilled.

"I'll let him know you're interested and you can let me know when you want to practice."

"Great," she said, glancing down at his work on her hands.

"So?" he asked as he finished painting her nails.

"Looks good, I think I would like a massage next," she stated daringly.

"Are you sure?"

"You said I could trust you and I have liked my feet and hands being rubbed; I think I can take it."

He could tell she was nervous but that the bold wild cat was coming out in her and he could tell that she was trying to challenge herself. He was starting to discover that she was competitive and liked challenges and he was very much looking forward to training her.

"This way," he said, leading her across the room with a door that had a pair of hands engraved in the wood.

Victoria followed him into the dark sweet-smelling room, in the middle of the room was a bed with a face cradle attached to one end. He walked around the room lighting candles and incense. He motioned for her to sit on the bed. Lifting up a large heavy blanket, he said.

"You will need to take off the robe and slippers and lay face down on the bed."

142

Victoria froze, she didn't mean to insinuate that she wanted a full body massage, perhaps just a back or shoulder rub but Sabastian's look was one of amusement and doubt that she would follow though. She couldn't back down now, turning her back to him, she kicked off her slippers and dropped her robe, quickly turning and jumping into the bed. However, she saw Sabastian had raised the blanket above his head so that he could not see her disrobe. Her trust went up a notch as she felt him lower the warmed blanket over her body from neck to feet.

"What kind of massage would you like?"

"You pick," she said letting the warmth of the preheated bed take away the edginess that had risen drastically as soon as her robe was dropped.

Sabastian knew exactly what massage he would do on her and got out a tray with more oils than what any other massage used. From jasmine to ginger, almond to basil, every scent was proven to cause heightened sexual arousal.

Victoria was rigid at first but the scent of the oil and his firm warm hand rubbing her body made her melt. He started with her legs and rubbed her in long firm strokes but then his hands started reaching higher on the outside of her thighs. She felt his hands stop and pull away and she knew why immediately.

"I tried to tell you yesterday, I made mistakes and learned from them," she said offhandedly.

"Christ, Victoria, what happened to you out there?" Sabastian asked horrified, looking closer at the large scar running along the outside of her leg six inches below her hips in a long diagonal slash.

"Just a fight, that's not the worst one," she said embarrassed.

"You have more?" he asked her.

"Ya, here," she said turning her arm that was resting above her head outward.

Sabastian could see a slash below her elbow that looked like a defensive wound.

"God, Vicky, how did you survive out there?"

"Oh, come on, Sabastian you must have seen worse than that?" she asked.

"Yes, but you're so small and this one," he said, grazing her hip, making her shiver beneath his fingers, "is so deep."

"I didn't even have to go into the ER for that one, it was only a flesh wound and it happened early when I had some padding there."

"So you went to the hospital for your arm?" he asked.

"No, that one was fine, it was when I was stabbed in the stomach."

Sabastian was running his hands through his hair, the courage this girl had to possess to withstand everything the streets had did to her and still be so strong was unbelievable. She handled the pain, both emotionally and physically with nothing but an iron will and courage he didn't think was possible.

"Does that mean the massage is over?" she asked, oblivious to his mood still lying face down on the bed.

"Can I continue? Do you want me to?" he asked.

"If you don't mind my hideous scars," she said not completely joking. No one had ever seen, let alone touched her scars and she realized she was self-conscience about them.

"Do they hurt at all?" he asked tenderly.

"No, not anymore."

He resumed stroking her legs and said.

"No matter how many scars you had in your past, you could never be hideous," he whispered in her ear.

Victoria sighed and relaxed once again into the bed, inhaling the intoxicating scents rolling around the room. Every time he would move to another part of her body, another scent would waft around her making her feel warm and liquefied. She felt she was melting into the bed and odd thrills would occasionally run up and down her body at his touch.

At first, she was focused only on his hands the way they moved up and down her legs and back loving the feel of him on her skin. She had never had this kind of closeness with anyone and it made her feel cherished. She had not been touched in years and this contact more than made up for that. After about twenty minutes of stroking her legs, he moved to her upper back and her focus went to a place she was not being touched.

She felt Sabastian started to rhythmically rub her entire body and was pushing her gently into the firm bed. His rhythm caused her hips to slowly rock back and forth, her pelvis rubbing deliciously and she could feel something like butterflies fluttering deep in her belly. She didn't even notice that the blanket was gone until he moved to her lower back and started to very softly and slowly go from small to large circles, going lower and lower until his long fingers were pushing into the top of her buttocks, continuing the slow rocking.

The large circles of his hands stroked her from the side of her rib cage just touching the outside of her breasts. Then they moved in a path down to her bottom, all the way down the outside of her legs and back up again between her thighs, then around to the outside of her hips. Every once in a while, he would push a little harder on her bottom in a sensual rhythm making the butterflies in her belly dance. Her heart rate had quickened and her breath was now little pants of pleasure.

Victoria shocked herself when a low moan escaped her lips and her eyes flew open, escaping the trance he had put her in.

She was suddenly angry, what was he doing? She was lying before him completely naked and she felt dizzy and vulnerable.

She stiffened. "You're done," she said angrily, trying to reach out for something to cover herself with.

She was panting with anger now, her face red. Turning only her head, she glared at him.

"What were you doing to me?" she asked.

"I was massaging you; did you not enjoy it?" Sabastian was both sincere and bemused.

"You were doing more than that," she said scowling at him. She grabbed the robe he held for her and covered herself, and made her way to the door, putting on her slippers as she went.

"Oh come on, Victoria," Sabastian said with a chuckle, following her out. "It's just the start of the process, I need you to feel and not think. You are thinking too much."

Followed her down the hall, smiling at the way she moved. Even as mad as she was, she still glided on her tip toes as she all but ran back to the round room. Sabastian was triumphant he had aroused her with the massage, but worried he had betrayed her trust in him. Taking her arm, he spun her around to face him before she reached her room.

"Victoria, I'm sorry but in order for this to work, you have to be honest with yourself and not be ashamed of your body or its reactions. You loved the massage and you want to try it again, admit it. Don't be mad, it's alright, you need to embrace everything that this place has to offer and that includes how I can make you feel and what you can learn from it."

She frowned at him intently, not knowing how to respond. She turned back to her room, shut, and locked the door in his worried face. She flopped down on the bed and thought about what he had said. She was not prepared for what had happened. It happened so gradually that she didn't realize what he was doing to her until it was too late. He had taken advantage of her and she had loved it. Standing up, she walked over to the mirror, dropped the robe and looked at herself, she was flushed and her skin tingled warmly from his hands.

Crap, he's right, I do want to do that again, she thought angrily, covering herself back up.

Seeing her meal was here, she took it and noticed her dresser was full of books about *Kuma Sutra, Finding Your Inner Sexuality, The Female Orgasm, How to Please a Man and Yourself, A Women's Guide to Fantastic Sex*, and so on. She stared at the titles, completely embarrassed and totally intrigued. She was still angry, but knew Sabastian was coming at her with a trainer's point of view and not a woman's, but she still felt vulnerable and confused.

Needing to understand what she was getting herself into she read a note by the book collection with instructions on which book to begin with. Grabbing the first recommended book, Victoria took her meal and went to her bed to get started. Looking at the title, *Exploring Your Sexuality*, she opened the book and tried to read, but her thoughts kept going from Sabastian's face, to his hands, then to the feelings he had awakened within her.

Chapter 32

Sabastian strode into her room unannounced and saw her lying relaxed on the bed reading. Throwing the book from her hands across the room, he stripped off her blankets, elated she was only wearing blue silk panties beneath the covers. He grabbed her ankles, yanking her toward him, and ran his hands up her legs all the way to her breasts cupping the soft flesh. Pinching the nipples softly, he lowered his lips to take as much of her breast into his mouth as possible and sucked greedily.

Standing back up to gaze down at her long lashes covering her blazing lavender eyes, his frantic sex strained forward. Reaching down, he released his erection from his shorts and he took it in his hands and grazed the soft head of it along the inside of her calf. He saw her watching him intently, frozen but intrigued as he ran tip slowly up her leg until she was squirming with need. Her hips arched up as he ran the crown of his shaft along the outside of her silk panties, up and down, over and over again until he could see her moisture soak both the pale blue fabric and the head of his cock, which bucked in his own hand.

Needing to slow down, he gazed into her strange erotic eyes as he slowly peeled her panties from her body. Leaning down, he kissed first her jaw and the corner of her mouth before sucking and kissing her lips. Taking her tongue his mouth, he sucked until she groaned and grabbed for him.

Pulling away from her hands, intent on driving her crazy with need, his mouth trailed a row of kissed all the way to her perk nipples rolling them in his hot mouth.

Her cries of lust drove him mad and the teasing he was intent on giving her made him lose his restraint. He positioned himself and growled as he slowly, sensually drilled into her dripping sex which seemed to swallow him until he was buried to the hilt.

He felt her wrap around him, so sweet, so soft. She moaned his name and arch into his body and that was all he needed. He pulled out of her and pushed in, with each thrust going a little bit faster until she was screaming and matching his strides. He felt her body convulse with the orgasm that rocked though her, intent on making her scream his name over and over again. He pounded on, grabbing her breasts in his hands, pinching the nipples lightly and enjoying the wave after wave of pleasure rolling through her body until he felt his own muscles tighten and his cock swell and jerk.

Sabastian's eyes flew open as his body finished what his dream had started.

"Fuck," he swore, lying his head back down into the pillow.

Sabastian knew he was losing control, now both when he was awake and asleep.

Lying in bed after his wet dream, he forced himself to focus and regain his discipline. This was so unlike him, but he couldn't help it, she was so soft, so small, and she had responded so beautifully during the massage. He had started to lose himself to her and had remembered wanting to be the one she was lying on instead of the massage table.

Thinking back, he knew he had messed up. He had actually earned her trust and he took advantage. He wanted to tell himself it was worthwhile, to see her respond under his well-trained hands, but was extremely worried he had truly upset her.

Sabastian shook his head. "She's only a job, get her trained and move on," he told himself, trying to be subjective.

As much as he told her to be honest with herself, the least he could do is be honest with himself. He wanted her and she was not just another girl he was training. Even though she was his promotion girl, she was much more. She was strong, bold, and willing, he could not wait to see how willing she was. It would take everything not to rush her and just take her the next time he saw her.

He focused on her eyes and her hair, the feel of her under him and his shaft started to fill again. Frustrated with himself, he knew he had to get some measure of disciple back into his life. He thought the first step to achieving this was to visit the mini manor attached to the estate, but it was not the kind of satisfaction he needed and he threw off the covers, got up, ill-tempered and restless.

Sabastian headed to his easel in front of the bedroom window, hoping to put his artist skills to work to relieve the tension flowing through his heated blood. He flipped back the paper of the vague female he had begun when he had first started conversing with Victoria through the notebook. He knew now it was her he had started to outline unconsciously several weeks ago.

He had never been very good at drawing people, as no one had interested him enough to sketch, so he had little practice. However, with the colored charcoal in his hands, he was soon staring into Victoria's perfect purple, blue eyes on the page. His hand swept over the paper lightly as he curved the outline of her heart shaped face and let his hand stroke down the paper until her face was framed in her glorious long dark blonde hair.

Sabastian dropped the charcoal and his fingers delicately traced the outline of her face, being careful not to smear his work. He noticed his breath was coming in short shallow bursts, he had been working so briskly over the paper and was consumed by the eyes of Victoria staring intensely back at him. Closing his own eyes, he cursed himself and the girl. Ripping off the page, he let it fall to the floor before heading to the shower.

Control, dammit, get some control over yourself. She's your only chance for more, get her trained and move on.

Turning on the hot water, he tried to erase Victoria and her mesmerizing eyes from his mind. Judging by his body's reaction, he was failing miserably and with another curse, he flipped the facet to cold and stepped in.

Chapter 33

Victoria was surprised when another meal appeared. Had she been reading for two hours already? She stretched, got up, grabbed her food, and dove back into her book. After dinner, she had finished the first book and was more than half way through the second book when she heard a knock at the door.

Sitting up, she called out. "Who is it?"

"Hello, Miss Victoria, may I come in please?" asked an unfamiliar voice.

"Uh, sure," she answered flustered.

A tall boyish faced man stepped into the room. A stunning Aboriginal with high cheek bones, long black hair down past his shoulders, and an overly wide bright smile grinned at her. His rich coffee colored skin made his smile jump out and also made him look eighteen but his muscles and broad lithe body told another story.

His smile was infectious and she smiled back at him automatically.

"Miss Victoria, my name is Maximus," he said politely with a smooth carefree manner.

"Oh," she said pulling the blanket off of her and standing up, "you're the martial arts trainer here," she said delighted holding out her hand.

"Yes, miss, in a manner of speaking," he said taking her hand lightly in his and shaking it once.

She frowned slightly, "I know you have to respect me and everything but the whole miss things drive me nuts, can you call me Vicky and can I call you Max?"

"Of course, Vicky," he said enthusiastically.

"Okay, great, nice to meet you, Max."

Aware she was still only wearing her robe; she crossed her arms in front of her and admired the man in front of her.

Maximus seemed undaunted and started, "Well, Vicky, I heard you have some skills and I would love to see them first hand."

"Okay, I've been sitting on my ass all day reading and it would feel really good to get out of bed."

"Of course, we can go and train now if you like. I will wait for you in the round room while you change."

"Okay, great, see you in five," Victoria rifled through her dresser and found yoga workout pants and a tank top with bra support in it and changed quickly. She found Maximus lounging relaxed on the couch but he jumped up as soon as he saw her.

"Okay, this way," he said leading her down the hallway.

Victoria liked Maximus right away, he was enthusiastic and friendly and hoped the lesson would go well.

Turning into the only door at the end of another hallway, they walked into a huge weight room with multiple workout machines. The exercise room would rival any gym. Treadmills, elliptical machines, bikes, as well as bench presses, and numerous sets of weights filled the room. She followed Maximus though the room to another door and entered a large padded room. It was perfect for training martial arts, well organized, and cleaner than any training room she had ever worked in. There was a large mirror on a wall set back from the padded mats that covered the floor and the back and side walls.

"Wow," she said running her hands over the walls, "it even smells nice," inhaling the scent of vinyl and lemon.

"I'm glad you like it," Maximus said, taking off his shirt.

Victoria gapped at him, he wore a light green muscle shirt under the T-shirt he had just taken off and loose brown sweat pants. His muscles were very impressive and they looked like they were made of glazed mahogany. It was his smile that made him look the most attractive as he wore it constantly, but his muscled body was a very close second. She noticed him gazing back at her and Victoria lowered her head blushing.

"Okay," Maximus said clapping his hands together, "show me what you've got."

Shaking the shy feeling from her, she walked into the middle of the room and kept her eyes on herself in the mirror, not wanting to see Maximus's reaction to how she moved. She focused and breathed then went into an easy warm up routine, moving effortlessly and smoothly, and forgot there was someone else in the room until Maximus spoke up.

"Wow, you weren't exaggerating on your skill level," he was smiling again and Victoria didn't know what to say.

"Sorry, Sabastian told me yesterday. Impressive," Maximus sounded eager and energetic.

"Okay, so I can see you are out of practice and even though you have the skills, you will need to work hard to get back up to the level you were at before you stopped training. When you are doing the sweeping slide kick, make sure you compress your center and really pop your leg out, like this," he demonstrated.

"Try to strike out your leg off the ground and maintain your balance when you do."

He did it twice more and Victoria watched him, then she repeated the kick until she was able to balance through the kick.

"Looking good, kid, a little higher and you'll have it. It's like riding a bike, once your muscle mass is up you can put more detail in your maneuvers and it will all come back," he said confidently.

Victoria was thrilled to be in a class again, able to practice the skills she had learned to love so much as a child. Maximus was great, at first, she was nervous being alone in a room with a strange man but he only showed her the moves she needed work on and let her use him to practice those moves on his body. She needed the distance to focus on what he was teaching her and he seemed to know that. He was respectful and professional but always joking and laughing with her and made her feel completely at ease.

Maximus went through several maneuvers she knew and they worked on them together until she had remastered them.

"Okay, okay, Vicky," he breathed after taking several rigorous snap kicks from her. "You'll be at the highest skill level I teach in a few months, so we are going to have to come up with some fun combinations to get creative and challenge us both."

They took a break on the mats sitting cross legged across from each other and talking it through, they developed a thrashing front assault that was a combination between two different art forms.

Victoria could do this all day; she was in heaven. She was surprised on how comfortable she was with Maximus, he was so friendly and seemed to always be happy even though she was using him as a punching bag. Maximus was a fantastic teacher, patient, skilled, and she could see herself becoming fast friends with the man. He would get up and help fix her technique, and never lost his humor while he worked with her. He was willing to experiment with her to make her more lethal. The trick was making sure all her movements were flawless, balanced, and could cause the most damage, no matter what size someone was.

After trying to get their new move down without losing her balance, he finally had to stop her.

"Okay, Vicky. You may not be done, but I am," Maximus said, grabbing a towel and wiping his sweaty forehead.

Victoria was also covered in sweat and knew that Maximus was nowhere near tired, but was stopping so that she didn't get over worked, thinking that was thoughtful of him.

"Sorry, Max," she said breathing hard. "It's been so long I didn't know how much I missed it until we started training. How are you doing?"

"Oh I'm fine, Vicky. Trust me, I'm having as much fun as you are. I think I will use you for demonstrations with the other guys," he said with a wink and a grin.

Her eyes widened, "No, thank you," and smiled when he laughed at her expression.

"Don't worry, kid, I wouldn't do that to you. Although it would be hilarious to see you kick the shit out of some of the guys just to prove they need to practice more," Maximus said laughing, wiping his arms down with the towel.

She laughed with him and caught the towel he threw it at her, wiping her brow. Victoria felt about Maximus the same way she would feel if she had an older brother.

"So you train all the men here?" she asked.

"Yup, most are not that into it and only do the bare minimum so it's really nice to practice with someone who has a true passion for the art."

"The guys don't love this?" she asked shocked. When she had trained years ago, she saw most men thrived on learning the skills and enhancing them.

"Well, they tend to get distracted by the other means of working out at the manor," he said with his trademark wink and grin. "There are a few that workout with me and do enjoy it, but I would say the only guy that has deep passion for learning how to fight and pushing himself and me to be better is Ethan. He's the one that's always here and is my best sparring partner."

The name meant nothing to her, so she asked, "Only one, hey?"

"Ya, well I practice with all the guys but without him, I wouldn't been able to challenge you. He helps me be a better trainer, although some of those skills he uses to work his specialty at the manor."

Victoria was about to ask about the specialty when Maximus read her thought.

"Don't ask, I can't tell you. Okay, Vicky," he said wrapping his sweaty arm around her shoulders. "Let's go."

"Yuck, Max," she said ducking from under his arm.

"What?"

He looked at her innocently.

"I don't smell, do I?" he said lifting his armpit to her face.

She used a move they had been working on and Maximus ended up on the floor, his arm twisted and his face hitting the mat.

"Mercy, mercy!" he screamed in mock pain.

"That'll teach you to keep your sweaty pits to yourself," she laughed, releasing him.

Maximus got up slowly, tripping and falling and groaning in an over exaggeration of being in severe pain.

"Oh, ouch, god, oooohhhh, ah," he moaned, trying unsuccessfully to keep the smile off his face.

Victoria gave him a light kick in the leg as she walked past, "Come on, show me to my room, so I get there safe."

"No way, you show me to my room so I'm safe," he said laughing.

Maximus waved bye as she headed down the hallway to her room.

"See ya, kid."

"Bye, Max, and thanks so much, that was great," she said graciously.

She saw him wave back and entered her room, heading straight for her bathtub.

Victoria fell into bed exhausted, knowing she would be thoroughly bruised the next day.

She woke up invigorated but sore and was glad she had reading to do and relaxed again all day until Max knocked to invite her to work out again.

He took it easy on her as it took a long time to work out her tightened muscles and the lesson was a bit shorter, but just as much fun. Maximus always called her "kid" and when she asked why the nick name, he referred to the famous *Karate Kid* movie and she didn't know if she was honored or insulted.

"Oh come on, the Karate Kid?" she asked embarrassed. "How old are you?"

"Oh come on yourself, look at you. You are probably the same size as that pint size kid LaRusso, probably smaller and just as unexpected. If you like, I can call you Miss Victoria and kiss your ass like the other guys do?"

"No, no, 'Kid' works," she said. "Can I call you Miyagi?"

"Please. You probably know more than me, you just don't remember it all. I just get to watch you and help you practice what you already know."

"Okay, I'll stick with Max and you stick with Kid, deal?"

"You got it, kid," he said, shaking her hand and flipping her to the mat at his feet grinning down at her as she lay looking up at him cursing him playfully.

The next day was the same, reading and eating and working out with Maximus but the fact she had not seen Sabastian in three days was getting to her. When she collapsed in bed, all she could think about was his warm oiled hands rubbing her sore muscles.

Chapter 34

Victoria was dragged out of her dreamless sleep at eight a.m. thoroughly exhausted. She had stayed up late reading and the meal tray slid into her room way too early for her to get enough sleep. Her body was still sore from yesterday's workout so she stayed in bed to continue reading. She caught herself blushing last night at the content of the book she had been reading, which was happening more and more often the further in the reading program she got.

She was still surprised Sabastian had not come to get her and was really starting to miss him. She had several more questions about Eximius and now that she was reading, she had several embarrassing but need to know questions that were floating around her mind.

She remembered his large bronze hands rubbing her legs the feel of the rhythm on the bed and cursed him.

God damn it, I do want another massage.

Knowing he was right, pissed her off.

After lunch, still tired, Max woke her up enough to have another hard work out. She was too tired to shower after training with Max so she decided to take a short nap to catch up on her lost sleep. Only ten minutes after she has laid down to rest a low knock on the door woke her.

She groaned and answered, "Yes?"

"Miss Victoria, may I please come in?" Sabastian's low husky voice asked.

"Umm."

She looked in panic around the messy room, self-conscience of her personal hygiene.

She realized he had seen her much worse in the alley, but things had changed since then and still didn't want him to see her like this.

"No, I'll be right there, and stop calling me Miss," she added, getting up.

She cracked open the door with the chain fastened and said, "Yes?"

She looked into his face, he was always freshly shaven every time he came to her and it made him look and smell so nice. Staring into his bright green eyes and smelling his fresh scent of citrus and musk made her head spin. She was more aware of her lack of personal care as she gazed at his perfect appearance.

"You are not mad at me, are you?" Sabastian asked, wondering why she was keeping him out.

"No. I've been reading and educating myself and am not dressed, sorry. Max has been keeping me busy, too, so I have been working out a lot."

"I know, so I have arranged for a team to serve you in the spa if that is Okay? They are all women and they want to do a full top to bottom beautifying routine on you."

"What?" she asked, unfastening the chain and opening the door wide.

"Please come with me," Sabastian took her hand, not waiting for an answer as he pulled her gently down the hallway. She was instantly reminded of what those hands had done to her the last time she was in the spa room. She had read a lot about doing what felt good. So trying not to think and only feel, she left her hand in his and followed the strong intimidating man down the stairs and into the long cool hallway.

They entered the spa room where two women in light pink scrubs stood waiting for them.

"What are they going to do?" she asked apprehensively, looking up at Sabastian.

"Well, it's not going to be as nice as what I did to you," he said smiling.

Her cheeks burned hotly and she glared at him.

He gave her a light push toward the women, "Go on, they won't bite."

She watched him leave and the two women, who looked to be in their early thirties, took both her arms and steered her toward a room that had a sponge engraved on the door.

The women were strong and both had light blonde short hair and tough hands. They were pretty and tall but somehow, they didn't seem like the women who worked for the company in a true sense. She tried talking to them, but they either did not speak English or were not allowed to talk to her.

Victoria spent the next eight hours wishing she was back in the "hands" room with Sabastian being rubbed down with oils. The women were brutal, they gave her a shower in which she was lying down on a vinyl covered bed and was flipped and rolled over and scrubbed with a harsh salt mixture. After that, she was caked in mud, left to harden and washed again, then wrapped in seaweed bound tight with warm towels and left to marinate. The women came back a half an hour later and unwrapped and washed her once more.

She was starting to feel water logged as she had been either wet or wrapped for the last few hours. The only time where she was not being worked on were when her meals were delivered to her by Sabastian who gave her a sympathetic look and a grin and left without a word.

She was beckoned to a room with a long piece of cloth and a little bowl on the door. There she was waxed, her legs, her arm pits, and very reluctantly, her groin area. Her tears swelled up fast with the last one, but by the time the tears had fallen, they were done. The women may have been brutal but they were proficient and skilled. Even though most of her skin was bright red and bleeding in places, it was incredibly baby soft and she could not stop gently gliding her fingers gingerly across her now super sensitive skin.

She was glad when she was brought to the hands room but this was no gentle relaxing massage. The woman pounded her sore muscles making her jump and tense as they worked out the stiffness and rolled her limbs mercilessly. Leaving her sorer than a workout with Max and decidedly more bruised.

Next, she was treated to a facial, which she found was painful just like Sabastian had said, although nothing could be as painful as the waxing she had just experienced so she sucked it up. She was relieved when they brought her over to the pedicure chair, however, there was no gentle massaging involved, they scrubbed her feet brutally with what looked like a cheese grater and a knife. She was tempted to jerk her feet up and run, but the other woman was working her hands that received the same torture and between the two of them, they had her trapped.

Thinking there was nothing left on her body to work on, they placed her in a salon chair and trimmed her hair. Her hair was then washed twice and conditioned and was left to soak. They oiled and creamed, working from her scalp all the way to the tips of her hair. They rinsed it out again and finally dried it with a cool blow drier brushing out the ankle long locks. They kept exclaiming about her hair in a soft whisper, apparently, they were amazed at its length and color and she was glad that they only took off a couple of inches at the bottom to a curved edge. They then braided it loosely down her back and put it in a soft bun on the top of her head. Her neck was sore from being back and forth from the hair washing basin and having her neck strained in place for too long. Her skin throbbed where they had waxed it and her entire body, including her face was sore and overly sensitive. It even hurt to walk on her feet as they have scraped away any protection she had had there.

Victoria was completely exhausted when Sabastian came to collect her, if she never saw the spa again, it would be too soon. She had been working out too long and hard with Max and the spa day had put her over the edge. She leaned on him as she walked, not getting enough sleep the night before and constantly tensing every time the women had touched her had left her shaky.

Sabastian noticed how wiped she was and scooped her up in his arms. She was so light and smelled heavenly, she was nothing but floral scent and sweet skin that made him want to hold her and breathe her in. He felt so protective of her, which didn't make sense, she was not his to protect.

Lifted off her feet, Victoria relished the feeling of his strong arms wrapped tightly around her, she curled into him like a cat and was surprised she didn't start purring. She curled her hands into her chest and let him take all her weight too exhausted to even hold her head up.

He walked with her for too short a time and placed her in her bed, covered her up, and placed a light kiss on her forehead, turning off the lights as he left. She was asleep before she heard the door close.

Chapter 35

Okay, he had enough, it was too much. He paced his room again for the hundredth time since Victoria's arrival and could feel his erection throbbing for release.

He had over used the girls in the mini manor and it still wasn't enough. He wanted a fight, an innocent girl who didn't want him until it was too late and was so caught up in what he could give to her. The moment the force became a real fight for domination was what he desired. Administering his special test to either professional girls or tester girls was the only thing that kept him from taking any unwilling female in the manor any time he pleased and effectively getting him kicked out of this job or worse.

With Mr. D, Jeremy, and Cherry gone, there was no one here to keep him in check but he still had to restrain himself from bursting into Victoria's room and cruelly stuffing his cock into her until she screamed both from pleasure and from the pain he would give her young body.

He roared in outrage at his hand on the doorknob to his bedroom fighting the urge to burst out and go to the wild cat's room. He turned away to his bed taking his erection out and stroking it hard and fast with his hand. He imagined her soft naked body fighting him, trying to get him off of her as he forced her body to accept his. He knew how wet she would be, even though she would deny she wanted a good fucking. The pain he would inflict on her as she came around his cock as he pounded into her, increasing both their pleasure with the heat of the leather whip. He thought of her screaming under him, begging him to stop until his stroking hand brought the hot sticky cum pulsing between his fingers.

He sighed, stroking his deflating length slowly, content at least for a little while. He needed more control than this and knew he could only hold it in check for so long. The anticipation was building every second thinking about her. His control would be set free as soon as his test began and he would have no restricting, respect, bull shit rules to deal with when it came to the young Miss Victoria.

Chapter 36

Victoria spent the next day in bed, sore, and bruised, her body had taken a beating from the so-called spa experience. The first time she got out of bed she walked over to the mirror and dropped her robe.

This had been the first time she had disrobed in front of the mirror since her first day at the manor. She noticed that her bones no longer protruded from her hips and her breasts had rounded out nicely regaining a fullness that had been missing. Her legs and arms had regained a lot of the strength they had lost while she had lived in the streets. She was surprised at the muscle memory they retained from being so active when she was younger.

Her skin was no longer pink, but she could see bruising over her legs in shades from dark purple to yellow. She remembered a few moves Max had worked on her and saw the marks clearly. Her workouts along with the so-called massage and waxing, her legs now looked like camouflage pants. She knew she bruised easily but this was ridiculous she thought. Her face was splotchy from the facial and she had pin pricks of dried blood around her groin, legs, and under her arms from the waxing.

She looked in between her legs and saw the work the women had done there. She had wanted to stop them, but by the time she realized what they were doing, they were almost done so she had reluctantly let them finish. On her mons sat a perfect symmetrical triangle. She touched the skin around the soft, dark blonde pubic hair and shivered at the sensation. It was so sensitive, almost painful, but felt nice as her fingertips gently grazed the ultra-soft skin.

She undid her braided hair and let it drop down her back. Her hair had never looked or felt so soft in her life. It was like heavy silk and hung loosely in soft waves from the braid down her back. She ran her fingers through it and the weight and feel of it made the whole experience worthwhile, exhausted as she still was. She let her hair hang loose behind her like a cape, letting the smooth silky feel of it brush the overly sensitive skin of her sides, bottom, hips, and calves. She walked over, and lay down on her bed and relaxed into reading, using her long mane of hair to cover her body like a blanket as she slipped into a book.

A few hours later, she heard a knock on her door. She was almost too tired and sore to care, but she got up and put on her night gown and robe before falling back in bed. Expecting to see Maximus and ready to say she was skipping practice today, she called out warily.

"Come in."

Her eyes went wide when the door opened and a strange man with wire rimmed glasses was standing just outside her door frame in the hall holding a small black bag. He was tall, skinny, but with sharp muscles rippling his arms and neck. Short, dark black hair topped his head and he had a mustache that looked very dashing on him, he was very handsome, like a young Tom Selleck but much slimmer. Sabastian was standing behind him so her tension from seeing a strange man wanting to enter her bedroom eased slightly.

"Good afternoon, Miss Victoria," the man said in a soft polish monotone voice.

"Umm, hello," she answered, pulling her blankets up around her.

"I am Dr. Michael Marshal, may I come in please?"

"Um, yes, of course," she sat up straighter, moving a few books out of the way.

He smiled at her and gracefully entered her room and placed his bag on her bed.

"I need to make sure you are well and also to run some tests if that's all right with you?"

She pushed herself a little straighter and looked at Sabastian for reassurance.

"He's the man who made sure you were okay when you got here and put you on your meal program to help you fatten up," Sabastian said with a slight smile.

She scowled at him, then addressed the doctor.

"Thank you so much, Dr. Marshal. How have I been doing so far?"

"You have been my best patient yet. You eat well and exercise more than you need to and your weight has been steadily gaining. Also the fact that you were drug free, much to everyone's surprise, was a good start," Michael said grinning shyly at her, "I need to weigh and measure you, give you a complete physical as well as give you an injection and take some samples. Do I have your permission to do so?"

Victoria could not refuse him, he was so polite, his manners were impeccable and it would seem overly rude to tell him no, even though she was nervous.

She nodded her accent.

"Thank you so much, Miss Victoria," Doctor Marshall said.

Stepping forward, Sabastian swallowed, cleared his throat, and asked formally. "First, Miss Victoria, I need to ask, will you be staying with Eximius? Would you like to enter the internship here and try for a position with us?"

Sabastian stared intensely into her eyes, willing her to say yes. But a small part of him was hoping she would refuse and leave here with their good blessings and hope she had a good life away from here.

Victoria was stunned. She would have to answer him right now? It was life altering and she was not sure she was ready. But looking into his intense green eyes, she nodded slowly.

"I need a clear answer from you with our witness," Sabastian said firmly, gesturing to the doctor.

Victoria cleared her throat and said, "Yes, I will accept the internship with you, Sabastian."

Blushing, she looked away and realized she had just confirmed that she would be having sex with him.

Sabastian reached into Michael's bag and took out some papers and handed them to her.

"This will need to be filled out after your examination. Take your time to look over it before you sign it, please," he said carefully.

"Okay," she said, not understanding the wisp of disappointment she heard in his voice. She took the papers from him and put them on the bed beside her.

The doctor had brought a chair close to her bed and Sabastian removed the flowers on her bed side table to make room for tools of his trade to be laid out. Sabastian winked at her when he noticed her concerned face as the instruments were laid out, so she relaxed, knowing she would be in good hands with him to watch over her.

After asking, Dr. Marshall took off her blanket and parted her robe and examined her bruised legs. She remembered how badly both her body and faced looked and again was incredibly self-conscious for Sabastian to see her

164

like this. She glanced an embarrassed look to his to see his reaction but all she saw was a concerned frown as he watched over the pair of them closely.

"You took quite a beating yesterday, Miss Victoria. How are you feeling today?"

"Just tired and a bit sore, but I'll be fine. Could you not call me Miss Victoria, it kind of bugs me?" she asked shyly.

"Oh no, I couldn't, miss," Dr. Marshal said, his face growing slightly pink.

She frowned and looked at Sabastian who just shrugged his shoulders still worried for her.

"Are most of these marks from working out with Maximus?" he asked.

"Yes, most of them. But the new ones are from the spa yesterday. I bruise really easy so..." she trialed off.

"Yes, I know that the first-time waxing can be especially hard on the skin and perhaps we should lighten up the workouts to only twice a week instead of every day," he recommended out loud.

Victoria did not like the sound of that.

"Really?" she asked. "But I love it and it keeps me from going crazy in this room."

"Well, perhaps, we can just watch to make sure it does not have any lasting effects and then reassess."

Victoria was relieved and relaxed as she let the doctor work in silence.

The doctor took her blood pressure and a blood sample, checked her heart and her breathing, tapped her belly and with the utmost delicacy and after asking three times for her permission, he checked her breasts for any lumps over her night gown. She held her breath the whole time during that check but didn't feel threatened, only awkward. Her eyes, nose, mouth, and ears were all checked, the doctor was always smiling at her and continually asked if she was okay, and for permission to do everything he needed to do his job more than once.

When he brought out a needle, he said, "This is a strong type of birth control that will last six months, it has very little side effects and is the best protection against unwanted pregnancy. May I?"

She nodded. Of course she would need birth control, it was one of the many questions she had not gotten to.

When she thought, he was finished. Dr. Marshall looked at her and said, "I am very sorry, Miss Victoria, but I need to do a pap smear on you, could you please lay down for me?"

Victoria was confused, she didn't know what a pap smear was, not having a mother past fourteen and a father who could care less about her, she was at a complete loss.

"What's a pap smear?" she asked uneasily.

Dr. Marshal looked sympathetic, "Well, Miss Victoria, I am so sorry but I need to check your vagina for any abnormalities and we need to swab it to test for cancer. I also need to check for any STDs. I am so sorry but it is our policy and if you need time to think about it, I can always come back later."

She looked at him wide eyed. He wanted to check out her vagina! This had to be some sort of joke, did doctors even do that?

"Is that something doctors usually check or is it something special done here?" she asked doubtfully.

"Yes, Miss Victoria, women get this test done all the time with a gynecologist and their regular doctor. The test is performed almost every year as soon as a woman is sexually active, before and after giving birth and when they are older to prevent cancer. It is one of the most frequent tests women get to stay healthy. I am so sorry this has upset you, miss, and I would love to bypass this test if it has made you uncomfortable but it is a requirement to move forward in the program. I can always wait for you to think about it; however, I believe that will only increase your anxiety about the test. I am so very sorry."

The look the doctor gave her was so apprehensive and he kept apologizing. It looked like he was more uncomfortable and upset than she was.

"Will it hurt?" she asked, scared to hear the answer.

"No, of course not. It can be uncomfortable if you do not know what to expect but it is not painful."

Taking pity on the over concerned doctor, she took a deep breath, "Okay, what do you need me to do?"

Michel smiled kindly at her and said, "Thank you, Miss Victoria. Please lay flat on the bed and bend your knees up."

He took her blanket and draped it on her stomach and over her knees.

"Now. Please relax, Miss Victoria."

As he dipped down behind the blanket, spreading her knees gently apart.

Victoria was aghast and her face burned red, her legs shaking. She was thankful that Sabastian was by her head, but uneasy he was watching her.

She felt warm hands between her legs at her groin and bit her lip. Closing her eyes tight, she tried to relax but had started to shake slightly.

Her eyes flew open when she heard a clinking sound by her head as Sabastian had picked up a metal duck bill shaped implement to hand to the man. But just then, Dr. Marshal's head suddenly popped up over the blankets.

Ignoring the proffered tool that Sabastian held out for him, he lowered the blanket to cover her and said briskly, "Thank you, Miss Victoria."

"You're done?" she asked, realizing that was almost too easy, sitting up. She had no reason to be scared, it didn't even feel like he did anything although was curious about the object Sabastian still held.

She was starting to be relieved the examination was over until she saw the look Dr. Marshal shot to Sabastian. Michael, deep red in the face suddenly gathered his tools and his bag.

"Good Bye, Miss Victoria. Thank you so much for being such a wonderful patient," he said formally as he left her room quickly.

Sabastian followed the doctor out, glancing behind him at Victoria in the bed, watching them go alarmed.

What did I do wrong? she thought. *Oh, God, there must be something wrong with her. Were her female parts messed up? Was she sick? Did she have cancer?*

She started to breath hard, *oh no something was really wrong.*

She got out of bed, wrapping her robe back around her, making her way to the door hoping to overhear them or maybe follow them and ask what was going on. She was concerned but also a bit angry.

How could they just leave me like that when something was clearly wrong? she fumed.

She had just reached the door when it flung open. There stood an enraged Sabastian, he was red in the face and shaking, his eyes a dark emerald color that shocked her. She took a step back alarmed ready to run.

"You're a v v virgin!" he raged at her. "You're a f f f fucking virgin."

He stared at her completely at a loss on what to do, stuttering for the first time in years he was infuriated and took a step toward her.

She backed up on to the bed frightened.

"Y…y…yes," she stammered.

She lowered her head, ashamed tears in her eyes, "I'm sorry."

Sabastian softened immediately, and took a step back, trying to control the urge to shake some sense into her.

Sabastian ran both his hands through his hair and concentrated to control his voice, "Shit, Vicky, why didn't you tell me?"

She looked up at the shortened version of her name and said meekly, "You didn't ask. I'm sorry," she repeated.

Sabastian looked at her hard and said firmly, "Don't you apologize to me Vicky, this is my fault."

His shoulders slumped and he dropped heavily on the bed beside her, his head in his hands.

"That's a bad thing here," she stated, clearly not having to ask.

"Look, you have to understand the kind of work we do here." He looked at her, "You are a rarity that any man would pay for. We have only had two virgins in thirty years here and they never stay, they get ruined."

He looked at her painfully.

Afraid to ask, she whispered the words, "What happened to them?"

"Umm, well," he said looking at the door, then up at the ceiling. "They get bid on," he said flatly.

She looked at him horrified.

Sabastian knew he was in so much trouble already that digging himself deeper for her didn't matter anymore. Normally a test girl would never be considered but once it was discovered she was both clean and a virgin, he would lose her for his test subject and be put directly into the system for high paying clients.

"A notice goes out to our clients and whoever bids the most on you gets you for a week. But the men are selfish and use the girls up and never show them much pleasure, so they never stay with the company. They get used for one client maybe a couple more and then they are done."

She was shocked, "Why?"

"Money and reputation," he stated simply.

"Okay, so let's say I'm not a virgin and just move forward?" she asked hopefully.

"We can't hide it, Vicky, Michael will put it in his report and it's on the camer—" Sabastian stuttered to a halt.

"Huh, cameras?" she asked shocked, looking around the room.

"Shit," he groaned, knowing coming clean was the best course of action at this moment, "sorry, Vic, you've had cameras on you since you got here."

"What?" She screamed leaping off the bed, "You have been watching me this whole time!?"

Sabastian leaped up; his hands held out in supplication in front of him.

"It's just to make sure you were safe and didn't harm yourself, that's the only reason. We needed to make sure you were eating, and getting better and not going to hurt yourself. We didn't know you and needed you safe. I'm sorry but I don't make the rules."

She calmed slightly, it made sense and she knew she must have been watched somehow but just did not think it was all the time.

"Are there any in the bathroom?" she demanded.

He hung his head.

"Really?" she said incredulously. "You enjoy the peep show?"

"No! I never watched you in there."

"Oh, ya, then who?" she spat.

"Roman, mostly, and Matthew, they work the monitor room. You weren't supposed to find out."

"And that makes it better?" she fumed that strange men had watched her all this time. She was appalled and wanted to curl up and die.

"No, of course not, but we have lost girls before who were on drugs and who have panicked making assumptions, they have hurt themselves. Watching the girls twenty-four seven was the only way to prevent it."

"So is that why you never answered my question, if you could get into my room or not?"

Sabastian sighed and walked over to the wall, leaning around he pressed a hidden switch on the back side of the night stand beside the bed.

Victoria scrabbled off the bed that had started to rise up off the floor. Sabastian pointed down and she leaned over the side of the bed and sure enough, there was a hidden hatch under the bed and when it rose up, it opened up enough to fit a person.

"Nice," she said sarcastically.

Sabastian pushed the button again and the bed started to lower down, "Look, I need to take care of your problem, I'll be right back."

Victoria watched him run from the room.

My problem? she thought. *Oh, right, the fact that I am still a child to his eyes and have absolutely no sexual experience. That problem.*

Victoria shook. What was he going to do? She didn't know what to do so she grabbed her book and headed to the bath tub, careful to keep the robe on her until she could hide in the softly rising bubbles.

Chapter 37

Sabastian sprinted toward Michael's office, bursting in.

"Hello, Sabastian, please come in," Michael said politely, spinning in his chair toward the intruder.

"What will it take Mike?" Sabastian panted at him.

"What will it take for what?" Dr. Marshal asked, confused.

"For you to change the results of her physical?" Sabastian glared at him hard. "Put down that she's not a virgin and I'll give you anything you want."

Michael frowned, "You know I cannot do that, Sabastian. I would lose my job and worse if anyone found out."

"Okay, how about you just write that you were unable to do a pap smear, that's true and you can do one on her later. You know she is free from STDs, that way you don't lie," Sabastian tried desperately.

Michael hesitated and Sabastian knew he was about to hear the catch to his request. The doctor may be a perfectly polite spoken gentleman and he would need a very good reason to break the rules.

"I will give you a month's pay," Sabastian offered.

"Three months," Michael countered softly.

Sabastian knew it was too dangerous to bargain lower, so he shook the smart doctor's hand before turning to leave.

"Just tell me one thing," Michael said. "Why would you not take the commission on a virgin? Instead you give up three months' pay and for what? What's she to you?"

"What do you care, you get paid," Sabastian said, not really knowing why he was doing it.

"Well, I want you to know that I get paid no matter what, so if you want your money's worth, you better make sure Roman goes along with it, too."

Sabastian knew he was right and bolted to the monitor room.

Sabastian ran right into Roman in the hallway, knocking him and a tray of food flying.

"Shit, sorry, Roman," he said, helping him up. "Where have you been?"

"Well, the last thing I needed to watch is another pap smear so since you and the doc where both in there with her, I took a break," Roman replied, looking down at the food he had been carrying now all over the floor.

Sabastian grabbed at the opportunity.

"I'm sorry, Roman, you go and get more food and I'll clean this up and watch her for you, take your time, this is completely my fault."

"Damn straight it is," Roman said, punching him hard in the arm. "There better be more pot roast left," he mumbled as he headed back to the kitchen.

As soon as Roman was out of sight, Sabastian dashed into the monitor room and grabbed a chair. He quickly erased the video till just after the doctor left and the discussion he had with Victoria after he had come back from talking to Michael in the hall. Even though there was no sound, the altercation was enough to raise eyebrows and seeing him lose it on her right after that particular test they would guess something was up. He started it again knowing there would be a glitch from the time the doctor left to her suddenly being in the bathroom. But seeing how no one reviewed the video unless something went wrong or there was a complaint, he felt safe enough.

The knot in his chest lessened slightly and he turned to cleaning up the hallway.

As he worked, his thoughts turned to Victoria, he had never trained someone with no experience and never been with a virgin and was completely at a loss on how to handle it. He couldn't believe someone of that age had never been with someone, but knowing her history, he didn't see a chance for her to have any kind of relationship with anyone. Being beaten and controlled by her father for years and living on the streets had kept her pure. He knew most women on the streets who were into drugs became hookers, but even if they were not into drugs, they still had to eat.

"Is that why she was so skinny?" he asked himself.

She never considered that option even to feed herself? The fact that she was contemplating this lifestyle baffled him. She was taking a huge risk; she knew nothing of sex. He stopped cleaning, *'Oh God, she had read those books.'*

His face warmed, embarrassed for her, how could he have given her those books to read? She had to be the bravest and most reckless girl he had ever met and only took his shit when he was pissed off. His head dropped; how could he have yelled at her like that? He must have looked just like her stepfather screaming at her in a violent outburst. He had screwed up royally and now, not only did he have to fix that but he had to take her virginity and he had to do it fast, before someone else found out.

Chapter 38

Sabastian went to her hours later, still ashamed of himself and knocked lightly on the door.

Victoria, who was reading in bed, expected him and said, "Come in Sabastian."

Sabastian opened the door gingerly and took the chair that was still beside the bed. He glanced at the book she was reading and flushed. *Sex for Women* written by men. He slowly took the book from her fingers and placed it on the table.

She noticed the worried hurt look in his eyes and misread it, "I am so sorry I didn't tell you. I never really had the chance."

Sabastian held up his hand to stop her.

Summoning his iron will to keep his eyes on hers and not drop them shamefully, he said, "My sweet Victoria, don't you ever apologize to me again, this is entirely my fault. I am so sorry. I never knew to ask; it's never happened to me before. I had no right to yell at you like that. The fact that you are a virgin is something to be proud of and I am so very sorry I talked to you like that. It just shocked me and I didn't know how to handle it," he finished frantically, watching her reaction.

His face had a look of torment on it and he lowered his head into his hands.

Victoria didn't hesitate as she placed her hand on his head and ran her fingers slowly through his soft wavy hair.

"It's fine, Sabastian, that was nothing. Anytime I can walk away from a conflict without bruises or a broken bone, I can handle it."

He looked up at her shocked and she returned his gaze with a slight grin.

"I'm okay, don't worry, it's nothing," she slowly moved her hand to slide down his cheek. He was too beautiful, too strong to be this worried about her.

She dragged her thumb across the cleft in his chin, her heart beating so fast. He was so close to her and her heart had sped up as soon as she touched him.

Sabastian was completely spellbound, slowly, he raised himself from beside her bed and leaned in cautiously and captured her mouth with his, keeping his eyes open to watch her. He moved over her and pressed his lips to hers, feeling the tenderness of her beneath him.

Victoria closed her eyes, relishing the feel of him pressing into her, inhaling his strong scent of leather, citrus, and musk that filled her senses. His lips were soft at first but then probed tentatively deeper and she opened to welcome his tongue between her lips. Letting her body overtake her, she reached to wrap her arms around his neck and pulled him closer, running her fingers through his hair.

She pulled at him and his kiss went from sweet and soft to sensual and hungry in a heartbeat.

Sabastian knew he needed to pull back before he lost control. What was she doing to him? He told himself again that she was a job and nothing more. He couldn't deny that he was losing himself to this girl, she drove him mad and yet he could not get enough of her. When he was not with her, he was glued to the monitors just to see her stretch luxuriously in bed. This had been going on for weeks and he knew the more time he spent watching her and, in her presence, he became more aware that she was different and it was changing him into someone he didn't know and could not control.

Sabastian groaned, feeling her open under him and had to hold back an over whelming desire to crush her with his weight wanting to feel her delicate creamy body beneath him. Summoning his will power, he softened the kiss again, but when she groaned and tried to pull him tighter, he broke it off, his jaw clenched. She had no right to want more, especially seeing what she was.

He looked down at her and relaxed his jaw so she wouldn't be able to see the restraint he had to invoke to resist her.

She looked hurt and then embarrassed and looked away from him.

He couldn't take the insecurity she felt and leaned down to place a butterfly kiss on her lips and smiled.

She turned to him, blushing.

"I'm sorry."

Gazing down at her, he brushed her cheek lightly with the back of his fingers, "What did I say about apologizing?"

"Sorry," she said grinning up at him.

"Christ, woman. Get up?"

He needed space, this bedroom was too small and smelled too much like her. He was drowning in her presence.

Sabastian got up and grabbed her robe. Taking her hand, he pulled her from the bed and out the door, throwing her robe over her shoulders. He led her quickly through the round room, toward a set of double doors and outside, stepping into a stunning, enormous, wall lined garden.

Victoria gasped, "Its beautiful, Sabastian," she said in awe, soaking up the sun.

Victoria had not been outside in weeks and the fragrant garden filled her senses. She needed to feel the warm breeze lick her skin so she dropped her robe and stood in her ankle long, silk, nightgown and started to walk through this garden paradise.

The garden was something out of a fairy tale, butterflies drifted about lazily, and the smell of flowers and trees engulfed her. The stone path went in over a dozen different directions and the garden was so large and thick, she couldn't see where it ended. There were blue lights illuminating the paths that gave a soft glow to the fading light of dusk outside. There were fountains, ponds and a mini river, waterfalls and all kinds of flowers, shrubs, and trees. The birds were settling down for the night and she could hear crickets and insects lazily flying around. She was enchanted and walked ahead of Sabastian brushing her fingers along the bark of trees or through the soft leafy bushes. She finally sat down on a swing beside one of the ponds to watch the Koi fish swim smoothly in the blue light of the lanterns.

Sabastian followed silently behind her enchanted not by the garden but by her cat like movements as she gracefully glided through the surroundings. Her movements were mesmerizing as she walked on her tip toes like a ballerina, hardly making a sound. Watching her walk had his body in a sweet agitated state as she moved around the lovely warm paradise. Her lithe movements and how she appreciated the work put into this floral landscape was an aphrodisiac to him and he adjusted his too tight shorts before stepping in behind her to give her a gentle push on the swing that sent her hovering over the pond.

Everything was so quiet; she hated to break the spell but had to ask.

"What will happen when my training is done? Will I be allowed to still see you?"

Sabastian hesitated, the questions that she had been holding back would come now and he had to be very careful in his answers to keep her in the dark.

Clearing his throat, he said huskily, "Yes, any woman can request a man at any time as long as it is more than forty-eight hours before a job," he stated this, like he read it from a manual.

"Oh, so do many women request, um, your time."

He hesitated, but then answered flatly, "No."

"Oh. Umm, have you been needed lately?"

"No, I have put off most of my duties since you got here, wild cat," he said, hoping to lighten the conversation with his favorite nick name for her.

"Okay, so I realize that I am in a house full of men that have needs, do you date, or just ask the women when you need to 'get some?'" she smiled, talking about sex so freely invigorated her.

"No, we can't date, nor have sex with anyone outside the manor. The only way we can get some," he said chuckling, using her words, "is if a woman requests us, or to visit the mini manor."

"Do I have to ask?"

"The mini manor is where the female staff live for the men to 'get some.' It has some girls working there that are there for the guys and also to help with men's chores. They do not mix with the company's women although they do work in the woman's manor to clean and cook. You met two of them in the spa the other day."

"Can they say no?"

"Yes, of course, they can. We are not barbarians that knock them out to have our way with them. They have every right to say no at any time, without an excuse and without reprimand. Remember we are all about respect here, even for the guy's girls. Of course, it is extremely rare that they ever say no."

"And why is that?"

He hesitated and decided to only tell her where some of the girls came from.

"Because a lot were drafted from the SAA or the Association as we call it."

"And do I want to know what SAA stands for?"

"It's for Sex Addiction Anonymous."

"Isn't that low? Taking advantage of women who have an addiction?" Victoria asked, not even knowing that such an addiction was possible.

177

"Well, they get to stay here and be paid well to enjoy something they love. Not only do they get what they crave but we actually help them recover from their addiction in the end, we just get the perk of helping them to that step."

"Oh, I guess that benefits all parties? How come your company girls don't come from there?" Victoria asked curiously.

"Some do, but they tend to have too much experience and cannot be molded as well as the girls with less experience, plus they are usually all about self-pleasure and in order for the clients to be happy the women have to give as well as received selflessly and equally."

"But I thought you said that the women are trained to enjoy sex."

"Yes, of course, but it's a two-way street. It's not the client's job to pleasure our women. The women have to be in tune with their bodies to be able to get satisfaction without a lot of work on the client's parts. The women have to make sure the clients are completely happy and fully satisfied, usually several times a night, without having to sacrifice any pleasure on their part. When on a job, the Eximius women take their pleasure, as it is generally not given to them. You read the books, right?"

"Yes, are you talking about a woman having an ummm…orgasm, during intercourse?"

It was an educated question from the books she had read, although it made her very self-conscience.

"Yes, most women can't do that, because they are not tuned into their bodies but every one of our women easily can. They can control their bodies and can orgasm at will. It not only makes our women utterly sensual, but it gives the clients a great feeling of power that they believe they can do that with our girls and no one else. That's why they are so popular and why they are so pricey. It gives our clients a feeling of control and confidence and they crave that power. Men need power to be successful and our company helps them do that. It's our girls that make them even more wealthy, successful, and powerful and they can't get enough of it. Sex with our girls is a powerful addictive drug that benefits everyone. Of course we know it's mostly the women's doing and the men are only there to enjoy the ride and take the credit. It surprisingly has little to do with sex. A lot of the men need only companionship and a stress-free night with an educated women with no commitments or games. They need them to also mingle well with their peers smoothly when at social events. Make sense?"

"Yes. I remember you said that it's not only the sex act that the women do, right?"

"That's right, they have to perform when at banquets, fund raisers, on the podium beside their men, and have intelligent conversations with their clients and their client's colleagues in every subject from politics to environment. They can also be called on to give speeches and talk at prestigious events. Not only to make the men feel good, but also look good to everyone around them. It's all about boosting their clients and if they do a good job, they get hired again."

"How do you advertise?"

"Word of mouth only, although it's always hushed and very discreet, as the men don't want other men to find out they are paying for these women."

"Okay, so do any of the women ever get involved with the clients like in *Pretty Women*?" she asked, referring to the Julia Roberts movie.

"Yes, it can happen, but you have to understand that the women are acting and when they see the client wants more than a date, they drop the act and the client can see who she truly is and that usually turns him off of pursuing her. That's why the girls have to be careful they do not show too much of their true personality. They are not trying to land a husband, only do a perfect job. We have had women fall in love with their clients, it's been mutual and they can be themselves around them and get married. So far, none of our girls have been divorced and they are all in happy marriages with kids, the whole nine yards."

"What about you guys?"

"Well, since we can't see anyone outside of work and the companies' women are very hard to impress, we stick to what we have and are happy with it."

"Okay, so you only see the company women when summoned?" she asked, looking around on the swing at him, seeing his smile. "And you have your own girls in the mini manor that you help with their addiction by having sex with them. That, by the way, is very generous of you."

She cooed, sarcasm dripping from her voice.

"Hey, you laugh, but it's true and it benefits both parties. It's a system that works well. Don't knock it before you try it, *virgin*," he emphasized the last word with humor.

Victoria was starting to get dizzy and put her foot down, slowing the swing. She turned to look at him.

179

"Okay, smart guy, when do you guys move on? Do you get involved with the girls from the company and run away together or just stay happily knocking boots with the addicts?"

"First of all," he said seriously, "watch what you say about girls in the mini manor, they deserve and get respect from everyone here so I wouldn't repeat that what you just said."

"Sorry," she said contrite.

"You don't have to apologize. No, the men can never get involved with any women from the manor. Being involved with any women who works here is strictly prohibited and it will cost you, not only your job, but also your pay. We are here to make sure they can do their very difficult job well with our support and protection. We teach them and help with their art and that is all."

"Sounds like you are the ones being used," she said watching him.

"Ya, well, most don't mind," he shrugged.

"You lose your pay? Doesn't sound like so much, so you lose a month or…?"

"No, all of the pay we have earned in all the years we have worked here gets taken. Everything gone and we are left with nothing. Mr. D cannot let some romantic fool steal away his company girls. There would be fights and conflict all the time among the men, competing for them. We come into this knowing that if we want to move on with our lives, we have to leave and start somewhere else away from the company and never to get involved with anyone here or at any other chapter of the company."

"So no guys here can be involved with any girl? How does that work if a woman is interested in one of the guys here, she can just keep requesting him, right? How does Mr. D control that?"

"There are strict rules with requesting men, if he's requested too frequently that man can get blacklisted from that girl and will not be able to either service or work with her. They can also be reassigned to another chapter, at the very least."

"Wow, no messing around," she watched him and during this conversation, she had realized the answers he had given had gone from textbook memorization to more passionate answers.

She decided to get back to her question list, which she had been going over in her head the last few days.

"Okay, so what about diseases?"

"That's what the lab does, all our women are tested for STDs of course. It's the clients we have to worry about and they have to undergo testing before they date any of our girls. They would be the ones blacklisted if they refuse or turn up positive for anything so they are very careful who they sleep with outside our women if they want to retain our services."

Sabastian reached out and lifted her lightly off the swing. Placing his hand on the small of her back, walking her deeper into the garden.

"How's your questions list? Is it getting smaller yet?" he asked, glad he had not had to lie to her too much.

"Yes, but I am sure more will keep popping up the more I learn."

"How did you enjoy those books?" he asked slowly.

"They were very informative," she said swallowing, glad it was dark enough to hide her blushes.

"Your inexperience absolutely astounds me?"

"Oh ya, why?"

"You've never been with anyone? No sex, I know that, but not even fooled around?"

Turning to face him.

"Well, let me put it this way, today was my first kiss and I was not disappointed," she said softly, looking up into his eyes that had suddenly darkened.

"Only one kiss in your entire life, huh?" Sabastian said his mouth suddenly moist, his tongue peeked from between his lips as he gazed down at her.

Victoria smiled shyly up at him, "Mmmm, yes," she whispered.

His fingers slowly encircled her forearms and he pulled her into his body, claiming her mouth gently, looking into her magical purple iris. When he heard her moan, he wrapped her in his arms, pulling her tightly to his long, hard length. Her arms were trapped under his grip, and he felt her melt into him, surrendering to his demanding mouth. He released her arms and ran his hands through her magnificent long silky hair. His hands moved around to the small of her back, encircling her tiny waist and pulled her hips into his. His erection throbbed painfully tight but he welcomed the delicious agony of it as he felt her body mold to his.

Standing on the tips of her toes, barely reaching his mouth, she let him pull her willingly into his body. Victoria lifted her hands to his hair running her finger through its softness, enjoying the feel of it between her slender fingers.

As soon as her hands flowed into his hair, he moaned and deepened his kiss backing her up into the garden wall. She cried out from the surprising impacted on her back and with her mouth open, he deepened the kiss. Her eyes closed wanting to only feel, to let her body take it all in, heightening her nerve endings, concentrating on him, and how good it felt to have him pressed into her. She felt a throb and a tightening sensually deep within her and moaned again, remembering the feel of his hands on her during the massage.

Sabastian wanted her, he ached for her and couldn't stop himself, she was so ripe and willing and it thrilled him that she was responding so eagerly to his kiss. What would happen when he was not just kissing her?

Sabastian wondered if she was naturally willing and responsive or if the books had taught her some tricks. He wanted her to respond naturally and not be acting from what she had read. He pushed her into the wall to feel her breasts hot against his chest. She tightened her fingers in his hair and he wanted to crush her, ready to explode. He knew if he didn't turn back soon, he would take her on the stone path of the garden and she wouldn't have time to enjoy her first sexual experience. She was still too small, too weak. With the desire she had built in him so quickly, he knew he would hurt her if he tried to initiate her tonight. She groaned again and pushed her hips into him and he wrenched himself away breaking apart and stepping away from her, leaving her panting.

"Sweet Vicky," and even with his words he knew he was breaking rules, so much more than just the house rules, but his own rules. He had to step back from this girl both physically and emotionally, this girl was not his and never would be his. He needed to get her trained and get her out of his system. He knew that once he had sex with her, he would pass her along with no more need of her, at least that is what he hoped.

Breathing hard, he swallowed, cleared his throat and tried again.

"Miss Victoria, let me escort you to your room."

She frowned at him, not knowing what game he was playing but going to her room sounded like a good idea.

When they entered the room, she turned to him with a shy grin on her face and asked, "I think I'm getting the hang of kissing. Would you like to bring my total up to three?"

"Of course I would, Miss Victoria," he bent down gave her a sweet soft kiss on the lips and pulled away before she could get her hands up to his hair again.

"Have a good night, Miss Victoria," he said formally and quickly shut the door behind him.

Victoria was utterly bewildered, what had just happened? She stood there still panting, her heart pounding in her ears, wanting him to hold her, to press himself into her, and he just left. Did she do something wrong? She stood looking at the door for five full minutes, going over their embraces, trying to see the point of which it changed and couldn't find it. She finally walked in a trance to the bathroom, getting ready for bed.

She tossed for hours restless and edgy her body craved something it had never had and she couldn't get it to settle.

So much for having control of the women's body, she thought, glaring at the books across the room.

Ridiculous that she was mad at books, she turned over and forced herself to think about something else and eventually fell into a troubled sleep.

Chapter 39

Victoria awoke to her breakfast tray sliding into her room, she stretched and yawned and walked over to the tall mirror. Glancing around her and up at the ceiling, she tried to locate the cameras that apparently had been watching her this whole time. She couldn't see any trace or even a hint of a camera anywhere.

She stood closely in front of the mirror and opened her robe, trying to keep herself covered and to only show her nakedness to the mirror and to herself. Her bruises were fading fast, except for slight discoloration on her legs. Her face was now flawless and soft, all redness and splotches were completely gone from her spa experience. Her skin glowed and was so smooth, she was in awe as she rubbed her arms and belly. She was still thin and probably could use another ten pounds on her body, but she felt strong and firm.

She knew it was all about the meals, smoothies, and snacks she had been eating all this time and she looked at her breakfast tray. Eggs benedict on whole wheat English muffin with thick ham and a generous amount of hollandaise sauce. Sausage and hash browns on the side with a fruit salad, milk, orange juice and water and a chocolate muffin for dessert, all arranged so artfully on her tray.

She started her meal in bed and thought about all that had happened and wondered what the next step was. After her meal was almost done, the table appeared again with a stack of books on it.

She sighed. *Back to work,* she thought.

These books had some more sex titles but there we a couple of self-help books as well. Titles like *How to Heal, Being Strong After Abuse, and You Are Not a Victim Anymore.* She rolled her eyes frowning at the titles.

I guess Sabastian thinks I'm messed in the head, she thought.

Putting the new books aside, she grabbed the book she was working on and her eyes landed on a man caressing a woman's face while he undid her dress.

The man's face was blank and she thought about the Eximius women and the job they did.

That was the one of the main things that made her hesitate, how could she just jump in bed with some guy because he paid her to do it? How could these women do that, glancing at the title of the book she had taken, *Loving and Needing Sex to be Happy* and rolled her eyes again.

"Of course," she said, frowning at the book. They did it because they liked sex and it didn't matter who they had sex with. But could *she* do that?

Not wanting to be caught in her night gown again, she jumped into the shower and got dressed in a light blue spring dress that had a modest neck line and stopped just short of her knees. She would study like a good girl and wait until he came for her again. Getting settled, she noticed the papers on her bed. Setting down the book, she picked up the contract that Sabastian had given her when the doctor came and wondered if she could still sign it, considering the fact that she was not as experienced as they had hoped. She thought perhaps there was another contract for girls in her unique situation so she thought it best to sign this contract as soon as possible.

Grabbing her pen, she wrote her name down on every space requested, reading in-depth only after she had signed every page.

There looked like there was the option for a one-year trial stay in the internship program and taking clients over that time was also optional. She read this part carefully thinking about the possibility. The woman must live in the manor until the one-year trail and her training was complete, then could choose to leave if she decided not to pursue a career with Eximius or if not offered the job. She signed this page; willing to commit the year if she could stay here safe and sound and be close to Sabastian and hoped that was still an option for her.

The contract also went though many rules of living at The Manor. While in training, the "intern" was not permitted in the, file room, the monitor room, or in the mini manor where the pleasure girls lived. She was also not allowed in the woman's manor unless accompanied. At no time was the "intern" allowed to leave the property for any reason until she had been offered the job and was official trained and working for Eximius. It went in detail all about studying her books, taking tests on the material, and what hours were to be put aside for studying. Also certain number of hours were to be put aside for practicing what was being learned in the books when it came to the physical part of the job.

She would be required to meet with the company physiologist monthly and to stay physically trim and within certain weight range for her height and undergo bi-monthly body treatments at the spa.

Most of the contract made sense to her and there was nothing that really turned her off, except the part about being open minded and willing with tests that were done throughout the internship. Apparently, there were multiple tests that would challenge her mind and her body. The contract talked about how the tests were there to educate and fully explore every woman's deep sexual desires and use them to benefit the company and the intern and that worried her. The tests did not follow any respect or boundary rules and the intern had no say in how these tests proceeded and that's what really concerned her. What kind of tests were these? This was the only section she wished she had read before she had signed. She wanted more information about these so-called tests to discover her deep sexual desires, in which she had no say in the matter.

Putting the contract on her dresser, she settled on the couch and picked up her new book which stole all her attention until her snack came through the wall. She walked over to it and checked the clock, *Yup, right on time*. She took her stuffed mushroom caps and strawberry smoothie and went back to her chair a little exasperated. Where was he? She ate and was once again absorbed in her book and only snapped out of it when another meal appeared. She shut her book and walked over to the door, she knew where his room was, she could go to him.

And then what, Vicky? Demand he start training me? she thought ridiculously to herself. Well, she wasn't going to wait all day for him, she took her book, grabbed her food, and left her room. The round room was empty and she was pleased to find the garden door open. Stepping into the bright light of the outdoor paradise, she picked a bench and sat down beside the fountain to read, soaking up the warm sun on her skin. She knew that Sabastian wanted to keep her healthy and was obsessed with her weight. Which made sense seeing how skinny she was, so she hoped a few missed meals would draw him to her. She was engrossed in her book and only occasionally lifted her head to watch the birds or butterflies in the trees and flowers to take a mental note of a particular piece of information she thought was helpful or interesting.

She was coming to the end of her thick book and the shadows had moved in the garden. She frowned at the garden door.

Where was he?

She jumped when the door suddenly opened.

A tall sculpted dark man stepped into the sun with a large tray in his hands.

Of course, she thought. '*Sabastian would send a henchman. Were all the men male models*?' and thinking that they probably were, she smiled at who was clearly her chef.

"Miss Victoria," he said with a slight bow, "your meal," he said, placing the tray on a garden table beside her bench.

He was tall, dark, and handsome, probably like all the men here, large muscles and a short beard made him look older than his eyes said he was. He was probably around thirty years old and he had a bright white smile, light hazel eyes, and very large tough hands. He was also very attractive with a kind face but she could not help comparing him to Sabastian.

"Thank you so much."

Her smile was brilliant. This was the man who had fed her so well these past weeks and she was so happy to finally meet him.

"Mister…?"

"Of course, I am so sorry, Miss Victoria, I am Nickolas," his voice had slight Italian accent to it, and it would not surprise her if Eximius had head hunted the best chef from Italy and brought him overseas to cook for them.

"And I assume you've been the one feeding me and fattening me up?"

"Yes, I have, Miss Victoria, and it has been my absolute pleasure to do so," he said proudly with a slight bow of his head.

"Could you please sit with me, Nickolas? Would that be okay?"

"Yes, of course, Miss Victoria, what can I do for you?"

"Well, first, you can call me Vicky, if that is okay with you. The Miss thing tends to bug me," she said with a smile.

"I'll try. However, you better get used to it if you plan to stay," he replied as he sat down on the opposite end of the bench, but not before pulling the small table with her food closer to her.

She opened the lid and saw the arrangement of artful cheeses, fruit, and crackers with a cherry lemonade and a water.

"You truly are an artist," she praised him. "Most days I don't want to wreck your creations but the smell always gets to me and I can't help myself."

"Well, if you did not eat, then there would not be any point of cooking for you," he smiled at her and gestured to the tray.

She picked up a kiwi and leaned back on the bench.

"So how long have you worked here?"

"I have been here eight years, miss."

Ignoring the miss, she asked, "And do you like it here?"

"Yes, of course. I hope to never have to leave," he said earnestly.

"You don't want a life outside the manor, or a family?"

"Not at this point, I am only thirty-one and have years ahead of me to start a family. Besides this is my family and I want for nothing here."

"So you're treated well?"

"Yes, we all take care of each other and work together to run this company smoothly, there is not a single soul here that does not want to be here," he said with pride.

"How many men are in the manor?" she asked, looking toward the garden door.

"Well, there are twenty-five of us living here but only five are here right now, many are with the girls on jobs, some are running errands, and others are out at another company."

She jumped at the chance to ask, "Where are the other companies?"

He shook his head, "I am sorry, miss, but I cannot tell you that."

"Can you tell me where we are?"

"Sorry, miss."

"Are we still in the states? You can tell me that at least."

Nickolas tightened his lips and shook his head.

"It was nice talking to you, Miss Victoria, if there is anything you need from the kitchen, please, feel free to ask."

She was about to ask him to stay to try to get more information out of him when the garden door suddenly opened with Sabastian standing there. Victoria stood up to see him, but he only glared at her and motioned for Nickolas to come through the door, slamming it shut behind the chef, leaving her alone in the garden.

Victoria could hear angry voices on the other side of the door. Nickolas and Sabastian were arguing, she could hear Nickolas's accented voice against Sabastian low monotone that was raised slightly. She walked to the door and tried to hear what they were saying but the door was too thick and she only caught who was talking not what they were saying. *This was stupid*, she thought and pulled at the door. She was outraged to find it locked! She slammed her hand on the door and yelled, "Are you kidding me? Let me in!"

The voices stopped immediately and Sabastian opened the door for her.

"To your room, Miss Victoria," he said angrily, pointing his finger in the general direction of her room.

Nickolas stared at her, his face slightly less pink than Sabastian's and tried to leave.

"Stay here," Sabastian said harshly to Nickolas, "You go," he said, addressing her, pointing down her hallway.

She was completely flustered and muttered, "So much for respect."

As she stalked past the two men. She turned at the door of her room and yelled at Sabastian, "I'm not a child."

She slammed the door behind her, realizing the irony of her action.

She waited in her room fuming, what the hell was going on. She wanted to listen in on the men still fighting down the hall but was afraid to get caught again.

Minutes later, it stopped and she waited impatiently. If he was not going to come, she would refuse to stay in her room like a misbehaving child waiting for her punishment. She had done nothing wrong. Tentatively, Victoria cracked open the door and glanced Sabastian leaning up against the hallway wall his head in his hands. It looked like he was trying to calm down before coming to see her and she immediately regretted opening the door. She was frozen and couldn't move, watching him as he raised his eyes to her. His green eyes were dark and stared into hers.

"Christ, get back in there," he said, walking toward her.

She snapped out of her trance and hastily turned back to her room, Sabastian right on her heels.

His anger had cowed her and she tried to figure out what she had done wrong to apologize and sate his anger.

"I'm sorry, I thought I was allowed to leave?"

Slight exasperation in her tone.

"Stop apologizing. Yes, you are allowed to leave, you are not, however," his voice rising, "allowed to talk to anyone but me from now on. You are to get your answers only from me, got it," he shot at her.

"So what about, Max, am I not allowed to talk to him either?"

Why was he so angry? she worried, *was he afraid she was going to find out where she was and take off?*

"It's different now. I will see about your classes later."

"That's bullshit, Sabastian," she spat back. "I didn't know and it is totally unfair of you to lose it on *my* chef," emphasizing the word my.

Sabastian's eyes widened, she called Nickolas her chef. He knew he was being irrational; Nickolas was allowed to talk to her, of course, and the conversation they had, had been harmless. Nickolas had done nothing wrong and that was probably why the chef had fought Sabastian so much. Calling him possessive which was true and a dangerous road to be on. He didn't want her talking to anyone but him, it kept him in control of the situation and the training program that he was putting her through. He didn't want her getting any information that was not carefully thought out. He had told her too many variations of the truth and had to keep everything straight in both his head and hers.

He had spoken seriously to Maximus before they started working together to let him know what Maximus could and couldn't tell her. She was vulnerable in her innocent condition and he found himself overly possessive of her. He couldn't risk anyone else knowing about her condition. If anyone found out she still possessed her virginity, both himself and Vicky would be screwed, figuratively and literally. If she said the wrong thing to anyone, they both might be discovered and that would be the end of them.

If someone let it slip what happens to her after she was trained, he would lose her for sure. He found he couldn't let her go, the VP position the furthest thing from his mind. He must keep her here at all costs and not risk losing her. Judging by the look in her eyes, he saw that if he didn't relax and handle her better, she would leave anyway.

He had tried to stay away from her today for a reason, trying to gain control and figure out a game plan. When he saw her talking so freely to Nickolas through the monitor room, which he had not left since his last talk with her, it made his blood boil.

Sabastian strolled to her dresser, picking up the contract she had signed earlier, trying to focus on anything else but her. Flipping through the pages, he saw her full name was Victoria May McCoy and that she had signed every line. He was hoping she would have at least asked about the contract before signing every space with her initials and full signature in her fluent hand. He was livid at Kevin who had wrote up the contract. The lawyer at the manor had made sure things were as legal as they could be at Eximius. He had used the fact that Victoria was terrified of being sent back home and he had amended part of the contract as a clear threat of keeping her quiet about the company. He hated how he had manipulated her like that and felt sorry for how his company was going to use her. Thinking to himself that it was not the company and that it was him. He needed her for his promotion and paused.

Do I even want her here?

He finally looked up at her, she glowered at him her breasts rising and falling, her cheeks pink and her hands on her hips.

"Christ," he muttered.

His body reacted to her with a shock that made his veins electrify and he could feel the heat searing between them.

I do want her here, but not for my promotion, Sabastian admitted to himself.

"What?" she asked, still defensive.

He was still trying to control himself, but she looked so tempting. She was absolutely gorgeous, her loose long hair flowing over her shoulders and down her back. Her soft smooth legs under the short feminine dress and her breasts moving up and down, he found his own breathing matching hers. Her cheeks were flushed and he realized he liked her like this, fighting back, strong, and passionate. The color of the dress, her long hair, blazing cheeks, she was too tempting.

He moved quickly toward her and she took a step back. He needed to change the anger she felt to passion and he lost control, unthinking.

"Your first training session starts now," he said lustfully, letting his body take control, he grabbed her wrist with one hand and yanked her hips into his roughly.

Victoria was shocked and almost went into defensive mode but her voice squeaked out a response to his onslaught first.

"W…what? No," she stammered, still confused and upset trying to pull away.

Sabastian dropped her hand immediately and stepped back, a well-trained habit to automatically stop all contact when he heard no from a woman.

Fuck, man, control yourself.

Shaking his head and blinking, he bowed his head slightly and said, "Yes, Miss Victoria," and walked out.

Victoria blinked, frozen.

What the hell was that all about and why the hell did she say no? she thought to herself. Walking blindly backward until she felt the bed behind her, and sat down heavily.

This man was driving her nuts, first he was begging her forgiveness; the next second, he was yelling at her, then after kissing her would leave her to simmer for hours. She had no idea what was going on, she was so confused and the stress was starting to get to her.

She paced her room like a caged animal back and forth for the next hour and ignored her next meal.

She had enough and walked to the door, she needed to talk to him and set things straight and she couldn't wait, no matter how much trouble she got in. She almost fell down when the door refused to move, she was locked in!

She banged on the door and yelled, knowing it would be no use.

The gray notebook appeared on the table beside her meal.

She grabbed it angrily and read.

'You need to continue your exercise program and gaining weight before we can move forward.'

"That was it?" she asked herself.

Keep eating and gain weight, she threw the book across the room and her tears welled up.

Fine, she thought, stubborn and motivated, *I'm nothing more than an intern to him and if I want out of here, I better get to work.*

She grabbed her food, and picked up the notebook, flipping to the last pages that held her exercise program. She threw herself into her weight lifting using the frustration and anger to fuel her, she loved nothing more than a challenge and she would prove to him that she didn't need or want him and only wanted the job.

Chapter 40

He knew he was being too rough for this girl, but he didn't care. He would finally be able to ease the ache that had not ceased since the wild cat had arrived. He grabbed her arms and tightened his grip and saw slight fear in the girl's eyes. The fear drove him on and his shaft throbbed painfully.

He didn't want to risk a bad report, so he needed to talk her through this, to let her know that it would be okay.

"Trust me, Gabriel," as he pulled her arms above her head and kissed her roughly on the mouth, pressing his frantic erection into her side. "You'll love this."

"I am not into that stuff. You know that," she said slightly fearful.

"But you never let me try," he pushed her into the wall pinning her and slipped his fingers to collect the sweet wetness between her thighs.

"Taste how ready you are," he lifted his fingers to the girl's lips and hesitating, she sucked.

He pulled her roughly to the bed, throwing her down and watched as her overly large breasts bounce with her body.

"If I go too far, let me know, but trust me."

He took off his shirt and yanked her legs toward him. She scrambled away from him panicked and stood near the end of the bed.

"I can't, you've already gone too far," she said, rubbing her wrists.

He cursed soundlessly fuming, he wanted to slap her, then fuck her, and slap her again. But this was no intern, this was a pleasure girl and she could very well kick him out of her room at any point. With the way he had upset her he would be in a shit load of trouble even with his boss gone.

His body screamed at him, every time she said no or he caught the fear in her eyes, he wanted desperately to pound her with both the whip and his shaft. He loved that fact she was fighting him, but he couldn't take it to the level he wanted and decided to get it over with to ease her mind and both their bodies.

"Gabriel," he said seductively and saw a shiver of excitement run through her, "you should know your body better than this by now."

He slowly walked up to her, herding her into the wall, until her back was pressed up against the surface again. He then reached out to tenderly wrap his hot hand around her breast gently rolling her nipple between his fingers. Smiling when she closed her eyes, he repeated the action on her other breast and was rewarded with a soft moan.

"Your body wants to be fucked hard," he smiled at her as her eyelids popped open wide.

He could see it coming, she was debating with herself. He knew Gabriel, she was too soft and would not explore. She only did vanilla sex and it was never any fun. To prevent the denial forming on her lips, he swiftly kissed her hard, silencing her. He grabbed her nipples ruthlessly in his hand squeezing roughly. She gasped so he bit her lip and lifted her effortlessly up and onto his pulsing cock, slamming her body down onto his.

He felt her body encircle his shaft and moaned in the painful tightness of her body wrapped around him. He could see she was shocked at the quickness of his assault and he felt her sheath grip along his shaft almost painfully and thrilled at the sensation. Gabriel was small and tight and the fear made her convulse around him and he growled in her ear. He wanted to fuck her up against the wall but he was losing control and had to soften his approach for her.

Still keeping his tongue in her mouth and his shaft buried to the hilt, he moved with her to the bed and laid her down gently.

Looking down into her wet eyes he said, "You're okay," he pulled his thick length out of her slowly and said, "You know my reputation and I am not in the mood to cater to you today."

He slammed into her hard and she cried out.

Leaning down to kiss her to prevent any argument, he pulled out again slowly and pounded into her tight body again. He could feel her respond and climb even as she fought him. He continued his assault; drawing out slow and thrusting powerfully into her unwilling body until he felt the change he needed to release her mouth.

He felt her pulse and her climb to orgasm built around him as he thrust urgently into her.

"That's it, Gabriel, come on, girl," he gripped her wrists, pinning them above her head and felt her arch her hips up to meet his.

"Fuck, come on," he growled as he ruthlessly drove into the small female struggling underneath him.

He felt her orgasm tear through her right before his body spilled himself into her with a powerful spasm.

"Ahhhhhhhh," Gabriel cried out, her body bowing unexpectedly as the pleasure hit, then flowed through her.

"Fuck, yes, girl, that's right," he continued his thrusting until he felt her muscle spasms slow, then cease altogether before pulling out of her panting hard.

He wanted to continue but knew he already had damage control to do. Leaning over her, he kissed her softly on the belly and worked his way up to her cheek. He waited until she turned to him and brushed her lips with his, hating to have to suck up after a less than fully satisfying copulation.

"Are you okay, Gab?" he asked, running hard hands up and down her legs and ribs cage softly.

Still panting, "Yes, that was umm, different."

"A good different?"

"I don't know, but at least, I know what the other girls have been talking about," she said, shaking slightly.

He sat up, "Honey, you have no clue. That was me holding back," he reached for his shirt.

"Well, if that's the case, I am not sure I would be able to handle more," she said slightly frightened.

Good, he thought, *you are not woman enough for me any way.*

He had been thinking about Victoria the whole time and Gabriel was no challenge and having to hold back, only increased his sexual frustration.

Trying to be tender but wanting to slap the girl and fuck her hard again, he bend down and kissed her lips lightly.

"That's okay, honey, you were great and I hoped you are now a little bit more aware. I'm here any time you want to experience that again."

"Umm, alright," she said unsure.

"You're okay, right?"

"Yes, I'm fine, just surprised."

"Yes, you would be. You never gave me a real chance in the beginning, you laid there passively and I couldn't work with you. You were not into it then, but you can learn if you want."

Not wanting to waste any more time explaining this with a soft useless female, he left before she could ask any questions, leaving her wondering on the bed.

He stormed to his room thinking about the wild cat waiting for him and the time where he would not have to hold back and when he would have a real fight on his hands.

Chapter 41

Sabastian kept his distance from Victoria, allowing Nickolas to converse with her via the notebook. However, he couldn't keep himself from the monitor room. Even when she was sleeping, he watched her. Roman had to wake him up after he had fallen asleep to get him to go to his room. After the third time this happened, he forced himself to get back to his regular duties at the manor and put as much distance between his wild cat and himself as possible.

He had come so close to taking her on the floor of her room. He needed to feel the softness of her skin under him and use her temper to benefit them both. She was still too small and not strong enough and he had to will himself to wait. The spa alone had left her bruised and sore and he knew only after only an hour with him and she would be in bed for days afterward. His mind and body drifted to that thought and he smiled inwardly.

Sabastian was attracted to her, that was obvious but it was beyond physical. He was protective and possessive of her and being physically attracted to her was not the problem. He was getting emotionally attached and the feeling was so foreign. He couldn't figure out what lured him to her so strongly. He had not really spent a lot of time with any of the other professional girls. Just training and they moved on, talking was never really a strength he possessed, but it seemed so easy with her. Sabastian was generally a private person, not letting anyone in and for good reason. When his emotions got a hold of him, everything else opened like a flood gate and he lost all control. Then he was dangerous, mean tempered, and violent, the last thing Victoria needed to ever experience again.

He spent years shutting down that side of himself and had not needed to exert discipline over himself until this wild cat came along. He hoped that once he screwed her, he would be over her. He wanted to run his hands though her glorious Rapunzel like hair and softly kiss her until she was butter in his hands. At the same time, he wanted to wrap that hair around his wrists and hold on tight as he possessed her body and claimed her as his and his only, a dangerous thought in this company. Just the thought of her beneath him making her moan again with his kisses made him have to readjust his tight black jeans.

Damn it, get a hold of yourself.

He needed to approach her like he had so many other women, get her trained and get her to move on. But a cold sweat chilled his skin at the very thought of her with Chandler, the next step in the program. He couldn't see himself being in the same house while she was taught how to pleasure a man after he had taught her to enjoy love making. He had to try to be professional and do his job. If he treated her like any other girl, it would be over soon. Hopefully, once he had sex with her, the lust he felt would dissolve, along with the feelings he had for her.

Sabastian focused on his computer and the program he had no experience with. Miss Cherry always did all the teaching about a woman's sensuality, how could he, a man, do that. He was the best at initiating a woman physically into everything she was taught from books, but this was a whole other story. This was, of course, his test to induct her into service with Eximius in order to get his promotion, but she was proving too much for him. He knew that even Miss Cherry would have difficulty teaching a woman how to discover and pleasure herself if she had never had sex before. He was at a complete loss, but he would make sure she read all the books and watched the films to further her education and hoped it would be enough to awaken her arousal. Once a woman had been sensually awakened that is where he usually stepped in to take over the program from Miss Cherry to help the new girl practice her skills and further her desire for sex.

He sighed, he had zero experience on how to enlighten a woman about herself. He knew how to make a woman feel utterly aroused and let her use him to pleasure herself. The mental part of it was beyond him and it would be a learning experience for both of them.

Frustrated, needing action, Sabastian went down to the kitchen. Nickolas was still confused on what had happened between them, but after Sabastian gave him charge of her, all was forgiven and he enjoyed reporting to Sabastian every day on her progress. Nickolas liked conversing with her, even though it was in Sabastian's words.

Sabastian scanned the notebook and saw that the last three days she had asked. "*When?*" and he didn't have a reply yet. He hadn't figured out how to control himself around her and was procrastinating. It had been three weeks and he knew he couldn't keep her in there forever. She had finished every book they had handed her and even finished the self-help books. She had been working out in her room with her weights religiously and going through her self-defense routines on her own. Movies, books, and a dedication to getting strong could only go so far and he felt her frustration, but in a totally different way.

He looked down at the last note.

"I am the heaviest I've ever been and have bigger biceps than you. You have not let me train with Max, I'm going crazy, and I'm done. I can't take this anymore."

He smiled at her bicep comment, at least she still had her humor.

"Tomorrow, but don't tell her," Sabastian said to Nickolas, hoping he would be ready for her after not seeing her in the flesh for so long.

Chapter 42

Sabastian knocked at nine the next morning.

She answered the door and Sabastian forced his eyes not to look her up and down in her short dress. He stared past her shoulder coolly and said, "Miss Victoria, will you please accompany me to the round room?"

He asked, offering her his arm.

Reading his demeanor immediately, Victoria walked past him refusing to touch him and walked smoothly down the marbled hallway to the round room. If he could play it cool, so could she. On the inside however, she desperately wanted the passionate man who could not stop himself from kissing her in the garden. She sat down squarely on the couch in the round room, looking up at him as he entered behind her.

Sabastian watched her sashay ahead of him in a light dress of yellow cotton which brought out the color of her long dark golden hair and showed off her legs wonderfully. Her legs had gained some diameter to them since he had last held them in his hands at the spa. The dress hugged her body beautifully and he longed to run his hands up that dress and feel her new and very much improved body.

He focused and said, "Miss Victoria, I would like to show you a film made by Eximius. It is to elaborate on the books you've been reading about women's sensuality."

Ya, right, he thought. She had sensuality flowing from every aspect of her, it was natural and not trained. Being a trainer of women, he had seen it before but only from a small percentage of women and all of them had had lots of sexual experience. But never from someone with little knowledge of love making or none in her case.

Victoria didn't answer him but looked at the screen in front of her waiting.

He turned on the player and sat to the right of her on the other couch, wanting to watch her and not the film, but trying to be subtle about it.

She sat on the couch with her feet planted squarely on the floor, her knees together, and her hands folded in her lap.

That would change soon enough, he thought with an inner smile. He was going to enjoy watching her react to the sensual film. However, twenty minutes into the film, she hadn't moved or reacted in anyway. She was simply watching the film.

God, he thought, *she's watching it like she's a school girl trying to get a good grade. How could she just sit there like that, frozen, with no reaction whatsoever?*

Watching her, trying to figure it out, she yawned.

Sabastian suddenly snapped out of it. How could he be so stupid? Had he completely forgotten what she was? How could she start to awaken her sensuality and gain control of her body when she had never even experienced intimacy?

"Shit," he told himself, *"she only had her first kiss a few weeks ago."*

Miss Cherry had always built on the sexual experience of the girls that had come to her and a vague memory of her asking him to help him with one girl crashed into his mind.

Her name had been Rosaline and she had had sex many times, but had never experienced an orgasm. Miss Cherry had asked Sabastian to spend three days with her before she could begin the program with her. He had spent those days giving her fulfillment but she had been a frozen robot, lying in the bed and he could not build a desire for the satisfaction he gave her. Rosaline had never recovered from her bad experiences of horrible sex and had opted out of the program. But he did remember they had tried to physically awaken the girl before trying to mentally awaken her.

Sabastian snatched up the remote and turned off the TV. *Stupid,* he thought again and scowled at himself. *I'm as naive as she is,* he thought, looking over at her.

Victoria looked back at Sabastian, wondering if he had lost his mind.

"Do you have any questions so far?" he asked, trying to cover up his gross oversight.

"No," she answered clearly and calmly, but still watching him closely. "This is just like the books only in more detail and with more visuals," she stated unaffected.

"Okay then, if you are not learning anything more, will you come with me?"

She didn't move, "I have more studying to do."

"I thought you were sick of your room?" he said, pointing down the hall.

"I am…I just want to have my freedom back and to workout properly with Max and perhaps enjoy the garden some more. Plus I want to read some of these books," she said, wondering over to the financial sections of the library.

"I can only read about my psychological well-being and sex for so long. What about the history of the stock market?" she asked pulling out a thick black book.

"Fascinating," he said sarcastically, not wanting to let on that she never needed to be educated as she would never be hired by real clients.

"You said that the Eximius women have to be educated in order to do their job properly and professionally," she replied with a touch of annoyance. "Besides, I love to read and learn new things, as my school was a little less than challenging."

"I thought you said you barely past grade nine."

"That was because of attendance, not because I didn't understand the material, I love to learn," she said defensively.

Sabastian knew she was smart, much smarter than him as he could not even figure out how to say he needed to give her an orgasm? It was absurd and he wished he could turn back the clock and go back to the garden. His eyes lit up.

"Let's go for a walk," he said, suddenly grabbing her hand.

Victoria had no time to react as he pulled her to her feet. With his hand on the small of her back, he guided her through the garden door. She felt the electricity jolt through her body at his touch and tried to concentrate on the garden to keep her head clear.

The sparkle of the garden was lessened by lack of sunlight obscured by the clouds, but being outside in the garden still thrilled her. She had been shut up in her room for too long and the weeks had dragged on so much longer than before without someone to talk to. She breathed in the fresh cool air and walked away from Sabastian, leading the way into the walled paradise, letting her confusion and annoyance fade away with the scenery.

Sabastian watched her flow away from him in no hurry. Her hands grazed the water fall, then rested on a tree as she watched the butterflies flit around. She drifted as lazily as the butterflies. She had him spell bound and he no longer cared about rules. He walked close up to her determined to bring her kiss count up to four when she scowled at him and turned away deeper into the garden.

He followed behind her bewildered on how to start, he didn't want to address this like a lesson. He wanted her to want to be with him. The other girls he had worked with had known what was going on and desperately wanted to practice their skills they had read about on him, so he had to do very little. Awakening a woman was always done for him by Miss Cherry, he would have to work on her and for lack of a better word, woo her.

Sabastian cleared his throat behind her and said, "It's a butterfly garden."

Victoria watched a huge monarch butterfly sip from a flower, then fly toward Sabastian, her eyes following the pretty insect to his face.

"A lot that is planted here is for them," he watched the same butterfly fly between them. "They fly from miles to come and lay their eggs; we will have hundreds of cocoons in the garden soon."

He walked over to a certain branch, "Come here." He pointed at a branch with a cocoon attached to it, "Look."

Victoria bent down to look at the little green cocoon hanging tentatively on the branch, "What is it?"

Sabastian moved closer to her to look at the branch, "It's another monarch, there are tons here. We're in their migration path."

He was so close to her she could smell him and her heart quickened its pace, she did not want to be cold toward him or him cold with her. He was trying and she thought it was sweet.

She stood up facing him a little too close and gave a forgiving smile.

Sabastian could not resist; he took her lightly in his arms and holding her he wrapped his lips around hers slowly and sensually waiting for the melting that would come. She did not disappoint and fell slowly in his arms, letting the kiss overtake any annoyance she had with him.

Sabastian felt the change and forced himself to keep the embrace tender and soft needing her to want more when he pulled away. When he did start to pull away ever so slowly, he felt her arms tighten around him and moan when their lips parted.

"Sweet Victoria," he murmured, "go to your room and I will come for you tomorrow."

His voice was beyond husky, full of promise. He watched her eyes go wide with comprehension as she reluctantly turned away from him toward her room. He smiled after her, not moving till she was out of sight.

Sabastian walked back through the garden, and through the round room to the Summit, which was a large room between the men and the woman's manor houses. It held every manner of trinkets for every kind of sex taught in the manor. The entire room was white, the lush carpet, the walls with white wainscoting, the metal bed was all white along with the sheets, blankets, and all the furniture. The room looked like it had been covered in a blanket of rich white snow as everything in it was the same shade of pure white and so was dubbed "The Summit." There was not a single thing in the room that was not the exact shade of white from the door knob to the bed frame. It was hard to see the furniture and other objects in the room when the light was this pure white making things blend into one another.

The dressers and wardrobe held various outfits to wear. There were toys, swings, vibrators, and other implements also hidden away in the cabinets, walls, and dressers. There was a bench in the corner and a large sturdy chair. Large metal rings hung in the wall and ceiling with various attachments also all white.

The room was used for the men to teach new interns and test subjects the skills required to work at Eximius. But the Summit was mainly a practice room for the professional women who used it when their client's appetites increased or they accepted new clients with certain tastes. They used the Summit to further their skills using whichever man from the manor they needed to perfect their art.

Sabastian looked around the purity of the room and his thoughts went to the girl that awaited him. He contemplated the enormity of the task ahead, trying to control the longing that had been building steadily over the last few weeks. He realized as he got to work that he was unusually nervous and that frightened him. He had never been with a woman who was untouched and hoped he would be able to control himself. His body responded even to the simplest thought of her hair or eyes and soon, she would be naked, offering herself up to him and he shivered. His erection throbbed painfully tight in his slacks and he took a deep breath. If he couldn't control his excited anticipation just thinking about her, he would be lost as soon as she stepped into this room. Trying, once again, to convince himself she was just another girl to train, he shook off the unease he felt and started to prepare Victoria's first sexual experience, hoping to make it special for her.

Chapter 43

Victoria thought her meals were weird the next day, after a light breakfast, she was served an unusual lunch. There was an arugula salad with asparagus tips, pine nuts, almonds, strawberries, and carrots drizzled with honey. Oysters with pineapple and avocado toppings and a slice of rich chocolate cake artfully decorated in chocolates swirls. She ate all of it, loving every bite and was now soaking in the tub with one of the more sensual books wanting to learn everything she could and trying to somehow to prepare herself. It was no use; she was too nervous. Every time she flipped a page, her fingers shook. This is stupid. How can you read about sex and schedule a training session?

Her excited nervousness was driving her mad, she got out of the tub and got dressed, choosing a long white dress with little red roses embroidered in it and risqué red under garments to match. She brushed out her long hair till it flowed around her, then put it in a loose braid over her shoulder. Grabbing her book, she went out into the garden to soak up the sun. She found a hammock and with the sun beating down on her and the birds and the butterflies flying around her, she closed her eyes and tried to focus on what she had read.

It was not long before Sabastian appeared and she gaped at him. He was freshly shaven as always and wore extremely tight black jeans with a tight white shirt, his muscles rippled under the almost see-through material, he might as well have been naked. He also wore a pair of black dress shoes and a grin that anyone who saw it would know what he was thinking. Blushing deeply, his grin is what held her attention bringing out the dimples that she absolutely adored. His white teeth flashed at her and she smiled shyly back at him before lowering her gaze.

He sauntered over to her and hovered above her. "Would you care to come with me, Miss Victoria?" he asked offering her his hand.

"Umm, okay," she answered ignoring his formality. Trying not to let her shaking hands reveal her apprehension, she let him pull her to her feet off the hammock she was lying in.

He took her hand and led her back into the round room, but walked her toward a set of down ward stairs, instead of her room.

"Where are you taking me?" she asked.

"You'll see," he said mysteriously.

His secretive behavior did little to ease the tension rippling through her.

Victoria let him lead her downstairs and down a long hallway to a door with a key code on it, punching in numbers, he opened the door. She let him gently guide her inside with his large warm hand on the small of her back into a very yellow room and her mood instantly lifted slightly. The smell of the room was so invigorating, a mixture of sandalwood and jasmine filled her senses and they reminded her strongly of the massage he had given her. She guessed that the scents had a purpose other than to make the room smell nice. There was a large bed draped in the same shade of yellow and looking closer, she realized the color looked strange. She looked over at Sabastian whose color also looked off and realized that the room was not yellow only the lighting was.

"Welcome to the Summit," he said proudly.

"Umm, what's with the light?" She asked.

"There is a color physiology that we use in this room, yellow is happiness, you were nervous, so it's what I chose to give you a little pick-me-up."

He took a remote from his back pocket and the light changed, the room turned bright white.

"Wow," she said looking around, "everything blends into everything else; the furniture looks camouflaged. May I?" gesturing to the remote.

"Yes, of course," he said, handing the remote over to her.

"We can use any color to enhance feelings. If you are only feeling and not thinking, the effect can be surprising."

Sabastian reached over her and pressed a button on her remote and the room turned instantly red.

The color burned into her eyes and she felt suddenly warm, like the color was produced by heat lamps instead of just light. She also noticed her heart had sped up and a tiny ripple of a thrill lashed at her skin.

"Passion," he purred in her ear.

Worry gripped her and shaking, she quickly pressed another color and purple engulfed the room, she glanced over at him, her eye brows raised.

"Power," he said simply. "It's a favorite of the girls."

"Why?"

"It helps them control power over themselves and who they are with, the guys like it, too. It helps both of them feel they have power either over the other person or themselves."

Another button produced a light pink color.

"Sophistication," he explained. "The girls feel proud of themselves and their confidence goes up a notch or two, it helps with tricky or new skills that need to be learned."

Pushing the remote again, she was plunged into darkness until her eyes adjusted to the dark grey room.

"Ummm," Victoria muttered, trying to see the remote in the blackness of the room. She felt better when she heard his deep voice beside her.

"Black is fear of the unknown and it tends to heighten intensity. It's only used with certain sessions."

Victoria jumped when she felt his hand on her shoulder, he grazed her arm lightly all the way down to her hand and pressed a button on the remote.

She turned to face him as a rich blue light turned everything to solid water around her.

"I like this one," she said gazed at him in the light, he looked different, wider, stronger, she could see his muscles more defined and he looked powerful and dominant. It made her shudder and she wanted to place her hands on his wide chest and feel the strength of this stunning man in front of her. It also reminded her of the time they had spent in his bedroom with the blue glow of his fish tank. She blushed and her hands twitched toward him.

He moved closer to her, so that Victoria had to look up at him. "Masculinity," he whispered huskily down at her. She could smell him so close to her and it over powered the smell of the room, his after-shave mingled with the citrus and musk of him made her pleasantly dizzy.

"We also use music, scents, and even food to increase sexual arousal."

"Oh," was all she could manage to say.

"Jasmine to arouse you and sandalwood to relax you. Everything you ate today has been proven to intensify your sexual desire."

Victoria swallowed.

He reached for her hands, taking them both in his and pulled her with him. Walking backward he led her over to the far wall with a large curtain. He stopped her and slowly walked around behind her, careful not to touch as he circled like a hawk. She stood facing the wall when she felt his hands rest on her shoulders and with feather light touches trailed his fingers all the way down her arm and ever so slowly, slide the remote from her hand.

"Close your eyes," he breathed in her ear.

Panic rising and adrenaline shot up as she obeyed and suddenly her eye lids turned red. He must have switched the light to the passionate red color.

"Open, slowly," he murmured.

She slowly opened her eyes and was blinded by the harsh white light in the room.

"Purity," he purred in her ear, brushing her hair aside and kissing her neck softly.

"This is your color, and I don't want anything to obstruct your view tonight or my view of you, sweet Victoria," he breathed into her ear kissing her neck, inhaling her fragrant woman's scent. "Let the colors be true to your eyes."

She smiled and sighed, taking a deep cleansing breath, still incredibly apprehensive, but trying to control her nerves which tingled at his touch and his words.

His one hand came to rest on her shoulder and ever so slowly with his fingers barely touching her skin, he slid his arm across the top of her chest from one shoulder to the other, inches below her throat.

Victoria felt her stomach drop and a quick panic rose up that she repressed, all he had to do was raise his arm up and squeeze. It would be over in seconds and there would be nothing she could do about it. His arm wasn't tight, it gently held her across the chest and his fingers caressed the soft flesh under her arm where the fabric of her dress stopped. The fear she felt was so sudden that she had not prepared for it and somehow it heightened everything he was doing to her. She had to trust him and went back to only feeling and forced her mind to shut down, even though she was still confused by the feelings the fear had caused as it had swept over her.

She was gently being pressed into him, her back to his hard chest and she felt his warmth seeping through the fabric of her dress and tried to relax. Nervous silence filled the room and she waited for what he intended to do with her next.

She felt him shift slightly and heard a click of the remote. Suddenly, the curtain in front of her on the wall slowly parted and she saw both of them standing reflected in front of a floor to ceiling mirror. The mirror was huge and took up almost the entire wall of the room. Her eyes went instantly to his through the mirror.

Seeing him encompassing her with his possessive arm across her chest, she was thrilled and loved the protective stance he took behind her. They gazed at each other and they stood there locked for moments. She tried to turn to look at him directly but his arm tightened slightly and she was effectively held in place facing the huge mirror.

Sabastian stepped back ever so slightly and he guided her braided hair from her back placing it to drape over her shoulder. His hand then disappeared between them and she felt the zipper on the back of her dress slowly be dragged down. She could feel his fingers trail a path after the zipper lightly down her spine as it opened, making her shudder at the feel of his hot hands on her. The zipper was long and it went past her hips and stopped just short of her thighs and that is where his fingers stopped after softly brushing the curve of her butt. Looking intensely in her eyes, Sabastian smoothly pushed the dress from her shoulders, letting the material drift lazily to pool on the floor at her feet.

Why red? he thought to himself.

She was standing before him in nothing but red lace bra and panties, courtesy of the clothes provided in her room.

She was gleaming and all feminine curves gazing back at him trustingly. Gone was the thin emaciated and stringy girl. He saw her as she used to be, beautiful and strong.

Sabastian gaped at her and had to close his eyes and take a deep breath to calm his body's response, which he only fleetingly held in check.

Victoria looked at her scared body embarrassed and tried to step away from him so she could turn around to face him, but his eyes flashed open and the hand across her chest tightened again, she heard him tisk with his tongue, scolding her to keep still.

"Don't move, Vicky," he said thickly, trying to get a hold of himself.

Her eyes turned back the mirror and she could not take her eyes off the scar on her hip and stomach cursing her flaws. She looked up to Sabastian's eyes which were intently reading hers.

Grazing his finger lightly over her scar, he whispered. "Victoria, you are absolute perfection," he murmured as he stroked the pink lines on her hip and stomach until she no longer cared that they marred her body.

Victoria felt his fingers graze her skin running from her hip bone, up along her ribs, and the side of her covered breasts, then to her shoulders and down her arms. She was too tense and her nerves buzzed with either fear or excitement, she didn't know which. She watched his slow movements in the mirror, trying to relax. She raised her arms to wrap around his neck behind her and was rewarded with a soft brushing kiss on her neck. She was still shaky and stiff and thoughts of what was about to happen kept flooding her mind. He continued his feather light touches over and over watching her intently in the mirror until her body loosened and melted. Letting her mind go, she let her body take over.

Feeling her finally relax, Sabastian moved his arm off from across her chest and used both his hands to run feathered touches up and down her body, finally resting on her covered breasts cupping them over the material.

Before Victoria knew it, he had unclasped the front clip and her bra sprang open and his warm palms took over where the bra had left. Cupping each breast softly in his palms, weighing each one in turn. His fingers slowly circled the satin skin, coming closer and closer to where the skin went from cream to pink. She watched as her nipples contracted in anticipation of being touched and was fascinated. She longed for him to hold her like this forever but a pulsing had taken over deep within her. She needed him pressed into her to feel that pleasure she had felt in her bed. She lowered her hands and tried to turn around again to face him, but he tisk-ed her and she stopped and he started to pull the bra off her shoulders.

Putting her arms behind her slightly, Victoria arched her back sticking out her chest to help wiggle the bra off of her.

Sabastian froze her movement, quickly holding her hands still in that position with the bra a loose make shift tie on her arms, keeping her still, he stared at her reflection. Her arms pulled back and her chest pushed out, his captive made a very pretty picture.

"Very nice, Victoria. Look at you. Beautiful," he said as he held her there, staring at her until she blushed and lowered her eyes. He then let the bra join her dress and she was able to lean back and relax into his chest again.

He saw her breasts were round and firm and thrust up proudly, much bigger than her thin frame would suggest. Sabastian's eyes gazed at her full breasts and noticed they had swollen slightly and she had started to push them out to meet his touches when he resumed his strokes. He saw her soft pink lips matched the color of her perk nipples and wondered what the coloring of her sex would be in comparison. Her nipples hardened before his eyes and he couldn't wait to taste the shell pink nipples and roll them in his mouth.

Watching her through the mirror intensely, his hands made their way from the soft skin on the side of her breasts all the way down to her hips going down her legs, hooking her panties in his thumbs as he went. His hands continued down until they were past her knees letting the delicate lace material join the rest of her garments. Relived of her clothes, she felt exposed but her nervousness had been replaced by something overwhelmingly pleasant.

If only you knew how badly I need you, he thought, but he knew his own need would have to wait.

Victoria took a short breath in as his long fingers splay out, touching as much of her skin as possible as they went from the back of her knees around to the inside of her thighs and up toward her sensitive mons. His hands were so warm when they reached close to her sex, she tensed and shivered. They passed lightly over her groin, grazing her stomach, then he wrapped his arms tight across her ribs in a bear hug causing her breasts to thrust skyward.

Sabastian could not keep his gaze from her, either to watch the reaction in her eyes or to see her body react with his touches. God, she was stunning, the last few weeks had added a softness to her and now she had more of a woman's contour on her hips and breasts. Her breasts were larger than he thought possible and he silently praised Nickolas for his fantastic cooking that had made her back into a woman with curves now so proudly displayed. She had strong muscles that were coated in a light creamy layer of silken skin that he ached to touch all over. He wanted to take his time with her and had to muster all his will power not to have her underneath him, screaming his name, and clawing at his back. He knew his time would come, for now, it was all about teaching and awakening her.

"My god, Vicky, I want you so bad, I want you under me, thrashing and clawing," he said lustily in her ear. "I want to hear you scream my name while I make you mine."

He trailed a row of sweet kisses along her shoulders and neck as he spoke, "I want to consume you, kiss you all over till you are begging for release."

His words made her body tingle and she gasped at his mouth came down to her skin. In her nervousness she realized, she wanted the same thing. To be under him while he crushed her body beneath his while kissing her all over.

Victoria watch his head bend to kiss her again, she moaned and tilted her chin to give him better access, closing her eyes. He stopped immediately and gave that same almost inaudible tisk-ing sound with his tongue close to her ear. Her eyes popped open and she saw him looking at her expectant through the mirror. As soon as their eyes met, he continued his kisses up toward her neck.

So, she thought, *the mirror has a purpose.*

She realized he wanted her to watch him. He wanted her to see everything he did to her and she had to concentrate on keeping her eyes open and not to close them in pleasure. Their height difference was substantial, and he had to bend down low to kiss her. His lips slowly made their way to her lower jaw and she turned toward him offering her mouth to him. He drew back slightly, watching her eyes and stilled. She looked hard into his eyes, trying to read his thoughts. She tilted her head up to him more and her lips parted and her breath came out heavy. Her hand reached up around the back of his neck and pulled him toward her. He resisted and a slight smile peaked his lips.

"Damn it," she yelled in her head, "kiss me!"

She pulled at him again and lifted herself onto her tiptoes reaching out for him. A slight frown crossed her face and his eyes smiled down at her, waiting.

What was he waiting for? she sighed and pulled harder and finally her thoughts reached her lips. "Please, Sabastian, kiss me," she pleaded.

Sabastian's grin disappeared into a look of pure longing and he slowly lowered his lips to hers, holding her eyes with his.

Victoria melted into the kiss, achingly slow and gentle, she parted her mouth as he ran his tongue around her lips, kissing first her bottom, then upper lip, then kissing her fully again. She wanted more, she pushed, pressing her lips into his, and testing the feel of her tongue in his mouth. When she pushed for more, he returned the pressure and deepened the kiss only slightly. That drove her on and she strengthened her mouth turning into him and pressing her bare breasts against his chest. She closed her eyes and moaned and he stopped pulling back looking down at her.

"You are amazingly beautiful, sweet Vicky," he murmured in her ear with awe in his voice.

Reopening her eyes, she wasted no time and kissed him deeply, keeping her eyes locked on his. The intensity increases as he took her lower lip into his mouth and sucked firmly, then nip it sharply before softening the kiss and her head started to swim, her body swaying dangerously. He must have felt her legs lose control because his arms wrapped around her back and curl around the sides of her waist and she no longer needed to stretch up to meet his lips, as she was lifted gracefully off her feet. Her eyes locked on his, knowing loss of eye contact meant he would stop. She felt him move with her until her legs were pushed into the plush bed.

Sabastian followed her down into the bed and pressed her with his body, sinking in the deep goose down feathers of the white duvet. He released her and gazed at her sprawled on the bed, her braided hair draped across her chest and along her stomach. How long had he waited to see her like this, naked sprawled before him, wanting him, and in the beginning, awareness of her female sexuality?

She gazed up at him with hooded eyes that sparkled and smiled and he couldn't help but smile back at her wickedly. She stretched before him, cat like and arched her back slightly toward him. Running her hands down her hips, then stretching them above her head, she closed her eyes and breathed deep, causing her chest to raise and fall from deep within the lush bed coverings. Her skin was pale against the white background and her bright purple eyes and her rich blonde hair popped in contrast and Sabastian focused on the color to distract his body. She was too pale and needed more sun on her body and he imagined her just like this, naked, sprawled out in the garden and bronzing in the sun.

Sabastian knew that this was so different than any other women he had trained or even been with in bed. Most of the other women knew what they wanted and took it, never needed to be aroused, not really, and if they did, it was more direct. There was little to no foreplay, no soft caresses, no sweet kisses, no love making which he realized that was what he was doing to this utterly gorgeous girl. He never knew, as a man, he would enjoy doing those things to a woman, taking the time to make her need him, want him, crave him. Just touching her to see her react to his hands, feeling her respond to his kisses and his words made him have to summon his will. He had to remember where

214

he was and what he was doing, if he messed this up, she would not be allowed to stay. Trying to get his head back in the game he focused on being professional and tried to hold his own needs and passions back, apart from her.

Sabastian grabbed the edges of his T-shirt and pulled it over his head, watching her eyes the whole time and hated the split second when she was not in his sight. He saw her eyes dilate ever so slightly and a shy smile touched the corner of her full pink lips.

Victoria craved to touch him, to place her hands on his chest and to feel the hard square muscles on his back. His lithe body, so dark compared to hers, so strong made her blood thrill that this magnificent man was here with her. Her eyes grew heavy as he knelt on the bed beside her and she reached out for him.

He leaned in closer, just enough for her to graze her fingers along his chest. She couldn't be silent, she had to voice what she wanted, guessing this was part of what men needed. She was more direct, "Lay with me and kiss me."

He immediately lay on top of her holding his weight off slightly with his arms and softly kissed her again and she melted under him. She wanted more. She pulled her lips away and the desperate need in her voice was clear, "Kiss me!"

He dropped onto her, crushing her beneath him, and kissed her hard, demanding, and taking what he wanted from her. Biting her full lips, and sucking her tongue through his teeth. His kisses were uncontrolled, passionate and her body reacted instantaneously. She arched her body into his and her hands ran through his hair pulling her to him, not letting him go until she was breathless and the room spun around her. Her hands went to his back and she lifted herself into him trying to get him to repeat what he had done in his bedroom. His shirt was gone but his jeans were still fastened and when he did push into her teasingly, she groaned at the hardness of him, but frustrated. She wanted to feel him, not his jeans and reached down for him.

Sabastian's need was building to a frenzy and she had barely touched him. He was throbbing and hard and the only thing that restrained him was the fact that his jeans were held securely in place keeping him from feeling her softness. He was at a total loss; he had no intention of fulfilling his need for her now. She had not even begun to truly experience what she so desperately wanted. She still had no idea what she longed for so badly, her body knew, but she didn't, no matter how many books she had read. He couldn't be greedy, he knew that, but he was too close to embarrassing himself, like he was an untried teenager.

The man in him screamed, he wanted to make love to her just to feel her wrapped around him, not teach her anything. He realized he was trapped; he could not prevent her from touching him. Any gesture of stopping her from doing anything in the beginning might cause her to become reserved. She would be afraid to try anything with a man if he stopped her from exploring and taking risks, especially this first time. If she reached for him and he stopped her hand, she would feel rejected, and would not initiate any control over sex in bed, perhaps becoming withdrawn. She was far from impassive as she was reacting to his every touch with wonton abandon and he loved that about her. However, he could not let her touch him, he would be finished in seconds.

She reached for his denim covered pelvis and snagged the top of his jeans. Not able to stop her, he willed himself to calm down and breathed deep and focused on her deep lavender eyes. She undid the top button and pulled down his zipper. He took over from there; afraid any touch from her would bring him to climax and would scare her. He undid his jeans, standing before her while she watched, staying focused on her eyes. With tremendous discipline, he lowered his pants and stood in front of her in tight black boxer briefs, his covered erection frantically straining toward her.

Victoria's eyes widened and her mouth went dry at the sight of him as he stood before her proud and breathtaking. Her eyes focused on the part of his body incased in the black cotton briefs and she longed for a look. Realizing she was staring at his most intimate of male parts, she looked away and lowered her lashes. She heard the familiar tisk of his tongue scolding her and she looked up into his eyes again. He was teaching her to watch, look her fill and to never be shy or reserved. She liked that he was showing her there was nothing to be embarrassed about and to have her fill in every way.

Emboldened, she stood up on the bed finally being able to see eye to eye with this gorgeous man and wrapped her arms around his neck pulling him into an embrace and rubbing her hips wonderfully against him. She felt her perk nipples brush through his soft chest hair and she leaned in to kiss him, wrapping her hands in his hair and feeling his hardness throb into her burning flesh. She loved the feeling of his skin on hers with nothing to separate them. She reached for his boxers and he immediately backed away.

Not wanting her to feel she did something wrong, he explained.

"Vicky," he whispered. "I want you to do whatever you want with me, you have to be free and unrestricted anytime you are with a man, but you have me on the edge of reason and I don't want to hurt you. Wait and you will have all of me with no restrictions. You are a special case and this is all about you and I cannot be greedy," he said thickly.

Victoria nodded slowly understanding. "Okay," she whispered.

He came to her gradually and she smiled, she only needed him to lay with her like when they were in his bed and to move with her again. She let him press her into the bed under him and he dipped his head to kiss her again but softly. She opened her lips and invited him in, running her hands through his hair and forcing him to deepen his kisses. As he kissed her, she felt his hand caress her leg all the way up to her breast. Placing his palm on top of her nipple, he slowly started to roll her nipple in tight circles in the middle of his palm.

"Oh, mmmm," she purred out, fascinated with the new sweet feeling of her tingling nipple under his palm. She arched her breast into his palm and felt her nipple harden tighter under his ministrations.

The sensation was so wonderful she wanted more, he cupped her other breast in his overly large warm hand and repeated palming her nipple in a circle, first one way then the other.

She arched again, "Ah, mmmmm, mmmm," her mouth opening in her moans for him to kiss. He plunged his tongue into her mouth and stole her cries of pleasure and his hands tightened around her breast and pinched her nipples lightly as she bowed into his hands.

He slowed his kisses. Letting her settle, and cupped her sensitive breasts in his palms delicately. Trailing kisses over her neck, his mouth moved closer to where his hands still lay on her chest and she raised her head to watch him lick and suck the top of her cleavage. His lips moved closer and closer to her tight pink peaks and she was thrilled at the indescribable feeling he was rising in her. All her nerve endings were on edge focused on him and where he left a cool trail of moisture on her skin. She shivered in sweet anticipation.

His lips parted taking her entire areola in his mouth and swirling his tongue around the tip.

"Oh, ahh, mmmmm," she cried out as she pushed her chest into him as he rolled her tender nipples. She felt lightning strikes flash down her belly and deep into her muscles between her legs, making them pulse and throb and her hips lifted in the air disappointed; there was nothing to push against. She moaned as he repeated the ritual with the other breast and his hand went to her first breast and rolled the wet nipple between his fingers pulling, then palming the nipple in circles while his tongue worked the virgin breast. She felt him graze her nipple with his teeth over and over again and the pulsing increased as she moaned.

"Mmmmm, ah, Sabastian," she groaned, straining into his mouth.

He stopped and straddled her with his knees at her hips sitting lightly on her legs, she was trapped and couldn't move and what was worse, she could not even push into him in this position. He was grinning down at her, her cheeks flamed red from the embarrassment at her reaction and she lowered her eyes to the side, away from his. He tisk-ed her again and she looked up at him, her eyes a rich blue, purple mixture, darkening with longing.

His hands cupped each breast and pulled them together, touching the nipples to each other and with a look of hunger, he dipped his head and took both nipples in his mouth.

"Mmmmm, Ah, Sabastian, mmmmmm," she cried impulsively, yanking on his hair with both hands, before throwing her hands out to her sides to steady herself, grabbing fists full of fabric.

Electricity shot down her belly in an even tempo, her hips tried to raise up of their own accord but were locked in place. His mouth and tongue swirled, pulled, pushed, and nipped at her tender tips until she was breathless, bucking against him and squirming trying to move. She felt her sex tighten, squeeze and release over and over again and the pulsing was in tandem with his tongue on her hardened nipples.

"Mmmm, ah, ah, ohhhh," she moaned beneath his tongue as the lightning hit her hard in a spot unexplored. Trying to figure out the connection between where his tongue played and her sex, she gasped.

He released her and she was able to breathe again, he kissed her deeply on the lips hard and fast before giving each nipple a light kiss that made her jerk toward him. He slowly worked his lips down her belly, working from one scar to the next cherishing her. Moving further and further down her body, Victoria eyes widened, realizing his goal.

No, she thought, *he couldn't.*

She couldn't allow him to kiss her there, it seemed indecent, but she felt her body excite at the idea of his mouth on her woman's center. She had read about it multiple times and like a naive fool, she thought it was only something she would read in a book.

Her legs tensed and tightened together. He raised his head to look at her worried expression and with a slight grin, he dipped his head down.

Sabastian could ask or even command her to open for him and to let him pleasure her, but knew that if she did it on her own, she would feel in control. He wanted her to be totally in control and to do anything with him but on her own terms. Since he needed to settle his own body down from her strong responses as he had molded her breasts to his mouth, he wanted to take as much time as either of them needed.

Victoria felt his lips brush her hips, then go across her belly and back again, infinitesimally moving lower and lower until his lips were lightly kissing butterfly like touches on her mons. She was so sensitive there and she recoiled like she was being tickled, but he stayed there kissing softly getting her used to the sensation.

Shooting his tongue out in little strokes across her mons making her skin wet, he then blew softly on the sensitive skin drying it with his warm breath as she purred and moaned. He suddenly lowered his head half way to her knees and dug his tongue hard and strong down in between her thighs and licked up until he was at the top of her mound.

At one point during that movement, there was a spot that felt like a jolt of electricity that made her jump. She had no control of it and the feeling was nothing like she had ever felt before, like an electric pleasure shock that her body responded to without her. He then blew warm air over the wet area he had just made and she relaxed her tight legs open. He surprised her by pushing her legs back together and with a broad strong stroke of his tongue, he licked from six inches down between her legs all the way up again and she felt the little shock in that one spot, this time though, her muscles tightened in anticipation and her hips arched into his mouth. He kept her captive, holding her legs tightly together as he repeated the motion. Moving at a snail's pace over and over again and the longing of him touching that tiny spot below her mons grew each time till she was panting with an unknown need.

"Ah," she moaned, arching then relaxing over and over as he repeated the delicious strokes with his tongue.

Over and over again, she felt the shock followed by the throb that would pulse her muscles deep within her belly that would continue until he shocked her clitoris again.

Finally, he stopped his strong broad, cat like licks of her pulsing mons and released the grip on her legs. With the greatest of pleasure, she parted her legs wantonly to his mouth. She felt hot breath on her and realized she was dripping wet all over her legs and on the bed and she knew it wasn't from his mouth. She was about to let the embarrassment overcome her and turn away from him, when he paused and said, "God, Vicky, you are so ready for me, you are so wet. I have waited a long time to taste you."

He lowered his mouth to her soaking center and sucked greedily at the most intimate part of her.

"Ohhhhhhhh, awwwwww!" she cried, bending into his mouth, giving everything to him and letting him take what he wanted. She was shocked at her body's response, how could he put his mouth there and oh, the sensation. It was nothing like she had ever felt before and it made her body thrash. His whole mouth consumed her, took every inch of her sex while his tongue darted all around her soft flesh. The feel of his tongue on her, thrilled her and she pushed hard, trying to take more of him in her. He was drinking from her, licking and lapping at her and she cried out again.

"Mmmmm, yes, ahhhhh!" he captured her hips in his hands and held her down, dipping the long point of his tongue into her soft sex lips, he then brooded his tongue as he lifted his mouth her up to her clitoris.

"Ahh," she cried grabbing at the sheets, thrashing. He dipped and licked up over and over and she felt the pulsing become a strong building, she was climbing higher and higher, her muscles tightening with every pulse, every step up, throbbing harder and stronger. A sweet ache was building and she desperately strained into his skilled mouth.

Sabastian suddenly stopped and she almost cried out. He raised his head to look at her and she looked into his eyes for several rapid heartbeats before he disappeared again between her quivering legs. This time, when he put his mouth on her, his tongue swirled and swirled in circles over the tiny collection of needy nerve endings. He imprisoned her hips as she thrust into his mouth, he dipped harder, deeper with his tongue and moved faster. She rose higher and higher her muscles tightening, her body posed on the edge of something glorious. It almost felt like a sharp pain but felt so sensational that she thrust

220

into his mouth harder, she was almost to her breaking point, he circled her fabulously faster and harder, his tongue dancing with her hips.

There was a single beat of her speeding heart where everything froze in time, just one beat where every cell of her being was focused on that one tiny part of her that controlled her entire body that his tongue licked so expertly.

Then she was suddenly thrown over the edge, shattering into a million tiny pieces. Her body bowing so violently into his mouth as the shockwaves of extreme pleasure thundered through her. She was screaming, convulsing, reaching down with fists full of his hair in her hands in total abandon shuddered into his mouth while he sucked at her center. Her body had lost all control and she lasciviously welcomed the hot ecstasy his tongue had brought her to. She floated to the ground riding his devious mouth through wave after wave of convulsions claiming her body, gasping.

"Oh my God, Sabastian, yes, mmmm, ah, mmm," she moaned as she threw her head back giving everything to him.

Absolutely in awe of what her body could experience with just his lips on her, she moaned and finally collapsed from the shivering sensations still coursing through her body. She now knew why the act of sex drove people to madness. The pleasure was so over powering and all-consuming it made her whole body tense, thrill, then relax with full-blown satisfaction.

Sabastian could not believe the power of her orgasm, it was so passionate, so thrilling. When he had finally let her open for him, she did so willingly and he had to look his fill before tasting her again. She was dripping and her shell pink folds were swollen, open wide for him, and glistening. When he had first made contact and had only started to part into her sweetened layers with his tongue, the taste and smell of her sex made him throb so frantically he had to jerk his hips off the bed. Her honeyed layers were the strongest aphrodisiac he needed. Not needing special food, smells, or light to send him into lust, all he needed was her squirming under him.

He had to be careful though, as his tongue had brushed her virginity so close and he needed to make sure he did not break the evidence of her innocence yet. He was careful not to probe too deeply with his tongue and was thrilled that she was a true virgin and he was tasting the very first orgasmic experience. He knew it would not be the only first he would experience with her tonight.

The look of her in the throes of her passion and his name on her lips almost made him lose his iron control. He was throbbing painfully; he was engorged and purple with need and was already sore. She was still moaning, rubbing her body back and forth on the bed, still riding the waves of pleasure. He lapped at her, taking all of her juices, drinking her in and sucked until she had started to tremble beneath his mouth. He licked his lips, then came up beside her and kissed her deeply; he wanted to taste her mouth with the waves of passion still riding her body and feel her moans on his lips.

Victoria's eyes flew open when she felt his lips on hers, and she moaned again this time consciously putting effort into the cries, letting him know that she loved what he had done to her. Stretching her neck to deepen the kiss, she could taste herself creamy on her tongue. When he pulled away, she licked the corners of her lips and he captured her mouth once more, tasting her sex together.

"Mmmm," she moaned again, looking into his eyes with hooded lids. She arched and stretched reaching her arms up high and rising her back off the ground letting all her muscles tense then relax at once slumping deep within the now too hot bed, eyes closed, satisfied.

She felt him disappear briefly before she felt his large warm hands on her body and the smell of almonds engulf her. He started on the inside of her thighs and with long firm strokes, his fingers spread wide slowly blending the warm oil into her skin. His hands moved upward and did not stop until they had reached the soft inside flesh of her elbows. His hands left her and started again, the inside of her thighs, outside of her hips, up her rib cage, brushing the soft skin on the side of her breasts and stopping at the inside of her elbow. He was methodical, slow and strong and she stretched in his hands every time they ran that delicious path up her body.

She was cat like in the after effect of her orgasm and he watched her relax still trying to calm himself down. But feeling her beneath his hands with the oils making her slick and shiny was not helping. He stroked her until her stretching subsided and she finally went weak drained of energy.

He stopped and came up to lay beside her, his head in his hand to watch her and she turned to him and smiled shyly.

"Mmmmm, I can see the benefits to a job like this," she whispered wickedly.

His thoughts turned dark for an instant, but he pushed them away and smiled, "Yes, now that you know what all the fuss is about, I get to teach you how to control that feeling."

"Sounds like a very fun lesson to learn," she said, quietly her hand coming up to stroke his chest.

He was wound so tight he jumped at her touch and she frowned. Realizing what had just happened, she looked down at him and saw him straining against his boxers.

"Oh, umm are you okay?" She asked.

"I'll be fine," he swallowed. "I was not expecting to react that strongly to you. You're a force to be reckoned with, Victoria," he said lustily rolling her name on his lips, smiling.

"We didn't have sex," she said bewildered.

He paused, then in exaggerated surprised, "What! We didn't?"

His face in utter bewilderment.

Victoria laughed and hit his chest.

"I thought you were supposed to be the sex expert and you didn't even jump me like promised," she giggled.

"I never promised to jump you, but if that's what you want," Sabastian leapt to his hands and knees over her, looking down into her eyes and paused.

Victoria looked shocked and tensed as he bent down and kissed her lightly on the lips. He then smacked the side of her hip and said, "Roll over."

Victoria didn't think that this is how it would happen, he was going to take her from behind, it didn't feel right and she was again apprehensive as she slowly turned over, wary, and froze.

She felt him leave and come back within a few seconds and then felt his warm hands with fresh oil start at the bottom of her calves and in strong small circles worked their way up her thighs, her bottom, her back, and finally her shoulders. Victoria sighed and relaxed into his hands, feeling worshipped she lay her head down on the bed watching him in the mirror on the wall. She had forgotten it was there and was glad it was so close to the bed as she wanted to look her fill. A few times he looked back at her and winked or smiled and she smiled and closed her eyes content. For the first twenty minutes, she enjoyed his strong hands on her. Loving the way he kneaded her muscles but soon she felt his hands brush the sides of her breasts and he was lengthening the time he spent kneading her bottom. He started to put more pressure into her behind with his palms, pushing her in to the bed.

Victoria wanted to relax but her body had other ideas as she slowly started to feel a sweet throb begin very lightly deep in her belly. She tried to thrust her hips into the bed covering as his hand worked her butt but it was too soft, there was no resistance and her frustration started to build. She groaned in dissatisfaction.

She heard him tisk his tongue at her and she looked into the mirror to watch him push into her backside again and again. She ground her hips into the bed trying to show him she needed more. He was watching her through the mirror pointedly, like he was waiting for something. A light bulb went off in her head.

"More," she said and Sabastian smirked as he quickly reached under her hips and flipped her over before placing his palm on her pubic mound. His fingers laced in the soft triangle of her pubic hair and started playing gently in the soft, warm wetness of her outer folds.

She gasped and groaned at the new sensation as she writhed into his palm. "Mmmmm, ahhh."

With every thrust Sabastian pushed back into wet lips with his fingers, pushing her to a rhythm that made her squirm deliciously.

Her body had started to climb again and she thrust faster, trying to speed up his palm, but he suddenly slowed the rhythm and her frustration started building more than her fluttering sex. He grazed his fingers into her pouting labia and brought them to her lips and offering them to her. She saw his eyes darkened emerald green as she opened her lips to take the offering, licking and sucking at his fingers.

She pulled away from his hand and gazed at him with long lashes, needing to be kissed. Reading her body language, Sabastian leaned down over her and kissed her roughly, tasting her once again, loving the mingled flavor. He repeated the action twice more. Victoria's hips shooting up into his hand each time, then sucking the cream and kissing him deeply as tendrils of pleasure flowed through her.

Sabastian groaned each time he tasted her on her own lips and he had to stop, he was too close to the edge again. He needed to distract himself so reaching for her braid draped over her shoulder, he slid the white hair tie off and slowly undid her long, dark blonde hair. He draped it around her body on the bed until he had made an erotic picture, framing the wild naked female displayed before him.

"Sabastian," she smiled and reached for him and tried to pull him down on her, but he quickly got off the bed and watching her face fiercely, he hooked his thumbs in his boxers and slowly pulled them off of his hips.

Victoria's eyes, round and wide, dilated in shock, she couldn't believe something so large could enter her body.

How could this be possible? she thought.

"It's okay," he said soothingly seeing her fear to his nakedness.

"Your body will make room and open for me, you'll be able to take me all in," he said reading her worried expression.

"Your body will mold to mine," he said it like he was trying to convinced himself as well as her. She still hadn't put on enough weight to satisfy him but her overabundance of passionate lust let him know that she was more than ready for him.

Victoria saw Sabastian standing there naked, so sure of his body and his confidence, he inspired her own. She was almost scared, but her awe pushed that feeling away and she longed to touch him. His long shaft, curved slightly up and had a large mushroom head. His full length was a deep red color and the tip of the head almost purple, gleamed with a clear pearl liquid. It looked so hard but soft at the same time, she yearned to feel it under her fingertips.

Victoria moved to the edge of the bed, trying to get closer, her eyes glued on him and was disappointed when he stepped back from her. She frowned and looked up at him. He looked worriedly at her and she was confused.

"Come any closer and I'll be done," he warned, his voice hoarse with lust.

Looking up into his eyes, she stood up on the bed and pulled him toward her and kissed him so deeply, expressing how much she wanted him. Putting all of her weight into his neck, she pulled him back down on the bed with her.

Sabastian knew little restraint, but mustered everything he had not to slam into her. He slowly placed a kiss on her lips, on each of her nipples and then slowly parted her swollen sex with his tongue, loving the taste of her as she pushed delicately into his mouth.

"Ahh, ahh, mmm, uh, uh," she cried every time his lips touched her. But like before his movements were too slow and teasing. The mounting frustration was too much and she finally cried out, "Please, more!"

He leaped up to her mouth, bringing her woman's cream to her mouth and felt her hips thrust upward and he crushed her with his weight and almost lost all control with his marble erection throbbing against her.

Victoria ground into him feeling the heat of his shaft so close to her sex. He lowered and positioned himself in the right place for her to push her hips into his, feeling, for the first time, the searing heat of his hard length against her sweet wet folds. Her sex seemed to wrap themselves around him and cover him erotically in a kiss. He stilled and made her focus on his eyes before he moved slowly up and down the slickness of her. He stopped right when his ridge caught her clitoris and move back up making sure to be slow. He had never been this aroused and an air of electric eroticism struck him every time he heard her groan under him begging for more. He stroked her up and down, moving his shaft over her again and again, making her writhe and thrust into him.

"Aahh," she cried and she pushed urging him on.

Wave after wave of intense need gripped her and Victoria moved her body with his, the moist flesh between them hot. She was climbing with heightened sensuality that gripped her body so intensely she was intoxicated.

Victoria felt him slow and almost cried out at the injustice of it. She lifted her head to watch him as he took his erection in his hand and positioned the soft tip of it over top of her aching clitoris and slowly started grazed her up and down not taking himself from her. Moving in it up and down and in tiny little circles, over and over again as she climbed and reached and arched and thrust, needing more of him. She could feel how close to the plummet she was and felt her body tense gloriously about to be released from this sweet torture when he suddenly left her.

Her eyes flew open to look at where he had gone, in shock that the moment she was about to feel the breathtaking explosion again, he had stopped all contact. She looked up into his eyes as her body pulsed wanting. He was watching her, his eyes ablaze with lust and a ferocity she had never seen in him before, sweat gleaming on his hard muscled flesh. She stared in wonder and knew her own eyes held that same urgent look.

"Yes, please, Sabastian," she begged, almost crying. "Please!"

The ache behind her swollen clit was unbearable and her body started to slowly relax from the intense tightening that had started in preparation of her fulfillment. Her hips lowered back down after several seconds of watching and waiting for him to continue in silence. She took a deep breath and willed her body to relax and her heart to stop its frantic beating. She was about to ask if she had done something wrong when she saw his eyes darken with pure need as he plunged into her softness hard and fast, penetrating her tight sex.

"Yi!" Victoria yelped, eyes bulging her hands clenched into fists.

Not expecting the brutal assault and the pain that came with it, there had been a split-second pressure then a pop as he tore into her virginity. She lay completely still, feeling him inside her and was in wonder. It was the quickness of his invasion that had shocked her, the pain recessed fast and was slight compared to the feel of him throbbing inside her. She felt her body stretched taut to accommodate him and her dripping sheath hugged him powerfully. She focused on him and could feel a deep strong heart beat deep within her and she thrilled at the sensation.

"Vicky, are you okay?" he asked breathlessly, looking down at her.

She nodded hesitantly and reveled in the glorious feeling of his body joined with hers.

He didn't move for what seemed like a life time and she felt herself pulse around him; needing the satisfaction he had brought her so close to moments before. She pulled in on his sex tentatively, willing him to move and squeezed newly discovered muscles and saw him close his eyes in ecstasy. She smiled inwardly and squeezed around him again and heard him groan. She pulsed feeling his length inside her and longed for more.

"Victoria, for Christ's sake, stop it, I don't want to hurt you," he growled thickly.

Sabastian had to hold onto every fiber of his being not to hurt her further, she was so tight and the only reason he had gotten this far is because he had sunk into her hard and fast. The fact that she was dripping wet and had them wrapped in the silken moisture also helped him enter her. He wanted to hold her down and finish what he had started with her. But waiting for her body to relax before he had entered her was the first step. He had so much more to go and had to wait. But she was tightening herself around him and he had to bite his lip to distract himself. He had taken her virginity and needed to do the rest of this right. The fact that she had taken him in pain and was still craving movement, made him admire her that much more.

Victoria gazed up at him with heighten sensuality, desire written plainly on her face and squirmed beneath him.

227

Why wasn't he moving? she thought.

"Sabastian?" She croaked at him huskily, her eyes questioning him.

His look of controlled need, turned to anguish as he pulled out of her a fraction and plunged deeper, hard, and violent and stilled, waiting for her to get used to the sensation and relax.

Victoria shrieked again, and realized he had pushed into her body further. He had not entered her all the way the first time. The fullness she had felt before doubled and her sex felt tight to bursting and the pulsing she felt, thickened. The pain that had come with his thrust was overwhelmed by the friction she felt as her body tightened, she felt a quick climb toward ecstasy that made her shudder.

Sabastian watched her, keeping very still, breathing hard and waited for her to adjust to his size knowing he still had not entered all the way. He tried to grind in a little deeper but she was constricting around him so tightly that moving was impossible and he knew he had to repeat his last action, hopefully, only one more time. He wanted to avoid thrusting into her so roughly, knowing each time he did he stretched her more and she experienced pain. As much as he wanted to avoid that, he knew this was best done in one session, so there would only be pain the first time and not for several times after. He mastered himself and waited for her to relax enough to let him move. He felt her tighten even more around his shaft and squeezing him pleasurably and he had to hold himself back from slamming into her over and over again. He felt her relax and instead of pulling out to prepare for another assault; he grabbed her by the shoulders and jammed himself to the hilt and closed his eyes in pure ecstasy as her sheath compacted around his full length triumphantly.

Victoria's gasped, her eyes closing tightly and held her breath as the indescribable sensations flowed through her sex. He was so big, so thick, she thought she was stretched to the limit the first time he had entered her. The pain was a glorious price to pay for each slick movement, however. If it hurt every time, he forced his way into her body she would welcome it if it meant she would feel him slide far inside her again and again. He had pushed until she was enclosed around him and the fullness she felt was all consuming. She could feel the tight curls of pubic hair surrounding his sex pressed into her own and loved the warmth and the weight on him centered on her most sensitive spot. She was so tight and tense, she jumped when he spoke.

"Breath, Victoria, just breath," Sabastian whispered to her with a look of self-loathing on his face.

Victoria opened her eyes as she felt his sweet gentle touch of the back of his hand brush the hair from her face. Looking up at him and seeing his concerned expression for her, she forced herself to breathe. She slowly relaxed her body and she let his fullness overwhelm her, completely opening for him, her legs going slack by her sides. She could feel a deep throbbing pulse of him or her, or both of them deep within her belly and she sighed. The pain of being stretched to her limit lessened with her relaxing and she could feel the pounding of him buried in her and was amazed that her sex started to pull at him again, still not satisfied.

She lay under him looking into his eyes and she felt their heartbeats mingle together both needing satisfaction, but still he waited for her and she knew the restraint he had and the iron control he was summoning would not last forever.

"Please, Vicky, are you okay?" he asked, concerned.

Victoria nodded as she felt her body mold around his perfectly. She needed more and welcomed any pain if only he would move again. She felt him angled his hips so he would be sliding into her from above and felt her body squeeze, tensing as he moved.

"Victoria, are you sure? Do you want me to stop?" Sabastian asked, noticing when she tensed.

"No," she arched slightly trying to feel more of him. "I'm fine, please, it's okay."

He slid slowly out of her, inch by inch, so slowly, watching her face. He was shuddering at the incredible tightness of her. The crown of him was in her soft entrance and he prepared to push his smooth head wonderfully back into her when he saw her tense again.

"Vicky, let me in," he gently commanded, trying to control himself.

Victoria looked up into his eyes, trusting completely and relaxed her body.

Sabastian never knew he held that kind of restraint as he nailed down his lust and propelled his way slowly back into her. Barely able to gain entrance because of the hold she had on him, he knew it was for the best as her grip forced him to move gradually. He pulled out of her again and dug his way back into her at a snail's pace that both of them could handle.

"Aaaauuuuugh, Vicky," he growled, closing his eyes at the sensation, shuddering hard, his arms shaking and his teeth clenched. He continued the pace, pulling so slowly out, feeling her tightened as he moved within her. Having to use much of his strength to keep her still and keep a hold of himself at same time was insane, she was so wet and so tight, he wanted to scream.

Victoria was shocked that her body welcomed him despite her fears, but she trusted him and his slow movements had lessened any previous pain. Discomfort receding, she felt the glorious movement of his shaft gliding its way in and out of her. The pain was increasing the pleasure somehow and it engulfed her entire body inside and out. She squirmed and push into him fighting his hands that held her hips in place needing more.

"Ohhhh," she moaned and she tentatively tested her body and tried to follow him with her hips.

She felt him clamp his hands down hard gripping her hips and locked her in place.

"Stay still," he demanded harshly as he pushed into her again slowly, feeling her body grip him tightly every inch along the way.

He was still trying to restrain himself and when she moved with him, he had to clamp down hard to keep his body in check.

"Aughhh," Sabastian moaned, the feeling was maddening. It was more than he had ever felt in his life and the sensations flooding though his body were so astonishing. He trembled, trying desperately to keep the motion as slow as possible to introduce her body to the feeling of him. He was almost undone so many times that he ground his teeth determined to set a sluggish pace and cursed himself for a fool thinking he could master this girl beneath him moaning and pushing him for more.

"You are so wonderfully tight, Vicky. You feel exquisite wrapped around me," he moaned into her ear.

Victoria felt her sheath convulse around him at his words.

"Mmmmmm, ahhhh," she cried unable to articulate any words. She egged him on, squirming and arching herself toward his shaft, desperately needing the satisfaction her body craved.

"Fuck, Victoria. You can't move," he said tightly between clenched teeth.

Victoria saw his raw need and tried to settle her own body down but he was making her senseless with need and only his hands immobilize her hip made her still under him. She loved the force he put on her body and the fact that he was also barely in control of himself.

"Mmmm, yes, ahhhh, mmmmm, please," she begged him again.

She moaned at every down thrust watching him.

"Sabastian, please!" she cried, her body rampant as it bowed into his.

Sabastian felt with every push toward him Victoria fought him and grew steadily bolder and he knew she had surpassed any pain and was now building toward the tremendous sensation he knew would rack her body soon. He wanted to ensure that she was ready. Her anxiety was completely gone and she was thrusting hard toward him taking every inch of and wanting more. Her words gave him the reassurance she was ready for him.

Victoria felt him release her hips and move his hands behind her knees to spread her legs wide and increase the tempo. She blissfully matched his accelerated pace, throwing her hips into his with each thrust.

"Ahhhhhhhhhhh," she screamed and threw her head back, arching her hips toward him and welcoming him into her. This time was different, stronger, yes, but she felt her walls contract hard around him and felt her climb increase on the inside of her belly deep as well as on the outside, doubling the sensation. She could feel the tightening of her sheath around him and the start of fireworks and shots of hot liquid pleasure up and down her sex in time with his thrusts. Her body was in frantic abandon as she let him possess her as she writhed and convulsed around his rock-hard erection.

Sabastian quickened his pace encouraged by her movement with him and her cries of pleasure, he could feel the tension increase, building to a crescendo. Knowing he wouldn't have even millimeter of space to move once she imploded around him. He needed to feel her orgasm and pounded faster watching the ecstasy on her face and her growing need prompting him to move recklessly, feeling her build around him and he drove her over the edge.

"Feel me," he growled, "Yes, Ahhh, cum, cum hard, Vicky."

His words were so erotic, it sent her into a flurry of sensation that ran through her entire body. Her eyes widened as she looked into his ferocious expression and she let him pound into her softness harder and faster and a scream wrenched from her lips as she was tossed over the abyss.

"Ohhhhhhhhhh, ahhhhhhhhhhhh."

Fireworks exploded inside her and her entire body bowed in a violent spasm that rolled over and through her. The feeling was so tremendous she let out another raw cry at the shockwaves of pleasure. Jolts of electricity shot from her delicate nerve endings to her nipples and back again. Her body jerked and her scream left her own ears deaf. She could feel him in her and felt her body spasm around his, finally having something to hold on to. As she screamed out her climax, the feeling was so intense she saw spots in her eyes and her whole body shuddered deliciously.

"Yes, fuck, Vicky. Augh," he growled down at her.

He continued to move with her writhing body, unable to maneuver in and out of her sheath as she was too tight. He let her ride him in her orgasm, pulsing around his shaft, she throbbed and vibrated and jerked around him and he felt every single shudder and it made him quake with his own need and the self-discipline he was barely hanging onto. Her shudders lasted for so long and she gripped him so forcefully he relished every second of her orgasm as much as she did. Her soft fleshy walls finally lessened diminutively and he was free to maneuver once more. He pulled out of her pulsing walls slowly but it was so sensually painful he savored every sweet inch of her.

Victoria still felt the trembling deep in her womb when he started to move again slowly out, then back into her and she gave sharp little bursts of pleasure at the back of her throat. She was so hyper-sensitive but she felt the waves being carried on gloriously. He was extending her climax and she curved into him loving the feel of him deep within her as she throbbed hard from the rupture still shattering her body.

He moved faster and faster, getting more and more fevered and she matched him, clawed at his back and screamed at him pulling him into her. She felt her orgasm extending by his hard body and she continued to shatter into a million pieces all around him. Suddenly, she felt a change inside her and it felt as though his full length had been replaced by marble. There was a growing pressure, him swelling inside her already constricted sheath, expanding her and she embraced the painful feeling of him engorged deep inside her and felt herself expand with him.

She saw and felt his body stiffen and his body convulsed violently and she felt him explode and empty himself inside her. He had stilled for a brief moment, then she felt him jerk and spasm. Loving every vibration as it ran from his body into hers. She felt every inch of him fill her and expand her sex that she shuddered with him still feeling herself throbbing from her own powerful release.

"Ahhhhhhhhhhhh," Sabastian screamed, the orgasm rocking his body and he thrust into her again and again so hard he fell apart.

"Oh, Vicky, yes. Aaaauuuugggghhh!"

Sabastian collapsed on top of her shuddering, still feeling her wrapped tight around his cock and he knew it would be while before she would relax enough to release him. He didn't want to crush her but he also wanted to stay buried in her sweet casing forever. Pulling out would be painful for both of them, so he rolled and placed her on top of him and she lay down on his chest shaking and moaning in his ear.

Victoria lay on top of his slick broad chest breathing hard, still vibrating and she had never felt so completely satisfied in her life. The feeling he gave her was more than she could've ever asked and she hated her ignorance and couldn't wait to question him. However, she would need to catch her breath as she was still savoring the pounding of their combined sexes now starting to finally slow down.

"Christ, Victoria," he whispered breathlessly.

Now that neither one of them were moving, she focused on him at rest both beneath her and inside of her. She could feel a slight soft pulse in her inner channel slowing with both their heartbeats as they rested and marveled at the sensation.

"Mmmm," she sighed, running her hands up his chest and around to his neck.

Sabastian arms enclosed around her tiny frame and he inhaled her fragrance.

"Mmmm, yourself," he smiled into her hair.

Victoria was hot and sweaty but didn't care, she could feel their heat mixing between their chests and she loved the warmth they created together. She felt his arms leave her and seconds later, they returned to wrap around her again just when a cool breeze began blowing across her back. She snuggled into him glad the heat of their bodies would not force them to separate with the air-conditioning he had turned on with a hidden remote.

She was focused only on him and the feel of his sex still buried in her, still hard.

It took a long time but she could feel his sex diminish slightly and knew he was going soft like she read about in the books she had been studying.

She moaned with the new movement she felt as she relaxed with him.

"It has taken a lot for me to relax with your nakedness pressed into me," he said as he kissed her hair.

"Sorry," she replied although not sorry at all.

233

"Relax and don't tense," he instructed.

He grabbed under her arms gently and slowly, he started to pull her off his member.

"Mmmmm," they moaned in unison.

Victoria did what she was told and relaxed in his arms and felt the slickness between their sweaty bodies help her slide across his torso. She was vaguely aware of her nipples rubbing across his chest hair as she was too focused on the feeling between her legs. She felt him exit her flesh and the feel of him sliding through her made her moan in his ear again lazily. The moment he was gone, she missed him.

Sabastian placed her beside him on the bed and he turned to look at her with a small upturned smile playing across his lips.

Victoria bent in to kiss the dimple displayed there.

"How are you?" Sabastian asked seriously.

She thought about that for a second and smiled.

"Very wet and empty," she giggled.

"Not sore?"

She thought about it again and focused, yes, there was a slight soreness there. The pleasurable pulsing had turned into muscle throbbing that was tender but not overly painful.

"I'm a little tender, yes, but a good kind of tender," she reassured him.

"What about you?" she asked, glancing down at him.

She looked at him interested. The length of his erection was resting lazily against his leg slightly deflated.

Sabastian laughed at her innocence and quickly kissed her on the lips and whispered, "Not knowing much about sex did not prevent you from performing so sensually. Victoria, you were so absolutely stunning. You were so open and gave as much as you took."

He kissed her again, "Wild cat, you are perfection. What do you think?" he asked.

Embarrassed at his praise, she answered shyly. "I read all about this, it's just different to experience it first-hand."

She glanced at his wet length resting on his leg still fascinated, her fingers twitching.

He read her thoughts. "I am already at half-mast wanting more, looking at your lips, your soft skin," he said rubbing her arms lightly. "You're an aphrodisiac all on your own and even without the slightest touch, I would be more than ready for you."

Victoria smiled but he clamped his hand over hers before she could reach for his sex. "Don't even think about it, missy," and brought her hand to his lips kissing softly.

"Now, I'm sure you've read and now know from experience that not only men can have orgasms, and I plan on giving you as many as you can take over the next couple of weeks, but not right away," he winked at her again and she blushed and asked.

"It felt like an explosion of fireworks shattering inside of me," she said in wonder.

"That's very well put. Did you enjoy the fireworks?" he asked with a triumphant smile, showing off his gleaming white teeth and deepening his dimples.

She ducked her head as her smile overtook her features and her blush bloomed over her entire body. "Um, yes," she murmured. "I can see why you called this room the Summit, it felt like I climbing a mountain and was thrown over at the peak," she said, blushing harder.

"It's called the Summit because of the color. Everything looks like it's been covered in a blanket of snow. Until the lights turn the color of the room to something more meaningful, but, yes, the name has double meaning."

He lifted her chin and leaning over her, pressing his chest into hers and gave her a mouth-watering sensual kiss that made her both melt and forget her shyness.

"You're beautiful, Vicky, I love your innocence and cannot wait to fornicate with you until your shyness has melted away into pure lust, whenever you see a man."

She raised an eyebrow at him, "Fornicate?"

"Well, I can't very well say, I want to fuck you, can I?"

Victoria's eye widened at him and she drew back.

"Vicky, you must be free to say and do whatever you want in bed, sometimes being crude is a good thing and a lot of the times it's a requirement with a client. A lot of guys and girls like dirty talk, it turns them on and makes them feel the words physically. Words have a lot of control over a person's mind, which, of course, controls the body."

"So just words can turn someone on?" Victoria asked skeptically.

"Of course and sometimes no touching is required at all, you can get full satisfaction with the best worded phrases or even just looks."

Victorian looked unconvinced.

Sabastian grazed her arms with butterfly touches and moved close to her ear and whispered erotically.

"Victoria, I want to fuck your cunt so hard you scream my name and tear at me until you cum all over my mouth. I want to bend you over backward and have you cream all over my dick while I lick and suck you inside and out. I want my cock deep inside you and want to bang you so hard while I fuck your pussy over and over again, fuck me, Vicky, fuck me hard, fuck me rough."

He bit her ear hard and fast, making her jump and leaned away to see her face.

Victoria didn't know what to think, she was horrified at his words and felt she should be insulted; however, she had felt her body tighten at his words and was shocked at the sensations now running through her. She shivered and swallowed hard.

"I, umm, see what you mean," she said.

"Sometimes it needs to be in the moment but other times, it can have an instant effect."

He pressed his hand to her groin and her body responded instantly as her hips pushed into his warm palm.

Embarrassed at her reaction to both his words and his hand cupping her mons, she jerked back from him and said, "Stop it."

He couldn't help but laugh, "Yes, Miss Victoria."

Then in all seriousness, he whispered. "Remember, feel, and don't think." He kissed her shoulder as he got up off the bed.

She suddenly thought of something.

"What happened to all the respect rules? You know. No cursing, always 'miss' this and 'miss' that, not allowed to do rude gestures or not to take advantage and all that crap? Where were your manners just then, Mr. Sabastian?"

"Ah," he said smirking at her, "you are not in the women's manor yet, are you? You have to be fully trained, living with the Eximius girls and on staff before you get that kind of respect from me, young lady. You are an intern and there are few rules protecting you from us vulgar men. Until you are an official employee, I can treat you like a real woman and I can respond like a real man

Also in the Summit anything goes and there are no boundaries unless you set them clearly. When we are with an Eximius girl, there are clear rules set in place before we have sex but other than that, in here we are free."

His smiled faded, turning serious, "Anything you are uncomfortable with Vicky, anything you don't like, any time you want me to stop, I will, of course, listen and not because of the rules, but because I want to only please you and need you to trust me." He paused, "Do you trust me?"

She raised her lashes up at him while he hovered over her beside the bed.

"Yes, Sabastian, I do," she answered sincerely.

Well, you shouldn't, he thought grimly.

Sabastian held out his hand and she took it. He lifted her off the bed and led her over to the pure white dresser, there he took out a pink nightgown and tenderly dressed her making sure to run his fingertips over her skin at every opportunity, smiling at the shivers that ran along her with every touch.

He took out a pair of red boxers in another drawer, put them on and walked her to the bed. They then stood looking at the blood-stained white sheet together. Victoria blushed furiously and Sabastian bent down to kiss her sweetly on the lips before taking the sheet off and directing her to sit down. Balling up the sheet and throwing it in the corner, he said, "I think I'll keep that as a trophy."

She gave him a quizzical look and said, disbelieving, "Really?"

He leaned over and kissed her sweetly on the lips, "Victoria, you are a prize any man would be honored to show off."

Victoria thought he was being corny but that didn't stop her heart from fluttering and her skin flaming from his touch.

Sabastian walked over to the wall and pressed a button. There was a familiar sound and tray came sliding out of the wall just like in her bedroom. It was much larger than the tray in her room and she suddenly had a sickening thought.

"This room isn't monitored, is it?"

Her eyes wide, looking around.

"No, of course not," Sabastian replied, bringing the food tray to the bed. "The entire men's manor including the bedrooms are monitored, the common rooms and the kitchen are watched. This is the only room that has no cameras in it. It's a training room. So the cameras were removed years ago to give the girls peace of mind and privacy when learning a new skill. The women's manor is monitored but only the women's bedrooms are turned on when they have the guys with them, otherwise they have their privacy, too."

"Oh," she said relieved. Looking at the food displayed before her, she realized she was starving. Her chef was hard at work again and it didn't take long before she was lying in the bed with a very full stomach. Sabastian lay beside, her slowly rubbing her thigh and humming to himself.

Victoria was completely at ease with this man, it was strange, she had never trusted a man before and yet this man had opened her eyes and made her see the world in a whole new light. She had a revelation that her life had been irrevocably changed and there was still so much more to learn. She had a lot of growing up to do and anticipation rolled through her not wanting to wait to continue her lessons on her newly discovered sexuality.

Going back on the last hours, she blushed remembering the things he had done to her and started to feel a slight tightening in her groin. Blushing even harder, she rolled over and was surprised to see Sabastian gazing at her.

"Watch this," he said and pressed a button on the remote.

The room unexpectedly went pitch black and there were suddenly thousands of stars and with a bright colorful movement of northern lights flowing like waves all over the ceiling. It was beautifully relaxing and she lay down curled in his arms, her hand resting lightly on his hard chest, staring up at the moving lights. The last thing she remembered was his lips in her hair as she drifted off into a blissful sleep.

Chapter 44

Victoria woke up needing to use the washroom. She glanced around the now dim grey, starless room looking for Sabastian but he was gone and she was disappointed.

Where was he? she thought.

Victoria felt for the remote. Finding it beside her she started pressing buttons in the dark until she was blinded by the white light she was aiming for.

Rubbing her eyes she glanced up at the huge wall mirror, she hardly recognized herself. Her hair was a tangled mess, her face looked flushed and her eyes glowed brightly. She walked up to the large mirror and hoping no one would walk in, she lifted her night gown up past her hips. She was red in places and felt a soreness between her legs that was not pleasant, but at the same time, not completely unpleasant. She throbbed down there and knew exactly why and saw her face grew crimson in the mirror.

Victoria moved her hands to her sex and felt around tenderly, she was still wet and the moisture covered her fingers. She moved them around slightly and felt a tingling rush and saw her nipples harden through her night gown. She had done that to herself and was intrigued, she moved her other hand up to her nipple and slowly circled. There were no lightning bolts down to her groin like before but the smooth feeling of her sex under her fingers felt very good. Watching herself in the mirror, she licked her fingers tentatively. She tasted different than when Sabastian let her lick her from her fingertips and knew it was because the taste was now a mixture of both her and Sabastian's combined pleasure.

Victoria put her night gown back down and walked over to the bed, sat and nibbled on what was left of the meal. She was bored and restless, the feeling between her legs felt heavy and swollen and she wanted to ask why and if it would go away or if she was permanently changed down there. The books she

239

had read didn't have any information on losing your virginity and what it would feel like, so she was completely in the dark and craved answers.

She started to pace the room and was surprised that even walking around she felt a heaviness pull at her sex and breasts with every step.

Distracting herself, she started snooping in the cupboards and drawers. She found lots of clothes, mostly lingerie, costumes, anything from school girl costumes to firefighter outfits, all in the slutty category. There were drawers of weird looking implements with batteries, ropes, and handcuffs. Penises of every shape, color, size, and variation with beads and cords coming out of them. She closed the drawer quickly, thinking how embarrassed she would be if she was suddenly caught. She walked over to the door and tried the door knob which was locked, so she knocked lightly.

"Hello," she called and jumped when an unfamiliar voice answered her.

"Hello, wild cat, how are you doing in there?"

Not liking that a strange man was using Sabastian's nick name for her she answered, "Um, fine. Where's Sabastian?"

"He's detained, but if you like, I can come in and keep you company."

The man sounded pleasant enough. She hoped he was like Nickolas who she had enjoyed talking to. Perhaps she might be able to get some answers out of him.

"Sure, come on in," she said after grabbing a robe to cover herself.

She stepped away from the door to admit the man who quickly turned around to close the door behind him. The man was dark and broad just like Sabastian but not as tall. His angular face was clean shaven, with sharp cheek bones. His face was narrow and he looked European with his short tasseled hair, black and shiny like a sleek car. His eyes were a light crystal blue that didn't match his dark coloring and they burned into her.

"Hello, Miss Victoria, I have been wanting to meet you for a very long time, my name is Ethan," his voice was quiet, but hard at the same time and she smiled a greeting at him.

"Um, Hi," she backed up to sit on the bed. His voice was as slick as his hair, very mesmerizing. He was friendly enough, but something about him made her tense.

"Uh, what do you do here?" she asked, trying to ignore her unease.

240

"I'm a trainer like Sabastian and I am hoping to be the next step in your internship, if you would allow me to," he said professionally, licking his lips walking closer to her.

Victoria heard his fine voice clearly and he sounded much like someone proposing a business idea to her, but his eyes and the way he approached her was anything but professional. Something about him wasn't right as he looked at her hungrily. The same look Sabastian gave her a few hours ago when in bed with her, but Ethan's look was predatory and she had her hackles up.

Ethan licked his lips again and moved closer to her.

"I don't think I'm ready for that yet," she said, twisting her hair nervously in her lap.

"Of course, Miss Victoria. I was not implying now, just soon. I have a lot to show you and you have a lot to learn. I hope you will enjoy the skills I'll be teaching you."

His tongue shot out to wet his lips again and his eyes licked her body up and down.

This man would not have known she had been a virgin only hours ago, thinking she was at least a little experienced. She shot a glance past him to the wall where Sabastian had thrown the bloodied bed sheet. She saw it was gone and relief swept over her briefly until she noticed Ethan adjust his jeans and saw the defined bulge there. Somehow, she knew this man would not have the restraint Sabastian did and was alarmed.

"I was hoping for five minutes of your time to give you a hint of the pleasure my skill set could show you," Ethan stood right in front of her so that she had to lean back to look up to see his face. "I know you'll not regret it, wild cat."

He was crowding her so Victoria backed up on the bed to get some distance to breathe. She was shocked when he followed over top of her, his hands on either side of her hips.

Oh, God,' she thought fearfully, *he thinks I am inviting him.*

She scooted further back on the bed trying to get more distance and that only gave him more room to press himself into her roughly, closing his eyes and he moaned. Her body reacted and she was appalled.

"No," she finally choked out.

A cruel smile came over his face only for a split second, then he raised himself off of her and stepped away.

"Yes, of course, miss, I am sorry if I have over stepped my bounds, please excuse me."

His professional, polite voice was back, Victoria watched him turn and leave quickly, scared that he would return.

I responded, she looked at herself in the mirror.

She couldn't believe herself; her body had betrayed her and she was so ashamed that her cheeks burned pink as her eyes filled with tears.

Sabastian found her like that, leaning back across the bed with tears slipping quietly down her cheeks and went to her immediately.

"My God, Vicky, what's wrong?"

"What the hell did you do to me?" she yelled at him, making him jump at her words.

"I umm, I don't know? You g...g...gave p...p...permission, you wanted to. I'm s...s...sorry," Sabastian stammered, trying to figure her out. She had been calm and happy before she had fallen asleep. What had happened to change her mind frame?

Victoria was immediately contrite; his stammering made her regret the accusation that he had done something wrong. It was all her and she did want it and now hungered for it even when her mind didn't, her body did. She had no control and it frightened her.

Still angry, but mostly at herself, she said sullenly, "I had to use the washroom and you just left, where were you?"

"Sorry, I...," Sabastian walked across the room and pushed on a wall which swung in to reveal a shining marble white bathroom.

"Oh," she said as she got up, brushing past him and shutting the door quietly. The bathroom was larger than the one in her room built for two and completely white to match the Summit. The tub and shower were much bigger, at least four people could enjoy it at the same time and she wondered how many people had enjoyed the water together.

Minutes later, when she was finished, she walked out to see him on the bed with his head in his hands.

Shit, she cursed at herself. *The poor guy.*

She sat down next to him, her leg touching his.

"I'm sorry, it's just, I feel different and I want you...to well...um, fuck me."

He slowly picked his head from his hands and gapped at her in amazement.

"Sorry," she said again blushing. "Was that bad timing, the dirty talk I mean?"

He answered her with a kiss hard and urgent pressing her into the bed.

I guess not, Victoria thought as she pulled at his neck and pressed her breasts into him.

He quickly pulled her up into his arms and carried her back into the bathroom. Opening the glass shower door, he tossed her inside turning on the cold water. Victoria screamed and pounded on the door that he leaned up against, tearing at his clothes before yanking the door open and stepping into the freezing water.

"What the hell are you doing?" she screamed at him, trying to push past him to escape the cold water pouring over her.

Sabastian grinned and grabbed her in a bear hug turning her away from the cold stream, protecting her body with his. Holding her tight, he reached behind him and adjusted the temperature. He kissed her passionately, keeping both of them warm against the cold stream, waiting for the hot water to kick in. As soon as the water changed on his back, he spun her around so she could enjoy the warmth and bend down to lift her night gown over her head giving her diamond hard nipple a little lick as he rose up.

"You're crazy," she exclaimed, smacking him hard, laughing.

Sabastian gazed down at her small frame, wrapping his hands around her waist, he said, "It looks like you could use some warming up."

Victoria watched him dip down as he drew one of her perked nipples and rolled it around in his mouth until they were no longer hard from the cold water but spiked because of his mouth. She moaned and threaded her fingers through his hair as he sucked the other nipple till it was firm in his mouth.

"Mmmmm," she purred, running her hands through his wet hair.

He came to her mouth and tasted the sweet sound on her lips, then to madden her further, he pushed her breasts together and swirled his tongue in and around both nipples, making her hands fist in his hair.

"Ahh, ohhh," she moaned and she pushed her hips toward him.

He was leaning back to gain access to her lovely pink areolas so when he felt her move toward him, he stood up and pushed her against the wall grinding his pulsing erection into her sweet wet flesh.

"Ahhhhh, Oh, yes, oh, oh," she murmured as she felt another rush of desire strike her hard and fast. She felt him grind into her roughly and her body quicken and she peered up into his dark green eyes watching her.

He pulled away from her suddenly, grinning down at her.

"Nooo," she groaned disappointed.

Sabastian reached behind him and pumped a large amount of body wash into his palm, turning her around to face the wall, he proceeded to wash her.

Facing the wall, Victoria felt his hands on her arms, back, and belly. He moved to her feet which he tickled as he lifted to wash between her toes. She was giggling and squirming under his ministrations when his hands went from playful to being serious as she felt his long strong fingers run up the inside of her legs. Skipping the small sensitive part she wish he wouldn't, he went to her breasts circling them in the soft creamy soap that glided across her skin and she felt her body respond with need. She pushed into his palms stroking both her breasts and her nipples and leaned back into his shaft feeling the hardness pressed into her back and squirmed.

"Augh, Vicky," he moaned pushing back into her.

She felt him move away and was disappointed until she felt his hard smooth mushroom head pop up between her legs rubbing so wonderfully on her clit that she cried out excited and started moving her hips back and forth over him. His erection had a slight curve that put his head to her woman's center and it felt like her body molded to his even when he wasn't inside her. The ridge of his large head caught her again and again and she groaned and waves of growing pleasure shot through her from her breasts to her groin and the throbbing increased in tempo. Sabastian continued to flex and keep her squirming while his hands worked her nipples with the lather of soap that was slick and warm.

"Ah, Ah, oh, yes, Sabastian, God," she groaned into the wall. Sabastian could not finish like this; he knew she would be very sore after today and wanted desperately to feel her squeezing around him before her body would need a break. He tore himself away from her and flipped her around. Seeing the raw need in her eyes as well as the disappointment, his penis bucked toward her and he took her in a kiss, biting down hard on her lip, then sucked sweetly at her full swollen mouth.

Victoria cursed him, why did he pull away at the wrong time, she looked into his eyes as he kissed her and felt her feet leave the ground. She knew what his plan was and rejoiced, wrapping her smooth soapy legs around his waist, hooking her ankles around his back as strongly as she could. He lowered her until she felt the domed head of his erection nudge its way into her swollen folds. Victoria's eyes widened at the sensation as he lowered her slowly onto his slippery hard sex.

"Ahhhhhhhhhhh, mmmmmmmmm, Sabastian," she moaned, drawing his name out, as slowly as he impaled her. She could feel his hips touch hers at the union of their bodies and her muscles contracted erotically, welcoming him. She felt pain but the glorious feel of fullness inside her sex thrilled her and made her arch into him and squeeze, ignoring the soreness. Wrapping her arms around his neck she tried to move, but Sabastian took over for her and grabbing her bottom cheeks firmly in his large hands, he raised her up then down achingly slow.

"Ah," she gasped, loving the sensation of the water down her back and him so deep in her body becoming one, welcoming the pain completely to gain the pleasure.

"Ahhhhhh," she moaned slowly as he drew her down again.

Sabastian could feel her body tighten on him on every down stroke and savored the feel of the upstroke with her. Her rhythm and responses were so erotic; it drove him to the edge of reason. He felt her getting tighter and tighter and knew that he would have to hold on to both of them as he quickened the pace pressing her hard up against the wall.

"Auuugh, Vicky," he growled low and deep in her ear as he drove her down, hard on his throbbing erection.

"Christ, Vicky, Fuck," he growled as his pace increased.

Victoria felt the change in speed and clamped around him wanting to feel every inch of him, he thrust harder and faster grinding his hands into her tense flexing ass and it intensified the feeling within and she welcomed it. Her throbbing had reached a new peak and she rocked on him with sexual depravity. Her wet nipples slid over his chest with every thrust and she climbed with him hard and strong. Feeling the rubbing of both his chest and his pelvis hard against her own made her clamp and tightened with need. She felt electricity run through her, from nipples to her clit and the tension increased colossally. His mouth covered hers in a demanding kiss, dominating her and he pulled away suddenly to yell.

"Cum with me, fuck, Vicky, cum with me, hard," he said gutturally.

It was like his words turned the switch and her body shocked her with powerful waves triumphantly all the way to a mind-blowing orgasm that sent her head back against the wall and her hips thrust violently forward. He was still thrusting inside of her as wave after wave of pulsing pleasure made her convulse hard, pulling at his hair screaming.

"Ohhhhhhhhhhhhhhhh, Sabastian, Yes, ahhh," she screamed as she felt him swell all-encompassing, rock hard inside her shuddering walls. He bucked, making her whole body vibrate with him, throbbing savagely with her. She rode his orgasm, lengthening hers, making her shudder and moaned under him.

"Fuck, Vicky, ahhhhhhh. Fuck!" Sabastian roared his lust in her ear.

Sabastian gave a few final thrusts before her sheath tightened around his sensitive engorged head. He buried himself deep inside her where he would be safe and kissed her tenderly on the lips, trembling.

Victoria collapsed breathing hard. She kept focusing on the strong hard throbbing deep in her groin that was slowing now that they had stilled in each other arms. Knowing he would keep her from falling, she fully relaxed, letting the pulsing of their combined sexes calm down together. Completely satisfied, she lay her head on his shoulder and murmured in his ear.

"I guess I wanted that, hey?"

"Well, if you didn't, you have a funny way of showing it," he murmured back to her, giving her ear a little nip.

She squeezed him again and giggled when she heard him groan.

"Wild cat," he said, pinching her ass.

She jerked away from his hand and saw him tense.

"What?" she asked.

"Well, my dear," he said. "Is this part sensitive?"

He reached down between them and with his finger dug into her flesh just above where he was buried and gave her a little push on her over sensitive clit. She jerked again and once again, he tensed.

"Ya, so? Why are you…?"

"When it comes to men and women, we are a reflection of each other, we may be polar opposites but we experience the same thing. I'm just as sensitive as you are after a fantastic fucking orgasm."

He raised his eyebrows up and down suggestively at her.

"However, I am just sensitive on the tip, when you squeeze, jerk, or even laugh, you tighten around me and I need to stayed buried in you to stay safe from your, umm, administrations."

"Oh," she said. "So you don't like to be touched right after?"

"Yes, I need some alone time after, just like you, before I can start to warm up again."

Sabastian enjoyed teaching her so much and liked the way she absorbed everything. He was also pleased she was getting over her shyness, although he would miss her blushes and hope that he would be able to continue to make her turn pink all over. The thought made him aware of where he was and slowly started to lift her off of him.

Victoria lifted her head tensing slightly at the soreness resonated around his sex and murmured her disappointment. Even with the pain, she loved the feel of him slipping slowly out of her sex and the final pop of his warm head coming out of her made her twitch and want to rub on him. Instead, she let him slowly lower her feet to the shower floor. As she slid down his body, her nipples rubbed through his pelt of soft wet chest hair and it sent a shiver though her. As soon as he released her, she swayed as a dizzy spell hit her hard and her legs buckled under her. Sabastian grabbed her quickly holding her tight in his arms and chuckled.

"Nice," he said gazing down at her.

Victoria blinked up at him, her head still spinning, "What?"

"A woman going weak at the knees and unable to stand after sex means you did your job as a man. It's a great way to show you had a mind-altering experience and he couldn't have done any better."

"Is this when you stick out your chest and thump it, you big ape," she sarcastically.

"Laugh if you will, but you can't deny it," he took his hands away from her and she swayed again.

He grabbed her hips and steadied her with a huge grin on his face.

She rolled her eyes at him, but clung to his neck anyway, willing her legs to work.

Sabastian lifted her hot slick body out of the shower and placed her gently in the cool marble bathtub, filling it with warm water. The tub filled quickly as he threw in two bubble bath bombs and they started to fill the tub with warm jasmine scented bubbles. He climbed in and sat in behind her, cradling her between his legs.

Victoria could feel him warm and hard behind her, his chest cushioned her and kept her from sinking into the rising bubbles. She felt his hands start to rub an ultra-soft soap on her back, arms, and shoulders, then he started to circle her breasts and belly letting the soap lather thick and creamy. She relaxed and let his hands wander over her body trustingly. She tensed and arched when he circled the soap on her nipples but she was too tired to focus on anything and every time his hands left her sensitive parts, she relaxed again. She floated in the water in total bliss and when he focused on her breasts again, she let a low moan escaped her lips and felt herself tighten under the water briefly.

"Mmmmmmm, Sabastian," she purred and she felt a new movement behind her. She could feel him grow hard and long pressed into the small of her back and was fascinated. Victoria reached behind her and wrapped both her hands around his growing shaft, feeling for the first time its thickness in her palm and squeezed.

"Mmmmm, sweet Vicky," he said, nuzzling her ear.

Victoria closed her eyes and focused on her hands, she rubbed her hands over the top of the smooth head and was amazed at its softness and fullness. It throbbed in her hands and jerked periodically as she ran her hands all the way down to the base and threaded her fingers through his pubic hair, then reaching further, she felt his soft testicles and she rolled them and squeezed.

"Gentle," he said thickly in her ear.

She softened her grip and let her fingers roll him around him lightly, treating his heavy mounds like breakable eggs.

"That's right," he whispered. "That is the most sensitive part of a guy and must always be handled with care."

"Is it always so fragile?"

"Yes, always be soft with them and the rest will be hard for you," he promised, licking her ear.

Her one hand worked its way up his shaft as the other rolled his balls tenderly with her fingers.

"Mmmm, nice, wild cat," he said, pushing into her hands, hardening even more under her ministrations.

"Now move slowly up and down, squeezing hard and twist the shaft once in a while."

Victoria did as she was instructed and loved that with only her hands she had so much control over this large male. She felt him stiffen harder and realized this is what happened when he was buried deep in her body.

"Auuuuugh," he groaned, pushing again into her slippery hands.

It was the signal she needed to quicken her pace just like when he had sped up during their love making and she rubbed the top of his throbbing head and tightened again. Moving faster and faster, she felt him, pulse and jerk, then engorge swelling in her palms as he pounded into her hands.

"Ohhhhhhh fuck, yes," he growled in her ear, thrusting and grabbing at her breasts in total exhilaration with the orgasm pulsing through him at her back.

Desire coursed through Victoria, she was very aroused, her belly throbbing and squeezing along in pace with her hands and she realized it was all because of what she had done to him. The feeling over this strong man empowered her and she could see the appeal of making men weak at her touch. She knew, of course, it went both ways, but it thrilled her nonetheless. Sabastian had told her that men wanted and needed sex to feel empowered. To do well at business, give confidence, and having control over women gave them that feeling of power and control. However she didn't think it applied to women as well and knew she needed to learn so much more.

She slowed her hands and lightened her hold on him as he started to slow his movement, softly moaning in her ear.

"Mmmmm, Vicky, you are wonderful," he whispered thickly.

Sabastian started rubbing her shoulders and back with soap until she was almost asleep when he stepped out of the tub.

"I have to go," he said softly, drying his body quickly. "I want you to eat and get some rest, then there are videos you need to watch."

She was alarmed, "When will you be back?"

"I have to watch starting tonight," he said.

"Oh, what does that mean?"

Grabbing a white robe from the wall, he said, "I have an Eximius girl I need to watch tonight on a job. I'll be back in two days."

Her eyes widened. "What, you watch her work!?" she was appalled.

"No, no, not in that way. It's a new client who has hired one of our girls for two days, he's on probation for the next three visits. Once he is cleared, then the girls can take a job with him without us coming for protection. We simply stand guard close by and have an alarm that we respond to if she needs assistance. We are not actually in the room with them, just nearby."

He smiled at her and kissed the top of her head.

"Although being watched on a job does happen sometimes and you might love the thrill of other people watching you fuck," he winked, "you are free to leave and call if you need any help, just push that button by the door. Have a good night, wild cat."

Victoria wanted to talk more about how the system worked and she still had questions about how her body felt different. But she watched him go with a smile. She got out of the tub, intent on listening to his instructions as she was hungry, tired, and sore. A tray of food was waiting for her, so she ate, then sunk into the freshly changed bed to sleep away her concerns and questions.

Chapter 45

Victoria didn't sleep well; she was restless and uncomfortable. When she finally was fully awake, she knew why. Her entire body ached from her neck all the way down to her ankles. Her muscles were cramped and every movement made her wince. What drew her attention away from the muscle aches and cramps was her pounding sex. Her tightened sex shocked her by a hard cramp in her womb and she vowed never to use those muscles again. She felt raw, used up, like she had just climbed a mountain she had not been physically prepared for. Even her nipples and her lips were swollen and sore and throbbed lightly. She lay in bed and tested all the parts of her body, coming to the conclusion that muscles she had never used before had been over worked and weak. It was as if she had not been exercising at all the last few weeks.

She rolled over and saw their gray notebook opened on the nightstand beside the bed.

"I know it will not be a good morning for you, so I will not say it, take two of these and get into the tub and relax, see you soon. S."

Victoria saw a bottle of pain killers and a glass of water and popped two pills in her mouth and drank thirstily. She then dragged herself to the bathroom, having to spread her legs wide to insure she did not rub herself in between her legs and laughed at the sight she must make, like she had ridden a horse for hours. She carefully lowered her body in the tub and let the steaming water melt the aches. Putting the jets on low, she let them pound her tender muscles.

Luxuriating in the soft scented water, she thought that no way was this pain worth it. Did all women go through this every time they had sex, she wondered? Why would someone do that to themselves? She thought that it wouldn't be worthwhile and no way would she be able to take the abuse and the aftermath of a night of hard sex. But lying in the hot water, thinking about their time together, she rescinded the thought and knew she would do it again in a heartbeat.

She spent hours washing herself and soaking in the tub going over everything she had learned and everything he had taught her, still amazed.

After her bath, she walked gingerly over to the door to locate the button Sabastian had told her about but before she had a chance to press it, she heard a familiar voice.

"Yes, Miss Victoria, how may I assist you?" Ethan's quiet voice asked on the other side of the door.

"Ummm, Sabastian said there were videos to watch but I'd like to read instead, could you bring me my education books, please?"

"Yes, of course, Miss Victoria."

He sounded pleasant like last time, but she didn't like the fact that he was her keeper. Before Ethan returned, she covered herself in her robe.

She heard a soft knock only a few minutes later and went to the door to open it. Ethan walked in carrying all her books in his bulging arms and set them on the white dresser and turned to her.

"I didn't know where you were in the reading program, so I brought them all," he huffed as he dumped the books on the dresser.

Turning around to face her, licking his lips and gazing up and down her body, he said, "How are you feeling this morning, Miss Victoria?"

She breathed deep and said, "Sore."

He leered at her, "You must have been wild, like your name implies."

His sneer of a grin made her uneasy.

"Ummm, well, I'm just not used to so much activity."

"I bet you aren't, you didn't have much experience before you got here, did you?"

She didn't know how much to say to this man, she didn't trust him and she needed to be careful.

"Some," she said slowly, "but not a lot."

"I bet you loved to be fucked good and hard," he said, stepping close to her. "I can sense that in a woman, you wanted it so bad."

He took slow stalking steps toward her.

She frowned at him and put her hand up to stop him from coming closer.

"Uh, what happened to the respect and none threating rules you have to follow?" she asked, changing the subject, trying to get him on the defensive.

He slithered closer to her, too close.

"I want you to stop," she demanded raising her voice slightly, hoping he didn't hear the shaking in her voice.

Ethan straightened and bowed, "Of course, Miss Victoria," he said, still leering at her.

"However, miss," he said, looking hard into her eyes.

"You know it's true and I cannot wait to see it firsthand."

His complete turnaround at her words gave her confidence, with this strikingly gorgeous frightening man.

"Please," she said, pointing at the door, "get out."

"Of course, Miss Victoria, our time will come and so will you," he said, licking his lips, and just like that, he was gone.

Victoria stayed frozen in place her heart hammering, she felt a fearful thrill run through her and was confused. She knew no one could hurt her in this place and repeated that over and over in her head. Her words had stopped him even though she could see that he wanted nothing more than to fuck her good and hard, as he put it. However, something in the back of her head came to the surface and she remembered the contract she had signed. The so-called tests to discover sexual desires that had no boundaries. The fact she had no say in what happened to her in these tests made her shudder.

She began to wonder what it would be like to have another man inside of her and could not tell if she was appalled or fascinated with the idea. She decided to leave the call button alone and hope Ethan didn't help his way into her room while she slept.

Victoria looked at the books that had been brought to her and picked up the book about the female orgasm. This was the one book that had confused her the most when she had read it the first time. She was dying to read it again, now being able to fully appreciate and understand its context. She settled in bed, still sore but trying to relax as she flipped the pages, intrigued.

When she awoke the next day, what she thought what would happen, did. Just like when you work out hard, your muscles really don't start to feel the whole extent of the abuse until day two.

She groaned and took a few more pills as she headed to the tub again. She went from the tub to the bed taking her books with her willing her muscles to loosen and for the pain to go away, popping pills as needed. Her food came to her the same way it did in her original room and knew Nickolas was hard at work again to keep her strength up.

She spent the days mostly naked or wrapped in her robe as the room had very little in it for regular clothes. She was thrilled with her newly awakened sexuality and freedom of being nude now that she was no longer being monitored. By the morning of day three, she knew Sabastian would be coming soon so she got up happy to feel that her muscles had soften slightly and the pain had finally faded to a dull ache. She was pleased that the after effect of sex had faded completely, answering her own question that she was only sore for a short time and not permanently changed in that tender area between her legs.

After the tub had massaged her slightly sore back and legs, she lay on the floor and stretched out her limbs.

Sabastian found her like that, dressed in her red underwear and pink silk tank top on a blanket on the floor, stretching out her legs.

"Um, good morning," he said, watching her, "how are you feeling?"

"A little sore," she muttered from the floor, looking up at him.

Sabastian offered her his hands and she accepted the help as he raised her slowly off the floor.

"Well, so much for the exercise routine," he said. "It was supposed to keep you flexible and supple for your lessons," he grinned at her.

"Ya, so much for that," she said grinning back, "I don't think any kind of exercise routine can prepare you for that kind of action."

She bent over, touched her toes, and then reached high over her head, groaning with the stretch.

Sabastian looked concerned, "Are you hurt badly?"

He put his large hand on the small of her back and led her over to the bed as if she was made of porcelain.

Victoria felt his hot hand through the silk on her back and a jolting shiver went from his hand down to her groin.

"No, I'm better now, it's really just my back and inner thighs that still hurt a little, but the rest of my body was tender, some places more than others," she said as she sat down on the soft mattress watching him.

"Right, of course," he said glancing down at her. "I'm sorry, I didn't want to cause you pain, but it was a necessary evil, do you hate me for it?"

"No," she sighed, "I was fine there yesterday. It was just so unexpected. I understand my unused muscles cramping, but that pain was so unusual."

"It will not hurt that bad again," he said quickly. "Every time the pain will lessen and the pleasure will increase. I promise."

Victoria looked up at him trustingly, willing him to be right and looking forward to increasing the pleasure part.

"So it won't hurt like that again?" she asked.

"No, not as bad, but you may still be tender for the next few times, but it all depends on how good of a job I did with you the first time."

"And how well did you do?" she asked smiling seductively.

"Hell if I know. You being a virgin is new for me, I've never had the pleasure before either."

"You've never been with a virgin?"

"Nope, you are my first and I must say it was more fun than I thought it would be."

Victoria smiled shyly looking down and blushed.

Sabastian grabbed the blanket on the floor and reached for her hand and hauled her up. He lifted her in his arms cradling her out the door.

"Where are we going?" she asked, surprised to be held so closely again and felt a thrill run through her.

"I am going to make it up to you," he answered.

"But I'm not dressed," she protested.

"Don't worry, wild cat, I'll protect you," he laughed.

She scowled at him till he assured her that no one would be around.

Sabastian carried her through the hallway, upstairs, and into round room and outside to the garden. There he laid the blanket on a hammock and placed her on top and said, "Don't move."

Victoria balanced herself in the hammock and felt the hot sun beating her skin warming her up instantly.

Sabastian was back fifteen minutes' later with a meal, drinks, and an arrangement of oils. He pulled the table close to the hammock and set the food and oils on it.

"These oils are for sore muscles and to promote relaxation, but first, I am going to feed you."

He popped open the lid of the meal tray and with a tiny fork proceeded to feed her stuffed mushroom caps, strawberries, warm sour dough bread, and exotic cheeses. When she was finished, he placed truffles in her mouth and let her drink a cool chocolate and hazel nut smoothie. He watched her take each bite as she licked her lips and groan at the tastes. Sabastian had to adjust his slacks more than once to get comfortable with her moaning with each bite.

"Are you satisfied?"

"Mmmm, yes, very," she said softly.

He reached for her and in one swift motion, lifted her tank top over her head.

"No, what if….?" she said, hugging her naked breasts with her arms.

"No one can come out here, I locked the door."

Sabastian stood up, bringing her with him and watching her intently, he slowly lowered her panties to the stone path.

She blushed down at him, shy and embarrassed, remembering the last time he had done this to her. Sabastian brought his lips up to hers kissing her tenderly and lay her back in the cloth hammock.

"Lay on your stomach and let me lessen the pain I caused you."

"Do you always talk like some ancient character from a book?" she asked bemused.

"Speech lessons to speak to our ladies. If ya wan', I could talk like this woman," he said with an outrageous bad Texas accent.

"No, that's okay," she giggled.

"Down," he said, pointing.

She obeyed and groaned as his strong but gentle fingertips rolled her legs firmly. The oils made her skin tingle cool, then warm into her skin and she could feel the pain melt away replaced by warm pleasure. Lying in the sun, her stomach full and his hot hands caressing her skin; she was asleep in minutes and only awoke briefly when he adjusted himself to better access her body and continued to rub her back to sleep. As far as she knew, he never left and never stopped rubbing the strong scented oils into her skin. She had no idea how long she slept for but when she woke up, he was there watching her, still slowly and sensually rubbing her back in large round circles.

"Mmm, that feels so good," she groaned languidly.

Sabastian got up off the hammock, wrapped her in the blanket, and lifted her in his arms. Walking her back to their room, he kissed her so urgently she read the need on his lips before she saw it in his eyes. She didn't know if she could handle this and she tensed.

"Shhhh, it's okay," he murmured in her ear.

He brought her back to the Summit and laid her down softly on the bed. Sabastian then started to rearrange her hair in a halo around her entire body. Artfully displaying her beauty with the golden waterfall background as she stretched her creamy body on the bed. He stepped back to admire her and took a mental picture so that he could capture her on paper later.

He had only touched her hair since he had laid her down on the bed and when his hot hands ran up her body from her strong calves up to her hips, he smiled when he felt her stomach tighten and her hip curve up to welcome his touch.

He could not have sex with her again, that would be cruel and selfish, even though he had missed her terribly in the days he had to work. She was ready for him as the moisture between her legs was starting to drip on to the covers. Sabastian needed to take this slow so he backed up and stood beside the bed, slowly pulling of his blue shirt and unbuckling his belt and his pants. He watched her as he disrobed standing naked before her, his body bucking toward his goal.

Victoria's eyes widen once again at his cock red and pulsing with need for her. She licked her lips needing him to fill her again with his body and reached for him. Frowning, when he stepped back, she used her lips to bring him to her.

"Sabastian. Please," she begged and was rewarded with a kiss. Soft at first but then more urgent as her body bowed toward his unthinking until he placed his entire length directly on top of her small body. She loved the weight of him and squirmed her body so that her hips were slightly above his to feel the hot length of his sex between her spreading legs.

Sabastian could feel the heat coming from her and pushed into her until he was slippery and wet with her cream. Rubbing slowly up and down the wet outer folds of her body, he could feel her ascent with him and he savored the moment as they reached for the same goal.

He was wrapped between her legs but carefully kept himself stroking her outer folds, feeling her jerk when the ridge of his head caught her sweet spot and her eyes rolled then closed from the pleasure he gave her.

He was losing this battle fast so he back off her and almost cried out with her as he disengaged their bodies. He sat on his heels between her legs and with strong arms, he lifted her up on his shoulders and sucked greedily at her dripping sex.

Victoria hands balanced her as his tongue worked its magic but she wanted more of him.

"Please, please, Sabastian, I need more."

Sabastian stopped and looked up into her pleading eyes but knew if he did as she begged, he would cause her pain. He lowered her down and reached with his hand to circle and palm her rock-hard nipples and squeezed her breast hard restraining himself from doing what she begged from him. Her hips pushed up urgently into his and he groaned at the pressure building insanely inside of him.

She clawed at him, reaching, begging, "Please, Sabastian," she moaned erotically. He could not help himself; she was too much. He grabbed her raised hips roughly and slammed into her body as she screamed.

Victoria felt like she had been stabbed, the pain mingled with the pleasure was beyond sensual and her body screamed in triumph. She was lost in the tenderness of her body until he thrust into her again and again. Every movement the pleasure replaced the pain until there was nothing but him filling her body with desire and the wonder of it held her in check until she felt herself tighten dangerously around his thrashing cock. As she tightened around him, the tenderness came back momentarily before her body imploded and she screamed her legs thrown out to the side as she threw her hips violently out to meet his thrusts welcoming everything he did to her wanting more.

Sabastian locked her shoulders with his hands holding her down as he pounded into her sweet flesh. Her orgasm trying to lock him in place he forced himself to continue to move as her walls reverberated and squeezed him painfully. It was the sweetest pain he could feel and he felt himself quicken as her body started to slowly come down from its high. He emptied himself into her as he swelled and pulsed into her tight body and cried out taking what he needed after what seemed like so long. As he started to slow, he could still feel the tremors of her climax coming down with him and his whole body shivered with pleasure for this beautiful mythical creature under him.

Sabastian sat back to watch her body continue little jerking movements from the remainder of the peak he had brought her to and relished the feel of her pulsing around him. He tried to pull out from her but saw her face tense from pain. Why could he not resist her? Why could he had not given her pleasure without the pain?

Victoria's body finally allowed her to relax and she melted into the bed. She felt only the pain, now that the pleasure was gone. It was a sweet pain with him still inside her and she winced again as he slowly pulled out of her body. She smiled lazily as Sabastian lowered down to kiss her softly on the mouth. But her eyes went wide when he lowered to her sex to kiss her tenderly, slowly.

Victoria could not take it and tried to move away, her body sensitive and raw. But Sabastian held her firmly in place as he kissed, nuzzled, and caressed her swollen sex until she no longer squirmed, trying to get away. She could feel herself quickening, the build-up seemed sped up and she was shocked when her body started to climb again so soon.

Sabastian wanted to indulge her in different ways and the fact she was so willing so soon thrilled him. He lifted his mouth off of her sweetness and sat back on his heels, lifting her hips to sit on his thighs. With strong arm, he held her hips in place and with the other hand, he placed the head of his cock right on her clit and slowly circled one way then the other as she bucked erotically under him.

"Please. Oh, oh, more," she begged, lifting her hips frantically toward him, rubbing herself on him and trying to open up to impale herself on him.

He would not pain her again and focused on only pleasure without any discomfort on her part. With his cock in his hand, stroking her swollen needy clit, his restraint was running out. He moved his shaft over and over her frantically as her body poised on the edge of the abyss. He could not take it and followed her as he laid her down to ground his body into hers working frantically back and forth, careful to stay only outside of her body but staying directly on her sweet spot. Her legs opened wide for him and she thrust her hips into his and screamed as she came hard. Sabastian let go then, letting his release flow onto her tensed up belly as she vibrated under him. He instantly missed the feel of her orgasm around his shaft but thrilled at the pleasure she had received with no pain to accompany it.

He watched as she shuttered with him, his cock still finishing as she liquefied under him and he grinned down at her. Victoria looked up and smiled sleepily, so he bent down to kiss her before he rolled to lie beside her.

Victoria instantly felt cool as his body left her unprotected from his heat. She reached down to find some covers and saw the cooling wet moisture on her belly and touched it curiously; Sabastian watched her face trying to figure out what she was thinking.

Victoria slowly moved the thick, creamy liquid on her belly; loving the feel as it lubricated her skin. Then tentatively, she lifted her fingers to her lips and sucked to taste him, looking over at Sabastian shyly.

"Fuck, Vicky," Sabastian suddenly cried as he jumped off the bed and scooped her into his arms.

"What?" she asked alarmed as he walked her into the bathroom.

"You are insatiable. You continue doing stuff like that and I will not be able to stop fucking you," he said in all seriousness.

He placed her gently in the tub and turned on the hot water to engulf her. He threw in some bath oils that quickly coated her skin.

"Relax and I'll be back later," he said, giving the top of her head a quick kiss.

Victoria had no time to respond as he strode purposefully from the room. She didn't know if she should be relieved or upset he was leaving her but settled in to the tub to reflect blissfully on what had happened the last hour.

Chapter 46

Victoria awoke in the Summit to a noise. She vaguely remembered climbing into bed after her bath and rolled toward the sound opening her eyes to greet Sabastian. She was shocked to see Ethan standing over her and she gave a slight gasp. She was fully covered by the heavy duvet but she still reached for more covers.

Going from alarmed straight to angry, she tried to control her temper as she asked.

"What are you doing in here?"

"Only following orders," Ethan said, smiling down at her. His fingers inched toward the top of her blanket and she grabbed on tighter recoiling from this strange man.

"What orders?" she demanded.

"To make sure you are on track," he said not elaborating.

She was about to ask when he suddenly turned away and tossed a remote to her.

"Watch this," he said as he quickly left the room, closing the door quietly behind him.

Victoria stared at the door for a long time, trying to figure out how long Ethan had been watching her sleep and shuttered. *Why would Sabastian send this man to look after her? Where was he? What was he doing? Was Ethan allowed to come into this room at any time? Was he part of her training?*

She was shaken up and decided to get dressed in case Ethan came back, ignoring the remote. She found a pair of silk boxers and a red tank top and threw them on quickly.

She sat on the bed confused and was tempted to push the button by the door to see if she could ask for Sabastian to come back to her but was afraid of getting Ethan instead.

Victoria was happy when she heard a familiar click and sliding sound and she got up to retrieve her meal from the wall table. She hardly looked at the food she ate; still deep in thought when she snapped out of her reverie to grab for the remote trying to distract herself.

The video was a self-help film from the company which talked in detail about a woman's sexuality, both her mental and physical part in becoming aroused and satisfied. At one point, it instructed her on how to touch herself. She blushed so strongly at the woman on the screen not able to copy her movements, but unable to take her eyes off what she did with her fingers and the pleasure it brought the on-screen woman. It was teaching her about her body and to react to only the thoughts in her head and the words that could be spoken to make her instantly aroused. She knew firsthand what words the film was referring to.

Being fucked good and hard, she thought to herself, then realized those were Ethan's words and shuddered.

She could feel her body readying itself for sex by the sensual squeezing she could feel between her legs. Both her thoughts and the video and the words they were saying about having control and power over her own body made her start to squirm. Her body reaching for the fulfillment she had experienced a few hours ago. Watching the video, her desire was mounting drastically.

Sabastian watched her from the doorway in the bedroom knowing that the video would be over soon, she couldn't see him and he smiled, seeing her fidget on the bed. The video was very good, he assumed, not knowing what it was really about only knowing it was the first in series of videos that taught a woman to control her body. He was jealous though, he wanted to be the one to make her squirm like that and he cleared his throat and asked, "Can I come in or do you want to be alone with your show?"

Victoria jumped at his voice, her face turning beat red.

"Y…ya, you can come in," she answered mortified.

Sabastian walked over and sat on the bed next to her and asked, "Why are you embarrassed, Vicky? Are you turned on?"

He grazed his finger lightly over the surface of the duvet and looked totally at ease with the question that made her cheeks burn hot.

"N…no."

"Really?"

He brushed his fingers on the inside of her thighs, feeling her reach into his hand when he reached the apex of her groin and squeezed, smiling when she moaned.

"Do you always respond like that when you are watching TV?"

"No!" she repeated angrily.

Victoria was still angry at him for letting a creep like Ethan watch over her and took to the defensive to hide her fear. Of course she was more upset Sabastian had read her so well and knew exactly how to make her voice her pleasure. The fact he knew her body better than she did was somehow infuriating.

Ignoring him completely, she got up and started slamming dressers open and closed, she yelled angrily, "Isn't there normal clothes to wear in this stupid room."

"Nope, only sexy lingerie and slutty role-playing costumes."

He was watching her from the bed, thoroughly amused, trying desperately not to laugh at her in her temper.

Victoria looked at him and only his dimples showed her that he was holding back a smile.

"Well, I am so glad I amuse you, Sabastian, but I need some normal clothes," her voice dripping with distain. She pulled lower drawer and found a red sweater and sweat pants. Not overly flattering but she threw them on determined to get some distance she stormed out of the room heading for the garden.

Sabastian followed her, enjoying her outburst.

"What are you going to do in here?" he asked her as she stomped around the sunny board walk surrounded by tiger lilies.

"I don't know, Sabastian. Get some air and some space maybe," she fumed.

"Say it again, Vicky."

"What?" she glowered at him.

"My name, I want to hear it on your lips again."

Mad that he was flirting with her and not taking her seriously, she started to yell.

"For Christ's sake, Sabastian, will you just…"

She didn't get to finish, he strode to her and grabbed her around the waist, pulling her hard to him. He covered her mouth with his, kissing her deeply as he squeezed her body into his.

Angry he was manhandling her, she tried to pull away but he wrapped his arms so firmly around her body it was impossible. Both his lips and his arms were stealing her breath and she gasped when his lips finally left hers.

He stepped back from her and said, "Miss Victoria, I need you to…"

Victoria cut him off, getting more and more pissed at this dominating male. She wanted to ask him where he had been and what he had been doing. She wanted to tell him not to leave her and to keep Ethan away from her. She did not want to need anyone and desperately needing Sabastian to keep her safe was scary so she built a wall and thought of the only excuse she could for her anger.

"Okay, that's enough of this 'miss' thing, it's driving me nuts. I am not one of your trained up working girls." She stepped toward him, "I do not want to be treated like some naive girl who just needs a little training like a dog and I do not need you reciting some respect code like a robot only following orders, its crap. So if you want to talk to me, just do it and stop this bull about total respect and talk to me like normal person."

She poked her finger hard into his chest, pushing him away.

"I am not your science project. You got that, Bastian boy."

Sabastian's rage was instantaneous and frightening, his hand shot out and grabbed her hand hard, squeezing painfully.

She was shocked and terrified, her body tensed, sensing danger, she wanted to react but suppressed her training, scared. He held her hand in a vise like grip and she froze. Sabastian was looking through her, not focusing and her adrenaline shot up and her tears watered from the pain.

"D…d…d…don't c…c…call me th…that ever a…a…again," the words tore from his lips shuddering.

She looked into his black emerald eyes and almost stuttered herself.

"I'm sorry," she said, panicking.

He still wouldn't focus on her, still looking through her, it was like he was somewhere else. She looked down at her hand and gave a light tug but Sabastian only tightened his grip. Tears ran down her cheeks, she couldn't escape; she was trapped and her hand felt it was in a slowly tightening vise.

"Sabastian," She whispered, pleading, barely audible, "you're hurting me."

Forcing herself to look into his frightening eyes, she saw him finally focus on her, then he looked down in horror. He released his grip on her fingers, holding her hand but softly now and placed his other hand on top, cradling her bruising hand so gently she was surprised his hands could ever cause her harm.

"My God, Victoria, I am so sorry," his eyes now look anguished as he saw her tears.

She only pulled her hand away from his warily then turned and ran from the garden.

Sabastian only hesitated a second, horrified at what he had done before taking off after her. He caught up to her just as she closed her bedroom door in his face, effectively stopping him from entering. He reached down for the handle to try to force his way in but she had fixed the chain in place. There was no coming back from this, he had physically harmed her and he couldn't take it back. He could break down her door but that would only push her further away, he could not rage in there like some mad man, but he had to find some way to erase her fear.

"Please, Vicky, let me in, I have to talk to you, I am so, so sorry. Let me explain, I have to explain. Let me in, I am begging you."

Silence.

Running both his hands through his hair, he whispered though the partially opened door, "Please, please, Vicky, open the door…Please."

It was no use, so he simply pulled the door shut gently and walked away.

Vicky was leaning against the wall behind the door out of sight and could hear every word Sabastian spoke. What had happened to him? She flashed back to the moments when she was held captive by her father and brutalized by him, the only difference is her father had loved hurting her and was always in the moment. She noticed her own eyes were out of focus looking at nothing across the room remembering the terrible memories just like Sabastian's had done in the garden and realized she wasn't the only one with a troubled past.

She heard his whispered pleas, sorry he was so upset. There was one clear difference between Sabastian and her father, Sabastian would never intentionally hurt her and her father would never beg forgiveness.

Sabastian had stopped pleading and had shut the door, Victoria reached for the deadbolt and hesitated.

Chapter 47

"Show me."

Matthew worked the monitors only part time but he was as proficient with the dials as Roman and loved the way the system worked. It had a full view of every common area in the men's manor. The monitors were not the best and he agreed with their tech guy, Timothy, that they needed to go to high definition. However, Mr. D insisted the monitors were only there to ensure everyone's behavior was up to his high standards and weren't there to watch in detail what everyone did.

The monitors also were in the women's manor but were only watched if there was a conflict between the staff. The same went for the men's manor; not viewed unless, of course, there was a new recruit to keep an eye to ensure the girl's safety. Matthew thought the main fault in the system was its lack of sound. Their boss told them that listening on the people who worked for him was going too far. He only needed eyes on the manors in order to run things smoothly and keep the girls safe, so no sound was ever recorded on the system.

Matthew played the recording of Sabastian and Victoria, or the wild cat, as everyone called her, in the garden.

They could see everything in the garden and followed the pair on their walk. They watched the altercation and were both completely bewildered at what had gone wrong.

The physical abuse was clear and Jeremy took out his phone and texted someone before asking, "I want to see every interaction between them, chronologically."

"Yes, sir, I already have the first few ready to go," Matthew stated.

Matthew did his job well and knew Jeremy would want to see the history of what these two had been up to the last few weeks, once he had reported the garden incident.

Jeremy saw that Sabastian had offered the girl her knives back, which unnerved him. Sabastian had hardly known this girl and she was unpredictable. Then he was bewildered to see that Sabastian had brought her to his room. Certain women in the men's rooms were allowed, however, Sabastian hardly ever let anyone in his room. To Jeremy's knowledge, he never had a woman in his room ever and the only time any of the guys were in there was when they begged to see his aquarium.

Jeremy continued to watch the monitors. The pair had had a pleasant talk in his room and the one altercation they had previous was when Sabastian had upset her in the massage room, nothing really to be concerned about. The only one who was angry was the intern and Sabastian had handled that professionally.

There had been times when, what he said made her angry, judging by her reactions but that was normal in the introduction period.

Sabastian used to be a renegade but Jeremy had not seen that side of him in years. Sabastian had shut down his emotions as required and did his job well. All the men did that, it was a job requirement, no feelings were preferred when doing your job, it kept the men apart emotionally from the women and kept the peace. No emotion meant no jealousy, no outbursts, and no fighting. It also meant that there were no conflicts especially between the sexes. The men would once in a while shake things up between themselves, but being men they might fight it out in the gym and were over it the next day.

Something about this girl had Sabastian rattled and she had brought back the emotions he was trained to suppress. He was acting out and the fact he had brought her to his room was the first warning sign.

Matthew had called Jeremy right away as he was trained to do when he saw the incident the garden. Any unwanted physical contact was restricted with an absolute no tolerance policy. It was one of their top rules, showing any kind of violence toward women here was dealt with quickly and harshly. Even the threat of violence, either physical, verbal, or sexual, was punished severely, with the exception of certain tests that needed to be administered in the internship phase. No man had any right to hurt a woman here and violence was second only to rape in this company, which had only happened once.

The rapist in question had been found in a land fill, naked, with his genitals ripped off twenty-four hours after the rape in the women's manor had happened. That was fifteen years ago and had not even come close to being repeated. The men were almost brain washed to immediately stop any physical contact when a woman said no. It was a safe word here and it almost never needed to be used with the respect rules in place.

The fact that Sabastian had grabbed her, had to be dealt with. Jeremy watched the rest of the video to see if there was anything else that would alarm him. Besides the very involved kisses, that were a much more than what he ever saw from Sabastian, everything looked like it was going okay. Jeremy was concerned, however, after the doctor's visit.

"What happened there?" he asked, pointing at the screen with the Dr. Marshall visit on it.

"Both the men left the room and then she goes from being in the bed and skips to her in the bathtub, what's missing?"

"I don't know," Matthew said. "It looks like she had her examination, then had a bath, not unusual. I just can't find the footage of her leaving the room and going to the tub."

He looked at the screen.

"It looks like we lost almost three minutes of film at one point," Matthew said, comparing the times at the bottom of the screens.

"That is unacceptable, find out what happened there," Jeremy said. Then left Matthew to work before heading to Mr. D's Office to inform his boss.

Chapter 48

Sabastian had his back against the wall in the hallway, his hands in his hair trying to clear his mind when he heard a click and his breath caught in his throat. Taking his hands out of his now tangled hair, he slowly turned toward the sound.

Victoria's bedroom door was slightly ajar. It wasn't wide open but he could see she had removed the chain. He walked forward quickly and paused before he pushed the heavy mahogany door open, trying not to rush in and scare Victoria more.

She was sitting crossed legged in the middle of the bed with a pillow held tightly on her lap. He walked through the doorway, wanting desperately to lock it to give him more time before they would come. But knowing how that would look to Victoria, he simply closed it behind him. He walked to the chair and pulled it several feet from the bed and sat down, hoping that was enough distance to make her feel at ease.

He asked, "Are you okay?"

She rubbed her hand, glancing down at it, "My hand's fine," answering quietly.

Sabastian caught that she didn't answer the question, so he asked again.

"Are *you* okay?" emphasizing the word "you."

"I don't know, Sabastian," she said softly. "What happened to you?" she asked, hugging the pillow tighter to her chest.

He wanted to tell her everything, but knowing he didn't have much time, he tried to think of a shortened version of his story. Not being able to think how to simplify it, he dove right in speaking fast hoping she would understand.

"By the time I was six, I could do my own laundry, cook, and clean. My mother was not exactly the nurturing kind and I was left alone a lot from a young age. My dad worked on the oil rigs so he only came home about four times a year. My mother partied a lot, drugs and guys almost every night and usually all day. She would come home with her friends and would join them in tormenting me because of my stutter or bossing me around. I would try to be out of the house most days but it was hard when you're that young. Sometimes being home and being beaten, teased, or humiliated was more secure than being on the streets alone in the dark. Plus I was used to it, it was the norm and I took it well, it made me strong."

Trying to ignore the look of pity on Victoria's face, he continued.

"My mom finally went out one day and never returned when I was ten. It was two months before my dad came home to find me alone and her gone and he was devastated. Even though they barely saw each other, he loved her. He was taken aback that he didn't know her as well as he thought and he blamed me for her leaving. It took me a long time to realize it wasn't my fault she had left, but I lived with the guilt for years after. Once my dad got over the fact she was gone, he realized he was now saddled with me. He contemplated adoption as he had no family he could dump me on but seeing how I had lived by myself for the last couple months, he left me alone again."

Ignoring her gasps, Sabastian kept his eyes down looking off to the side unfocused as the words flowed from him.

"Once again abandoned, he gave me money and his credit card along with instructions and was gone. I would have loved the freedom if I hadn't been by myself for so long, but at least I was used to it. I used the credit card to buy anything I needed. I forged all school papers and even signed up for football using friends or buses to get to games. I was the captain of the basketball team and thrived on the activities. I had friends over, set up my own birthday parties, I was okay. Maybe even better now that Mom had left and didn't bring her friend's home with her any more. Although I wanted her back, I also dreaded every time I heard a car pull up close to the house. My dad would show up every few weeks at first, then started taking longer shifts, and plenty of overtime. I think he needed the money because he was still paying for the credit cards my mother was using. I think he kept them active, trying to track her down."

Victoria knew her responses to Sabastian's history was making him uneasy and she fought to listen and keep her reactions to herself, but it was difficult. At least she had had someone who loved her unconditionally when she was little, Sabastian had no one. She was absorbed his soft deep voice, his distant manner, forgetting why he was talking completely lost in his story.

"When I was about thirteen, I started getting into trouble at school, the only rules I had to follow were school rules, as I was so used to doing what I wanted. I had no discipline and I was soon kicked out of school and that included all the sports I loved to do. So I went the only place I could play and that was downtown Chicago. I was still young then, a credit card, a house, friends and it turned ugly. I started using drugs, getting into fights on the street and joined a gang. It wasn't long before the head of the gang, singled me out and started training me to fight, as I was pretty big even then. I was heavily muscled from football and working out, so he trained me to fight and I was put into the ring against other gangs' fighters. It was like cock fighting, both gangs would settle minor arguments or territory with the fights and of course bet tons of money on the outcome, but mostly it was for entertainment. I was young but strong, at first I generally got the shit kicked out of me every few days."

Victoria made a move to reach out to him but thought better of it and settled on the edge of the bed.

"When I wasn't in an official fight, I was bated into street fights as others would goad me to get my temper up so they could see how good I was or just jump me for fun. When I started to get better and was winning more often than not, I would be put up against two guys or even three. If it was one sided, it wasn't fair, so they had to even the odds, no matter how well I did, I never got a break. When I wasn't cock fighting, I was the lap dog to Kick, the gang's leader, getting what he wanted, pushing others around for his amusement, and generally being treated like trash. There was no way out for me, I was hooked on drugs and had nowhere to go. I was always surrounded by other guys that would hassle me, hound me, push me around, and was never left alone. I had no privacy, they wouldn't even let me sleep most nights, waking me up to make me fight, which I usually did. I was once again beaten, humiliated, and tormented and it was a comfort somehow. It brought me a feeling of security as it was all I had known when I was young. They were the closest thing I had to a family and at least they were always there for me."

"I wanted to go back to my simple life, going to school, playing sports, and hanging out with friends but it had been years since I was kicked out of school and I was trapped. My father had cancelled my credit card long ago, so I had to fight for my food and my drugs. I hated it and was going to end it all, just stop fighting and let the other gang members do the ending for me. But that is when Mr. D found me, he was looking for a girl when he found me, they took

271

me as well as their collection that night. He cleaned me up, gave me a home, and a real family that truly cared for me and took care of me properly. I got my privacy back, which I cherish and he gave me a chance to start over, I was so completely enthralled at his generosity, I owe him everything and I wish I could…"

Victoria, her mouth gapped open, with tears in her eyes, jumped when two strange men entered the room.

Sabastian stopped talking and immediately got up. Victoria, who was gripping the pillow so tight her sore hand throbbed, stared at them.

"Sabastian," the tall older gentleman with salt and pepper hair said, "would you kindly come with us please?"

"Yes Sir, Jeremy." Sabastian gave her a look of regret as he turned to leave.

Victoria jumped out of her bed, thinking fast for once.

"Wait a minute, you were not invited in," she said to the two unknown men. "You cannot just walk in here any time you want, what happened to respect?"

Jeremy turned toward her, "I am so very sorry, Miss Victoria, and I truly regret having to break rules, but it is for your own safety. Sabastian will be removed from your program and you will be working with someone else from now on."

Sabastian had already walked to the door knowing if he fought it would only make things worse. He had assaulted her and expected they would come for him sooner or later. He was just glad he was able to tell her a bit about why he lashed out.

Victoria was terrified of him leaving.

"No, you can't take him. We were talking. Let him stay, he won't hurt me!" she reached for him and was surprised when both men stepped back.

She looked confused at the men, then slowly reached past them for Sabastian's arm.

Sabastian saw that Jeremy didn't know what to do. Jeremy could not physically restrain her, especially after she had been manhandled. Jeremy turned to Sabastian expectantly.

"I have to go, Miss Victoria, I am so sorry about what happened in the garden. I hope I have not soured its beauty for you," he said, back his formal speech in front of the other men.

She pushed away her feelings of frustration at his polite and rehearsed tone and gripped his arm tighter. "Please stay," she pleaded softly, her eyes letting go of the tears they were holding onto.

Sabastian lifted the arm that she held and gently took her hand from him. "Goodnight, Miss Victoria," he said so concerned for the pain she felt for him. He turned and left her standing there, still seeing the distress written in her eyes.

The men led the way and Sabastian followed then turned around quickly and said, "The name my mother and her friends used, as well as my street name was Bastian boy," and with his last words, he silently closed the door behind him.

Chapter 49

Victoria had been so engulfed in his story that she had completely forgotten why he had started the confession. It was to tell her why he had lashed out at her.

Bastian boy was his name given to him by his mother and from the thugs on the streets and she must have invoked powerful memories of the life he lived before he was brought to Eximius.

I guess I am not the only one with a crummy background, she thought.

She stood in the doorway and the ache she felt for him crushed her. She had endured an occasional beating from her father but her mother had always been there to save her, to rescue her, and take the brunt of the abuse. She had known such a strong love from her cherished mother and could not think what it would be like to have no one to love or even take care of you as a child.

She could see him, six years old, doing laundry or cooking simple meals to make sure he was fed. She could see him on the streets being humiliated and beaten with no will of his own, no freedom and no one who cared about him. She couldn't get over his story and saw that her life had been a walk in the park compared to his. It took her a long time to finally take her mind from his past and to think about her own predicament.

In a daze, Victoria turned to sit on her bed. Sabastian was going to be replaced and she shuttered. Some strange man, who she had never met, was going to teach her about sex and the thought sent a chill up her spine. Would the new guy figure out she had been a virgin only a few days ago? What would happen to Sabastian if they found out or her for that matter?

She crawled into bed in her clothes and let her tears fall for Sabastian and the new unnerving situation she found herself in.

Victoria awoke to her breakfast the next day, which she ignored, turning in bed, she slept some more. When her next meal came two hours later, she went to the bathroom and then slumped back into bed, trying to sleep. Her last few weeks of exercise and routine urged her to get up, but she couldn't and just lay there staring at the ceiling, thinking about what she was going to do. When her third meal went untouched, there was a knock on her door.

She jumped up and went to the door and called out, "Sabastian?"

She heard an unknown voice muffle.

"No, miss."

"Then go away," she said angrily, locking the door forcefully.

No one answered so she went to the washroom, grabbed a book, and started to study, trying to focus on the words but they blended together. She couldn't get her mind off of him.

What happened to him? Where was he? Were they doing something to him? Did they not realize it was my fault he grabbed me? He didn't see me in the garden. I had to bring him back. He was so far away in his dark thoughts.

She cursed herself for being so bossy, she just had to put him in his place.

"Well, now look what happened, stupid. He's gone and some guy who thinks I have experience is going to try to jump me! Then what?" she asked herself. "How am I going to get out of that one?"

Another meal was passed through the wall with her notebook, she jumped up hoping I was him.

"Dear Victoria, please eat for me. The only pleasure I get is when you enjoy the wonderful food that I create for you."

It was Nickolas trying to guilt her into eating. Well, her guilt box was full at the moment. She put her book back, went to sleep, ignoring the knocking door, and the food that kept coming.

The next day was the same, she only got up to use the facilities and drink a little water, ignoring all attempts to communicate with her. She knew they were watching and every time the door knocked, she would flip her middle finger to the ceiling toward the unseen cameras.

On the morning of day three, there was a knock on the door again, she ignored it and flipped the bird to the camera she could not see again. Then she heard a voice on the other side of the bedroom door.

"Miss Victoria, you will need to either eat or let me in. If you do neither, we will be forced to enter without your consent for your own good."

Shit, she thought, she had completely forgotten about the hatch under her bed. She couldn't let some strange man into her room, not knowing what they would do to her.

"Fine, I'll eat," she yelled petulantly through the door.

She went over to the tray and took it over to her bed. Whoever was at the door must have been satisfied and left. Victoria barley nibbled on the food, delicious as it smelled, she didn't have an appetite. She was devising a plan and needed time, so every meal that came, she ate at least half of it before sending it back, hoping to keep whoever wanted in, at bay. She was going to need her strength anyway, if her idea worked out the way she planned.

Chapter 50

Delayed again, his outraged increased, he couldn't take it anymore. He wanted her so bad, her soft skin, her hair, her eyes, and her innocence made him painfully hard and he wanted to get back at her from the pain she caused him. He wanted to hurt her like she was hurting him as he bucked in his slacks. He had gotten close to completing his fantasy and had been denied and he knew he needed to watch his timing. If he planned his next move wrong or was interrupted, he would only have an hour or two and he wanted a whole night of taking her again and again, her fighting him and him cruelly forcing her to enjoy the pleasure he would make her body take.

He fumed, paced, and cursed in his room like a dog with a bitch in heat on the other side of his cage. His erection throbbed and pulsed hard again, thinking of her and the test he would eventually administer once he could be let loose.

His skin shone with exertion of holding himself back and finally, he knew he couldn't take it anymore and stormed from his room, grabbing a large black case as he went.

Slowing and moving quietly, as he didn't want anyone else to know he was here, he silently walked into the room unannounced. It was late and she was asleep on the bed and he smiled, that was good, he would have time to prepare himself.

He got undressed, completely naked, his cock still reaching out for anything to satisfy it and he opened his case. This was almost as good as it could get, not quite, but almost.

Reaching inside the case for a black handle, he walked over to the bed. Pulling off the covers to reveal the sleeping girl completely naked; he saw her come out of a deep sleep slightly and his arm shot out, the black handle held tightly in his hand. The whip flipped over his arm and struck the girl hard on her hip and back.

He pounced on her as soon as his arm had finished the slashing motion and he covered her lips before she had time to cry out.

"Shhhh," he whispered soothingly at the frightened eyes of the young girl under him.

He could see tears in her eyes from the blow, but she focused on him and relaxed slightly under his grip and he wanted to hit her again for her compliance.

Still putting all his weight on her body, his hard hand over her face, he leaned in close and said, threating, "You have only one chance to say no Michelle and this is it."

He hated these rules, he knew he couldn't take any women without her permission and that is why the intern's tests were his ultimate satisfaction. He also knew this girl and knew what her response would be, but he still had to ask and that infuriated him more than he thought possible.

His hand moved from her mouth to her throat and put gentle pressure on her wind pipe so she could still answer him.

He saw her eyes dilate looking into his face. He could see she was scared; he had never been this brutal, this fast and he could see she was curious to what he had in store for her and he smiled as her mouth curved up slightly.

"Yes," the woman gasped under him.

He swiftly yanked her off the bed and on her knees before him, making her shriek.

"You do not have my permission to make noise," he yanked her back by her too short blonde hair, "You got that?"

"O…k…k," Michelle stammered.

He brought the whip to her skin so fast, he needed to teach her to listen better. He repeated his question.

"You got that?" he asked again, brutally pulling her head back against his groin, pressing his prick into her cheek and she felt her nod against him.

"That's better," he growled down at his captive.

"Stay," he commanded and walked to the wall to turn on the lights.

He turned to see her on her knees gazing at him, he saw the places the whip had made her skin pink and it made her more beautiful to him. Her eyes were wary, but intrigued and he saw she wouldn't fight him. He decided if he wanted a fight, he would have to push her and wanted to see how far he could take her. He had taken Michelle a few times and she was very willing and very good, having experience in being a slave to a dominates needs, but he had not really pushed her limits, at least not until now.

"You will not say no, understand, you had your chance," he hovered over her and his erection jerked toward her closed mouth.

He saw her nod her head and he thrust himself at her soft full lips, "Suck me."

Michelle's mouth opened automatically and her lips wrapped hungrily around his engorged head, sucking strongly. Her tongue wrapping around and around the tip quickly. He groaned and felt her hand wrap around his shaft and his cock thrust, full of sensation as his arm brought the whip down hard on her soft small back.

"I told you only to suck," he growled at her and felt the hand move away from his throbbing penis and her sweet soft tongue increase its movements. He grabbed her hair and thrust into her harder, making her gag deliciously on his full length. He gripped her hair as he pushed into her, twisting her head back pounding into her mouth as he came hard and fast.

"Fuck, yes, bitch, suck me, suck me," he repeated as he thrust into her sweet hot mouth. His cum dripped out the corner of her lips as she sucked him relentlessly. He loved the girl's enthusiasm and hoped it would continue.

He suddenly lifted her mouth off his now sensitive head with her hair and raised her up to him. Face to face, her hard nipples grazed his chest. His arm swung around and the whip struck her skin. His eyes bore into hers and watching every movement of her body and the reaction to the pain. He whipped her again and saw her eyes twitch and dilate with pleasure every time the snap of the black leather strings stung her flesh.

He lowered his mouth and bit lightly, then hard on her nipple, grinding it between his teeth until she moaned.

His mouth left hers and he clucked his tongue at her.

"Uh oh, you will need to be punished for making a sound," he smiled at her expression as he lifted her feet off the ground and carried her over to the bed. Roughly, he laid her across his naked lap and dropping the whip, he brought his hand down hard on her ass and felt her body clench. She was doing so well he didn't want to push his luck and risk a report. Giving her what she needed and starting over again would be so much fun anyway. He felt his prick rise up hard and fast with the thought of what he was about to do to this helpless girl.

Spreading his knees wide and centering her hot pubic mound over the empty space, he leaned over and put his hand between her legs. He hit her again in the same spot and he felt her start to fight away from the sting. His cock jumped at the resistance, she wanted him to stop. He saw her hands on the bed start to try to raise herself up. He heard her try to articulate her displeasure and he hit her again before she could say anything. Every time she tried to speak, he hit her, forcing her to struggle and try to get out of the position he had her in.

He wanted to push her more but she was already on edge, so his hand came down once more as his other hand thrust into her soaking wet sex and her scream turned to pleasure in a heartbeat. He knew he had her now and hit her again, her cream flowing down his hand and dripping down his wrist. With every downstroke, his finger dug deeper into her slit and she squirmed and moaned. His cock bucked against her hip with every slap of skin on skin and he had to hold himself back.

He needed to teach her about her body, she was upset but now she must be able to see the way her body craved the cruelty and hungered for the blows. This time, he pushed his hand on her curved red bottom, rotating her hips on his fingers pushing as deep into her as they would go, before striking her again.

"See how wet you are, Michelle, you fucking love it. You want me to take you, fuck you so hard you blow up around me," he whispered as his fingers pushed roughly into her soaking wet folds.

"I want you to fight me, Michelle, fight me hard and I will give you what you want."

He hit her again hard and his fingers dug into her sex with each blow, she didn't struggle though as she was so close to cumming. She squirmed on his hand as she waited for the sting of his hand to increase the pleasure with his fingers. He let his hitting hand do the work as he smacked down hard three times in succession and felt Michelle's tight pussy grip his hand pulsing and bucking.

One more blow after she came made her shriek and he lay his hand softly on her behind and moved it in slow circles around his fingers as she came down from her fulfillment. She moaned under him and his cock throbbed painfully into her hip. Moving her off him and onto the bed, she went limp with relief.

He placed her on the bed and grabbed a silk tie and before she knew what was happening, he covered her mouth, effectively silencing her.

He saw her eyes pop open alarmed and he grabbed her hands and pinned them above her head before she got the chance to take off the gag.

His erection shuddered as her struggles increased, he tied her hands together and then tied her heels together and bent her knees up and apart. He heard her muffled attempts to talk.

"You had your chance to say no, Michelle, now shut up before I have to punish you again."

She quieted, but the excited fear in her eyes was still there and he shivered. Leaving her, he took a long piece of rope from his bag and tied her ankles to her wrists behind her back.

He gazed down at his work, her arms behind her back, her heels tied together with her legs spread wide. His erection turned to marble as he climbed on top of her.

Not touching her, he bent down to her ear and said menacingly. "I loved how you fought me, I see you're scared and I fucking love it. You think you're done, but I've only just begun."

He was more than ready and could no longer denied himself. Placing his hands on her knees, spreading her legs wider, he buried himself into her still dripping engorged folds, pushing himself to the hilt and paused looking down at his captive. He saw her troubled eyes widen, still worried.

"Good, Michelle, did you like that?" he asked not really needing a reply, he pulled out slowly and felt a slight grip on his shaft as his entire length left her body.

"Fuck, you love it," he said; bracing the girl under him, he started his assault and pounded into her ruthlessly.

He slid in and out of her easily and could feel the fresh flow of her juices wrapped around his cock. He thrust and push and felt her tightening, she was quivering beneath him and his shaft jumped inside her. He saw her eyes close and her body arched up into his and he frantically penetrated as deep and as hard as he could. He thundered into her faster as her walls closed and vibrated violently around him and he cried out.

"Oh fuck, yes," he came hard as he heard her muffled cries of pleasure rack her body and spasm her entire frame under him.

He reached over and ripped the tie off her mouth so he could hear the cries of her orgasm as he continued to pound into her softening flesh.

Her over sensitive body jerked under him and he ground his hips into hers, feeling her try to move away and smiled smugly.

"Oh come on, Michelle, daddy wants more," he said as he pushed into her.

"I can't, I'm done," she sighed, struggling against the ties on her feet.

"You're done when I say you're done."

"No, I said I'm done."

He didn't want to argue with her and he knew he might have already pushed it too far; he wetly pulled out of her sex and untied the knots at her back.

"You don't want me to fuck you anymore?" he asked, testing her.

"No, that was almost too much," Michele said, rubbing her wrists on the bed.

"But you liked it, right?" he was talking softly to her, trying to see if she really was okay, he loved his job and couldn't afford to lose it.

He brightened when she said, "I said it was almost too much, it was overwhelming and unexpected but so much more than I have ever experienced. You have my permission to do that to me any time you want."

She smiled at him.

"No report?" he asked, knowing her answer.

"Hell no, my ass is a little sore, but I loved it," she knelt up on the bed to kiss him.

He didn't like her kissing him, but it was good to know he wouldn't be punished for his lack of control.

He saw her lay down on the bed, rubbing her ankles wincing slightly and his body stirred. He wanted to push her, fuck her, and have her fight him again. Every time she had said no stirred his desire to take her once more. His thoughts went to the new intern who he would be able to do what he wanted with and his half-erect cock filled up slowly.

Michelle glanced up at him and saw the state he was in and with worried eyes, she shook her head.

He slowly crawled onto the bed, pulling her legs under his body as she struggled.

"Ah," she said again and his penis thrust out.

"I am going to fuck you for real this time," he said, pushing her legs apart and entering her so fast she couldn't escape. She screeched under him and struggled. His eyes rolled into his head as he felt her truly start to fight him.

She had been satisfied twice and her body was over-stimulated and not interested. However he needed more, he needed to be true to his nature and get full satisfaction and she was going to give it to him, whether she liked it or not. She tried frantically to pull him out of her as he followed her and her struggles pushed her into the back of the bed. She had nowhere left to go so he pulled her up on his thighs and lifted her up and let gravity and his hands on her hips pound on him like a jackhammer.

She was still fighting him, saying his name, trying to get him to stop but he was so consumed by his fantasy with Victoria he didn't register the woman he was forcing to ride him to a complete satisfaction.

He lifted her with his hips and yanked her down on him in a hard fast rhythm, thrusting over and over again until she really started to battle him struggling hard. He felt her walls squeeze his erection violently each time she tried to get away and it drove him to the edge of reason. She was fighting him, tensing her body around him, and finally, he felt her stop fighting and move with him once.

He immediately threw her to the side and mounted her from behind spreading her legs wide and grabbing her hips and he felt her relax into him, accepting. He slapped her soundly on her tender behind and she fought him again with more vigor. She squeezed him with her struggles and he stuffed her relentlessly. Digging his fingers into her tender over used flesh as he forced the orgasm unwilling from her body, making her suddenly cry out. As suddenly as she came, his body jerked and convulsed frantic with the effort, finding the raw release he so desperately needed.

"Auuuuuuugggggghhhhhh, ffffuuuuccccckkkkk," he growled as he surged himself into her, letting lose the pounding climax that had been seeking.

He slowed slightly and finally released the girl who had collapsed on the bed under him. Rolling off her, he knew he had some damage control to do but needed time to breathe first.

He rested his hand on her back and slowly rubbed her and was glad she did not recoil from him.

After several long minutes of panting, he rolled over and whispered in her ear.

"Now that was a good fucking, Miss Michelle."

Michelle turned her head to him with tears in her eyes and he knew he had pushed it too far.

Shit, he thought, *I need to do some smooth talking to get myself out of this one.*

Ethan knew he was getting away with more than he dared with his boss gone. He would have never attempted this rendezvous if his boss or even Miss Cherry at the manor.

Hoping to lead her to believe this was for her own good, he said.

"I did that because I knew you would like it. You loved it, didn't you?" he was worried for his job and detested having to console her.

Michelle stayed silent breathing hard and looking at him with her head still resting the bed.

He reached out, rubbing her back, and kissed her lightly on the shoulder, "Mmmm, Michelle, you did wonderfully, you were beautiful in your passion and it couldn't have been better. I thought you needed to know how much your body could take and how much you would like being taken like that. Tell me you loved it and would still do that again."

He leaned down and kissed her again slowly and softly on the lips, feigning concern. Relief hit him when he pulled away from her lips and he saw a slight smile curve her swollen mouth.

"Ya, it's okay. I just have to adjust to what happened. It was unexpected and hard to handle but if you could do that to me again, I am sure I'll be able to take it."

He was elated and kissed her softly again rubbing her back. "Oh, Michelle, I think we could do so much more together. I just never knew what you could take and I always have to be so careful with you girls."

"I thought there were at least two or three submissives in the Eximius manor?"

"Oh there are, but I am not allowed to play with them, not in the way I want to anyway. I can't leave marks on them and in the end, they're in control. But with you, I can play with little rules and have you at my mercy," he grinned wickedly at her worried face.

He flipped her onto her back and leaned into her kissing her slowly, softly on the lips and rubbing her side until he heard her moan. He knew then that she would respond to him the next time he decided to fulfill his fantasy with her.

Still thinking of Victoria, he got dressed and took his case with him. He had only used one thing in his bag. He wouldn't be able to use most of his toys with the wild cat as she would be a handful with all the defense training she had. But using his hands would be the greatest aphrodisiac of all any way.

Michelle had been a welcome surprise. He had pushed her over the edge both physically and sexually. He never thought she would be that willing and yet unwilling at the same time and thought she would be a good fill in until he could actually perform the test on the very unsuspecting Miss Victoria. Now all he needed to do was wait for the right time and catch her unaware.

Chapter 51

Victoria studied and ate all day, trying to figure out how she was going to get away with her idea. She took a long nap in the middle of the day which was not unusual as she had been sleeping on and off throughout the day for the last few days. When she awoke, she was edgy, so she took a long bath. Whoever was watching would like that, it would look like she was getting back into her routine.

At midnight, she put on a long, dark navy night gown and turned off all the lights, she covered herself up with blankets and laid down. She fussed and tossed and turned for about twenty minutes, trying to slowly arrange the pillows just right under the covers, hoping that whoever was watching was not looking too closely. Feeling foolish that she was trying to pull off a classic prison escape but not caring. She waited over an hour before she started to move carefully toward the button on the night stand beside the bed, cautious to stay under the covers.

She would have to move fast and silent and hoped she had the nerve to go through with it. Making sure her arm was still hidden under the blankets, she reached for the secret button. It took a while to locate it and when she pressed it, the bed silently rose off the ground. As it raised upward, she slid her body to the edge of the bed, making sure the blankets draped down to the carpet to cover her as she dropped to the floor. When she hit the floor Victoria rolled until she was under the bed frame.

She found herself crouched in a low room with soft blue lights along the floor and saw a small door at the end of the low ceiling about fifteen feet away. She moved quickly to the exit, hunched over, and opened the door at the end into a very bright kitchen and squinted to see in the light.

"Good evening, Miss Victoria."

"Ah," she screamed, covering her mouth, pressing her back toward the wall.

"Nice night for a stroll," Nickolas said, smiling down at the fruit he was chopping not looking at her.

Her heart was beating so fast she had to catch her breath.

"Jesus, Nickolas, you scared the shit out of me."

Wide eyed, she frowned at her chef, still frozen in place. She was hidden slightly behind a huge rack of bread rolls in a very bright clean stainless steel professional looking kitchen. Everything was so organized and spotless and the smell of fresh bread and herbs filled her senses.

"The round room is to your left. I trust you know the rest of the way from there?" he said, still working on his fruit.

She gave him a brilliant smile, "You're not going to tell them?"

"I don't have to, if they're watching the monitors, they can see you right now, the whole manor is monitored, not just your room. If you want any time with him at all, I suggest you move fast. And try to look like you haven't let me see you, so I don't get busted as well," he said with a chuckle.

Nickolas turned away from her to pick up more fruit to chop and she took the opportunity he was giving her and bolted behind him, elated.

She followed his instructions and was at Sabastian's door in seconds, happy she hadn't seen anyone else. She couldn't stand in the hallway lightly knocking waiting for him to wake up, so she tried the door which was open. She slid inside the room quietly, which was lit only with the soft aqua light of his aquarium. She looked toward the bed and was taken aback to see him sitting up in bed watching her enter.

Sabastian was so pleasantly surprised that she was here in his room, she looked glorious in her long silk gown and her extensive hair in a braid over her shoulder. Once again, he imagined undoing that hair and letting it fall loose around her naked body while he lay with her.

"Victoria, what are you doing here? Who let you out?"

"I did," she said triumphantly, "What are you doing up?"

"Light sleeper," he said grimly.

Of course, she thought, he had to sleep with one eye open for a very long time.

He wasn't wearing a shirt and looked naked under his covers. She loved to see his naked chest again, remembering the feel of his hardness contrasted with the soft sprinkling of hair covering it. The blue light of the tank gave him a masculine look, defining his square muscles more clearly with blue shadows and she longed to touch him. His wide chest expanded into even wider shoulders, which turned into large arms with well-defined biceps. He was so stunning she was tempted to run her hands all over his body and blushed at the thought.

She walked over to his bed and sat on the edge, watching him. His eyes followed her like a hawk and she could see the light of his aquarium reflected in his eyes.

"Why can't you work with me anymore?" she asked him curiously.

"I assaulted you, Vicky, that's a big no, no here. No man can ever assault a woman, physically or otherwise. I'll be lucky if I'm not kicked out when Mr. D comes back to review my case. For now, I'm grounded," he said bitterly.

"Grounded? Come on, you have to stay in your room like a ten-year-old?" she asked bemused.

"Well, I was never was grounded when I was a kid, so I'm making up for it now," he said with a bitter smile on his lips.

"So you can't see me? Even to talk or umm, teach me?"

"No, I've already lost six months' pay with that little stunt in the garden and may be finished here if I push any farther."

"But I'm just an intern." She argued.

Sabastian could not believe she was here in his bed, begging him to be with her. "You have to go," he said regretfully.

"You lost half your annual salary because you held my hand too tight for a few seconds?" she was aghast.

"Any assault is punished and that is the minimum payment that must be made, you don't get it, they don't mess around here, all women are precious and are to be treated…"

"Ya, ya, I know, with respect," she said rolling her eyes.

"And kindness," he said softly. "I had no right to hurt you and I don't deserve to be with you in any way."

She frowned. "I can sneak out every night and come here," she said, her face lighting up with the idea.

"They already know you're here."

"How? I was very sneaky," she said proudly.

"There's other sensors in you room, not just cameras," he said gravely.

"Oh come on," she said exasperated, "You've got to be kidding me."

288

"Nope and you have to go before we both get caught," he said, not really meaning the words or caring if he got into trouble. He was smiling at her, he loved her daring and longed to touch her.

"If you turn me in, will you get brownie points?" she asked.

"Not sure, I've never had an escaped convict in my room before."

He climbed out of bed and reached for her. She saw he was wearing a pair of dark silk boxers and nothing else, she blushed, and looked up into his eyes. She stood up slowly, shaking she placed her small hands on his broad chest and tilted her head up ever so slightly to look up at him.

Her hands buzzed electric on his skin and she said timidly, "I can't be with some strange guy."

"Well, then, you're not going to last here long," he stated flatly, looking through her.

She knew that he was right and paled.

"Sabastian," she whispered his name so softly she wasn't sure he had heard her until he lowered his mouth to hers. As slowly and as softly as possible, she felt his lips on hers and he was kissing her so sweetly; her eyes watered from the tenderness she felt flowing through him.

She leaned into him, molding her body with his, with only the feel of a thin layer of silk between them, the sensation made her entire body tremble. His powerful physique emphasized her small frame and made her feel delicately feminine. He was so warm, so hard, and so firm everywhere that she craved him to hold her close while she quivered from his touches.

Sabastian felt her shudder and pulled her closer to him. Her soft warm body was what he needed now, he deepened his kiss and she responded by sliding her hands from his chest slowly up to his shoulders and reached up into his hair. Sabastian groaned and pulled her even tighter to him, wrapping one long arm around her back while the other one cupped her face. He knew they didn't have much time. He felt her legs go weak so he lifted her with one arm around her waist over to the bed where he laid her down, his lips never leaving hers.

Underneath him, she sunk into the bed and he laid his entire hard length of his body lightly on hers and felt her push back with her hips.

His body shuddered as he felt the softness of her flesh under the thin layers of silk and wanted desperately to have her naked beneath him so her skin could be molded with his with no barrier between them. However, the slippery fabric made it easy to slide himself along her supple body and his most insistent parts lunged at her. He savored the delicious agony of his pounding erection as he pushed into her urgently. Feeling her full breasts push into him on his chest, he rubbed into her savoring the feel of the fabric slide up and down between their bodies like warm oil. He felt her hands tighten in his hair and he deepened the kiss further, making her moan and her hands ran down his back, clawing at him.

He tore his lips from hers, "Christ, Vicky," he said huskily.

Gazing down at her, she was so sensual, her eyes were dark and she was breathing like she had just ran a marathon. Her breasts rose and fell with each labored breath and he was mesmerized at the delectable female flesh under his. She was watching him, her lashes long and sleek over her unusual eyes.

She pulled at his arms and begged thickly. "Please, Sabastian," as her hips raised to his wantonly. He crushed her then, pushing his hard length against her soft sex and she gave a sharp cry of excitement as she lifted her lips to meet his.

Victoria's kisses were fevered now and she pushed in to his hardness, trying to keep up a rhythm their bodies had started. She was almost crying with yearning and a pulling sensation inside her belly that she didn't know how to control. Her belly and deep inner muscles had been tightening in a steady rhythm ever since he had touched her and she felt a familiar growing need rising far within. She was climbing toward the delicious peak higher and higher and she thrust her hips into his needing him closer to her.

She kept trying to pull him to her tighter and tighter, he was crushing her but it was not close enough, she needed him closer, she needed him inside her again. She dragged her nails down his back lifting herself into him. He was so gorgeous, so strong, his masculinity making her feel so small and vulnerable. She wanted him so bad, needed him to show her everything he knew and to help with this driving need that was growing steadily deep within her. She heard him groan and it threw her into over drive, thrusting her breasts into his chest and spreading her legs wide. He had started to push into her mons slowly but hard and she drove back into him loving the feel of his hardness on her most intimate parts. He tried to move away but she followed him and he pushed into her again slow, grinding her into the bed. She could feel the substantial full length of his cock rub deliciously against her tender mound and the firm push of him into her made her discover a carnal part of herself she didn't know existed.

Sabastian reached down and yanked her gown up to her waist, removing his boxers down to his knees, too impatient to take them off completely. He pressed his erection into her, running along the slick outside of her cleft. Her legs were spread wide, but he pushed along the outside of her wet lips needing to build up her climax before he plunged into her. Not feeling the squeeze of her sex around his he was able to keep some semblance of control. He moved over her, building up a sweet rhythm which she matched with her cries of pleasure.

"Ah," she moaned, "Ahhh."

With every push, she groaned and tried to follow him every time he pulled away, feeling bare without him; her sex tightening with each stroke.

Sabastian felt her tense so he pulled back away from her body a little more. He felt her hips raise up and her legs widen to invite him in. The tip of his sex grazed hers and he slowly pushed his way in to her wet clenching body. He closed his eyes as she closed in around him and he groaned loud at the intense sensation. Her body was so wet and she was so ready he had to force himself to move slow as he pulled out watching as her hips flexed up gripping his length wonderfully. His eyes burned into hers as his hips tensed pushing his body to join hers again and thrilled at the hold this woman had on him. In and out of her, increasing the friction slowly, he wanted her to cum sweetly around him and shuttered with every thrust feeling her climb.

"Ah, ah, ahhhh," Victoria could feel the building stronger and she was getting tighter and tighter, her nerves on edge. She looked up into his eyes and saw an intensity that surprised her but seeing herself in his eyes, she wasn't frightened. She was so close, her body trembled at the plunge she was about to take tighter and tighter she prepared herself for the release. She wanted to be close to him when the sensation hit her so she reached up to kiss him, when she was suddenly blinded by a harsh light.

"Fuck," cursed, Sabastian. He leaped from her pulling up his boxers and grabbed a robe to cover himself up.

"No," she cried desperately as Sabastian lifted his warm delicious weight off of her, making her feel exposed and empty. Her body was still pulsing, throbbing and she couldn't stand the fact that he was gone, she shook at the loss. Outraged, she turned to the door, they had taken him away from her already and they were going to do it again.

She sat up and yelled at the shadows in the door frame.

"Get out!" she demanded.

Sabastian was shocked at the maliciousness in her voice, most girls would be screaming or trying to hide or cover up, but not his Vicky. She was pissed and ready for a fight.

Sabastian came around the bed to stand between her and Jeremy and Chandler who he had known would come to find her here.

"She came to me," Sabastian explained. "She knew where the button was for the hatch under the bed and snuck out."

Chandler tried to look around Sabastian at the first real glimpse of the girl everyone called wild cat, who was well named by the looks of her. It took all his restraint to not grin at the wild looking girl with the after effect of passion still on her face.

"Please beg our pardon, Miss Victoria, but we need to escort you back to your room," Chandler said, taking a step toward her.

"Fuck you," she spat at him and Sabastian's face lit up with a huge grin at her intensity.

He stepped to the side to block the men's view of her, possessive. Locking down his enjoyment of Victoria's passionate response with a professional look, he answered formally.

"That won't be necessary, Chandler, she is perfectly safe here, thank you."

Victoria couldn't believe these guys were fighting over her so politely like she was some palace queen worried they might shock her sensibilities, for Christ's sake, they lived and worked in a whore house.

"Miss Victoria," Jeremy said, still addressing her, "kindly follow us to your room."

He opened the door wide and gestured for her to follow him.

"No," she said stubbornly.

She had a devised a plan for this scenario. The two men had refused to stop her from grabbing Sabastian when they tried to take him away before. They could have easily stopped her, or even blocked her, but they had both backed away from her. She had doubted they were afraid of her, but it was against their training and treatment of women to ever be physical or threating toward them, just like Sabastian had said. She was bound and determined to stay and she knew they wouldn't take her kicking and screaming back to her room. She hoped that not being a true employee would not matter and held her breath, waiting to see if they would call her bluff. She crossed her arms staring at the men.

Sabastian couldn't have been more proud of her, not taking any crap from the guys and holding her ground. It was a shame it wouldn't work the way she wanted.

"Sabastian," Jeremey said low.

Sabastian turned, winked at her, and followed the men out, closing and locking the door behind him.

Victoria froze at what had just happened. That was not the result she had hoped for or even considered.

"Ah, shit," she murmured, slumping.

She wasn't expecting that. They left her in Sabastian's room. She heard the door lock and let out her held breath. She lay down staring at the ceiling, her heart still pumping from both Sabastian's intoxicating touch and the confrontation she had with the men, if you could call it that. She figured they wouldn't be back, at least not tonight so she curled her body around his pillow breathing in his musky, citrus scent. It took a long time for her mind and her body to settle but eventually drifted into a dream of water, waves, and lightning bolts.

Chapter 52

Sabastian followed Chandler and Jeremy down the hall completely distracted of the situation he and Victoria were now in. He was thinking about the way she had responded when his body had covered hers and how utterly sensual she was. Her aroused flesh under his as he had pushed himself into her hot silk covered body had his head spinning and his pulse boiling through his veins, electrifying his over-stimulated body.

His cock ached from the edge he had been pulled from and the dull painful pressure was getting stronger between his legs as he would not be completing the climax Victoria and himself had built together. He ignored his tightening blue balls as he needed to concentrate on controlling his thoughts now that he was away from her as he followed the men down the hall. Only after a few deep breaths thinking of the gravity of the situation they were both in, was he able to think clearly.

He knew the men would come and was happy they had taken their sweet time. He had been able to have some fun with his intern still in his bed only a few steps away and he smiled.

"So, fellas, how your night going?" Sabastian asked casually.

"Having a good time, Sabastian?" Chandler replied.

"Well, I was," Sabastian smirked at him as they walked down the hall and up the stairs.

"She looks like you named her well," Chandler said.

Sabastian didn't like that but let it go with a laugh. "I guess you had a good look then," he said nonchalantly.

"Was she worth it?"

"Just another piece of ass that needs to get trained up," Sabastian replied, trying to remain impassive.

Jeremy stopped in the hall and looked at Sabastian closely, trying to determine what was going on with him.

"What?" Sabastian asked.

"She's your promotion chance," Jeremy stated. "I am surprised you are so relaxed about breaking the rules with her."

"It was not my fault she came to me. I saw a chance and decided to do a little training with her and since you jokers haven't done anything with her, I decided to continue the program," Sabastian shrugged his shoulders and leaned up against the wall, like it was no big deal.

"Besides, I was bored and she was there, nothing better to do," he added, hoping his casualness was not being over played.

Chandler burst out, "It's not my fault I haven't worked with her yet, the female refuses to eat. She's been starving herself ever since I got assigned to her. I tried the notebook but she won't even pick it up, we were going to go in there today but she started eating all of a sudden."

Jeremy was still watching Sabastian closely, following the conversation.

"Yes, that was the plan. However, I believe she was only eating to keep us away and to get out of the room, which, by the way, she was successful," Jeremy looked pointedly at Chandler.

"Ya, sorry. I passed out and only woke up when the sensor went off," he rationalized.

Sabastian was troubled to hear Victoria had been fasting, but couldn't get upset over it in front of Jeremy. He was also not impressed that they had been planning to take over for him, even though Chandler was technically next in line once he had finished his initial training with her.

Keeping his emotions in check, he said, "You couldn't even get her to eat, you're screwed then. It looks like you have to start all over with her. You might be able to talk to her in a month if you're lucky and if she feels generous."

"Well, it seems like she is generous with you, Sabastian," Chandler said.

"Yes, that she is," he said with a wicked grin.

"Well, you might as well prepare her for release as I am sure you have failed your test and she is now no good to us or you," Jeremy stated stoically.

Sabastian thought fast. Letting her go would be the best thing for Victoria. She would be set up with money and a job and a decent place to live as well. It was what all failed interns were offered as extra incentive on top off the discloser agreement they had signed to keep quiet about Eximius. If he could convince Mr. D she would be in danger on the outside, she would also receive a new identity to stay hidden from her past. But a sharp stabbing pain in his chest told him that he could not let her go. He would never see her again. He felt the guilt of the selfishness of wanting to keep a prize that was never going to be his. He told himself not be stupid. Keep the reckless crazy girl here, put her through her paces and get his promotion. That was the only thing that mattered. There were plenty of girls out there, what made this one so special? He was trying to convince himself when Jeremy interrupted his thoughts.

"Come with me, Sabastian," Jeremy said, heading toward the elevators.

"Chandler, you guard the room."

Sabastian was suddenly alarmed. If he was going to Mr. D's office to be assessed, he was far from ready. He followed Jeremy to the elevator and rode it up in silence, trying to think his way out of the mess he was in.

Jeremy led Sabastian through Mr. D's apartment to a computer at his desk and sat him in the chair in front of it. He looked at Jeremy who was busy with the mouse and realized he was about to have a meeting with his boss face to face via web chat. He was not prepared but straighten his back and ran a hand through his hair, trying to look presentable.

Mr. D appeared on screen, and squinted at Sabastian.

"Good morning, Mr. D," Sabastian said clearly.

"Not from what I hear. I heard you assaulted your intern, explain yourself."

"I will admit I wasn't in my right mind, sir, and I lost control, but it was not directed at her. It was a complete misunderstanding and she has not only forgiven me but had started to starve herself because I am unable to work with her anymore."

"I said explain yourself, Sabastian!"

"Yes, sir, sorry. We were walking in the garden talking, when she told me to stop treating her like a 'science project,' were her exact words, and in the conversation, she called me...Bastian boy. I blacked out and lost it just long enough to grab her hand without thinking. She was generous enough to hear me out right after and I explained to her my history and why that nick name affected me so and..."

"What?" Mr. D asked, "You told her your history? What exactly?"

"Everything I told you when you brought me here, sir, from the beginning."

"I had to almost beat that information out of you for months and you give it willingly to your test girl you have only known for a few weeks?" Mr. D exclaimed.

"Yes, sir, that's how terrible I felt. I'd hurt her and the only way to get her to see that I didn't mean it, was to completely open up. Douglas has been telling me that for years, I thought I would try it, to earn back her trust."

"Did it work?"

"Yes, sir, I talked and she listened and after I was removed from her service, she came to see me and I decided to see if she would let me continue the program with her. Sir, she is willing and very trusting and I think she will work for the company and for me. She is my chance. Please let me continue."

"Where are you in the program?"

"I have finished the introduction and am starting the beginning of the program. She is intrigued with our company and wishes to join. I couldn't have asked for a better test. She is sensual, beautiful, and amendable. You will like her very much."

"That is not what you said last time you spoke about her."

"I have been working hard to earn my promotion and was able to turn things around."

"What makes you think that you'll get your promotion now? You hurt her and that's the end of it, you have officially failed your test."

Sabastian panicked suddenly, desperate to keep Victoria here. Losing her was not an option and he frantically tried to think fast on how it might be possible to get her to stay.

His promotion depended on if he was able to make Victoria think she was being offered a job. She needed to think she would be offered a position that did not exist for her at Eximius. She would never actually be hired by the company to work with their high paying clients. These clients paid for the elite and they got the elite and the elite were not vagrants from the street. The women were models and actresses who were smart, young, and beautiful, who have been carefully selected and trained in the art of pleasure. Only a very exceptional girl would be promoted from a test girl to an actual working position with the company, able to take on clients of her choosing and it had never been done before.

After Victoria was trained up and accepted the phantom job, she would only be offered the position of a pleasure girl in the mini manor. A slightly smaller house than the manor that the Eximius men and women lived in; the mini manor was attached to the main complex. The women were hired to help run the manor, train up woman and men in the art of sex as well as for the casual pleasure for the Eximius men and women when needed. All test subjects used for promotions had either been let go, or put in the mini manor if they choose. This was a required service as the many working Eximius men had no access to the professional girls unless they were training a new skill or were requested by the women themselves. It was a necessary service in this highly sexual environment. It was very frustrating for any man living with so many beautiful women who had been trained to pleasure someone sexually in almost every way possible.

Mr. D had ties to the SAA, Sexual Addiction Anonymous, and that was where he collected the bulk of the woman to work and serve in the mini manor. A dirty trick, preying on woman who had a problem, but it served both parties very well until the women decided they had enough and moved on. Then, of course, they were supported and got the help they needed. But in the meantime, they served a very important role in the business and they were paid very generously.

When Mr. D was thinking of expanding, he needed trusted men to run the new chapters, so the test was created. That way the promotion test girls could also fill the gaps in the mini manor and work for the Eximius employees. Yes, they would be very well cared for, but would never be on the payroll servicing high class, important paying clients. These women had two choices and only one lead to the promotion that Sabastian desperately wanted.

The one choice was to think that they were being trained for a true Eximius woman and be "hired," but in fact would be able to live in the mini manor as a pleasure girl, or they could go back to where they came from. If she took the job to be a pleasure girl, then the trainer had done his job so well that the test girl would want the job anyway and choose to stay with the company, even though the big payout would not be there.

There were many perks and the girls were treated well and taken care of, but the money and job to take clients, travel the world and truly be in charge of their lives would not be available like the professional girls. Mr. D believed in helping those who could help themselves, because even if a woman said no and opted to move on were still taken care of by the company. It was a bit of Karma and a lot of paying them off to keep the company a secret. Not like any of them ever knew where they were while at the manor. They never had access to real names or any information to lead to the downfall of the company but it was extra insurance. But Victoria was a street rat, deemed unworthily to be considered for a real job with Eximius and it was Sabastian's job to train her up to think she had a chance if she wanted it.

The answer came to Sabastian suddenly and hoped it would work. "Mr. D, I think I will be able to train her up to Eximius level."

He saw eyebrows raise in the screen and continued quickly.

"I know it has not been done before, but she is drug and alcohol free, hell, she doesn't even smoke. She's completely clean and very willing. If I can get her through the program and get her to that level, will that be acceptable?"

Mr. D was silent for a long time before he said, "Wait outside," dismissing him.

Sabastian needed an answer and hesitated wanting to fight for her but knowing his boss it was out of his hands. If he tried too hard, Mr. D would become suspicious. Any emotion with a girl at any time was unacceptable and she would be gone by morning. He just hoped that he had played his hand well enough to sound like he just desperately wanted another chance for his promotion.

"Yes, sir," Sabastian got up trying to stay professional and left the office to wait.

The fifteen minutes while he waited dragged on forever. His mind buzzing with thoughts and feelings he had no control of. He realized he had frantically tried to convince his boss to keep Victoria, considering letting her go had not crossed his mind during the conversation. He was being selfish, he knew. Was it because he wanted to use her for his promotion or was it something more? Nothing had really changed, Victoria's program would stay the same, but now she may have a chance to actually be an Eximius girl. Sabastian didn't know how he felt about this. If she was kept in the mini manor, she would always be there never moving forward, but if she was an Eximius woman, she would work for the company in the true sense and never be his. He had been desperate and had only thought about keeping her here. Once she was gone, she was gone for good and he would have no chance of finding her once relocated.

Sabastian had developed a cold sweat with his thoughts circling confusingly in his head and was chilled even in his robe by the time Jeremy came back out.

"Okay, Sabastian, you are back as her trainer, however, one more incident and you will be demoted to pot boy for the next two years and we will take half your pay over the last three years. If either of you get more than physically involved, you are to pass her along immediately to Chandler with no chance for another test!"

"Yes, sir, I've got it, she's just another job, just like all the rest of them."

Jeremy moved closer to him and said low and seriously, "I am seeing a lot of emotion in you lately and that is what will make you lose both her and your promotion and possibly your job. No emotion with her, it is dangerous, especially with your history."

Sabastian took a deep breath. Jeremy was right and he knew what he needed to do now.

"Jeremy, if I am fooling you into thinking I have feelings for this girl then I'm better at this than I thought. It was the only way to gain her trust. She would not have opened up to me and been so willing unless she thought I cared for her. It's all a farce and it's worked beautifully. I need her to think I have feelings for her, which is why you're seeing the emotions. She needs that emotion to open up and then she'll be able to move through the program. Don't worry, Jeremy, I'm in complete control of myself like always. Good night, sir."

And with that, Sabastian turned and walked down the hall before Jeremy could see through him.

He knew he was enthralled by this woman and the last thing he wanted now was to be blacklisted from her. He was determined to be professional from now on. Thinking about her warm and willing and almost naked in his bed, he could not help but smile as he went to find another place to sleep for the night.

Chapter 53

Victoria awoke in the strange place but her sense of smell told her she was wrapped warm and safe in Sabastian's bed before she even opened her eyes. She had been more than frustrated when Sabastian left but had lapsed into a dream she couldn't remember that had both soothed her and made her feel deliciously warm.

She glanced around his dark room. His fish were swimming lazily around the tank and the warm blue light shimmered along the walls with the water movement and made her feel like she was in an underground cave. She stretched luxuriously in the bed and looked up, slightly startled to see a pair of bright green eyes staring at her from directly above her head. Sketch was balanced on the wide head board of the bed, looking straight down at her. She smiled and was reminded of Sabastian's green eyes.

"Morning, Sketch," she said to the small black feline.

The little black cat cocked its head sideways and leaped lightly down beside her, settling on her belly.

"Now what kitty?" she asked, petting the soft black fur.

Victoria displaced the cat after a moment and rolled out of Sabastian's bed. With the navy sheet wrapped around her night gown she looked around the dark room. The light was starting to come through the windows which were still covered up and she was tempted to find the switch to open them and find out where she was, but she realized she no longer cared.

Her gaze was pulled to an easel and the many drawings scattering the floor beside the large windows. She saw many buildings but they were almost completely covered by a woman's form in various sensual positions. They were all in drawn in black charcoal and were done in impressive detail, considering that all the drawings were faceless. There were curves of the woman's back, her breasts, her side, the outline of a face, and her bare back from the neck all the way to her feet.

Her eyes fixed on at least three drawings which had more detail than the rest. Illustrations of a woman with hair flowing down over the woman's back. Sabastian must have lied about having women in his room because he clearly had models pose for him in various positions. Sabastian was unbelievably talented, the detail in the drawings, even though done in charcoal, looked like black and white photographs. She bent down to lift a few of the detailed drawings when a flash of color caught her eye. She pushed a couple of the drawings aside and she was suddenly shocked to see her own purple eyes staring back at her.

Her heart jumped as she gazed at the long lashes looking up at her from the page, the detail and color in the eyes were incredible. She found herself lost in the distinct copy of her unusual eyes, which were the only thing on the white paper. Sabastian must have memorized her eyes and had put his skilled hands to work to copy it. She looked closer at the drawing and could see a tall masculine figure who looked like he was approaching her drawn into the reflecting light in the iris. Her hand grazed the picture lightly and she bent to take a closer look at the detailed drawings scattered on the floor. Spreading the artwork around so she could see more, she looked closely and saw the faint outline of a scar on the woman's hips and on another sketch, she saw a light scar on the stomach and another on the arm. Each drawing of the woman in different position from beautiful posed to sensually erotic had features that could only be hers. Like the hair, eyes, or scars. There was even one picture where Sabastian had captured the way she walked on her tiptoes so perfectly it looked like it was moving on the paper.

Her fingers grazed the scar on her arm and could see the placement of the blemish on the page was in the perfect position in the picture.

These were all of her! she thought to herself, shocked.

Victoria gave a sharp yelp when a bright light turned on behind her. Ashamed she had been caught rifling through Sabastian art work, she turned around slowly bright red, ready to apologize.

She turned, but no one was in the room with her and the bedroom door was still shut. However, the blue light of the tank had been switched and now a bright white light illuminated the tank. Victoria approached the aquarium and saw the number of fish tripled in seconds. She regretfully walked away from the easel and over to the aquarium. The fish swam right up to her on the other side of the glass and they followed her as she walked past the aquarium. She was delighted they were interacting with her and giggled when they followed her fingers around the glass. The tank lights must be on a timer she thought as she played with the fish.

"They want you to feed them," came Sabastian's voice from the doorway.

She yelped again and spun around to see him leaning up in the door frame still in his robe, so gorgeous, showing his dimples in a slight smile.

Swallowing hard, she asked, "Can you?"

"Of course," Sabastian said, moving to the tank and reaching under the cabinet.

"I don't have any food thawed out for them, so we can just feed them dry food. They don't care, they'll eat anything."

Embarrassed Sabastian had almost caught her looking at his easel, she could not bring herself to ask about the art work so she focused on him as he lifted the lid of the aquarium.

Sabastian sprinkled a generous amount of food in the tank that was gone in less than a minute. The fish darted up and down, in and out, flashing their brilliant hues as they caught the tiny balled up food pellets. The speed in which they moved mesmerized her, as they had just been swimming so lazily moments before.

She watched fascinated; she had never seen anything so colorful in her life. Watching the fish gave her such pleasure, she could see why Sabastian enjoyed the hobby.

After several minutes of watching the fish, she broke the silence.

"So, how much trouble am I in?" she asked warily, keeping her eyes on the colorful aquarium.

"None, of course. *You* can do no wrong here," he said emphasizing the word "you."

"I could probably get away with anything here, huh?"

"Well, you could try," he said grinning.

"Come on," he offered her his arm and she took it shivering from an electric current that seemed to flow from his body to hers at their touch.

"You do, however, have to go to your room and eat. I hear you have been refusing meals the last few days and that is something *I* will not let you get away with."

Victoria sighed; she had seen that one coming. She let him lead her out his bedroom as they headed to her room together.

"Are you still my trainer?" she asked shyly, her face warming up.

"Yes, surprisingly your little stunt worked," he replied pleased.

Victoria shivered with pleasure that her daring escape had worked.

When they arrived at her room, she saw the meal tray and asked, "Will you eat with me?"

"No, I have some things I need to do, but if you eat and exercise, I'll be back as soon as I can. You cannot leave your room at all, even though the door is unlocked. It is a trust test to stay here for me, then if we can trust you, we can continue. Is that okay?"

"Do I have a choice?"

"Nope," he released her arm and ever so gently grazed her hair with his fingertips as he left.

"Back to routine," she muttered to herself, but secretly thrilled about the future.

Victoria's thoughts went back to Sabastian sketches of her as she ate. Apparently, he had been telling the truth about not having women in his room. She couldn't fathom how he could've drawn her in such perfect detail, especially since she had never posed for him.

Was he more than my trainer or did he draw all the woman who came here?

Absorbed in her thoughts, she ate with relish, excited about being free to be with Sabastian again.

Chapter 54

Victoria ate, and worked out to relieve her frustration as minutes turned to hours, which turned to days waiting for him, it seems like a lifetime ago and she was beyond pissed. How long did the man expect her to wait? The ache he had started in his room had only grown to a roar of need and she was beyond frustrated.

She had been given new books and she had to stop reading as it only reminded her of him pressing his strong gorgeous body into hers. She was looking for a distraction when a USB chip came through the wall with a note that read *"Watch this please."* Disappointed the note was not in Sabastian's handwriting, she frowned at the little chip and sighed. Turning to her computer, she inserted it and lay on the bed to see if something new would distract her.

It was a video about self-discovery. The woman on the screen was going through being in control of your own body. Being able to physically and mentally manage your body's reactions and using them to fulfill sexual desire to create completely controlled sexual experiences. After a lengthy explanation, Victoria watched the woman get naked and lay on the bed. Her legs spread apart on screen as the woman tilted her head back the camera zoomed in and Victoria was enthralled and shocked as the instructor came to a full orgasm without any contact with any part of her body. After the woman had floated down from her demonstration, she proceeded to show how to begin to gain that measure of mental control with her fingers and Victoria was determined to learn this skill. Getting more comfortable, she spread her legs gingerly and started to explore.

Sabastian had spent the last three days on damage control. Still trying to convince Jeremy and Mr. D he could handle his assignment and to be able to continue his work with Victoria. Once he had worked out the terms for him to continue, he had to attend sessions with Douglas, the manor's psychiatrist, making sure he was keeping his emotions separated and only doing his job as required. He had kept his distance as part of an agreement with Douglas and had only been keeping tabs on Victoria through the men in the monitor room. He received a few texts once in a while, updating him, but that was all. He needed to insure she was eating and being active and so far, she had not disappointed him. He forced himself to stay busy as he ached to see her again and he made sure he never went in to watch her on the monitors as Jeremy and Douglas had been keeping a close eye on him.

He was debating going to her later today as it had been several days when he received a text.

His reached for his phone to read the latest update on his ward and cursed himself as he sprinted to her room.

He slowed himself so he would not scare her as he opened the door to her bedroom. She laid there on the bed her fingers in between her legs. Sabastian's eyes found hers and went dark instantly. His mouth went dry staring at her on the bed, naked, her legs open wide and her fingers moved in a small circle over her clit. He took her in hungrily and felt himself grow steel hard with a rush of desire that was unsettling. Sabastian was speechless as he stared at her throbbing with need.

Victoria was so shocked that she remained frozen, knowing she was caught, but her groin jerked at his entrance and she didn't care.

Watching him watch her, she saw him grow long and hard, stretching out his loose pants quickly and her mouth went slack. Seeing him want her that bad made her feel powerfully female and wanton.

Choking down any embarrassment at her position, she breathed his name, rolling it on her lips barely audible.

"Sabastian."

Sabastian smiled and moved to her, slowly bending down to her ear and whispered a single word that made her first pale, then turn beat red.

He moved away from her quickly and handed her, her robe.

"Shit!" she murmured, covering herself up frantically.

"The fucking cameras," her head down, hands covering her face completely mortified.

Sabastian felt so sorry for the young girl on the bed that he suppressed his amusement and reached for her hands still on her face.

"Would you like to go to the Summit with me, Victoria?" he asked, the double meaning obvious as he bent to kiss her hands in his.

Victoria nodded, still keeping her face down looking at her feet.

Sabastian put an arm around her small shoulders and walked with her.

"It's nothing that they have not seen a thousand times over," he said amused.

"Oh God," she exclaimed, almost in tears.

Sabastian picked her up and did not put her down until they were both in the Summit. He placed her on the edge of the bed as he turned to close and lock the door.

Sabastian turned to her and smiled trying to lighten the mood, he asked teasingly, "Will you let me see the show you put on?"

Victoria was instantly anger for at him for teasing her but mostly for leaving her for so long. She used her anger to distract herself from the embarrassing situation she had found herself in. She had been ready to confront him for leaving her with no contact and was ready for a fight.

She stood up facing him, determined to get answers.

"What is wrong with you? Where the hell have you been?" she demanded a little too high pitched.

Sabastian smiled at her again and moved so close to her he was almost touching her breasts. He looked down at her and heard her breath catch in her throat and was thrilled she didn't step away. He loved how easily he affected her and reached for her possessively pulling her into a hard kiss.

She pulled away breathless and tried to stay mad at him.

"For Christ's sake, Sabastian! Three days. Where have you been!?" she yelled, trying to resist him pushing him away.

He kissed her again hard and fast, drowning her words with his lips and moaned into her mouth.

She placed both her hands on his chest and pushed. Ripping her mouth away from his, she said clearly.

"No, Sabastian."

He released her immediately and stepped back, only to watch her panting and red with angry passion before him.

She was so completely turned on that it fueled her anger and she flushed under his stare and his grin.

"There's only one way to reverse that word," he whispered seductively.

Still breathing hard, her eyebrows raised slightly.

"And that's to say yes," he crooned at her and lifted his hand and motioned with his index finger to her to come to him.

She took a step back and he frowned at her.

"Vicky, what have you learned about feeling and not thinking, you want me, I can read it in every movement your body makes, don't deny it. Your breathing, your flushed skin, even your breasts tell me what you want. I missed you."

He crooned at her again, trying to sate her temper. He sighed as she did not move and tried another approach hoping it would work.

Stepping forward again, his eyes raked up and down her body seductively.

"You can feel the need deep in your pussy, give into it. I want to fuck you, Victoria, let me suck on your clit and make you cum. Fighting it will only suppress it and you won't be able to enjoy what my cock and I can do to you."

He was deliberately talking dirty to her to get a reaction. He was so arrogant it made her sick, whether he was right or not. The words he spoke were deliberate, to make her want him to do dirty, primal things to her and her wet walls gripped themselves strongly listening to his throaty voice. Just the word fuck made her body react. She continued to scowl at him, not speaking or moving.

Her eyes raised in shocked bewilderment as he suddenly walked past her out the door, closing it behind him.

No, she yelled in her head, her body screamed at the injustice. He was right and she knew it. She didn't want him to leave. She sat down hard on the bed and sulked like a child who did not get the ice cream she was promised.

Lying down on the bed defeated, she thought, *now what am I going to do? So much for the questions I had for him about the video.*

Closing her eyes and thinking of the video coupled with what Sabastian had done to her made her skin tingle. After several minutes, she was too warm and tossed the robe aside. Lying naked on the bed, she could feel her woman's heartbeat flutter again and she focused on that feeling, the same one she had been taught to concentrate on when craving fulfillment from the teachings of the video. She could feel herself build slightly and her eyes popped open, surprised. She tested the feeling and squeezed. There it was again, the fluttering build, but she was missing something crucial and cursed Sabastian for leaving.

Sighing, knowing it was her fault Sabastian left, she willed herself to calm down unsuccessfully for over an hour. Sitting up, she could feel the buildup of moisture that had started over an hour ago. Her desire had grown stronger, thinking about her body and its cravings and was in awe on how her mind could control that part of her. She was turned on and she tentatively brought her fingers to her sex and felt herself engorged and hot under her touch. She lay her entire hand over herself and tenderly slipped a finger inside her folds. It was warm and wet and felt so tempting. She was happy to realize she was no longer sore and she pushed her finger in deeper exploring. It felt nice, yes, but when she felt her own hand, she knew what to expect. Not knowing what Sabastian's hands were going to do to her was the best part, the anticipation of the unknown was the thrill she needed.

Victoria raised her fingers to her lips and sucked gingerly tasting herself.

Sabastian entered the room to find her in bed sucking her fingers and smiled knowingly.

Victoria knew what she wanted and she would be damned if she would mess this up again. She spread her legs wide and said very clearly.

"Yes, Sabastian."

Sabastian closed the door and stalked toward her slowly, peeling off his clothes as he went, enjoying the rich dark purple in Victoria's eyes as she watched him.

He moved to hover over her in the large white bed and slowly put the slightest pressure of his weight on her small frame.

Victoria bowed into him so fast that Sabastian had to pull back. As much as he wanted to plunge into her, he still needed to take it slow, not sure she was fully recovered.

Victoria felt him pull back and she almost screamed no at him. But sighed as he lowered his lips to hers and kissed her softy as he slowly pushed his marble cock into her aching wet flesh. He filled her body completely and the feeling was so exquisite she moaned loudly. He pushed deeper and deeper into her so leisurely until she was pushed up the bed as he reached the peak of her sex. He moved in and out of her at a steady but soft pace, her body drew him in blissfully and she marveled at the feel of him inside her too ready body. What little tenderness still remained in her body was overwhelmed and replaced with pleasure and a growing need within her belly. Her legs opened wide for him as she pushed her hips to his, meeting him halfway gripping his chest to stay close.

"Mmmmmm, mmmmm, mmmmm," she moaned with each smooth thrust. Building so easily, each push increased her climb and she clenched his shaft, seeing what she had been missing with her own fingers. It was the fullness of his length and his throbbing deep within her, his weight, and his movement all drove her closer to the impending orgasm that was sure to come. Running her nails down his back, she arched into him again and again.

He increased his tempo faster and faster and she opened wider to accommodate his ruthless pounding into her body. She thrust back up at him, taking as much of him as possible and savoring every thrust as her hands reached above her head to brace herself against the head board. His groans of pleasure, hearing and feeling the slap of skin on skin made her body shudder for more.

"Auggghhh," Sabastian cried, looking down into her face as she gazed up at him with hooded eyes. His silken shaft was firmly caressed by her inner walls and he knew he would come fast and hard and hoped the small sensual woman underneath him would be able to handle it. There had not been a single minute he had been away from her that he did not think of her. With a need to feel her under him again and knew he would have very little restraint if any. Hearing her moan each time, he pumped into her too wet sex, filled him with pure hot predatory abandon.

"Ahhh, ahhh, ah," Victoria was building fast now and the assault on her body was welcome. She felt Sabastian let himself go a little and lose himself in her, being rougher with her not as afraid to hurt her and her body locked at the beginning of the climax, he pounded into her body.

"Vicky, cum. Cum with me, fuck!" he grumbled at her low, his muscles locking up tautly and she felt the sweet explosion of release rack her body.

"Sabastian!" she screamed as her body seized up violently into him, shattered and trembled beneath him, taking him all in and feeling every shiver run through both their bodies joined together in the massive crescendo that had left them enervated and breathless.

Sabastian thrust several times more to lengthen her pleasure and finally stilled sated. Leaning over her, watching her and feeling her body convulse with his as he joined her in the pulsing float down from their joined orgasm.

He could watch her all day like this, thrown into the passion that consumed her body.

When she opened her eyes, he asked, "Are you okay?"

She tested his question with a slow tightening of her sex and moaned when she only felt the pleasure of her muscles wrapped completely around him.

"Mmmm, yes, I feel wonderful," she whispered thickly up at him.

Sabastian went to pull himself out of her but she squeezed him greedily.

"I can't stay in there forever," he chastised her.

"Mmmm, why not?" she asked, squeezing her newly worked muscles harder and not letting him go.

"Because if I do, I will be overcome and need to fuck you again and again and again," he promised, grinding his hips into her every time he said "again."

She yelped and flinch from the quivering sensitivity still coursing through her center.

"Ah, ah, ah," her body jerking every time he hit her shattering spot.

"And that will only lead to soreness for you and then you will have to wait days to do that again."

He ground into her one last time, pressing down hard and vibrating his hips, then stopped, and she finally released him.

"Ohhh," she sighed as he slide out of her, empty once more.

Sabastian rolled over and said, "Let's wait another day to see if you're broken in yet."

Victoria had to lean up to look at his serious face, he was smiling broadly at the ceiling.

"What am I? A baseball glove?" she asked insulted.

"That's a good metaphor as I would love to oil you up again," he grinned.

Turning to look at her expression, he realized he had hurt her feelings.

"Sorry, I just want to make sure you are okay. How do you feel?"

"Still embarrassed."

"Why?"

"Because they saw what I was doing back in my bedroom," she moaned.

"Who the hell cares, Vicky," he said, leaning in to kiss her.

"You should not be self-conscience or modest. You should spread your legs for anyone and give them a show and know your actions can turn on any man to the point of insanity. Be proud of your body."

He reached between her legs to collect the wetness still there and raised it to his lips.

"You were turned on and are secretly thrilled there was someone watching you."

She looked mortified and was ready to deny it but was distracted as she saw his fingers dip between her legs again for another taste. But this time his finger stayed in her folds teasing and she had no choice but to moan as her head tilted back. His finger went from playing outside to tentatively pushing inside the sleekness of her body and her arms dropped to the bed to push into his firm fingers.

She could not take it how he so causally played with her and how she was moaning and squirming on the bed wantonly in seconds. She watched as his hand came away from her body and toward her mouth.

"How do you feel now?" Sabastian asked as he licked his fingers slowly.

"Wet," she grinned at him, forgivingly.

He frowned, still waiting for an answer to his question.

"Not sore?"

"I feel fine, really. I feel good, relaxed, satisfied," she insisted.

"Okay," Sabastian got up and got dressed and Victoria watched him disappointed he was leaving her.

"I came here to give you your next company video and also give you a piece of my mind when it comes to rejecting something you clearly want."

She blushed and looked away.

"Vicky," he said drawing her eyes to his, "never let emotion stop you from fulfilling your body's needs or the needs of others, got it? You cannot afford that luxury. Physical needs always surpass emotional needs here. Let your body crave and be satisfied, don't ever be ashamed or reserved. You cannot feel guilty about your sexuality. If you do need to think or be emotional, do it later and let pleasure always be in the front of your mind," he was serious as he spoke and she absorbed every word.

"Okay…Is that what everyone does here? No emotion and only sex."

"No, of course not, our women use their emotions professionally and in the right context but it's an act. That's when then they can be who they truly are in bed and thrive on the lustful emotion that overwhelms them at the right moment. When on a job, your true feelings do need to be repressed because you need them to act the part of the perfect companion. But if you have a strong emotion like anger," he smiled at her pausing, "let it fuel your appetite, anger is a powerful tool and will heighten your pleasure. You will learn that later, but for now."

He tossed a DVD case on the bed.

"You get to learn more about control, need, and pleasure."

Sabastian finished dressing and walked out and she watched him go.

Is everyone here an emotionless sex robot? Sabastian doesn't act like he just doing a job when he is with her. Although he just might be really good at what he does, she thought.

She found the TV in the large wardrobe and put the disc in the player and settled on the bed.

The video was in more detail about the woman's libido, sexuality, and arousal which intrigued her more than aroused her. Thanks to being satisfied by Sabastian and she was able to focus the content it was teaching her. She knew the cravings, the needs, and the body's desire to have certain things done to it. She again wondered if she could master her own body and not to think but only to feel her way through a sexual encounter. She thought to herself that she could not possibly be in love with Sabastian and since he had driven her to a frenzy of need almost every time he touched her, she guessed she must be getting the hang of it. She was so physically attracted to him, that was a good start and she admired and trusted him, perhaps that's all love is.

She also knew that he would protect her, something she hadn't had since her mother was taken from her. She believed Sabastian would do anything for her and longed for him to touch her, talk to her, and be with her. Her feelings a mess, she lay on the bed thinking about his touches and his words and his concern for her and sighed deeply, knowing she could trust him in all things.

Chapter 55

Victoria stayed in the Summit and spent her time re-reading several of the books she had not fully understood without the experience she needed to appreciate what they were trying to teach her. She would feel her body react to certain pictures and descriptions, always looking back on what Sabastian had done to her. She had changed and was aware of her body and its desires now. She loved the awareness and the passion Sabastian had awakened in her and couldn't wait for their next lesson. It was late afternoon and she had spent hours lying in bed, reading, and she was tempted to look for him when she heard a knock on the door.

"Hello," Sabastian said as he opened the door.

"Hi," she replied as a small demure smile playing along her lips.

Victoria felt her body react at his presence, but her shyness overcame her and she felt her face grow warm. She had been hyper aware of her body and her nipples tingled at the sight of him and she knew she craved his touch. Just seeing his large hands and his dimples and his soft hair, she longed to kiss and press herself into him.

"What have you been reading?" he asked glancing at her book sitting almost too close to her on the bed.

"Umm, how to get the most out of your partner," she blushed.

"And?"

"It's very interesting."

"Anything you want to try?" he asked, grinning at her wickedly.

Victoria lowered her head and tried to control her reddening cheeks and bravely turned to a page in the book with a picture on it and showed it to Sabastian, not looking at him.

"Yes, that's a good one," he said seriously, brushing her leg.

She was wound so tight that she jumped.

"Do you want to do that now with me?" he asked and she could hear the repressed humor in his voice.

She kept her head and eyes lowered and slowly nodded her head. A raising sense of excitement blossomed in her chest and her heart increased its pace as he leaned over her and slowly lifted her satin dress over her head; thrilled she was naked underneath. He moved over her and she could smell his strong male scent as he kissed her neck, licking her skin.

Victoria groaned and lifted her hips to meet his, frustrated by the feel of denim between them. She raised her lips and felt the need in his body that was as strong as her own.

"Sabastian, mmmm," she moaned as she watched him lift himself from her and sit back on his heels.

"That one," he said gesturing to the book, "is all about a woman's control, so as much as you would like to remain shy and blushing, which, by the way, is making me want to take hard and fast. You will need to take over."

His words sent a shiver through her quickening her pulse. Victoria, however, didn't have the faintest idea of where to start, but she knew that he couldn't do this dressed. Pushing herself into a sitting position, she mirrored his position sitting on her heels in front of him. Slowly, she reached for his shirt, willing herself to keep her eyes on his. She lifted the crimson shirt off of him, laughing when he had to help her when it caught on his head. She couldn't resist and placed her small hands on his broad chest and ran her fingers through his light sprinkling of hair that covered the smooth skin. She smiled when he closed his eyes.

"Mmm, wild cat," he groaned huskily, running his fingers lightly on the underside of her sensitive arms.

Victoria's skin shivered and she had to repress an urge to climb onto his lap. She glanced down at his jeans and hesitated.

"Please, Vicky, you don't have to be gentle with me," he whispered and he raised his hand and cupped her cheek and lightly kissed her.

With his warm hand on her face and his encouragement, Victoria held him in the kiss and reached down for his button and zipper lowering it and felt him suck her lip deepening the kiss. He sat up and let her lower the jeans to his thighs. Breaking the kiss, she looked down at his underwear with his erection underneath and saw it straining toward her. Curving her fingers into the waist band of his boxers she pulled, then took the black fabric away from his hips and lowered them to join his jeans. He was watching her and she wanted to look away, but she couldn't and stared fascinated at his throbbing sex.

She lightly grazed the soft skin on the tip of his erection and saw his penis jump at her touch. Smiling at the influence she had on him, she wrapped her hand around his shaft and squeezed, then with her other hand, she rested her palm on his tip and slowly circled the head of his large mushroom head and increased the pressure when he moaned again.

"Vicky, Christ," he said, grabbing her arms. "When it comes to you, I have very little patience. Even thinking about you makes me hard and seeing you, even fully clothed, I have to lock down my control. But your hands on me. Naked in front of me, I won't be able to hold myself back any longer. So if you would like to try the book's position, you will need to stop before I lose myself to you."

Victoria's confidence skyrocketed and the power she felt over this dominate man made her bold. Smiling up at him she moved her hands up and down his shaft squeezing harder.

"Fuck, Vicky," he cursed and he pushed her onto the bed underneath him, taking off the rest of his clothes as he went.

Victoria relished that he couldn't control himself with her and raised her hips to meet his greedily, no longer interested in the book. She felt his hands reach under her hips, lifting the bottom half of her body off the bed and pulled her onto his bent legs. Her body closed around him as he drove home into her slippery flesh. As soon as she felt him enclosed to the hilt inside her, she squeezed him hard and she saw his eyes blazed down at her.

Keeping his hands firmly on her hips, he slid out of her and brought her to him again, keeping her off the bed and onto his cock. Keeping up a slow rhythm, raised off the bed, she could feel his warm fleshy sac slap her butt and the image made her flex on him with pleasure. She saw he was trying to go slow but the grip her sex had around his powerful erection made him forget himself and she saw his face change dramatically from measured control to pure need.

"Vicky!" he rumbled deeply, his eyes squeezing shut. He slammed her with his hips hard and fast, holding her shoulders and bringing her to meet his thrusts and increased the tempo. She felt her body quicken under his thrusting but she had only just begun her climb to ecstasy when she saw his body tense and felt him swell wonderful inside her.

She arched into him feeling her body stretch pleasurably with him. Being able to feel him erupt, spilling himself into her without the distraction of her own body was fascinating.

"Augh, Vicky," he groaned as he completed his climax roughly with several more thrusts before lowering her back to the bed and taking his body from hers.

Breathing hard, it took Sabastian awhile before he could speak again. Victoria leaned up and watched him come down from his climax, enjoying his fulfillment.

"Now you can play," he said smiling up at her.

She smiled back at him. Victoria's body craved his and with the need still pounding her own sex, she was bold and crawled up onto his thighs straddling him, pressing her lips into his urgently. She groaned as she felt his hand wrap around her breast and tease her nipple. Her wet walls pulled in, she felt the moisture pool and she had to have more.

Sabastian felt her need still unfulfilled and laid down. As she positioned herself over him, she felt him fill hard, hot and ready underneath her. She hesitated; this was the position in the book she was trying to copy but didn't know how to begin.

She lay astride him and lowered her hips down on his, placing his shaft along her outer folds and rubbed wetly up and down his length. She could feel his head catch on her clitoris and her body jerked with every stroke.

"Ohh, ahhh," she moaned, closing her eyes as she rode him.

Her eyes flew open when she felt Sabastian's hands grab her behind and pulled her up slightly, effectively pulling her off of him and she looked at him questionably.

"Raise up," he commanded gently.

She rose her hips up and both saw and felt as he raised his penis till the silken crown rested at the entrance of her throbbing sex. Taking his hands away, his mushroom head stayed nestled in her folds and she lowered herself on him. Victoria closed her eyes and moaned as her body swallowed him.

Sighing, she raised her hips and repeated the process.

She loved this feeling; she could control every aspect of the sex and loved the hardness of Sabastian beneath her. Opening her eyes, she saw him gazing up at her and she put her hands on his chest and raised her hips again.

"Oh, Vicky, you are so beautiful," he whispered huskily as he watched every movement she made.

Victoria's body clenched at his words and she sped up her hips moving smoothly up and down on his hard shaft, savoring every inch of him. She leaned forward to kiss him but felt the angle of his cock change dramatically inside of her and she collapsed onto him breathing hard.

"Ah, ah, ah," she cried and ground her hips into his body exhilarated at the new angle she had created.

Moving faster and faster, grinding her hips and feeling the movement slide in and out, she felt her body mounting higher and higher.

Her woman's center had taken over everything and she couldn't think clearly and was finding it harder to concentrate on keeping up the rocking that would bring her to fulfillment. She was panting hard, her eyes closed, reaching, climbing, building, but her muscles wouldn't cooperate. Desperately, she tried to move faster but lost the rhythm and she raised herself up to look to Sabastian for help. She saw him smile up at her, but seriousness covered his face as large warm hands on her back continuing the wonderful rhythm she had started. He moved his hands to her hips to raise her slightly off of him, then pounded ruthlessly into her from below and she imploded around him so fast it was shocking.

"Oh, Sabastian, ahhhhhhh," Victoria screamed, coming apart, she let her body's earthquake take over. She felt him continue to thrust hard and fast, swelling deep inside her sheath while her body milked his. Her orgasm stiffening her entire body as she cried out, her nails raking across Sabastian chest.

"Auuuuugggghhhh," Sabastian growled thrusting faster, emptying himself inside her too tight cleft. Arching his hips and savoring the feel of this beautiful woman as he felt her pleasure ripple into his.

Victoria finally collapsed onto him as her sex shots waves of pleasure sporadically through her. Feeling his deep breaths under her, raising her body, lifting her gracefully up and down. She squeezed him tightly feeling his length still inside her and loving their heartbeats mingle together and sighed with absolute pleasure.

"Mmmm, sweet, sweet Vicky," Sabastian whispered in her ear, stroking her back softly.

Sabastian could still feel her sex tremble around him and he had to control the urge to flip her and continue fucking her until they were both sore and raw. He had felt when she lost her strength and couldn't keep the rhythm of motion she needed to climax. At first, he had controlled himself from taking over and had enjoyed watching her face and body above him as she pleasured her body with his. He was thrilled when her lavender rich eyes had found his, pleading for him to take over and bring them both to the heart racing crescendo. He had felt her tighten so hard around him and that was all he needed to release himself into her, letting her fall onto him still pulsing from his own massive climax.

She was astounding and so sexy that Sabastian knew that the urge to fuck her had not decreased but had increased tenfold after each time he had held her in his arms. He thought he would be able to get her out of his system after they had sex, but was sorely mistaken.

Victoria smiled into his chest, "Mmmmm, I liked that," she groaned replete.

"I can tell," he said, brushing her long tangled hair away from her face.

Victoria raised her head and smiled shyly at him blushing.

"You are something, Victoria," he murmured.

Victoria raised herself off of him and they both groaned when they felt their bodies detach. She scooted up to rest on the back board of the bed and tuck her legs under her chin.

Sabastian got onto his hands and knees and crawled to her kissing her on the lips.

"Don't hide," he said and tugged her legs free from her arms, he massaged from her ankles all the way to her breasts, holding them gently in his palms.

"I couldn't do it," she sighed.

"Like hell you didn't, Vicky, that was amazing, it was wonderful and the fact that you let me take over for you was so damn hot," he smiled at her encouragingly.

"But I…"

Rubbing his hands along the inside of her thighs, he whispered seductively, "All you need is practice if you want to be able to keep the rhythm by yourself. But if you fail a hundred times, I will be more than willing to take over for you every single time," he said firmly, his eyes smoldering into hers.

Victoria smiled and felt herself respond to the lust in his voice.

"Really?" she whispered.

"God, Vicky, there is nothing you could do wrong. A guy wants to take over, he needs that most times. He likes the control and if you need me to take over any time, I will tell you I will be more than willing to throw you down and finish you off until you cum all over me screaming my name. You are a pure sensual woman and every time I think of you, I grow hard fast, which is something I'm not used to. You are a natural and the fact that you would still trust me and let me have sex with you after the pain I caused you shows me that you love it and want it as bad as I want you," he finished, stroking her gentle curves.

Victoria responded to his words, she was amazed that even the thought of her made him lustful and it made her sexual confidence skyrocket. The way he so passionately felt about her made her blush and surge at his voice. His words burned inside of her and she smiled aware of her body's pull toward this gorgeous, strong man. She felt his hands over her legs and belly and her nipples hardened in anticipation of being touched.

"Even my words make you want to be touched, you are so erotic and willing, look at what you have done to me," he said, looking down.

Victoria looked down and saw him grow and went to reach for him but looked up into his eyes when his softly took her hand and raised it to his lips.

"No more, Vicky, I don't want to make you sore. I want every experience to be a good one, with no more pain after," Sabastian bent and kissed her and rolled off the bed.

"But I feel fine."

"You may not feel the after effects until later and I want only to be good after effects," he said as he dressed.

"You're leaving?"

"Sorry, I have to work, I came to make sure you were comfortable and have everything you need today."

"Yes, I think so, do you want me to go back to my room or stay here?"

Sabastian leaned into her, "Well, in here, we have privacy and if you feel the urge to jump me, you can."

She giggled, "Okay. I'll stay. Can you stay with me? Will you sleep with me later?" she asked, reserved but hopeful.

Sabastian heard the need in her voice, he knew that he would not be able to hold himself back from her soft curves. Sleeping with an intern was a big no, no as there were rules against attachment and he didn't want to be blacklisted from her and have her taken away from him again.

"I can't. I have to work. I need you to read and watch the videos and I will come to visit you in a couple of days. Will you be okay?"

Victoria's face fell, "Yes, I'll be fine," she said and covered herself with a blanket.

"Vicky, I want to stay. Trust me nothing would make me happier than to hold you and watch you sleep, but that's not the world we're in and we both have to accept that," Sabastian's heart hurt seeing her face fall and he cursed the rules he was trying to follow. He had to harden her and make her see that this was not a love affair or a game to which they controlled the rules. Leaning down to her on the bed, he took her shoulders in his hands and said forcefully.

"Miss Victoria, I am your trainer and I am only here to show you how to fuck and love it. There cannot be more or we will both lose too much. Do you understand?"

Victoria knew he spoke plainly about the situation they were in and nodded then smiled slightly, trying to hide her disappointment.

"Good. Have a good day and I'll see you soon."

Victoria watched him go and then curled into a ball and willed herself not to cry and to think about this like a partnership. One where she was being taught how to make love without any of the feelings involved and only learn the physical act of fucking, and leave the emotions behind, completely bewildered on how to go about doing that.

Chapter 56

Sabastian went to her every three days to see what she had learned and answer any questions. He wanted her to keep gaining weight and to continue working out, so her muscles would become accustomed to the new exercise regime. Every time he came to her, he physically reminded her of the pleasure involved with learning her chosen lifestyle and also to let her experiment with him.

On the days between their sessions, she went to Maximus to train, she needed to control her frustration and newly discovered lust with hard sessions of karate and kickboxing, throwing herself into what used to be her only physical outlet. She would work out for hours and Max was great. Kidding with her, pushing her, and knowing what she needed to fall into bed exhausted, too tired to crave Sabastian's hands on her. On days when Sabastian came to her, she would always be wet and wanting as soon as he walked through the door and it didn't take long for her to be panting and clawing him.

Their coupling was nothing but pleasure, making her courageous in bed. He was getting rougher with her and she loved every time he let a little more of himself go with her, showing her his true sexual nature.

She was also elated when he had let her go on top of him again, curving her hips in different positions. With every angle, she felt him rub strongly on different area of her vagina, each one a revelation. She angled her hips and was able to bring herself to an all-consuming orgasm with Sabastian barely moving beneath her. Reveling in the control it gave her, over both his body and hers. It had taken several minutes of heavy breathing lying on his chest to get her heart to stop pounding, as he rubbed her back. She knew she would have to work on stamina in this position, now that she was able to keep up the rhythm till the end.

Sabastian had also taken her from behind and on their sides while he played with both her breasts and her sweet spot. His hands were everywhere on her when he took her and she adored the feel of them playing with her body. He had also lifted her onto him against the wall, just like when they showered and he had told her to grab a well-placed white bar in the ceiling and helped her hold herself up as he brought them both to fulfillment.

They had played with the lights of the room and she could physically feel the difference between the lighting. Blue was by far her favorite, as she loved how it enhanced Sabastian's raw masculinity, which made her feel powerfully female and vulnerable. The scents he used on her skin would drive her into a frenzy as the almond and jasmine made her head spin with need. There were also several selections of music on which to make love to, which dramatically changed each sexual session.

She found she needed to stretch her body to limber up before his administrations. Even though the tenderness in her groin was gone, her muscles tended to give her the most trouble and she spent hours in the tub soaking or letting Sabastian rub her body with oils until she melted and he took her again in another position that made her sore once more. It was a delicious cycle that she craved would never end.

She loved fucking, her body craved his and only his touch made her scream, even a bath or shower made her tremble and she couldn't wait until he came to her next. She did wonder where he went and what he did while he was away from her, so as they lay on the floor breathing hard after their last encounter, she asked him.

"What are you doing when you are not with me?"

Sabastian stopped rubbing her back and sat up, "Well, I have watching duties, I also work in the kitchen and the spa, as well as the lab once in a while. You know this whole place doesn't revolve around you," he teased.

"So you're security for the girls when on a job?"

"Yes. After the girls have been on three dates with us as protection, she fills out a report. If she confirms the client is not overly eccentric or wants to hurt her, then the client is free to hire out anyone after he's been cleared."

"Do girls really get hurt?" She asked worried.

"It's happened before, yes, but our clients are generally good men who either have certain tastes or need a good woman to be there during business deals. Sometimes they just need companionship and a great evening with an intelligent woman."

She scoffed, "Good men, come on."

Sabastian sighed, propping up on his elbow to examine her and said seriously, "The clients we get here are great guys, yes, they have their flaws, but who doesn't. They have particular tastes or need a partner who is educated that they cannot find in their circles, so they come to us. Having particular tastes that would seem unusual to others is something they do not have to hide from us and they can be truly free to fulfill their needs without fear of them being found out or judged. Most men need what our women can give them, confidence and satisfaction in all things and our women love to meet their needs as well as their own. It's a win-win situation; our girls crave their clients just like their clients crave them. Several would do the work for free and some have even met with clients outside of work."

"They can leave whenever they want?"

"Of course, they're not imprisoned here, this is their home."

"And they leave to have sex outside of work with the clients."

"No and those who have, have been reprimanded for it, if their partners don't get tested, they are exposing themselves and others to STDs. They're smart and use condoms but that's not the point."

"Oh, so they are not supposed to go out on their own?"

"Not to hook up with someone, no, but to go shopping or travel, or meet friends."

"They have friends?"

"Of course."

"Do these friends know what they do for a living?"

"No, their job description is a business consultant. They work with CEOs, helping their business thrive through support, guidance, and service."

"Nicely put," Victoria said, "It sounds professional."

"It is. What part of this company is not a hundred percent professional?"

"Well, I actually know what you do."

"You have no idea what we do," he said defensively. "You think it's all about sex but it isn't, it's about power."

"Ya, over women," she said distastefully.

He frowned at her, "No, not just over women, over themselves. Our clients are the biggest men in their businesses, making millions upon millions of dollars and yet some have no control over their personal lives. You cannot be the best at something without sacrificing something else. Their lives revolve around their job and yet can be insecure about themselves. They are men with particular needs that hardly ever get met. They use our girls to be successful and thrive in their business. To be able to focus on their job without physical needs getting in the way. They can't have relationships because it would interfere with running their company. They can't just get a girlfriend and get married, it would take too much time away from their passion of being successful, and it would be too much of a distraction. Victoria, without the Eximius girls, they would not be as successful as they are, they may pay thousands of dollars to be with our girls but make millions because of them. Our girls are one in a million and we treat them like that. Get the ignorant thought of you being trained to work in a whore house out of your mind, because sex is only a small part of what services they give their clients. The education that you are getting is not all about the men, it's mostly for you. So you get what your body craves when with a client. We want you to enjoy that part of it, so you love and appreciate your job."

Sabastian had gotten up and started getting dressed, he tossed a book on the bed.

"Here. I suggest you read up; you are sorely missing the education needed to work with our clients."

Victoria looked down at the book *Stock Market Strategies for the Modern Man.*

By the time she looked up, he was gone.

Victoria gapped at the door after him, he was so protective of this company and the women here that she was jealous. She picked up the book and started to read, trying to figure out the material and how it would help her talk to these high-powered business men, but she was rattled Sabastian had left her so abruptly.

Chapter 57

Sabastian was incensed, the girl didn't get it. How could he show her how the system worked? He checked the clock and knew he only had an hour to get ready for his next assignment. Discontent, he paced his bedroom, then a thought hit him and he bolted out of the room, needing to prepare.

Victoria was on chapter three when Sabastian burst through her door, he walked straight through to the bathroom and when he returned, she had an apology ready for him. However he walked right over to her, yanked her off the bed and wrapped a robe around her nude frame.

"Come on, we don't have much time," he stated walking her out the door.

"What, where are we going?" she asked alarmed.

"We have to go."

"Are you kicking me out?" she was appalled, she didn't want to leave. She wanted this life, this job, and him. How could she have screwed this up so royally?

"I'm sorry I didn't think your company was professional, I'm sorry I..."

"Stop apologizing and no, of course, we aren't kicking you out, you are coming on a watch with me."

"What?" she stopped walking to look at him, "I'm coming with you on a job?"

"Yes, I'll explain later, first you need to get dressed fast and get to the spa right away, we only have thirty minutes."

They had arrived at her old room and on the bed lay a beautiful floor length black evening gown. She stared at it in awe, it was so gorgeous.

"Hurry up, I'll be back in five," he said, shutting the door behind him.

It only took her a minute to get the gown on and while she waited for him, she stood in front of the mirror. The dress was so tight it molded around her, it hugged her curves and cut down low in between her breasts stopping where her ribs parted under her breast bone. It had support that thrust her breasts up and in, showing off her voluptuous cleavage. She turned in front of the mirror and saw the same low-cut design on her back, leaving it exposed almost all the way down to her tail bone. It was a sensual but elegant dress. She gapped as she caressed the skin that was showing, which was a lot.

Sabastian entered her room and stopped. He was stressed and running late but the sight of her in that gown made him stop dead in his tracks with his mouth hanging open.

"Sorry, did I take too long?" she asked nervously.

Sabastian shook his head, trying to clear it.

"Umm, no, uh, come here."

He took her hand and led her out the door and down to the spa.

"Not the spa again," she said worriedly.

"Don't worry, they just have to do your hair and makeup, it'll be painless and quick."

Sabastian left her to the same girls that had waxed and plucked her weeks ago and they got to work on her hair and makeup in tandem.

Sabastian was back in fifteen minutes; she could barely see him through the girls but she saw enough for her eyes to grow wide with appreciation. He was dressed so sharply in a stylish black tux, he was breathtaking. His wide shoulders and broad chest with his hair slicked back looked so hot, she felt her body respond despite her nervousness. His tight black pants with matching shining dress shoes completed the package. He strode to her leaning down and placed a very high heel shoe on each foot and then proceeded to wrap her legs in the straps that crisscrossed all the way up her calf. The shoes molded to her feet and sparkled like black diamonds, exposing her toes through the end. They were as stunning as the dress.

"Umm, Sabastian, I don't think…" Victoria started.

"Finished," one of the spa woman said, stepping away from her.

Sabastian took his eyes from her feet and looked at the spa girl.

"What about her nails?" He asked.

"She needs a mani and a pedi, but just a touch up will work, give me a second."

The girl left and was back a minute later and with the help of her partner, both women proceeded to shape, then paint first her toes around the high heels, and then her fingers a light natural pink color.

Sabastian finally looked up at Victoria and his mouth fell open, gapping at her once again. She was stunning, her long hair was wrapped elegantly in a high bun on the top of her head sleek and shiny. The hair dressers had hung several long strands of hair so they draped over her one shoulder in soft curls that hung down to her waist. Her face had been covered in makeup but not heavily so, accenting her eyes with blue and purple and her lips were shiny with dark red lipstick. Her cheeks needed no blush as they were reddening under his gaze. He knew right away she would have no problem fitting in at this event.

"Sabastian," she started to say.

"You are absolutely stunning, Miss Victoria, you'll be fine," he offered her his hand and pulled her up slowly.

"But…"

Victoria's feet flopped, her ankles giving out and she fell toward him as soon as she tried to put weight in the new heels.

He looked at her bewildered, catching her in his arms.

"I've never worn heels in my life," she said mortified, looking up at him in his arms.

"Oh, shit, ummm," Sabastian was at a complete loss.

"Miss Victoria," said the spa girl, she had short light blonde hair and tiny beauty mark on her left cheek. "May I assist you?" she asked kindly.

"Yes, please," Victoria said gratefully.

"My name is Sandra, please stand and I can teach you."

Sandra looked at the overly stressed Sabastian and said, "We will meet you in the round room in five minutes, Sabastian."

Sabastian let out a breath of relief and left quickly.

Victoria spent the next few minutes learning balance and how to walk steadily in the heels. With Sandra's advice she was able to walk across the room without tripping twice. All she had to do was move naturally on her toes but she was over thinking and tripping when she tried to use the pointed heel. It was very awkward and she trembled with each step but when she walked on her toes to the round room her steps had begun to smooth out.

Sandra handed her to Sabastian and said, "Keep close to her and let her balance off of you and she should be fine."

"Great thanks, Sandra," Sabastian said at ease.

Victoria went to him and held onto his arm, "Sorry, I'm not very graceful."

"Don't worry, in that dress, no one is going to be looking at your feet."

She smiled and kept her eyes on her feet, finding their place on the floor as he took her through a different door that led down a flight of stairs.

She pulled back suddenly and stopped at the top of the stairs.

"Sabastian, I am not that good," she said worriedly, referring to her newly acquired skill of walking in heels.

He smiled and pulled her into his arms cradling her as he carried her down two flights of stairs and into a huge parking lot.

There were so many cars she was floored, there we no less than three limos, all black. Eight black sedans, all identical. There were several flashy sports cars, in reds and yellows, a pink jeep all decked out and an ancient bright green ford that looked rebuilt.

Regarding all the cars, she asked, "Are we in a parkade?"

"Kind of, this is our garage," he carried her over to a black sedan with blacked out windows and opened the back door for her.

"Miss Victoria," he said sweeping his hand toward the seat. With her hand in his, he helped her in the backseat and disappeared when the door closed behind her. Victoria was sitting on sweet smelling soft leather in complete darkness. She couldn't see out the side or front windows as a blacked out divider was between the back and front seats. She heard a door open and close and an engine start and she was thrown into the back seat as she felt the car drive and head upward. She found the seatbelt, fastened it, and called out.

"Umm, Sabastian?"

"I can hear you, Vicky."

"Why can't I see anything?" she asked.

"Cause you're in in the black sedan."

"Yes, I can see that, Sabastian," she said sarcastically. "Why am I in the black sedan?"

"Well, I cannot have you running away and telling everyone where our little harem is, now can I?" he answered her, sarcastically back.

Victoria kicked the back of his seat and slumped in the soft leather. She heard him chuckle and say, "Come on, Vicky, it's not that bad. I am, after all, taking you to a very posh party. Relax, you will love it."

"And what makes you think I will not go running and screaming to the first person I see claiming I have been kidnapped and, and…"

"Pleasured beyond your wildest dreams," he finished for her laughing again.

"Damn you, Sabastian," she said.

"If I know you, you are trying too hard to do a good job and have also been enjoying the lifestyle, plus, I think you like the education you are receiving."

Victoria could hear the smile in his words and cursed him again.

"Okay, you're right," she conceded. "But what exactly are we doing? We're not going to be peeping toms tonight, are we?"

"No, of course not. I just need to show you the job you are applying for and teach you how important it is to everyone involved."

They rode the rest of the time in silence. Victoria's mind buzzed, trying to remember all the stuff she had read in the etiquette books and how she was going to present herself at this party. She was agitated. How could she walk and talk among the elite crowd of the rich and powerful?

She felt the car slow down and make several tight turns. She had no idea how long they had driven for and didn't really care as she was so engrossed in her thoughts and nervousness. The car slowed and then started to inch forward like they were stuck in heavy traffic for a long time until they finally stopped and she heard a car door open and Sabastian say, "No, I have it, thank you."

Seconds later, there he was opening her car door for her in all his glory. His wavy hair, his wide shoulders and his grin, complete with dimples. Even though she was unsure, that all melted away as soon as she took his hand and he lifted her from the car. She leaned into him and he put a hand lightly on her back steading her shaky steps.

She was escorted right into a very luxurious hotel in the middle of some huge city. She glanced around but could only see generic tall buildings surrounding them and that the hotel they entered was very grand. They were caught behind several other couples slowly making their way into the entrance of a large meeting hall. Dozens of round tables surrounded a large dance floor where hundreds of people milled around talking or dancing. There was a live band and everyone was dressed so elegantly, in mostly black but there were a few colored dresses scattered in the crowd.

Victoria clung to Sabastian's arm, hoping she didn't embarrass herself by doing a face plant on the floor, courtesy of her very high, but gorgeous shoes.

Sabastian led her around the edge of the room. He walked gracefully, even though she was leaning most of her weight on his arm. He smiled and shook hands with a few men and he introduced her as Miss Mellissa Wignet. Victoria didn't know what to do, but lightly shake the hand of any person she was introduced to. She smiled nervously to each elegantly dressed gentleman, forgetting their name instantly as they continued to circle the room.

After the last couple they met, Victoria whispered, "How do you do it?"

"Do what?"

"Lie so convincingly, do you even know these people?"

"Some of them, yes, but as long as you act like you are one of the elites, it doesn't take much. Most of the very rich barely know who work for them, let alone any of the people they meet or invite to their events."

"So what are we doing here?"

"I want you to try to spot the Eximius girl. She is very hard to miss."

Victoria glanced around the room and spotted a crowd of people over by the head table slightly off to the side. There stood a man who must be the reason this gathering had taken place; he was clearly why everyone was here. Many people were talking to him or waiting to talk to him, he was tall, skinny and very good looking, suave was the best word to describe him, the type of man who could charm his way into or out of any situation. The crowd shifted and she saw those who were not engaged with conversation with. "Mr. Suave" were enamored and in deep debate with a woman.

She was not just any women, dressed in a deep blood red dress, she was both stunningly beautiful and classy. Her dress left one shoulder bare and the other wrapped and her shoes were a perfect match to the ensemble. When she shifted, Victoria saw almost her entire back was bare and flawless. Her hair, which was a very dark shade of rich coffee, fell gracefully in layers down to the tops of her shoulders, short but still very dramatic.

She was talking with an air of confidence and intellect and the others guests around her were nodding, completely engrossed in what she said.

Sabastian moved them closer to the crowd. Victoria could see and hear them clearly now. Mr. Suave stood close to her and was both listening to her and talking with her to their surrounding guests. Victoria could see that the men were drawn to her and she commanded their attention and their respect with every word she spoke.

Victoria paled; *how could she do that?*

This woman was flawless in her movement, her looks, and her intelligence. Victoria would never be able to do that job. She would have never guessed in a million years that this woman was a paid escort.

The woman looked up briefly, made eye contact with Sabastian, glanced fleetingly at Victoria, and went back to her conversation.

"That is Miss Rosaline Whitmore," Sabastian said proudly.

"Wow, I could never do that," Victoria said, speaking her thoughts out loud.

"What, have an intelligent conversation with a group of idiots? They are all suck ups anyway. They surround themselves with people who might grant them favors. Most of them are not that bright, but a few of them are and that's what you need to be prepared for."

"Don't you need to be closer to her?"

"No, I really don't need to be here at all, it's her third time with the senator and he's pretty harmless, he has gotten good reports so far and is very cooperative. I only need to stay within a minute of their location when they are alone for the evening. Things do not generally go wrong out in public. It's when they are alone behind locked doors when things can go astray. The girls are very good at reading their clients and know when things are going to go wrong well before it does. See the watch she's wearing? It has a button on the side that sends to my watch, one push is warning, a double push is help."

"What usually goes wrong?"

"We'll talk about that later," Sabastian said, reaching out his hand to a man approaching them.

"Hello, Mr. Taylor, so nice to see you again."

"And you, too, Sabastian."

Mr. Taylor was another finely attired gentleman, only slightly shorter than Sabastian and was almost as broad in the chest, he had a pleasant smile and looked to be in his late thirties. He was handsome but not in the model sense. He had a slight curve to his belly and a sweet face.

Sabastian motioned to Victoria and said, "This is Miss Mellissa. Mellissa, this is Mr. Johnathan Taylor, he owns several oil companies overseas."

"How do you do, miss?" Johnathan took her hand and kissed it lightly.

Johnathan looked at Sabastian, "Is this lovely lady one of your business consultants?"

"She's a new intern. We are currently seeing if she has the skills to be hired on with our company," Sabastian said smoothly.

"Well, Miss Mellissa, I look forward to being the first to test your skills to help me with my business."

Not taking his eyes from hers, he said to Sabastian. "See to it I am the first in line, will you, Sabastian? It looks like she has the skills I need to further my business profitability. If, of course, you do not mind taking on new clients, miss?"

Johnathan directed his question at her and Victoria was stumped on what to say. It took her a few seconds to remember the speaking advice in her business books. She made eye contact and smiled, letting the words flow from her, surprising both Sabastian and herself.

"Of course, Mr. Taylor, I would be delighted to go over your business ideas and put them into play. I am sure we can arrange a meeting in a few months when my calendar clears up. Sabastian will be able to set up an appointment at that time."

She gave him a dazzling smile.

Johnathan smiled back at her, obviously charmed, "You are absolutely delightful, Miss Mellissa. I look forward to working with you. Sabastian, you save this woman for me, I have a feeling I will be able to find many uses for her," Johnathan winked at her and left.

Choking down his instant rage and jealously, Sabastian turned to Victoria and asked calmly, "Where the hell did that come from?"

Victoria let out the breath she had been holding, "Why?"

Looking worried, "Did I do something wrong?"

Sabastian took a deep breath and gave her a tiny kiss on her cheek, "You were great I never expected that and you blew him away. You were subtle, charming, and very confident, he was basically drooling over you."

"Well, I guess I've had many years of practice playing a role on the streets," she said. "Is he a good client?"

Trying to be professional, Sabastian got a hold of himself, "Yes, he is. He treats our girls very well and doesn't have any weird quirks. He would make a good first client."

Victoria wondered what it would be like to sleep with Johnathan and found that he was very handsome and polite and thought if Sabastian said it was okay, she might consider it.

Suddenly, her attention was drawn to the podium, along with everyone else in the room. Rosaline had taken a spot at the microphone and everyone instantly hushed waiting to hear what the alluring woman had to say. With her client standing just behind her, she gave the crowd a dazzling smile and dove into a well-prepared speech. Victoria was so impressed when she spoke, she held everyone's attention and her speech was completely memorizing while she addressed the crowd of hundreds gathered before her with confidence.

She spoke with such passion about crime against women and went into such depth of the rules and regulations within the government on how to both protect and educate the women of the city. She quoted famous people, spoke eloquently, and her views were so enriching that Victoria would have voted for her client, even if he was selling children on the black market. She had a feeling that whatever subject Rosaline would have chosen to talk about, that it would make anyone a believer in her Mr. Suave. She could see clearly that with just her, this man would be reelected.

Ending her speech, she said, "My friends, I present to you our senator and my dear friend, Mr. Wilkshire."

Victoria lost interest as soon as the man walked up, shaking Rosaline's hand and hugging her swiftly. He smiled and waved at the crowd as he approached the podium.

Sabastian took her hand and led her to an empty table, he waved down a waiter and asked for chilled fruit juice and took her hands.

"Do you see, Vicky? The fact that our women are paid to do this does not matter. It is a job that they love and get a lot of satisfaction, both professionally and physically. They are very well respected at the manor and even more so by their clients. They are also well-respected members of the community and fight for what is right. They use their pay to better the world and enrich the lives of countless people around them."

He looked over at Rosaline who was still backing her client on the stage with a proud smile on her face.

"She has built three girls' schools in Africa and another girl at the manor, funds the foundation, Wrong to Right, which helps rape victims find homes for their babies. That is only a few, not all of the women do things like that but many like to give back as they have everything they could possibly want because of their job. Not only are their lives enriched by this job, but they help others and Victoria they truly love the work they do. You're narrow minded, you need to stop your prejudice and see them for what they are. Intelligent, strong, independent women who love being challenged, working hard to prove themselves, making a difference in this world, and also love to fuck."

Victoria gapped at him, his speech was so well articulated and passionate but the word fuck caught her off guard and she ending up gapping at him crudely.

Sabastian smiled and handed her the juice that had arrived at the table.

Victoria sat there absorbing it all, seeing it first hand in person was a real eye opener. What is the difference between these girls and real professionals who do this same job? The only one she could see is that they slept with their employers, how many thousands of women did that to get ahead anyway.

Sabastian was watching her, waiting.

"How many of them are married?" she asked. That seemed to be the only morally wrong thing she could find in this situation.

Sabastian sighed and put his head in his hands, clearly exasperated.

"Come on, party's over," he walked around to her chair and offered his arm to balance on as he led her out.

"What about your charge?" she asked, glancing over at Rosaline.

"My replacement has just shown up," he said taking off his watch. She watched as another dashing dark man approached them and saw Sabastian slip the watch into the man's hand without making eye contact or pausing at all. It was so smooth she only saw it because her eyes were focused on the watch.

He led her outside and the valet had their car to them in minutes and she was put into the back seat.

After several minutes in silence, she heard him say.

"Yes, Vicky, some are married. Mostly married to further their careers, they are not in love and very few have kids. The married men are smart and take their girls away on business trips to enjoy their company. None have ever gotten caught or have stopped because of guilt, seeing how most are not in love with their wives and need what our girls give them and what they aren't getting at home. But the percentage of married men is very low."

"Oh," was all Victoria could say. She was quiet for a long time, absorbed in her thoughts.

"So how do the clients pick which girls they want? Do you take them to parties like this one and show them off?"

"No, never. They are not allowed to choose any woman from the manor. It's not a line-up Vicky. The clients fill out a very detailed and personal questionnaire and we offer the client to whoever we feel is best suited to take on the job. We are able to match every client to our girls as long as they answer one hundred percent truthfully and whichever girl matches the profile and wants the job takes it."

"Oh, so Johnathan is not allowed to just pick me then?"

"He can, but if we feel you are not a good match for him, we will replace you with someone who can handle him with your features."

"Okay," Victoria was silent again, absorbed and wondered what other girls at the manor would have her features.

"How long will it take to finish my training?"

"It takes about a year minimally to train a new girl. Most girls do not make it through, but the few that do, take at least year, but that does not include specialties."

"Specialties?"

"Vicky, you are still so new to both your body and the act of having sex, you have no idea of the world of love making. There are several of our girls with specialties, they learn these because they crave them and there is a need for them. But you will have to wait at least a little while to experience them. I will let you know that you will hate most of them and the training that comes with studying them. But you never know, one might catch your fancy and you will add that to your resume."

"Do I have to try them?"

"Yes, you will not know you like them until you have tried them several times, you have to experience them, then practice them, and be comfortable with them. Only then will you see if it something you would like experience for yourself and to offer to your clients when working."

Victoria was once again lost in her thoughts, so much so that she jumped when Sabastian was at her door offering her his hand out of the car.

"Did you have a pleasant evening?"

"Yes," she said, shocked they were back so quickly.

Sabastian led her from the garage to the round room and stopped, "Would you like to go to your room or the Summit?"

Victoria was surprised, was he asking her if she wanted to have sex with him or not? Or was he asking her if she was staying or planning to leave?

"The Summit," she answered. "My answer is the Summit, always."

She glanced up at him and he was watched her sharply.

Walking down the hallway, he said, "You will not be officially offered the job till after the next part of your internship, which will either make or break you here," he said grimly, "You will not like it but," he paused, "perhaps you will."

She didn't know what to say to that, so she asked, "When will that begin?"

"Now," he said, opening the door to the Summit.

"Now? As in right now?"

"Yes."

Sabastian walked her over to the bed and sat her on the edge. He bent down to remove her shoes and asked.

"How are your feet?" Grazing her instep with his fingernail.

She shivered, "Fine."

He moved his hands very slowly up the inside of her legs; he hooked her panties underneath.

"You look stunning, Vicky," he brought her panties to his nose and took a deep breath inhaling the fabric.

Gently, he lifted her off the bed and pulled her into him, reaching around to slide the dress from her shoulders, kissing the fabric off of her as it went. Just like that she was naked, her skin tingling from his touches and her breath was coming in short fast bursts. Sabastian bent down to kiss her hard on the lips taking her by surprise seeing how his hands were just so tender with her.

This was different, he would usually take time to be rough with her, until she was desperate for his touch. Was this the kind of difference in sex he was talking about? Even though he had not touched her in any sensitive spots, she could feel her body tightening wonderfully in anticipation, readying itself for him, the moisture building between her legs.

"Mmmmm," she groaned under his lips, feeling his hands wrap around her back. He suddenly pushed her to the bed and ground his hips into hers and she arched into him accepting his quick arousal and the rush of desire flooding her senses. Sabastian pulled his lips from hers and lifted her chest up to his mouth taking her nipple hungrily in, swirling his tongue all around and she arched into him again.

"Ah, mmmmm, oh, yes," she cried. Her body was throbbing and a firm pulse was building so sweetly. He dropped her suddenly to the bed to push her breasts together to nip and tease the tips of both nipples sucking hard and she grabbed his hair in her hands and moaned again.

"Ah, Ah, Ahhhhhh."

Sabastian gave her one last long pull with his mouth on her nipples before lowering his mouth to her swelling sex moving his tongue quickly over her.

"Ah, ah, ah," she cried thrusting into his greedy mouth, she was building so fast. She cried out again when his hands flew to her breasts taking both her nipples in his fingers, pinching hard while he rolled them, the pain was so welcome her body bowed, taking more of his thrusting tongue inside her.

Her climax was climbing so strong she relished in it, trying to savoring it and she felt the wonderful pull as her entire body clenched its way toward its goal.

"Ah!" she cried again but not from pleasure. He was gone, she opened her eyes to look down at him but he was walking away from her.

"What?" she managed to asked to his retreating back. "Sabastian, come back."

He turned and winked, "Good night, wild cat."

"Did I do something wrong?" she asked, alarmed.

"Never, sweet, Vicky. Have a good night," and he was gone.

"No," she called after him. She tried to get off the bed but her legs were too shaky she couldn't stand. The pulsing that had begun to climb was aching for him, reaching for him and he was gone. She sat on the bed, trying to catch her breath, willing her body to relax.

"What the hell had just happened?" she asked herself. Her body was pounding and her face was red with longing. How dare he leave her like that, unsatisfied, wanting so badly and for him to take it away from her so abruptly? Her need was replaced by anger, she flung herself in bed fuming and knowing this was only the start of her, so-called, new experiences. Sabastian was right, she didn't like it!

Chapter 58

Victoria awoke groggy, she had been restless last night and as a result, didn't get enough sleep. She went directly to the shower to wake up. When she got out of the bathroom, Sabastian was sitting on her bed with her breakfast, picking at the ham on her plate.

"Good morning, Vicky, did you sleep well?"

"No," she said, glaring at him.

"Well, that's a shame," he patted the bed. "Come and eat and watch a video with me."

Still wrapped in her towel, she grabbed her robe, covered herself, and settled back into the pillows with her meal.

Sabastian leaned back and lazily turned on the TV, rubbing her legs softly up and down, not going any higher than mid-thigh.

Even though she was still pissed at him for last night, she wished his hands would go higher. She focused on her meal and the movie playing. It was another film but there was less talk and more action. The screen showed men and women having sex in many different positions, slowing down and zooming in at crucial parts. It was going through how to get the most satisfaction from each position and how to move smoothly from one position to the other. It was meant to educate a woman on how to bend, move, and curve their body to their partners to both give and take gratification. It was so sensual, focusing on the hips of the moving couple, the times when the man entered into very wet folds and when the woman brought her body to meet his. Then it would zoom in as either of them would adjust their angle to change the dynamic of the intercourse.

Sabastian watched Victoria's eyes dilate out of the corner of his eye and start to fidget about ten minutes through the film, right where it was detailed and up close. He saw she was extremely aroused and saw her legs open slightly when his hand ran up her leg. With every pass up, he got closer and closer to her groin and without touching her hardly at all, she was moaning every time he raised his hand higher.

Victoria nearly convulsed when Sabastian's fingers gripped her breast through the fabric of the robe. Her nerves jumped and responded to his playing fingers on her hardened nipple.

"Ah, mmmm," she groaned her lips parted, panting with need.

"What do you want, Vicky?"

"I want you to have sex with me, Sabastian," she said plainly without embarrassment, not trying to hide it at all.

Sabastian climbed on top her, flipping her robe open to reveal her creamy skin. He knew this was a dangerous game he was playing of which he had little control.

Victoria lifted her hips toward him, her legs opened wide. She was so close, she only needed him a few minutes as tendrils of pleasure had already begun the building sensation deep in her slick inner channel.

"Mmmm," she cried as he lowered his hips into hers. She raised her hips up and ground into him, feeling the painful need for him engulf her.

"You want me to fuck you like this?" he asked as he pushed into her hips.

Sabastian was still fully dressed but knew he didn't need to take off any of his clothes to satisfy this responsive girl squirming with need under him. He hated what he was doing to her and himself.

"Yes, please," she begged, writhing and trembling.

"You want to be fucked so bad?" he asked, pushing into her softness again.

"Yes," she breathed, offering herself up to him.

"Sorry, sweet Vicky," he leaned down, kissed her lips and walked out.

Victoria's eyes watched him leave and shouted.

"You jerk," and threw a pillow at the door, her body collapsing to the bed. She needed release and he refused to give it to her. She was in a frenzy of longing, her body desperate and her skin flushed aroused crying out for him. She was surprised when she felt hot tears running down her face. She dashed them away and realizing the video was still playing, she quickly shut it off. Whatever game he was playing, she was not amused.

She pushed the contents of her tray across the bed and went to get into the shower again, hoping that would calm her down.

Out of the shower, twenty minutes later, still hot and throbbing, Victoria cursed him again. She should just leave her room, find him and fuck him. Maybe that is what he was teaching her; to take control.

She sighed and pick up an etiquette book and tried to spend the next few hours reading and relaxing, trying to control her urges.

When Maximus came, she welcomed the distraction and only minutes through the work-out she knew that Maximus had been told to work her hard. Victoria was sweating profusely and exhausted when she got back to her room over two and a half hours later.

She bathed and settled to read when there was a knock at the door hours later. She was lying on the bed, reading naked, and didn't care when she answered the knock.

"If you are coming back to torture me some more, go away."

"Oh, come on," Sabastian said, letting himself in. "It's not that bad."

He was grinning at her but worried. He was wearing only thin cotton shorts and no shirt, but as devastatingly handsome as he was, she was determined to show him she was still pissed.

"I should castrate you," she said, trying to keep her eyes on her book.

As he moved closer to the bed, she could smell him and looked up. He was covered in sweat; he had clearly been working out. He smelled so musky and masculine that her sex flexed unbidden. She summoned her anger to cover her instant and infuriating arousal.

He sat down on the edge of her bed and asked, "What are you reading?"

"*Making It Worth It*, a business guide to strong companies," she answered nonchalantly.

Sabastian raised his hand toward her and grazed her shoulder.

Victoria jumped away from him, "What are you doing?"

"Nothing," he grinned, his finger moving closer to her and trying to brush her chest.

"Bugger off, Sabastian, I don't have time for your games."

"Who are you kidding, you have nothing but time."

"Whatever the lesson is, get it over with, you're driving me insane."

"I am sorry, are you sensitive?" he asked innocently.

"Ummm, I…"

"Are you throbbing already?" he asked, scooting closer to her.

His male scent over powered her and her vaginal muscles convulsed and pulsed so deliciously as a strong thrill ran through her. She realized that yes, she was sensitive and yes, she was very much throbbing. It had happened as soon as he knocked on her door when she was mad at him and she abruptly realized the lesson he was teaching her.

"How do you feel, Victoria?" he rolled her name on his tongue, grazing her bare shoulder with the tips of his fingers.

She had to take a deep breath to calm herself. She couldn't answer him, her throat was constricted and her mouth dry. She swallowed and the pounding increased as her walls flexed hard not having anything to grab ahold of as they pulled inside her body.

"Mmmmmm," she groaned and arched slightly toward him. Her nipples were erect and her belly had thousands of butterflies flitting around inside her at the anticipation he had built in her with only words and the teasing he had offered her earlier.

"You want me inside of you," he whispered huskily, breathing in her ear. He moved closer to her and moved his light finger touches to the top of her cleavage.

Her eyes flew to his, worried and fearful he would tease her to a frenzy again and didn't trust herself to answer him.

"It's okay, wild cat," he said low and husky.

His hand lowered to her ultra-sensitive nipples and circled lazily around the areola and her entire body went tense at his touch, the building increasing ten-fold between her legs.

"Mmmmmmm," she purred, her eyes closing in pure pleasure.

She was throbbing with need; she looked into his dark green eyes and saw his need was there hot and strong and wondered why he was waiting.

He took both her nipples in his hands and rolled them slowly, over and over. She cried and arched into his hands.

"Oh, oh, oh, yes, Ah."

She felt his hot breath on her neck and his musk filled her senses. He squeezed and pulled at her nipples hard and fast, moving in sweet circles and the buildup was both surprising and welcomed.

"Come, Vicky, let me see you cum hard and then I will give you what you want," he whispered sensually in her ear. His head dipped to tongue her erect nipples as his hand played and pulled at the other breast palming, then pinching in a steady rhythm.

Her body was building drastically and her sex pulsed in an erotic rhythm that speed up with his hands. Sabastian paused as he brought his hand together to lick and suck and bite her tender nipples in his mouth, groaning as he played. He increased the tempo on her nipples, biting, licking, sucking over and over again rolling each tip as his hands cupped her breasts expertly.

Victoria was so sensitive and needy that she suddenly erupted in his hands, her body pounding and throbbing in on itself as it arched with pleasure. She was amazed at the orgasm that claimed her body with only him playing with her breasts and her nipples sang with the satisfaction. She watched him with anticipation as he quickly positioned himself and she lifted her hips so he could drive home inside her pulsing wetness. She screamed with his entrance arching so hard into him, he shouted with her.

"Auuugggghhhh, Vicky," he cried and he pounded into her ruthlessly hard and fast into her still convulsing cunt.

Victoria felt his hands on her hips. He grabbed her and lifted her from the bed and she felt him pulling her with his hands while thrusting fervently into her wildly pulsing flesh.

He was relentless and she let him pound into her again and again and again with long, hard strokes. They writhed together in perfect sync and she felt herself start to ascend. It was so unexpected after her first climax, but her over stimulated body welcomed him hungrily. She felt her sex grip him, savoring the feeling. Finally having him inside her was so hot it sent her head spinning. He hammered into her with such speed and force that tension mounted as they sought release. He roared his lust as he exploded into her at the same time she imploded around him, milking him sweetly. Victoria's body jerked and convulsed, absorbing the multiple waves of pleasure ripping through her. He slowed slightly on his last thrusts emptying himself into her as she felt the swelling pulse inside her subside; she collapsed with him on the bed. She had received two unbelievable orgasms, strong and fast, she learned the lesson well and couldn't wait for the next one.

"I hope I didn't upset you too much?" he said as he exited out of her sweet wetness.

"Yes, you did," she said feigning anger. "But you also more than made up for it," smiling up at the ceiling.

He bent over her, "The more sensitive you are, the faster the reprieve and your clients will have to do very little to satisfy both of you. Few men know how to satisfy a woman, that's why so many women fake orgasms. But if you are primed and ready, so sensitive, any touch will make your body respond, you will cum hard and fast with little effort on his part and he will love you for it."

"But he can't tease me for hours before we meet."

"No, he can't. It's all in your head, Vicky, it's why you have been watching the videos. Now it's up to you. Over the next few days, you are to prepare yourself and I get to come in and screw you and see if you have studied enough for you to reach satisfaction with little work on my part."

"Sounds like fun."

"I will come in two days, then one, then half a day, then finally only one hour, every time you will be primed and ready for me. You will want to have sex and you will cum hard and fast. Got it?" he commanded.

"Yes, sir," she saluted him, smiling, enjoying the challenge.

"Okay, have fun," he winked at her and pulled on his shorts and went to leave.

"Wait," she said, kneeling up on the bed, "could you at least kiss me? It felt wrong not being kissed while doing that."

She motioned to the bed.

Sabastian sighed; she was getting too attached that needed to change. "No, get over it, Vicky, I am teaching you to fuck, nothing more," he said hastily and he walked out.

Sabastian leaned up against the outside of her door. She had asked him to kiss her and he had wanted to lean in and so gently take her lips into his and caress her bottom lip and tongue, to hear her moan into his mouth. She was not his and he needed to get over her, she belonged to the company. Sabastian decided he needed to have a talk with Benjamin, hoping he could help her get over him and him over her. She needed someone else.

Sabastian found Benjamin in the round room picking out a book.

"Hey, Ben."

"Hey, Sabastian, what's going on?" Benjamin asked, looking from his book.

"Wild cat needs someone new."

"Really?" Benjamin asked, turning toward Sabastian.

344

"Ya, she's ready, she is now working on building her arousal, the priming stage."

"Is she doing well with that? Because that can sometimes be an issue with many girls?"

"Not her, I could have been a three headed donkey and she wouldn't have cared."

"Well, that's promising, do you want me to prime her or only fulfill her when she's ready?"

"I think we'll give her three days, not two like I told her and you can see where she's at, but be careful, she's not experienced and is still very fresh."

"Okay, will do," Benjamin turned back to the book shelf.

Sabastian smiled to himself. He knew Benjamin was a good choice for his wild cat. But something in his gut had twisted and a headache had started to pound in his skull. So engrossed in his thoughts, he didn't see the figure one story above the round room listening in on their conversation.

Chapter 59

Victoria was in her room for only one day waiting and mentally preparing herself before her nerves got to her. Focusing and studying about intercourse all day put her on edge and she needed an outlet to her pent-up energy. She had been trapped in rooms for too long and needed some space and decided to head to the garden for some fresh night air to read.

She went over to the door and tried the knob; it was open but she couldn't walk around in just her robe. She had very little clothes in the Summit so she pressed the button by the door, something she had not used yet.

"Hello?"

"Yes, Miss Victoria."

Victoria heard the voice and realized it was Ethan again.

Oh, shit, she thought. *Not him. I should have asked Sabastian to find me another keeper.*

Hoping Ethan didn't come in her room, she said, "I need to get out of here, but I don't have any normal clothes, could you please get me something to wear?"

"Yes, of course, Miss Victoria."

She waited and realized that Ethan would be going through her room and didn't like the thought of him rifling through her possessions. She should have just asked for Sabastian, but he was probably working.

Ten minutes later, there was a light knock and Ethan walked in with clothes in his hands.

"Here you go, Miss Victoria," he handed her a pair of white shorts and a pink shirt with a matching blue lace bra and pantie set and white socks. He also set a pair of runners on the bench for her.

"Thank you." She took the clothes and saw him watching her and waited for him to leave.

Looking up and down her body, licking his lips, Ethan said, "Is there anything I can help you with?"

"Uh, ya, you could leave, I need to get dressed," Victoria answered, trying not to sound rude.

"I think you need my help with something else," he said, taking a step toward her.

She backed away not trusting him and his cold, ice blue eyes.

"You're working on your arousal training, right?" he asked.

"Um, yes," she said tightly.

"So if you have been doing it right, you should be primed."

Ethan stepped closer to her and she felt the bed hit the back of her knees and she fell backward. "You should be able to take on any challenge at this point," he leered down at her.

"I'm not r…r…ready," she stammered up at him, feeling her heart surge with adrenaline.

"Oh, wild cat, you are ready."

Leaving no time for her to react in defense, he leaned in and grabbed her arms, pressing his fingers cruelly into her soft underarms. Victoria couldn't' fight back in this position, she needed space to do that. He held her in a vice grip and Ethan barley even registered her resistance. He pressed his lips to hers hard, making her taste blood as he cut her lip on her own teeth and his tongue forced its way into her mouth. He let go of one arm and pulled her hips to his and bent down to press into her. Victoria took the opportunity to use one of her defensive moves to jerk out of his grasp and pull her mouth away from his panting.

He looked amused and she saw his eyes dilate on her breasts that had come free of her robe. Ethan's hand bolted out and grabbed her hard squeezing her whole breast in his hand and pinching her nipple callously in his fingers.

"Ah," she cried in pain, but she also felt horrified at the painful pleasure on her woman's center.

"That's it girl, cry out for me," he whispered lustfully, pulling the robe away from her body.

"Get the hell off of me!" she finally managed to say. Reaching her hands up, she pushed him hard, but he might as well have been made of stone as he didn't budge even an inch.

"Oh you don't mean that, wild cat, you want to be fucked, you have been thinking about it all day and you need me to take you hard and fast. Admit it."

She shook her head and he grabbed her again hard, shaking her shoulders and yelled, "Admit it!"

"Not going to happen Ethan, get out," she commanded with as much force as possible.

Victoria could see a lustful anger boiling in his eyes and flinched as he held her tight to his body grinding into her. Taking her hair in his fist, he bent back her head forcefully and planted a deep ruthless kiss on her lips.

Victoria couldn't move her head and had to submit to his mouth, his tongue digging into hers. She felt his hard throbbing erection against her groin and she had to mentally control her body to keep herself still. He pressed into her and groaned into her mouth and she knew the only way to escape him. She bit down hard on his lip, tasting his blood and was tossed as he threw her to the bed. She could see a triumphant smile play across his lips as he wiped the blood away and advanced.

"Get out!" She screamed at him, panting hard. "Out!"

Ethan hesitated, then asked, "Are you sure? Do you really want me to leave?"

He took off his shirt and she paled; he was advancing on her.

"Yes, out!" she said, trying desperately to control herself. He was dangerous and she knew it. Her body was throbbing with need and it scared her so much, she was shaking and tears were pooling in her eyes.

"Out," she whispered, her eyes lowering to hide her fear.

"Fine," he said, retreating to the door. "I'll be seeing you soon anyway, it's all a part of the training, each day brings you closer to me and nothing you do will change that."

He retreated, putting his shirt back on and left, slamming the door hard behind him.

Victoria sobbed and covered herself up. What the hell had just happened, was he allowed to do that? She was so ashamed at her body. He was too much, too strong and too violent, he reminded her too much of back home and being trapped and brutalized.

She sobbed again and took her clothes to the bathroom. She could see her arms were red from where he had grabbed her and her mouth was tender, but other than that, she was okay. She took several deep breaths and washed the tears from her face and put a cold cloth on her eyes to prevent them from swelling. After several minutes, she had her breathing under control and her face had returned to a normal color. She started brushing her hair when she heard a knock on the door and froze, her adrenaline peaked from fear instantly.

"Hey, Vicky, what are you doing?" Sabastian voice asked from her room.

Victoria sighed a breath of relief and answered. "I'm getting dressed, give me a sec," she said clearly, controlling her voice.

She braided her hair over her shoulder and got dressed quickly, glad the shirt was long sleeved and stepped out to put on the shoes Ethan had brought her. She glanced at Sabastian wanting to tell him what had happened but ashamed of herself and her response to Ethan.

"I have to get out of here," she said, putting the bright runners on.

"What, you don't mean....?" he looked so worried that she laughed.

"No I don't mean I want to leave; I just need to get out of here," she said pointing to the bed. "I'm bored."

Covering up her uneasiness to what had just happened with Ethan nicely.

He looked insulted, "Do I bore you, Miss Victoria?"

Exasperated, she said, "Sabastian, you keep me very entertained, but we can't spend every day in bed having sex and me thinking about sex twenty-four, seven. Come on, I need more than that. I have memorized all the books and videos; I have practiced and primed. I need a break." She also needed a distraction.

"Oh, have I been working you too hard?" he asked with mock sympathy.

She glared at him and tried to smack him when he dodged and slapped her soundly on the ass.

"Okay, you asked for it, let's go," he said, heading to the door.

"So what's the plan?" she asked, following him out. "The garden?"

"Well, I thought I should introduce you to the manor."

Her eyes brows quirked up, "Which one?"

"Both."

"Really?" she asked, following him out the door and up the stairwell.

"Ya, you should meet all the guys here."

"Umm, okay, do they know I am coming?"

"Nope, they are all working or hanging out, but don't worry, they won't mind being interrupted by the famous wild cat."

"Why am I famous?" she was intrigued.

"Because you beat the shit out of Edward and me when we collected you," he said smiling his dimpled smile.

"Right, will I be able to see Edward and say sorry?" she asked.

"Ya, I think he's around."

Sabastian pulled Victoria behind him, ignoring the men in the round room to turn down a hall and opened a large wooden door. They entered a huge laboratory with several glass tables, white, plastic rolling chairs, and all kinds of machines either plugged in, blinking lights or whirling.

"This is the lab. This is where we make sure our girls are going out with safe clients and this is Richard," he said, his hand outstretched to the only figure in the room.

Victoria stared, as a huge dark man got up from a chair that looked like it would break under his weight, and approach them. He was tall, well over six feet and his barrel chest stuck out impressively from a lab coat that was draped on his shoulders. His chocolate skin was carved and looked overly muscled, but not unattractively so. His hair was short and his goatee surrounded full lips that looked like they had been kissing for hours. Even though his build was extremely intimidating, his warm smile, sweet dark eyes, and bright white teeth told her he was anything but a threat.

She put up her hand to shake his, "Nice to meet you, Richard."

"Hello, Miss Victoria, so nice to finally meet you."

His low baritone voice rumbled slightly when he spoke. So softly he took her hand in his, which disappeared in his massive palm and kissed it lightly.

"This joker hasn't been giving you a hard time, has he? Because if he is, I would gladly sit on him for you," his face serious.

Victoria pretended she was thinking about it when Richard released her hand and made a grab for Sabastian who dodged easily out the way.

"Ya, right, you black hulk, if you could even catch me."

She laughed at the two men, obviously friends. Her Sabastian would be crushed by this giant and she was thankful he was only joking.

"You're lucky, you're fast little man," Richard replied with a laugh.

Even though Sabastian was not nearly as tall or wide, he was far from small and she smiled again at their banter.

"Come here, you luscious creature, let me show you my work and we'll leave scrawny here to his own devices."

He offered her his arm and Victoria glanced at Sabastian who smiled reluctantly at her, gesturing to go ahead. She took the proffered thick arm and followed the dark hulk of a man to the table where he had been working.

Within minutes, she learned about blood work and how it was separated and tested. Also within those minutes, she realized Richard was nothing but a big teddy bear who loved his work. He made her feel completely comfortable as he taught her about the job he did. This was such a nice change and a relief from the experience in her room earlier with Ethan.

She was learning there were others that worked here and helped Richard when they were busy, as well as how to keep everything organized to ensure there were no mistakes.

She thanked him for his time and wondered if he was a trainer as well, only because he was so sweet and gentle with her and made her feel so comfortable. She shuttered at the thought knowing that when men were over taken by lust they changed and she was certain Richard would rip her apart.

"We'll see the guys in the entertainment room next, then you can meet the men in here after," Sabastian said as he walked through the round room again and down another hall and opened a large black door. The room was very dark with an enormous screen TV centered in it with two levels of multiple lounging chairs like a movie theater. There was an army game being played on screen and it paused as soon as the five guys playing it realized she was there.

"Sorry, guys," Sabastian apologized, "I'm giving Miss Victoria the tour."

All five gorgeous men stood up at the same time and said, "Miss Victoria."

The ridiculousness of the situation made her burst out laughing.

"Come on guys, seriously?" she asked. "You don't need to do that; it freaks me out."

All five guys sat back down, amused and relieved.

"You said she was a wild cat, Sabastian," one of them said. "And you're right, bring her on in, she can be one of the guys."

"Ya, here," another man said, offering her his game controller, "Come sit with me, honey, you can play my game as long as I can sit with you."

Sabastian scowled at the men; he knew when the guys were in their own manor they acted like real guys. Constantly shoving, teasing, and swearing, and knew that, like Victoria, he would be driven crazy if they all acted like the polished gentlemen, they were trained to be all the time.

"Why would she want to sit near you, Maverick? You stink," a man in the front row said back to him.

The dark man named Maverick answered, "Ya, well, at least I don't smell like rose petals and lavender all the time."

"Hey, you would kill for my steady hand, I know the ladies certainly appreciate it," the man said, winking at Victoria.

Sabastian motioned to the guys in turn, ignoring their banter.

"The blonde one in the back is Robert, he mostly watches and works in the kitchen. That's Douglas, he is our company shrink, but doubles as a watcher and does kitchen work. Maverick is the cocky one in the front…"

"In more ways than one, honey pie," he said winking at her and Victoria blushed at the man who had large white teeth in a very handsome dark brown face.

Sabastian continued, ignoring him, "He watches and trains. And the one with the steady hands is Blake, our spa specialist who also a works the lab. And, of course, you know Maximus."

Victoria smiled at Maximus as he waved and winked at her with his large boyish grin that made her feel at ease in this room full of strangers. She looked at all the gorgeous men sitting in front her, everyone was heavily muscled, so handsome and overly attractive that if this job fell through, they would have no problem finding jobs as professional models. She couldn't help compare each one of the men introduced to her to Sabastian and each one fell short one way or another. They were all in their twenties and thirties and looked comfortable and relaxed, hanging out being guys, doing a job they loved. They didn't look repressed or taken advantage of, they looked like they were living the dream and she wondered about their background stories.

The guys were now joking back and forth, clearly showing off for her and she blushed again thinking that any one of these guys could be someone she could be sleeping with soon.

Maverick was still holding out the game controller and winking at her and she turned to Sabastian for help.

"Ya, well, that was great guys. Nice show," he said, turning to leave to a very loud chorus of boos and heckles.

Sabastian led her back to the round room where there were a few more guys hanging out.

"Hey, guys, I am introducing Miss Victoria to everyone."

The men started to stand, but she rolled her eyes. "Don't say it," she said sternly as she heard them start to say miss.

"Relax, guys, she's fine. Just an intern, be yourselves," Sabastian reassured the men.

Victoria frowned at that, but if just being an intern meant the men were not bowing and kissing her ass and would relax around her, she could swallow the insult.

The men continued what they were doing as Sabastian led her around the room. She met William, Jacob, Roman, and Nathanial. All of who she liked instantly, they were funny polite and very enamored by her. All of them had jobs similar to the first group, except for Nathanial who she was told was a submissive and she looked to Sabastian quizzically, who shrugged and said, "Later."

They walked over to another broad muscled man who was scanning books and Sabastian said, "And this is Edward."

Victoria looked at the attractive but surly man she had attacked in the apartment and looked down to his leg, trying to see if there was an after effect to the knife wound she had given him.

"I'm fine," Edward said, almost bored, following her gaze.

"I am so, so sorry. Are you sure?"

"Yes of course," he assured her.

"I panicked, I'm sorry," she repeated.

"Please, you had every right to be scared, but I must say I was impressed you were able to do so much damage."

Victoria's face reddened, ashamed.

"If I had known," she started.

"Well, we tried to talk to you."

Looking back on that night, she had given them no chance to even get near her let alone talk to her.

"I'm sorry," she said again.

"Okay, Edward, lighten up," Sabastian interrupted, saving her from the guilt.

"Oh, come on, you have to admit she was a stubborn piece of work," Edward argued.

"Yes, she is, but that is one of the things I like about her," Sabastian replied, wrapping his arm around her waist and pulling her away from Edward.

Victoria smiled up at Sabastian, loving the feel of his arm wrapped protectively around her waist, but then said, "He has every right to be mad at me."

"Who cares, there's no permanent damage, except maybe to his ego and that needed a hit anyway."

Sabastian smiled down at her, "Forget it, he's just mad you got the better of him and it serves him right. It will teach him to take you and the next collection job seriously."

"Okay," Victoria muttered, thinking back to that night in the alley that seemed so long ago. "Can I check out the book collection you guys have?"

"Of course, I'll be over here," he gestured toward another man across the room.

"Those books there will be your next step," he pointed to her left and she walked over to check them out.

She saw Sabastian move over to the side of the room to talk with the fair man she had not met. Meeting everyone was so overwhelming, she had already forgotten most of the names in the first group.

Glancing through the titles, she picked up a book and turned to join Sabastian and ran face to face with Ethan. She jumped back, recognition gripping her, and she back away.

"Sorry," she mumbled. He was too close and she took another step back.

Ethan glanced over at Sabastian who was across the room, not looking their way and bent low to her. Victoria's heart was beating so fast from fear and held her breath.

"Yes, will bring me to you, wild cat," he whispered. "One little word and I will be able to train you right."

She stepped back, trying to regain some distance. "No Ethan. Back off," she said firmly, glaring at him.

She pushed past him hard and went to Sabastian and the man he was talking to. Sabastian turned when she approached and noticed her flushed face and rapid breathing. He was about to ask her what was wrong when Ethan stepped toward the group.

"Gentlemen," Ethan said smoothly.

"Hey, Ethan, you know Victoria?" Sabastian asked.

"Not as well as I would like," Ethan replied grinning down at her.

Sabastian saw Victoria was fidgeting and twisting her hair concerned.

"Ethan works in the spa and kitchen and also trains submissives."

Victoria caught on the last word, confused. "You mean he trains Nathanial over there?" she said, gesturing to the man playing cards with William.

All three of the men burst out laughing.

"No, of course not," Sabastian said, chuckling at her.

Victoria frowned, she didn't appreciate being laughed at and her cheeks went red, missing what was so funny.

"You have not taught her anything," the fair man stated.

"Well, we haven't gotten around to it," Sabastian defended.

"I can explain it to her anytime," Ethan said seriously, putting a hand around her shoulders, and Victoria tensed.

"Like hell Ethan," Sabastian said even more serious, wrapping his arm around her waist and taking her from Ethan's arms to his side.

Ethan backed down, "Okay, okay, I can take the hint."

He dropped his hand, then reached for his phone that had just pinged in his pants.

"Oh, looks like duty calls," he licked his lips, winked at Victoria and waved to the men. "See ya," and he disappeared out the garden doors.

Victoria raised her eyes to Sabastian, still waiting to be let in on the joke, visibly relaxing now that Ethan was gone.

"Sorry, but Ethan doesn't train men, only women. Yes, Nathanael is a submissive but for the women only. Ethan dominates women who enjoy that kind of play and Nathanial is a submissive for our dominate girls to practice on."

Victoria was still very confused.

"Let's get you past all the basics before we dive into the specialties, then I can explain in more detail later, for now, I wanted to get you to meet someone," turning to the fair man he had been talking to.

"Victoria, this is Benjamin, he is going to work with you tomorrow just like a client would. Would that be okay?"

Victoria was taken aback and looked at this fair man in front of her.

He was tall, like most of the men, and a little thinner, but his defined muscles showed he was no light weight. His very light blonde hair was almost white and he had dark brown eyes that contrasted his light coloring dramatically. His glasses didn't hide his kind eyes and a sweet face. A cleft in his chin added to his very attractive face.

"Umm, I guess that would be okay," she said unsure.

"If you like Miss Victoria, I can just come and visit you tomorrow, we can meet in the garden and then I will let you take it from there," Benjamin offered.

Sabastian looked at the two and knew Benjamin would be the perfect next step for his wild cat. He knew from the other girls that he was very considerate with them and made sure the women were taken care of in every way when he bedded them.

"That sounds nice, what time?" she asked, trying to get used to the idea.

"I will come to collect you after lunch, at one o'clock, is that okay?"

"Okay," Victoria said, shrugging uneasily.

Sabastian took her arm and led her away.

"This isn't a date, Vicky, you need to act like he's a client and be prepared for him. A complete stranger and you need to be both physically and mentally ready."

"Yes, I know," she said quietly, thinking.

Sabastian showed her the medical room where, thankfully, Dr. Marshall was elsewhere as she didn't want to come face to face with the only person who knew she was a virgin before she had come here.

Back in the round room, she studied the manor's unique design. The outer rooms on the main level all surrounded the round room. There were seven hallways that led to the main work or common areas, kitchen, game room, medical room, the gym, her original room, the lab, and the monitor room. There were four stair cases leading down, one to the spa, the Summit, the garage, and another unknown area. There were two staircases leading up to the men's quarters, three upper levels with fifteen rooms each. See could see that the only natural light that came through the round room was the round skylight above. Then there were the double doors to the walled garden. She didn't see any doors that led outside.

"How do you leave?" she asked.

"Well, you can leave out the garden and out the garage. Why are you thinking about bolting?"

"Never," she said, smiling at him sweetly.

"So how do you visit the ladies?"

"Through the garden," he said, heading toward the double doors.

"Let's go meet the gals," Sabastian said, opening the door up for her and stepping out into the sun after her.

Chapter 60

Victoria followed Sabastian down a stone path that wound its way through the garden to the far wall where a large door stood. Sabastian punched in a code into the key panel and the door opened up to a huge span of lawn in front of her. It was an outdoor natural grass hallway about twenty-five feet across, surrounded by a tall flowering hedge of lilacs that was at least ten feet high. At the end of the hall stood another wall about a hundred feet away with the lawn running right into the front step of a door.

Sabastian offered her his arm and started to walk her across the lush cool grass.

"So this is how you get to the women's manor?" Victoria asked in awe of the crisp manicured park.

"One of the ways, yes."

"You are allowed to just show up without being invited?"

"We have to be either invited or working to enter. But seeing how I'm training you; I get to push the rules a bit."

Approaching the door, Victoria grabbed the end of her braid and twisted it, suddenly very apprehensive. She desperately wanted to meet and talk to these girls and see first-hand what they really thought of the job Sabastian had been telling her about. Sabastian punched in another code at the door on the outside of the wall that mirrored the one they had just come from.

"Each guy has his own code to enter, that way there is a way to track who comes and goes." He explained.

Sabastian opened the door for her and she stepped into another stunning garden like the one they had just left. Walking down the path to the building, they entered though another set of double doors. It was a mirror of the men's round room but the colors were light, cream, and soft. Where the men had black marble walls with small white lines running through them, the woman had cream marble with lines of bronze, the ceiling was white, and the wooden flooring was a lighter oak color that blended with the wainscoting and oak accents around the room. The furniture was cream or white with matching cushions, but the *décor* was not what attracted Victoria's attention.

Draped across a lounge chair with a book in her hand was a vibrant red head who spoke as soon as her eyes found Sabastian.

"Sabastian! Who called you?" the woman asked surprised.

Her eyes fell on Victoria behind Sabastian and stopped.

"Oh, sorry. Hello," she said, looking Victoria up and down.

"Good day, Miss Valerie, it's my pleasure to introduce to you, Miss Victoria."

Victoria noticed Sabastian's tone and demeanor had changed and guessed he was playing the polished respectful gentleman required to be used in a company girl's presence. She did not like the change in him and frowned at his back.

"Hello, Victoria, how long have you been here?" Valerie asked in her sultry voice.

"Around two months, miss," Sabastian said for her.

"What the hell are you thinking?" Valerie exclaimed sitting up. Her voice raised, clearly alarmed. "A couple of months, are you fucking kidding me? Christ, Sabastian, is she even clean yet? You are putting everyone at risk."

"Please, Miss Valerie." Sabastian said calmly, raising his hand up. "Miss Victoria did not need to go through the detox program as she was clean when she was collected."

Valerie's red eyebrows shot up, her eyes large, "Really? Clean?"

"Yes, miss."

"Wow, okay, sorry," she said impressed.

Victoria couldn't help but stare at this creature in front of her, even sitting she could tell she was elegantly tall. Valerie's face was nothing but perfect angles complimented by light freckles, her hazel eyes shone with interest, but what Victoria couldn't get over was her hair. The color made the entire room pale, making her the center of attention. Victoria had never seen a shade of red so brilliant. It hung straight down loose down past her shoulder blades. Her face was ethereal and her eyes so exotic she looked like she had Asian in her lineage. Her legs and arms were very slim and even her fingers looked graceful. She was wearing a pair of grey sweat shorts and a white tank top with a nude bra underneath, she was the picture of comfort and even though her clothes were very plain and unflattering, it didn't take away from her beauty.

"You should see me when I am all dolled up, sweetheart," Valerie's voice rang out.

Victoria blushed, realizing she had been staring. "Sorry," she muttered, looking at her feet.

"You really think she's going to make it, Sabastian, she looks too sweet and she's clearly introverted."

Valerie was looking Victoria up and down.

"You are going to need all the luck you can get to train her up, seeing how I heard you were training her on your own."

"Yes, Miss Valerie, however, she has been doing very well so far."

"Where did you find her?"

"On the streets in Denver pulling off a very convincing old woman act."

Valeria looked impressed, "The old hiding in plain sight routine, hey, smart."

"How far has she gotten?" Valerie said, referring to Victoria's training.

"Getting to the priming and testing phases."

"Oh, honey, that is the best part," Valerie said smiling. "It will make or break you here, have fun with…"

Valerie stopped in her tracks as a heart stopping scream ripped through the air. Victoria jumped her eyes wide. She saw Valerie roll her eyes.

"Augh, Ethan," Valerie said, exasperated.

Victoria's eyes shot to Valerie.

"I'm sorry, Miss Valerie, we are working on getting Miss Charlotte a sound proof room next month," Sabastian said apologetically.

"Ethan's up there with someone?" Victoria asked alarmed.

"Well, Char asked for it, though I wouldn't want to be with him in that mood. He passed through here like an enraged valiantly about ten minutes ago."

Victoria looked horrified.

"Don't worry, Vicky, it's all in good fun," Valerie said to her.

There was another scream, this time followed by an obvious male's yell of pleasure and Victoria's hair on the back of her neck shot up.

Valerie smiled, ignoring the upstairs sounds and patted the chair beside her, "I guess you have questions for me?"

Sabastian cleared his throat and looked at Valerie stiffly.

"Oh come on, Sabastian, you've been the only one talking to her, you know she needs answers from a woman."

"Please, Miss Valerie, I would like her to speak with someone a little less ummm…"

"Colorful?" Valerie snorted. "Please, if she doesn't get color, she is doomed, look at her, she is pale as a ghost. Come here, Vicky."

Victoria glanced at Sabastian who released her arm and said, "Please be careful, Miss Valerie."

Valerie rolled her eyes at him as Victoria sat down beside the vivacious red head.

Victoria didn't think she would get a chance to speak with someone so soon and the questions piled up in her head.

Valerie interrupted her thoughts, "You want to know if it is true, right?"

Victoria nodded, "Do you really like it here?"

Valerie looked over to Sabastian, exasperated, "Did you not tell her?"

"Several times, miss, however it is much more convincing coming from a woman."

"Poor girl," Valerie said, turning and smiling back to Victoria, waiting for her to ask her questions.

Victoria thought this was not the time to be bashful and hoping not to sound rude she said, "It's just that you sell…"

Valerie interrupted her immediately.

"I used to think just like you. This company just sells sex with women for money. However true that may be, it's no one's choice but ours. Vicky, we want to do this, we love it and we get to rub shoulders with the rich and famous. We are cherished and needed, these are just bonuses to doing a job we not only need to do, but enjoy so much, it would kill us to stop. We are challenged and have so many adventures, get to travel and are so well respected, not only here, but by our clients as well. We are also better taken care of here then we have been our entire lives by the people who were supposed to love us unconditionally. Are you starting to get it yet?"

Victoria was awed by the passion that Valerie spoke to her about a job she loved and defended adamantly.

"Everyone here feels that way?" Victoria asked.

"Yes. The only way to put it is my life is complete here, I have never been happier or more fulfilled. You may think that this is a demeaning job, but working as a secretary at a shitty job that you hate while being treated like a hooker and handled by men who think you belong to them is something that stupid women deal with every day. Treated like a piece of meat, no respect, having to put up with assholes to keep a job they hate, just to put food on the table. Now that would fucking suck. That, to me, that would be a demeaning job. I don't care how much they teach sexual awareness classes to men; most are pigs who take advantage of any young girl who works for them, thinking they own them. It couldn't be more opposite here. If we are out with a client and by the end of the evening, we don't want them to feed the kitty, we don't," Valerie smiled wickedly.

"We call our watchers and we leave, no harm done, although most of us never do because we love to sink the sausage, plain and simple. Burying the bone at the end of the evening of fine dining, dancing, and smooching with the elite of the elite is like icing on the motherfucking cake."

By the end of her speech, Valerie was grinning broadly and Victoria noticed Sabastian had closed his eyes and was shaking his head.

Valerie turned to him with a huge smile and asked, "Colorful enough?"

"Yes, Miss Valerie, your views, like always, are very colorful."

"I have a hundred more but I prefer just plain and simple screwing," she said with a wide glorious smile on her cherry red lips, leaning back in the lounge chair. "Although stuffing the taco is fun to," she said, laughing at Victoria's expression.

Trying to focus on the points she was making, Victoria asked, "So you can say no at any time?"

"Of course, us girls always come first," she said, raising her eyebrows suggestively up and down, making Victoria laugh.

"Clients second and no one had ever been reprimanded for leaving in the middle of a job. Very few do because they look forward to mattress dancing so much," she said, turning to Sabastian.

"Jesus, Sabastian, look at her blush, you have a long way to go with this one."

Victoria was still trying to take it all in, but couldn't help but laugh at this fun, passionate girl who was as vivacious inside as she was out.

"How did you get here?" Victoria asked, instantly regretting the question.

Valerie's face fell, losing her dazzling smile and she frowned, looking at Sabastian.

Sabastian went over to Valerie and whispered something in her ear and Victoria frowned at the two of them.

"Ah, okay," Valerie answered, nodding her head. She tucked her bare feet under her crossed legs, getting comfortable.

"Long story short, I was knocked up at fourteen and thrown out. My first boyfriend pressured me into sex, denied it was his and told my family I was sleeping with every guy in school to cover his ass. Even after I aborted it, my family still wanted nothing to do with me. I begged to come home but they were done with me, no money, and no help. My father, with my mother screaming at me behind him, threw me into the street kicking me hard, fracturing a few ribs calling me worthless and useless. That's the last time I saw them," she smiled.

"You can see how being here with people who love and take care of me and respect me, means so much," she motioned around her at the beautiful room both the girls were sitting in.

"I spent about a year on the streets and got heavy into drugs, trying to hide the pain of rejection. Heroin and alcohol were my vices. I had a job waitressing and it paid for my addictions. I lived on the streets because I couldn't get a place to rent so young and I refused to waste good money on rent when I could buy more drugs," she paused and looked at Sabastian before continuing.

"It was almost impossible to hide my hair and age but I made it about two years before the pimps heard about me and started to track me down. William and Douglas found me curled in a ball with four guys beating the shit out of me because I refused to join their pimp club. I was unconscious and they were still kicking, intent on killing me to send a message to the other girls who would think about refusing such a fine offer. The next thing I remember is being with Dr. Marshall in the infirmary. I was not a pleasant patient, hey?"

She turned to Sabastian who hesitated then chuckled and shook his head.

"No, Miss Valerie, you were not."

"Ya, I went after poor Michael so many times, broke his nose at one point. Tore apart the medical room more than once and had to be strapped down and knocked out several times. Plus when I got to the cream room, I believe you guys had to totally renovate the entire room. Do you remember what I thought you guys were doing to me?"

"Yes, I do," Sabastian said.

"I thought they were going to force me into a satanic cult and make me give birth to more satin worshipers."

Valerie looked far away, "Coming down from heroin gets you pretty crazy. I was seeing things, hallucinations, and nothing made sense. I will admit I was wacko. It took a lot of work on Miss Cherry's part to get me to see reason and over a year to get detoxed."

"Miss Victoria thought we were going to harvest her organs and she was clean."

"Ha, really, wow that is even crazier," Valerie said laughing.

Victoria scowled at Sabastian.

Valerie gave her a light slap on the leg. "Come on, you have to laugh about it later," she said smiling.

"Anyway, by the time I was ready to be trained, I was eighteen and chomping at the bit but of course Mr. D will not hire anyone on officially until they are twenty-one. I got three years of education, caught up on my high school, received my diploma, and learned three languages as well as became an expert in every client's field, so that when I was brought up to the majors, I was ready. Man, was I ready!"

"So now I have been working for four years officially and have loved every second of it. The only thing I dread is having to go when I am finished."

"Why would you have to leave?" Victoria asked, completely engulfed in this woman's hard story.

"Well, I can't stay young forever, I haven't heard of anyone lasting over forty years old, but as long as the clients keep asking for you, you can stay. Although, only a few years here, you are set for life, so retiring at forty is a pretty sweet deal. I don't know what I would do with my life though, I'm so happy here I can't think of any other way to live."

"And you have no regrets?" Victoria asked.

"My only regret is beating the shit out of poor Michael, although I more than made up for it with him by letting him stuff the turkey," she said laughing.

Victoria smiled and tried to stay on track, in light of her kidding mood. "There is nothing you want that you can't have here, you are not restricted in any way? You don't feel trapped or pressured?"

The questions flowed from her now.

"Come on, girl, look around. This is paradise, I can do whatever I want, whenever I want. I have money to burn, a full-service spa, and a great apartment upstairs. I take whatever clients I want, when I want and even have fine men on the side to help with my porking when needed. Take vacations anywhere in the world, at any time, for as long as I want too. The only thing I would like to have is a dog, a beautiful Irish setter with a red coat. It's for the best though, with my schedule and my studying, I wouldn't have the time to spend training, so that is one of the rewards I will be giving myself when I retire. Trust me girl, this is all on the up and up, if you're lucky enough to get proposed to at the end of your training, take the job, you will not regret it," she paused smiled and winked. "But no pressure."

"Proposed?" Victoria looked at Sabastian who had come over to offer his arm.

"Well, we need to make sure you want and will love the job and that you are suited to the task. Then we will officially propose a position to you and you have the choice to take it or leave it."

Victoria took Sabastian's arm and followed him toward a hallway.

Turning to Valerie. "Thank you, Valerie," Victoria said, smiling.

"Yes, thank you, Miss Valerie. That was very informative," Sabastian said exasperated.

"I'm sure it was. Come and talk to me any time you need a little more color in your life, Vicky," Valerie said, putting her feet up on the lounge to get back to her reading.

Victoria had absorbed the conversation intently. It was truly enlightening hearing from one of the girls, even one as crude as Valerie. She trusted Sabastian and never thought that he had lied to her, but it felt good coming from someone who had been there and in much the same situation as she had been.

Walking through the cream round room and down a hallway like the men's manor. Sabastian opened a door, guiding her with gentle pressure on the small of her back. They stepped into an equally large entertainment room with a huge screen. Victoria saw what looked like a horror film, paused.

Turning on a light in the dark space, Sabastian said, "Hello, ladies, I would like to introduce Miss Victoria to all of you, if that's all right?"

Victoria almost laughed, here was an opposite reflection of the men she had seen in the other manor. Seven beautiful women, all in various styles of comfortable clothing were draped on the furniture. There were two blondes, three brunettes, and another redhead, though not as stunning as Valerie, and a striking black hair girl who smiled and waved.

"Thank God," a sweet voice rang out in the back.

"Ya, good thing you came in, Gabriel was about to have a stroke," another voice shrilled out laughing.

"I was not," a sweet voice answered.

"Oh, come on, you had your eyes covered the last ten minutes."

"Please, ladies," Sabastian said. "This is Miss Gabriel, Miss Anita, Miss Evangeline, Miss Anastasia, Miss Jillian, Miss Sara, and Miss Isabella."

Each girl raised her hand in turn and smiled at Victoria warmly.

"Hello," she managed to mutter. Each woman was as beautiful as the next, it was like she had just walked backstage to a beauty pageant.

"Would anyone would like to help me with initiate Victoria to a woman's specialty?"

Victoria looked at Sabastian who smiled at her with wicked eyes and her nervousness shot up again.

"Doesn't Miss Cherry pick out that girl?" the girl named Sara asked.

"Yes, she does, however, I am in charge of Miss Victoria and I would like a volunteer."

"How new is she?" asked Jillian.

"As fresh as they come, Miss Jillian."

Jillian jumped up and approached them, "I would love to," she bounced up enthusiastically.

"Ladies, thank you for your time," Sabastian said and led both Jillian and Victoria out of the room into the hallway.

Jillian faced Victoria out in the hall. Jillian was a bit shorter and had brown copper hair that was layered on her shoulders. Her adorable face was round and she looked like a cherub angel. Her eyes were a soft brown and her lips were full and sensuous. Wearing an oversized sweater did nothing for her figure, however Victoria could see she was well endowed in the bra department.

"What stage is she on?" Jillian asked, looking Victoria up and down.

"Priming," Sabastian answered simply.

"Mmmm, that's the best part," Jillian said, slowly in her honeyed voice.

"I love your hair, it's so long. I wish mine would grow that long but no matter what treatments I get, it splits when it hits past my shoulders so I am forced to cut it, but yours." Jillian gazed at her hair in awe and ran her hands along the length, "Nice."

"Thank you," Victoria said, a bit uneasy. Jillian was too close, but she couldn't back away as the girl's hand was still in her hair.

Keeping her eyes on Victoria, Jillian rubbed her full lips together like she was evening out lipstick and asked Sabastian, "Never?"

"No, Miss Jillian."

"Mmmm," Jillian hummed low, smiling.

Victoria felt like they were having a private conversation about her, ignoring her completely and it annoyed her, she was about to say so when Jillian brought her hand close to her cheek cupping it.

"Nice," she repeated.

Victoria leaned back away from her slightly, but didn't want to be rude so she stilled.

Jillian was staring hard into Victoria's eyes, then her eyes moved to her lips and Victoria knew what she was going to do to her, a split second before it happened.

Jillian stepped into Victoria and so slowly and softly pressed her lips into hers, pulling Victoria's mouth to her lips as she kissed her.

Victoria froze until she heard Sabastian say so quietly behind her, "Feel, don't think."

Victoria had never felt anything like this before, Jillian's lips were so full and warm and so very soft, the only way she knew she was being kissed was by the gentle pressure on her own lips. Jillian was not moving much, letting Victoria gets used to both the feel and the idea of being kissed by a woman.

She felt Jillian's hand wrap around her waist and very lightly coax her closer. Victoria leaned in and let herself be pulled into the other woman's body and felt her breasts push up against Jillian's chest. A moan escaped Jillian's throat and Victoria couldn't help respond to her pleasure and she let the woman deepen the kiss exploring. Jillian instantly leaned into her, pulling her closer and pressed her tongue between her lips and Victoria opened for her. An involuntary moan escaped Victoria's lips and before she knew it, her hands were at the woman's back and her hips pushed forward. Jillian opened and pushed her tongue and surprisingly, they were passionately kissing, moving their mouth and tongues with each other in a dance. They were both moaning and moving together and Victoria felt herself tighten deep within and broke the kiss panting, shocked at herself.

Jillian smiled at her pressing her lips lightly to Victoria's again.

"Yes," she murmured, "very nice."

Emotion swelled in Victoria and her eyes filled with angry scared tears, so taken aback by her body's reaction.

Jillian stepped forward again and reached out to Victoria who froze.

"Shhh, it's okay, Vicky. A woman knows what another woman wants and needs and I will be so honored if you would let me show you everything there is to know about being homoerotic."

She rubbed her soft fingertips on Victoria's cheek, catching her tears and licking them off her lips.

The move was so sensual, Victoria felt herself react and her skin tingle with the pleasure of watching this gorgeous women's movements.

"I, uh, I don't think I could...um," Victoria stuttered.

Jillian grabbed her hand lightly, "Don't worry, Vicky. You'll be in very good hands." She squeezed her hand again to accentuate her point, smiled, and turned back to her movie like nothing unusual had happened.

Victoria stood there stunned, then whirled on Sabastian.

"You couldn't have warned me?" she asked furiously.

"No, it's your reaction that I needed to see. If I would have prepared you, your reactions wouldn't have been natural. Letting her kiss you is the first test to see if you would accept a female partner."

Victoria was mad, even though it made sense, although it did not lessen her shock.

"That's not fair," she pouted.

Sabastian leaned in and kissed her swiftly, "Well, if it makes you feel any better, you reacted perfectly to her and judging by your body language, you will enjoy your time with her very much."

"Well, it doesn't make me feel better," Victoria said, knowing that being with a woman would mean missing a crucial part of sex that she had come to enjoy immensely.

"So what, do we service women as well?"

"Yes, actually, we do, mostly very wealthy woman who have a life, kids, and husbands, who do not know about their needs for a same sex partner. We do not have many but the need is there. However, our girls are trained to pleasure each other for male clients who like to hire more than one girl at a time."

Victoria was taken aback that the company also serviced women and did jobs that required multiple girls, but she knew that with all the different kinds of sex she had been reading about that anything could be required from the Eximius women.

"Well, I guess that makes sense, so there would be two of us with a client when hired?" she asked, trailing off in thought.

"Yes, sometimes more," Sabastian stated.

"Oh," Victoria said, still distracted after Jillian, wondering what her physical response to the woman really meant.

The rest of the manor tour was a blur. It had some of the things the men's manor did. Same kitchen, large games room, movie room, and an enormous gym. Although it was missing the lab, monitor room, and her room. Everything else were women suites, which Sabastian said were just like her cream room but larger. She could see the apartment doors beyond the balcony above her in the cream round room. The doors all decorated individually by the girls living in them.

Some girls had hung pictures on the doors or walls next to the apartment doors, some had flowers, art work, or little wooded signs with sayings that she could not make out. They ran into a few more girls but they were all a blur of long legs, soft hair, and beautiful skin, all attractive, and all friendly. She was dying to have another conversation like the one with Valerie but she knew the answer to the one very important question every time she met someone new. They were happy, well taken care of, and in control of their own lives.

Leaving the woman's manor through the garden and outside on the grass hallway. She asked, "Are all the women friends?"

"No, not at all, there are some that can't stand each other, but it's very easy to avoid those you don't like. Busy schedules and a large manor keeps the peace and the fact that there is nothing to fight about makes it simple, but not everyone can be friends, same goes for the men."

Victoria was tired when Sabastian led her to the garden in the men's side of the manor. They sat on a bench watching the butterflies drift in the air before them.

"That could not have been everyone? Where is everyone else?"

"The other girls would either be with clients, out shopping, or on a trip, a lot like to travel and do so with the private jet. The guys would be in the kitchen and a few are watching. There is Gregory, he works in the file room, and the good doctor and a few assistants are probably taking blood from clients. Matthew who works in the monitor room, but is probably in the women's manor on a service call."

"Service call, is that what you call it?"

"Ya, well, the guys get a call and they go to service the women. What else do you want me to call it?"

"Soooo…the Eximius girls call you and you come running," she grinned.

He shrugged, "The girl's text us and we go where we are needed."

"Why don't they just come and get you?"

"Because no one is supposed to know who is with who. We try to keep it as private as possible, that way there is no jealously among the guys. No one talks about who they sleep with. The guys are not allowed to brag to the other guys or even tell which women they are with. The only way guys know who has slept with who, is that they know the trainers sleep with all the new girls, but then they move on, unless requested later. The girls tend to know which guys are being called and to who, but women here do not fight over guys. They tend to be too busy working to really care much, plus with no attachment rules it keeps things uncomplicated."

"So you said you don't get requested much."

"No," he said flatly.

"Why not, you're good at your job," she said, blushing looking down at her feet.

He smiled at her, "Well, I'm not normally so open, I don't share any part of myself with anyone. I do my job and carry on; the girls use me to practice and then they go to the next step. I don't need to put them through the program or pitch to them like I've done with you, so there is little talking and mostly action."

"Oh, so you said Miss Cherry works with the new girl's, right?"

"Yes, but she took off after we collected you, so I got to take you on as a test for a promotion."

"A promotion?"

"Yes, I will be able to head another branch, move there, and take over if you accept a job here," Sabastian said, surprising himself at his candor.

That is why he was working so hard, she thought. *The more time he puts into me, the better I will do and he will get his own franchise. It has nothing to do with me, he put all this effort into me to make sure I will stay.* She was crestfallen, *He would be gone once I get trained.*

Her mood soured and the butterflies suddenly annoyed her, fluttering to close to her face, she stood up waving them away.

"I'm hungry," she stated flatly, keeping the ache in her heart from making her cry.

"Okay, I believe you have an appointment in twenty-four hours, you need to prepare for anyway. Are you okay with the arrangement?"

"I'll be fine," she said, shortly annoyed at his flippant tone of the fact that she would be having sex with another man for training purposes. She turned and headed to her room.

Sabastian followed her and stood in the doorway, noticing the change in her mood immediately. Thinking that she was nervous about meeting Benjamin, he tried to help.

"You need to prime all day today and tomorrow, so you are well prepared for Benjamin."

Victoria turned to him apprehensive, not wanting another man but knowing she had to get over this hurtle and be open to new partners.

Sabastian saw the worried look in her eyes and said, "He's the sweetest guy, Vicky, he'll take good care of you. You have nothing to worry about, I won't let anything bad happen to you, trust me, you are in good hands," he smiled warmly at her and closed the door behind her to the Summit room.

Pissed, his headache was back. Sabastian reflected on Valerie's performance. Man, she was good. She had listened when he had whispered how to play the conversation and come up with a great story so fast it shocked him, He just had to keep up with her as she worked her story for Victoria.

Valerie had been a college student who was on the verge of dropping out when Eximius found her. She told her sad story of being on the street beautifully. Of course, she had never taken any drugs or been on the street even for a minute but even Sabastian believed her when she went into the details of her fake recruitment. Valerie loved drama and Sabastian had told her to play the part of a test subject that had taken the internship after being abused and rescued off the streets and now had a wonderful job that she loved. Of course the job she loved was true, just the back story was bull. Test girls never were officially hired and if he succeeded, Victoria would be the first.

Sabastian went to his room to try to figure out why every time he thought about Victoria with someone else made his head throb and his stomach drop.

"She's just another girl," he told himself. *Then why does she affect me so strongly?* he thought that feeling would disappear once he had initiated her in bed, but in fact the feelings had gotten stronger each time he bedded her, talked, or spent any time with her. He was really getting tired of not having the iron control he always had when dealing with women and his own emotions. He knew once she had been trained and passed around, he would become desensitized and start treating her like every other Eximius girl.

She was a good student nothing more, but deep in the recesses of his mind, he knew that she was so much more than that to him.

Chapter 61

"Tonight."

He gripped himself painfully through his jeans and squeezed.

His mouth hung open and his erection bucked under the denim.

He would finally have her tonight and knew the timing could not get any better. He had even asked Jeremy, who had given him permission. Even though his particular test was usually administered after several other partners, he had been very persuasive and talked him into it. Mr. D would have never even considered it. Jeremy was sick of Sabastian breaking rules while he was in charge and thought this would speed the girl's progress along to move her out of the men's manor.

Ethan had heard of the wild cat breaking out of her room and going to Sabastian. He used that information to convince Jeremy that the only way to expedite the process was to get her initiated fast. He saw that Jeremy like the idea of getting some distance between Sabastian and Victoria as well.

He had taken another woman today, but it had been totally unsatisfying. He had been under her control even as he had whipped and fucked her from behind, wishing it was Victoria screaming at him. The girl was too willing to undergo his administrations and knew that the fight the wild cat would give him would be his ultimate release.

His wait would be over in a few hours and his body throbbed and he started to slowly prepare his mind and body for tonight.

Chapter 62

Victoria was nervous as she prepared, but she ate, had a long bath, and started her priming exercises until she felt a longing deep within, pulling at her and she had to stop before the frustration got too heavy for her to handle. She watched her videos to make sure she was focusing right and once she calmed down, she started again.

The videos made her hyper aware of her body and helped her focus on her erogenous zones and imaging what she wanted done to her. From her ears and neck to her inner thighs, her belly, breasts and feet, to the inside of her elbows and knees. The thoughts of Sabastian stroking or licking her in those extra sensitive spots made her tremble until she needed to calm down the sensual struggle.

Focus, concentrate on the feeling, let the pressure and the pull deep inside her build until she felt moisture, then lay down to settle. She realized while she was priming herself, she thought only of Sabastian. Using their time together to prepare her body for the next man she would be with and strangely enough a new person was the image she used when trying to calm down. Being with another man got her to body to settle and she knew being with someone else made her very uncomfortable.

She was upset Maximus had not come for her as she would have loved the distraction to ease her apprehension, but knew why she would not be working out today. She had to focus on the task at hand and didn't need any other distractions.

When she was not focused on getting her body primed, she thought about what Valerie had said and what Jillian had done with her lips. She was intrigued as she wondered what it would be like to live and work with the other girls. If she did well with her training and tests and this first time with a new partner, she would eventually be proposed to and be able to accept the job that they might offer her. Still uneasy about what lay ahead, she knew that when she was focused and her body's need had built to a frenzy again, she hoped that no matter who came through that door that she would be ready and willing to do whatever it took to make the pleasure run through her and satisfy both Benjamin and herself in order to stay here.

She wished; however, it would always be Sabastian. She knew him and loved talking to him and thinking of his hands on her body and his mouth on her. She was quickly turned on again and had to calm herself with a large amount of self-control even as her fingers inched to her sex, she got up to walk around instead.

It was two hours since her last meal and her body and her mind were very tired. She had one more day to go before she needed to be truly ready and she decided to do one last priming exercise before she crashed for the night. Lying in bed with the lights out and the silk covers wrapped around her naked body was the only tool she needed to prime herself and she lay there moaning and squeezing her sex.

She jumped when there was an almost inaudible knock on the door, she was not sure she had heard it until she heard a soft voice.

"Please let me in, Vicky."

Victoria's heart raced, her body clenched and her skin started to electrify ready and wanting. However, she was instantly apprehensive. She flicked on the lights, grabbed her robe, and threw it on. She was relieved Sabastian had sent someone for her tonight and that she would not have to wait as the anticipation was stressing her out. Excited, trepidation curled around her as she opened the door.

Ethan stood there grinning at her, he quickly pushed his way in, turned around, and locked the door.

"What are you doing here?" she asked, stepping back quickly from him, looking for something else to cover herself up in.

Ethan was wearing only a light white shirt and a pair of long black boxer pants, a lounging outfit that looked loose and comfortable. He was devastatingly attractive and he had a dangerous look about him that both thrilled and frightened her. His eyes were sparkling bright blue and his wide chest and overly bulging biceps told her he was strong and hard and the last place she wanted him was in here with her. He was attractive, but that was overcome with fear of this unpredictable man advancing on her.

"Sabastian sent me, of course," he leered at her and licked his lips.

Victoria shivered as the hair on the back of her neck rose up stiffly.

"Why? Benjamin is supposed to come and not till tomorrow."

Taking a blanket off her bed and throwing it over her shoulders to cover herself more, she asked, "What did Sabastian say?"

"He said to enjoy myself," licking his lips again, he advanced.

"Wait, what?" she asked, stepping back from him.

"I cannot wait to make you sore again, after you are with me," he stepped closer to her. "You don't know pleasure until I have had a chance to work you over."

Victoria wanted to talk to him, she wanted to know more about what the hell he was doing here. Would Sabastian send someone else? He said she was not going to like the next steps, but she was sure it had to do with the teasing he had put her through, not this. Ethan was too menacing, he was too strong, coming onto her like she was his to do with as he pleased and it made her shake.

"What happened to the respect rules? You're threatening me, that's not allowed."

The grin left his face and he scowled.

"Well, Miss Victoria, in my line of work, threats and force are not only needed, they are desperately wanted by some of the women at Eximius as you will soon find out."

"Listen here, Ethan, I don't know what your game is, but I do know you cannot touch me without my permission and I will not take your threats. I had to put up with that bullshit all my life and I am not about to repeat that mistake," she spoke harshly and stood her ground.

This man, though stunningly dark with his white blue eyes and sharp features, didn't back down easily. He took another step into her and forced her back into the bed post, effectively trapping her. Her eyes widened as his hand came up to graze her bare arm and she shuddered involuntarily. He suddenly grabbed both her arms and clawed into her flesh, pressing his entire length hard up against her, grinding into her and she winced from the pain of the post at her back. She heard him inhaled deeply beside her ear and she froze acutely aware that this room had no monitors in it.

His voice came out like a hiss as he dug into her flesh with his hands and his body.

"This is a very important test that I am required to do to you. You signed up for this and I am going to enjoy breaking you in properly, Victoria," he dragged out her name both menacing and sensual at the same time.

He then bit her hard on the neck under the hair line and ground into her again. Victoria winced and tried to move away, but at the same time, a thrill ran through her that she had no control over and her body trembled responding.

"And you are going to love it, crave it, and beg for it in the end," he said, against her neck.

Bending down, looking into her eyes with a maddeningly expression, he viciously took her in a hard kiss, biting her lips when he pulled away. Victoria shuddered again as he grabbed her breast hard with his hand, engulfing her in a painful squeeze that left her breathless with shock.

"Ah," she cried in pain and tried to back away from him but he just pushed her back into the bed post and ground into her again, pulling her blanket off her shoulders. She was so confused and had to fight herself before she could fight Ethan off.

"I thought you were with someone else today?" she asked, trying to keep him talking and to give herself time to think clearly.

"Not enough for me, honey. I need more, besides Charlotte never lets me play the way I want to. I thrive on teaching you a specialty you will either love or hate. Let's find out."

With a cruel smile on his lips, he pushed into her hips again.

Victoria could feel his hard shaft grinding into her and started to plan her escape. She pushed him back with her hips and she heard him groan in pleasure, thinking she was responding. She then backed her hips away fast as she threw her knee up toward him, her elbow swung to knock him aside and she tried to use his body against him like all her training taught her to do. Ethan moved so fast it shocked her, he twisted his body around, and pushed her backward against the bed post with his tight grip on her arms effectively missing the blow she had directed at his balls. The harsh lustful look he gave her told her that she had made the situation so much worse and she froze thinking hard.

Victoria mind suddenly flashed back to the conversation with Maximus. She remembered Ethan was the only partner that challenged Maximus and who had a real passion for self-defense. She was in real trouble and her body tensed, fear taking over her training.

"You little bitch," he said with a large grin on his face. "You are a wild cat."

He had her pinned again, her arms trapped behind her back, his hips immobilizing hers. Unable to move, Ethan reached up between their bodies and thrust his fingers hard up into her slippery sex, almost raising her feet off the floor.

"Yi," she cried, the pain was sharp. His fingers thrust into her twice more, making her wince as he breathed hotly in her face, watching her with a look of pure lust. He pushed his fingers into her a last time and her sex anticipated the movement and hugged at him. Her face flushed from embarrassment as she watched him pull his fingers from her sex as he sucked them hungrily.

"Mmm, Vicky you are so wet for me, I knew you wanted it," he threw her to the bed, taking off his shirt and followed her down.

Her eyes widened, he was so much stronger than she thought, his muscles over powered her senses and she knew she would never be able to fight him off. Refusing to give in, she summoned her courage and twisted on the bed, moving fast to strike, but he yanked her ankles hard toward him and sat on her legs, he then pulled her robe away from her body and gazed down at her with hungry eyes.

"Fear can be a powerful aphrodisiac, Victoria, can you feel it? You are dripping for me."

Victoria couldn't let this happen, she could feel the adrenaline coursing through her body, warning her. *"I don't want this,"* she kept thinking to herself.

Reading her mind, Ethan argued with her out loud, "I know you want this; you want to be fucked hard by Ethan, don't you?"

Referring to himself in the third person, she realized Ethan must be unbalanced. He grabbed her breast and pinched her nipples hard.

"Ah, no," she curved her torso, doing a sit up with him perched on top of her, fisting her hand and pulling it back to hit his Adam's apple.

Ethan dodged the well-placed jab and grabbed both her hands in one of his huge hands and held them together above her head. Victoria was now completely immobilized. His weight was so heavy on her it was hard to breathe. His eyes narrowed and he licked his lips again.

"Mmm, my dear, you are panting for me, you are wet for me, you are loving this, aren't you?"

Victoria couldn't speak, she shook her head and her eyes widened as she watched his free hand graze over her skin. He suddenly pulled his hand away from her body and brought it down fast, slapping her hard on the side of her hip, the smack echoing around the room.

"Ah," she yelped as she flinched from the sharp smack.

He repeated the process, his hand grazing from her neck, gently down between her breasts, and down her belly to her pelvis, then raised his hand up and down hard and fast on her other side of her hip, leaving a stinging pain behind. Her body becoming ultra-sensitive to every movement as he struck her.

"Ah, stop it," Victoria cried, tears coming to her eyes. Her skin was tingling and she shrunk from his hand and when it came down on her again. This time, he pulled hard at her nipple pinching it and pulling her whole breast up with it. The pain mingled with pleasure and she was so confused it scared her even more.

"I want you to say, you want me to fuck you," he said to her twisting her nipple in his fingers.

"No," she shrieked at him, denying him.

His hand came down hard again, on the top of her breast and she cried out, "No."

"Good," he relished.

Ethan opened the robe to reveal more of her body and yanked down his pants halfway, forcing her legs open, he bent down and bit her nipple hard.

Her body instantly arched up from the pain in her breast, at the last second, she saw his plan to use her body's natural reflex to gain entrance into her and she twisted her hips hard to the side, making him miss his target and throwing him off her.

Victoria continued to roll until she was off the bed and stood ready for him and paled as she was able to see his erection at last and was suddenly even more frightened. He was so thick he would have split her in half if he got his way.

Ethan was on his hands and knees, looking both frustrated and consumed with joy at the game he had her trapped in.

Ethan was going to fuck her brutally and she was so consumed with the thought that she would eventually give in and enjoy it that she knew she had to fight even harder to prevent that from happening. Her body was ruling her mind and she was scared to death of what that meant. How much had she changed in this Eximius world that her body would take over and let any man force himself on her and that she would want it. She shook her head from the terrifying thoughts racing in her mind and prepared for a full-on fight, she could not let this happen. She had to maintain control over herself and her body at all costs.

She watched as he pulled his pants off quickly and leaped at her, making a big mistake. She countered his weight and threw him almost effortlessly in the back wall. Ethan got up fast, racing to her as Victoria bolted for the door. He slammed into her back, pinning her up against the door, breathing hard in her ear.

"Don't tell me you are not having fun, wild cat," he said as he turned her to face him.

Victoria was pinned but was able to reach up and ripped her nails across his face drawing blood.

"Auuugggghhh, fuck, yes," he cried out, his face full of excited lust as he bent to lift her up.

Victoria countered again, twisted and was able to free herself but now was further from the door. She was in full self-defense mode and was ready for him as he stalked his way to her, this time more calculated.

She saw him position and mentally calmed herself and prepare to spare with a partner that would not be forgiving or gentle as Maximus had always been.

His body tensed before he rushed her but stopped all forward momentum to counter any moves that she would have used to use his weight against him. He kicked, grabbed, and flew at her fast. Victoria was able to either counter or evade most of his maneuvers but he was too fast knowing the sport well. She saw his face and was horrified at the expression of lust mingled with pure joy at the fight he was winning.

What seemed like long minutes but had probably only been seconds, she found herself pinned face down on the floor, him panting over her.

"Fuck, girl, you are good," he breathed. "But not good enough."

Victoria felt his rough hand lift her hips. She felt his hot thick sex press into the back of her thigh and felt sick. Ignoring the slickness between her legs at her sex seeking his, she twisted fought and kicked at him hard, absolutely exhausted now but unwilling to give up. She tried to struggle, tried to shimmy her hips away from his as he pushed into her trying to gain entrance. She twisted again and he cursed as he lifted her bodily from the floor.

She was horrified when she found herself air born landing hard on the bed with him fast behind her.

He was impossible to fight. Not only was he naked with no clothes to grab onto, but his skin was so slippery that she could not get a grip on his large limbs. Victoria herself was covered in a layer of sweat but was so skinny that his large hands had no problems holding onto her. Her hair had come undone and was a tangled mess around her body, covering up more of her body than the robe that lay in shreds on her heaving shoulders.

Victoria shuffled back on the bed as he landed after her and she shot out a leg. Ethan grabbed at her dodging the kick and taking her hair in his hand wrapping it along his forearm tightly. Victoria sobbed as he yanked her head back not from the pain but the fact that he had won. He had ultimate control of her now. Control the head, control the body, her training lessons came to her and knew that is exactly what he was doing.

"Now, my little girl, we get to have some real fun," his lustful grin scared her more than his words. "Most women fantasize about being raped. Well, it's my job to see if being forced to fuck is everything you dream of. I am here to make your dreams come true," he smirked at her.

She couldn't give up. Since Ethan only had one hand to protect himself, she lashed out with her arms and her legs, striking him hard in the stomach with her knee. She made contact with his face, his shoulder, and his chest, not really doing any damage but able to keep him on the defensive. She couldn't move away from him but he couldn't protect himself either.

"Augh, yes," he growled as he fought her, holding her hair with force and slapping her hard across the cheek.

Victoria's head throbbed and she stilled, refocusing her eyes enough to see that his erection was still hard and throbbing. Her eyes panicked and she struck out again clawing at him.

"Yes, come on, wild cat, you can do better than that," he groaned as he kissed her brutally.

Victoria barely felt the pain, her adrenaline defending her from feeling it so far. Her body tingled but the pain was not registering. The one thing that did register is for every second she fought him, she saw he grew more and more aroused. He used the violence to drive his need and she saw his eyes were overcome with unbridled rage induced lust. She could not become like him but her body both wanted it and was too weak to fight him from taking what he wanted. She was on the edge of giving up as he repositioned himself to finish what he had started.

"Oh, come on, bitch," he growled in her ear feeling her strength start to ebb away. "Come on! You have more left in you."

Her moans were inarticulate as she felt her strength finally leave her weak and panting.

Victoria was blinded by him, not able to see anything but his face full of power, her eyes blurred.

"Come on," he growled at her and he bent his head and bit her hard on the shoulder, trying to get more fight from her.

Victoria knew if he got what he wanted, he would tear her apart. He was too big to handle and she closed her eyes, trying to block him out. As he reached down between their bodies, she kicked at him feebly.

"Perfect," he whispered to her almost lovingly. "Absolutely, God damn perfect."

Brushing a loose strand of hair away from her face gently.

She tried to push him away but without the protection of the adrenaline, her body was now filling rapidly with a throbbing pain.

"Stop," she pleaded her voice hardly more than a whisper.

"Let me go," she begged desperately, tears in her eyes, pushing on his chest.

How could Sabastian do that to her, how could he send this mad man to rape her? Her body was so sore, her neck, her arms, everywhere he had hit her.

Ethan knelt over her and then touched her on her hair, softly caressing her head.

"You don't get it, do you?" he said vehemently. "I own you for tonight, you are mine to fuck as I please."

"No, you can't," she cried.

"Oh, you don't have a choice, my little wild cat. You will love every time I stick my cock in you."

He leaned down close to her face and put his hand on her neck and pushed slightly, blocking her air.

Unable to breath, she felt empty, drained, and so tired that the feeble attempts to fight him off drained her even more. She lay there watching him with fear clearly written in her eyes as he spread her legs and positioned himself.

"This will just hurt a bit but you will love it in the end," he threatened in her ear as his penis nudged her looking for an entrance.

Victoria closed her eyes again, trying to control her sobs and waited for him to continue his assault on her already pain racked body when his weight was abruptly lifted off of her.

"What the…?"

She heard him say and looked up.

Sabastian had Ethan by the throat and she saw his fist connect solidly with Ethan's face hard before dropping him on the floor. Sabastian moved to him, kicking him hard in the ribs, then kicking him again while he tried to defend himself on the ground.

She had never seen Sabastian so angry; he was filled with uncontrollable rage.

"What the hell are you doing here, Ethan?" he screamed down at the naked writhing man on the floor. He kicked him again and again until Benjamin came in and grabbed Sabastian by the arms, dragging him back.

"Sabastian, stop," Benjamin said, gripping him hard in a double arm lock.

"That b-b-bbastard was t-t-t-trying to rape her!!!" he screamed stuttering.

"He was only doing his job, Sabastian, his timing may have crap but you can't beat the shit out of him."

"He didn't have p-p-permission," Sabastian jerked toward him and Ethan flinched on the floor.

"How does it f-f-feel, Ethan?" Sabastian asked him. "You like having the c-c-c-crap kicked out of you? You sick f-f-fuck!"

Ethan was getting slowly up, "You asshole. It needed to be done eventually and I was sick of waiting for you to stop codling her. She needed to be introduced to my specialty," he said, wiping the blood pouring from his nose onto his arm.

"She wasn't even warned," Sabastian screamed at him, finally getting a grasp on his stuttering "You needed permission from me first, you son of a bitch, she had no idea and she wasn't ready."

"We don't tell them when it happens, that's the point and you know that. Jesus, Sabastian, get a hold of yourself, you are too involved. I saw an opportunity and I took it, plus Jeremey approved so I did not need your fucking permission."

Sabastian lost it and leaped out of Benjamin's arms at Ethan who was ready for him this time. He spun and deflected the attack and Sabastian was sent hurting into the wall. His head crashed into it with a sickly thud.

"No!" Victoria shrieked as she watched Sabastian thrown to the floor.

"Shit, you guys," Benjamin said, almost exasperated.

Grabbing Ethan roughly by the arms, Benjamin threw him out of the room naked, shutting the door.

"You stay here," he said to Sabastian who was struggling to get up and continue the fight. "Or I will go straight to Jeremy to report this. Right now only I know and if Mr. D gets a hold of this, you'll both be on the streets. Calm the hell down, I'll take care of Ethan. When you come to your senses, then you can talk to him and figure this out, for now, stay here."

Benjamin left and Victoria heard the clear click of the door being locked from the outside.

Sabastian stood there, staring at the door breathing hard, his face red, clear frustrated fury written all over his features. After a deep breath, he turned to Victoria who had backed herself up against the head board with her arms wrapped tightly around her knees, curled into her chest.

His face softened immediately as his eyes met hers, his face contorted into clear pain for her and he slowly moved toward her. He saw her body red, the bruising starting already and her face swollen.

Sabastian saw her body tremble and her tears would not stop flowing silently down her cheeks, she looked wide eyed at Sabastian. He moved toward her carefully, afraid she would shatter if he moved too fast. Her eyes lowered in overwhelming shame that tore a sob from her lips.

"Oh, dear God. Vicky, are you okay?" he asked her, his voice full of compassion. He sat slowly on the bed, trying not to jostle her.

Victoria couldn't look at him, she was so ashamed, her cheeks burned and another sob choked her, her body still shaking so hard.

"Vicky, please talk to me, God, are you hurt bad?"

Victoria stayed silent, her head down in her arms and tried to block him out. She tried to go to her safe place inside herself, trying to keep Sabastian out.

Sabastian could see her shutting him down.

384

No, I'm losing her, he grabbed her by the arm and pulled her arms apart.

"Vicky, talk to me," he demanded.

Her eyes shot to his, angry.

Good, he thought.

"You, you sent him to me," she accused.

"No! Never," he denied. "I would never send him to you. He came on his own. He must have found out what you were doing and took advantage."

"No shit," she said bitterly, closing her eyes, letting the tears continue to fall. She drew her knees back up, wrapping herself again. She tried to shut herself down and to go a place that was not in this twisted reality, but her body kept her here. The pain and the tremors running through her was something she couldn't escape from and a sob ripped its way out of her again. Wrapping her legs tighter to her chest, she tried to close herself down.

"Let me do that," Sabastian said, getting up off the bed.

Victoria watched him gather the large blanket off the floor and wrapped her naked tender body in it. Then he lifted her between his legs and surrounded her body with his, holding her close in strong arms.

Victoria was so tense and her body trembled in his, but his warm hands moving softly across her back calmed her slightly.

"Hush, it's okay, you'll be fine, I'll take care of you," he murmured the soft words in her ear.

Victoria didn't hear much of what he said, only the tone of his deep voice and his strong warm arms wrapped around her, soothed her. He calmed her with his presence and slowly, her tremors subsided and she lie there, her head against his chest as he ran his fingers through her hair and whispered in her ear.

"You said you wouldn't let anyone hurt me," she whispered accusingly after the long silence.

"Yes, I know, Vicky, I am so, so sorry," he said aguishly. "He was supposed to be asked to test you when you were ready. I am so sorry," he repeated, then whispered to himself. "I'll kill the bastard."

Sabastian knew the test would come eventually but not Ethan, he had another dominate in mind who was not as intense or crazy.

Listening to his voice but not hearing the words, she went over what had happened and was so confused. She was able to think now and her face burned with humiliation, she closed her eyes tight. A sob followed her thoughts and she felt Sabastian stiffen and tighten his arms around her.

"How bad are you hurt; can I please look at you?"

Victoria slowly nodded and she lay down as he unwrapped her.

"God Vicky," he said, going over her body.

Sabastian was shocked at the assault she had taken. She was bruised with several individual finger marks all over her body. Her face was red and swollen starting to color. There were nail marks on her hips and her entire hip area was red. He turned her over and saw her back rubbed raw and bite marks in her neck bitten so hard that they were already darkening under the skin.

"Fucking asshole!" Sabastian spat, losing it.

Sabastian's jaw and fists were clenched and he had to fight hard to control his voice before he spoke again. "You'll be okay," he smiled at her as she turned around.

"Come on, let's get you into the tub."

Leaving to draw a bath, he came back and carried her to the warm water and lowered her in, leaving the jets off and slowly washed her body with a soft cloth.

After he had washed her, he lifted her out of the tub and carried her to bed, wrapping her in the silk sheets that had aroused her not long ago. He gave her some pain killers and then covered her tender body with heavy cool blankets. She sunk into a restless sleep with Sabastian lying curled around her body protectively.

Chapter 63

Victoria woke extremely stiff and sore. She felt Sabastian curled around her so she kept completely still and thought back on what had happened the night before. She had worked so many years to gain a sense of control over her life with her self-defense lessons. It was the only time in her life that she had any control and had mastered herself. But she knew that staying here would make her lose any self-control she ever had.

Tears flooded her eyes, knowing that she would never see Sabastian again if she left this place, but she didn't love him, she could not. After all, he was only here with her to train her up to be a good companion for other men and to get his promotion.

Victoria lay there, torn on what to do. She wished she could turn her mind off and only feel, but right now, all she felt was pain. A sob shook her body and Sabastian suddenly woke up beside her.

"Vicky, are you okay?" he asked gently, waking up instantly.

Victoria sniffed, "I'll be fine," she said, turning toward him.

Sitting up, he asked, "Is there anything I can get for you? Would you like a bath or some more pills or something to eat?"

Needing time to herself to think, she nodded and said, "Something light to eat please."

"Of course," Sabastian jumped out of bed and hurried to the bedroom door that had been unlocked during the night at one point, "I'll be right back."

Victoria watched him go then after several minutes, tentatively sat up, wincing. She reached for a robe and walked to the bathroom. She washed her face and hands and was horrified when she opened her robe and looked in the mirror at her naked body. She was covered with bruises, scratches, and bite marks. Her groin area was red and still swollen. Tears silently slipped down her cheeks as she washed.

"Fuck!"

Victoria turned around startled at the voice in the bathroom doorway and quickly covered herself up when she saw Sabastian standing there watching in horror, wide eyed.

Sabastian took in her darkly bruised body, trying to clear the red rage that had settled over his eyes. He pulled his gaze from her legs and back, and up to her tear filled blue and purple eyes. Sabastian was torn, he wanted to go to her and hold her but also wanted to tear out of her room to track down Ethan and kill him.

"I'm okay," She said bravely, "I've had worse."

Her words hit him hard and thought of her as a child being beaten and scared. Taking a deep breath, Sabastian decide it would be better to stay with her, he walked slowly to her.

"Sweet Vicky, you don't have to be brave for me, I know you will always be okay but you didn't deserve that."

Coming up behind her, Sabastian softly took her shoulders in his hands and turned her to face him. Cupping her face so tenderly, he placed a soft kiss on her lips and smiled at her.

Victoria knew she needed to play her role well and said, "it's all part of the training, right?"

"No, well, ummm, kind of," he muttered, taken aback.

Taking her waist, he led her back into the bedroom and cursed under his breath when he saw her wince when she sat down on the bed.

Trying to keep a level head, he said, "Yes, it was a test but one you weren't ready for."

Victoria looked at him appalled, "Could anyone be ready for that?" she asked.

"Well, you would need to read about it," Sabastian said, trailing off, seeing her reaction.

Victoria rolled her eyes, as much as she loved books she was sick of reading, "Just tell me," she demanded exasperated.

"Okay, well there are several kinds of specialties that the girls can do with a client. There is BDSM, which stands for bondage, domination, discipline, sadism, submission, and masochism."

Victoria looked at him, completely at a loss.

"Okay, we call it hard sex mainly. Domination and is when a man or a woman dominates the other person for pleasure, both theirs and their partner's.

They control the sex through subjecting the person with rules and rituals of submission. The submissive has to obey and be able to act obediently within the rules of control, the dominate puts in place. Then there is Sadomasochism, which does all the same stuff but uses pain to bring pleasure."

"Like how?" Victoria asked, still at a loss.

"Okay, well a dom would tie up the other person, perhaps whip them and cause pain arousing both of them at the same time. The dom would control all aspects of the sub with both pleasure and pain, sometimes with humiliation. The sub basically becoming a willing slave in bed and lets the dominate do whatever they want to them."

"Is that what Ethan did?" she asked, swallowing.

"No, the fucking bastard is a rapist as far as I'm concerned and uses BDSM as an excuse to get away with it. What he does is not how that is supposed to work. You need a high level of trust in order to be in that kind of relationship and do the dom slash sub thing properly. However, the test he tried performed on you is to test your compatibility for that particular specialty."

"What about the other things you said, umm, the sadist and the other one?" she asked, not remembering what he had said.

"Bondage means being tied up, I'm sure you figured that one out. Sadist is a person who likes to inflict pain on others to get aroused and the person who likes being hurt like that is a masochist, who get aroused being hurt either physically or mentally or both."

"So how many women here do that?"

"We have a few and we match the women to the clients who have those particular needs."

Victoria's thoughts reach back to the letters beside some the woman names in the files she read so long ago.

"And they do it on purpose," she looked horrified.

Sabastian nodded, "Yes, some people get off on it, love it and are in this business to find partners to satisfy that craving they need for the combination of pain and sex to increase the pleasure and get full satisfaction."

"So is that what Ethan was doing?"

"No, what Ethan was doing, was satisfying his own sick pleasure at your expense under the cover of trying to see if you would respond. The only time he gets to really let loose and be in total control is when he tests out a new intern. When he is requested, even though he is playing the dominate, he is still under the control of the girls and has to continue to obey all the respect rules. He's both a sadist and a masochist and playing out a real rape scene with a new girl who fights back is the most pleasure he can ever receive and he hungers for it to the point of being obsessed. Like I said, there needs to be a level of trust and consent before a person can be violently handled and Ethan always skips that step as he wants the real thing and always has. That kind of sex is a thrill that both people should enjoy. I have told Mr. D for years that Ethan takes it too far and even though it does work on some girls and those girls love being with men who roughly handle them. Ethan is too much and he takes it over the top."

Sabastian did not want to tell her that he had another dominate in mind, one he could trust but did not want to give her the impression that a lot of men liked dominate sex.

Victoria was truly horrified. If he knew this about Ethan, why would Sabastian put him in charge of her while he was working? She had been put through the paces of being trained and she had allowed Sabastian to play with her and put her in the situation where Ethan had access to her. Her heart swelled with choked emotion, filling with pain, and knew Sabastian didn't care for her at all and only wanted her to move forward in the so-called program. Her resolve hardened her plan and as much as she wanted to ask the question as to why he let Ethan watch her, the answer would be too painful to hear. Her body's discomfort was nothing compared to the hammering in her heart and she tried desperately to control her emotions. Sabastian may have not wanted Ethan to take her and had beat the crap out of him, but he did nothing to prevent it. Her face grew warm and she couldn't prevent the tears from rolling silently down her cheeks so she covered her real pain with a question.

"What about you?" she asked, trying to keep her voice level and failing. She was scared to death of the answer.

"No, I took the intro course but that was it. However, I do not judge people who are into it."

"Will he do it again?" she whispered.

"No, never. He was too hard on you and you are hurt and as much as the scenario was going to be played out anyway, he took it too far. If it was me, I would never have hurt you," he said, brushing her arm lightly.

You already have, she thought, and tried to keep her mind in the conversation.

"But how could that work?"

"Well, there is a difference between being taken roughly and aggressively without being hurt cruelly. So there would be pain to make you sensitive but the pleasure would override it to the point of wanting the pain only to increase the pleasure in the sex. Ethan doesn't do that, he only takes and doesn't give and that's why he goes too far. When you are in the internship, it should be all about your pleasure and no one else's."

"Oh," she said distracted.

There was a knock at the door and Sabastian said, "Come in."

Nickolas came to the bed and put a meal tray on the table.

"Miss Victoria," he said solemnly in his kind accent.

"Hi, Nick."

"I have brought you some great food for healing and relaxing, I hope you enjoy it," Nickolas said with a comforting smile.

"I always do," Victoria said, lifting the lid.

Nickolas left and Sabastian asked, "Can I feed you?"

"No, I'll manage," she said, wanting to get some control back, not wanting to be treated like a child.

"Okay, I'll run a bath for you," Sabastian left for the bathroom.

Victoria sat crossed legged on the bed and nibbled on the food she couldn't taste.

"What am I doing here?" she asked herself. *"I can't do this, it's too much."*

Absorbed in her thoughts, she did not notice Sabastian watching her from the bathroom doorway.

"It's ready," he said, watching her closely. "Are you okay?"

"I'm fine," she answered blandly. Not looking at him as she entered the bathroom, closing the door behind her. She left Sabastian worried in the other room as she sunk into the warm soothing water.

Chapter 64

Sabastian brought Victoria to Dr. Marshall who did a quick examination assuring him she would be fine after some rest. After moving Victoria back to her old room, Sabastian spent the next several days watching her recover every step of the way. He had to force himself not to kill the bastard Ethan when he saw her bruising darken by the next day. He rubbed her body with medication and oils and made sure she was completely comfortable moving with her into her room to keep an eye on her.

Victoria was at war with herself, while she healed. The time she was spending with Sabastian was so wonderful. They did nothing but talk and spend time with each other with no other agenda but to keep each other company. He never left the room, holding her all night and talking to her, playing games and watching movies with her, talking endlessly about everything, except about what had happened. Of course she loved the attention, even though she felt she was fine after only a couple of days. She found herself wincing on purpose when Sabastian was watching her to prolong their time together. She knew she was milking the recovery but did not want the days or the nights to end. Sabastian slept with her every night, never leaving her side, his body wrapped protectively around her own.

She had hinted a few times about feeling insecure about being watched on the monitors while she healed and was happy when she heard the argument, that Sabastian won, about turning off all the monitors for her room. Sabastian even got Max to double check that they had all been disabled. He would be staying with her twenty-four seven and there was no need to invade her privacy during this time, she had heard him say. After Max had confirmed that they had earned their solitude, he had Max feed Sketch and bring him his art supplies.

She enjoyed laughing and talking with him while his hands moved over the paper like water to draw her. She loved posing for him and had fun with the different moves as he adjusted her limbs in the perfect position to sketch. She would continually break her pose to sneak peeks at his work always laughing and darting away when he yelled and tried to grab at her playfully to prevent her from seeing his half-finished drawings of her. After she had done this several times, she was confused when he did not try to stop her from getting up to see once again. When she circled the easel, there was the curve of a lovely black cat instead of her. Giving him a playful smack and yelling at him, he ripped off the cat page and taped it to her mirror laughing at her while she pretended to be mad at him.

Victoria knew this fairy tale would end soon and even though she was falling deeper for Sabastian, she knew he was only here to protect his investment and secure his promotion. Soon she would be a hundred percent fine and the training would begin again. When she had first accepted the internship, she only had Sabastian in mind for her lover. She had been naïve about other men but now that she had almost been with someone else, it was too much. She would not be able to handle this without Sabastian and seeing how he was training her to be an escort to be enjoyed by multiple men, a future with him would never happen.

This was not the only reason for her plan. The episode with Ethan had shocked and scared her but not in the way that it should have. Her body had taken over her mind and she was mortified how she had reacted to the way Ethan had handled her. The pain and the fight was something she was too familiar with and the way her body had accepted and craved that kind of brutality scared her so much that she was in confused tears almost every day. She had to be careful not to show Sabastian as she could not help but be honest with him if he started asking questions. She was not sure she would be able to hold back the truth about how she was at least intrigued about what had happened to her. She hated and mistrusted Ethan and would never want to have sex with him but he had brought something out in her that she fervently denied every time she thought about it. Instead she blocked any thoughts and tried to enjoy the sweet company with Sabastian and what would be their last days together.

She remembered Sabastian telling her she could leave at any time, she was not a prisoner here and she would be offered money and a job if she decided to opt out of the internship. But as many times as she tried to imagine the conversation, she could not tell him she was leaving; she was barely able to leave on her own and she knew any conversation with Sabastian would quickly change her mind. She would not be able to say good bye if he asked her to stay, even though it would only be to protect his chance at his promotion. She prepared and waited for her chance and hoped she would be able to leave easily, breaking all ties to Eximius and Sabastian, hoping a clean break would be enough for her to stay away.

Sabastian had watched Victoria carefully, looking for any lasting signs that she was not okay. She acted like she was perfectly fine but he was too afraid to ask her the serious questions that needed to be asked. He had loved this time with her the past several days and did not want it to end but he was constantly telling Jeremy to wait as well as Douglas, Eximius' psychiatrist. Not only did she need more time to think about what had happened but he did not want their time together to end. He had never spent this much time with a woman just talking like normal people, spending time together, learning about each other, and just being friends with no other agenda needing to be filled.

Finally, Jeremy said she had enough time and that if she could not talk about the test, she would not work out anyway so he agreed to one more day. Her bruising had started to fade and Sabastian needed to know for sure about her mental state to really ensure she was okay. He needed to start a new plan to get her back on track, not even sure if she would agree to have sex again. He was more than pissed and unsure of what to do. Where the hell was his boss Mr. D? It had been weeks and he needed someone to talk to and Mr. D and Miss Cherry would have been able to work though this problem with him. He guessed the first step was the talk with the doctor. Knowing he should have brought Douglas to her days ago, he went to collect him and devised a plan to get her back on track.

He was unable to sleep on the morning he planned to get Douglas to talk to her and woke up insanely early. He lay in bed beside her and mentally took in every curve of her body and the warmth of her skin. He did not know what would happen after her talk with Douglas. She could decide she was finished and wanted to be bought out and relocated as was her right. He would of course beg her to stay and he was not sure he would be able to take the rejection if she said no. That is why he had avoided the conversation for so long. He could not, would not let her go and that thought in itself scared him.

Sabastian slowly uncurled his body from hers and crept out of the bed they had shared for not long enough as far as he was concerned. He gave her a light kiss on the head and left her leaving her to sleep soundly, hoping he would be back in time to see her wake, not wanting to upset her by his absence.

Chapter 65

Victoria knew she had played her role well the last few days. The books as well as her lessons in self-defense had taught her more than just how to control her body but also her emotions and she hoped she had fooled Sabastian enough to keep his suspicions down. She felt his kiss and heard him finally leave her alone in the room for the first time since he had moved in to care for her over a week ago. She waited only a minute and then proceeded to fly out of bed, grabbing her bag that she had carefully packed when he was not watching her, which had not been easy.

Her pack was intact and had everything in it from her mask to her knives. She had extra clothes, blankets, and food packed carefully away. She had enough for a week of survival before she would need to establish a place to stay and find food.

Victoria grabbed her clothes putting on many layers fast and threw her pack on. The tour of the manors had given her the path she needed to get out quickly and easily. Knowing they would not be far behind; she tied a dark silk sheet tightly to her bag and draped it over her back. Making sure to braid and tuck her hair into her sweater, she slipped out the unlocked door, hoping that Max had been honest when he had told them they were no longer being monitored.

She was relieved to see no light coming into the hall from the sky light in the round room, which meant it was still dark outside, her timing was perfect. The only person up was probably Sabastian so she looked around the corner carefully to the empty room before dashing to the garden doors. Out in the cool air, she ran straight to the farthest wall away from the grass hallway that led to the woman's manor. Taking a risk to which wall would lead to the outside, she hoped the east side wall was the only barrier to the mansion's property. Taking off her pack, she slung it over the top corner of the field stone wall so that the sheet that was tied to it draped down toward her. Backing up she ran at the corner of the wall, placing her feet on the sides of the ninety degree corner to propel her way half way up before grabbing the hanging sheet firmly in her hands. Hand over hand, she was able to take weight off of her feet and to balance her body as she scaled up the high wall.

She clawed her way up the wall, breaking her nails immediately and saw her fingers were raw and bloodily as she reached the top. She silently cursed her manicure as she pull herself up over the peak. Straddling the wall, she flipped the pack on the inside of the garden wall and the sheet on to the outside of the wall. Her fingers throbbing, she put as much weight into the sheet as she dared still using the rough stone wall and lowered herself down, landing hard and falling backward. Standing, she backed up and jumped and grabbed the sheet, pulling until her pack was in her hands. Moving fast, she threw it on her back with the sheet over top and down her body like a cape, camouflaging her well in the dark.

She kept her head low as she ran through the large lawn and manicured flower beds. She was surprised at the size of the property, it took her a long time jogging to finally come to another large fence. She climbed it fast and hopped over the spikes on the top and ran on. She never looked back. Whenever she saw street signs, she averted her eyes, not wanting to know where she was and where she had come from. She didn't want the temptation to be able to find her way back and ran hoping that she was not being hunted again.

She ran as fast as she could, but turned away from the lights of the big city she saw in the distance, she knew if they were close behind her, they would assume she would go straight toward the city, so she ran to her left, keeping the city on her right-hand side and then proceeded to zigzag her way toward the lights in a random pattern.

After over an hour of running, Victoria sat down and breathed a lung full of air, exhausted. The sun was coming up, she looked toward the sky line on the horizon in front of her. Staring at the city carefully with the sun finally coming up, she could now see the outline of city buildings. It was strange, she recognized it somehow. Digging into the recesses of her mind, she got up and moved to get a better view and realized with a shock it was New York City.

She was both scared and relieved. It would be so easy to hide in New York with the amount of homeless on the streets, she could stay in this city and a team of men would never be able to find her. Her initial plan was to get to the closest city and pan handle till she had enough money for a bus ride far away from here, but New York was the perfect hiding place. However, New York was not Denver and she didn't know the city and hoped her street skills would be enough to keep her alive until she could establish herself.

She would be in the clear and thought if they didn't find her by now, she would be on her own again. Thinking of what she had left behind, she forced down the strangled loss, gathering in her chest and focused on what lay ahead. Collecting her pack again, she tucked the sheet into her bag, which would look weird in the day light and trotted quickly toward either her freedom or her downfall.